REPRESSED

AN ASH PARK NOVEL

MEGHAN O'FLYNN

Distributed by Pygmalion Publishing, LLC

IBSN: 978-0-9974651-4-3

For my husband
who would probably try to get me back if I went missing.
But don't pay the kidnappers too much, honey. I can gnaw my arm off
or something. So really just offer them half the price of a new arm, and
if they let me go, we'll come out ahead. And we can spend the other half
of the "arm money" making decisions at least two thirds as
questionable as bartering with a kidnapper.
Incidentally, my decision to marry you
was one of my best.
I love you, babe.

WANT MORE FROM MEGHAN?
There are many more books to choose from!

Learn more about Meghan's novels on
https://meghanoflynn.com

There is a demon in my head,
No angel to confront him;
With whispers sharp as razor wire,
His voice becomes my anthem.
He never sleeps, just watches…and waits for me to
    break.

On bloodied knees, I scream,
To loose the monster within;
But no wail of anguish can erase,
Teeth like glass in shredded skin.
And they listen to me scream, waiting for me to
    break.

And when my cries have faded,
He is still, no use to plead;
And I alone try to recall,
Why I watch him bleed.
There I stand, forever alone, waiting for my soul to
    break.

"Deep into that darkness, peering, long I stood there wondering, fearing, doubting, dreaming dreams no mortal ever dared to dream before."

~Edgar Allan Poe, "The Raven"

1

_____

THE HOUSE WAS HUSHED, steeped in the steely gray of dawn as he made his way to the kitchen and flipped on the lights: the white tile floors, the white cabinets, the light-green soapstone, all of it at once harsh and as vital as the pulse in his veins. Each morning it was that split second of jarring blindness that finally connected him to his body. But that connection wouldn't last. Detective Curtis Morrison was not so much a stranger to his home or to himself—it was his mere existence, the world of men and earth, that seemed utterly foreign.

Around him the noises of morning murmured to him, less sharp than the light, but just as poignant: the click of the heater, the agitated tapping of a backyard woodpecker, the cat's gentle mewl, and, as he moved about his morning routine, the hiss of the coffee pot, rising like an ocean wave and cresting over his eardrum. In these quiet moments, before the present caught up with him, he felt he was on the brink of a precipice, a place where if he concentrated hard enough, he might hear hushed voices from another dimension—from the world where he really, truly belonged.

Telling him how to get home.

From the cabinet, he pulled down Shannon's coffee mug, the one that read "Arguing with a lawyer may prove ineffective," and set it on the counter hard enough that the clatter sent the cat skittering from the room. He stilled, staring at the mug. It was his job to be in control. Thinking like a detective was a skill comprising fire and ice—the passionate pursuit of justice and the cool logic of calculated deliberation, all centered on the *now.* Which was good. The past was hazy at best, and he couldn't bear to consider what it might have been at worst. The ugliness that lurked in his soul was like a malignant blister begging to burst at the first irritation. Common for cops, maybe; guns and violence and blood were a part of the daily routine. Few remained unscathed.

Breathe. Connect. Center.

Morrison padded upstairs to the bedroom where Shannon sat against the upholstered headboard with their daughter, Evie, both wrapped in the blue comforter to ward off the late spring chill. The entire room felt as if it were swaddled—cozy. Shannon said the colors reminded her of the sea. And if the room was the sea, she was a siren, waiting for him as the first rays of sunlight filtered through the curtains and bathed her blond hair in reddish-gold. She raised her hand to block Evie's face from the glare, and he set Shannon's mug on the wooden end table next to her, squinting briefly at his own hands. He knew they were his, yet he'd not have been surprised to learn they'd belonged to someone else all along. Perhaps common for other cops. Perhaps not.

He sat beside Shannon and ran a hand over her thigh, over her leg trapped inside the cotton shell of the comforter.

"What's up, Iron Man?" Shannon's voice was still hoarse with sleep. She put her hand over his fingers, still resting on her shrouded knee. "Ready to go catch some bad guys?"

Nope, not ready. He released her and pulled his guitar onto his knee, relishing the cool of the strings—more familiar than any part of his body. Shannon squeezed his bicep, Evie smiled at him, and suddenly all was right with the world, whether he truly belonged to it or not. They couldn't see the sorrow through his smile, and there was a pleasure in that   not in the hiding, but in the knowledge that they were safe from the pain he carried, the secrets that remained etched on his gut like scars from a jagged blade. Here, with Shannon and Evie, he was just Daddy. Some days he could almost convince himself that he had never been anything else.

While Evie gurgled at him, he strummed and sang: "I loved you from the first, baby, baby girl..." By the time he rode into the second chorus, Evie was squealing with delight, and Shannon was laughing, stroking Evie's head like they were actors in a sappy holiday commercial. But that peaceful tranquility hadn't been easy for her, not lately.

He strummed the final notes of the song and set the guitar beside the bed, then walked downstairs with Shannon to the living room past the white and gray couch Shannon had insisted they buy because it didn't remind them of her ex-husband or of Morrison's bachelor years. He hadn't argued—his pre-detective days were fraught with a wildness he had worried he'd never tame. These days he felt more domestic, but that didn't make him less of a liar.

Or less of an addict.

Shannon touched his shoulder. "You okay?"

"Yeah." He wasn't worried about himself. The bottle of antidepressants on the dresser was some comfort, a safeguard against him coming home to Shannon crying in the kitchen with her hands over her ears, Evie in her crib wailing. "I can't do this," she'd said that night. "I want to drop her at the fire station."

Maybe they should have expected it—she'd had some depression after her surrogacy with her brother's child. Morrison had assumed that episode was related to Shannon going home from the hospital alone while baby Abby went to live with her fathers.

He'd been wrong.

Morrison tried to force the memory from his brain, busying himself by pouring fresh grounds into the coffee maker—one more pot, enough to top Shannon off and keep Petrosky alert and focused for whatever the day had in store.

"You ready to deal with your partner all day long?" Shannon asked from behind him as if reading his mind.

He turned and made a silly face at Evie, and her cherub cheeks grew wider as she grinned back at him. He tickled her foot and met Shannon's eyes: ice blue and collected...but concerned. About him. "As ready as I'll ever be," he said, forcing a smile.

"Good. You need to get back to work. A month off is long enough."

"Tired of me harassing you, eh?"

"I didn't mean it that way." She shook her head. "Sorry."

"No sorries here, Shanny. Just love." He kissed her cheek. "I'll be back around lunchtime so that I can meet the candidates." He poured the coffee into two stainless-steel mugs and refilled Shannon's when she held her cup out to him, the inscription already marred with a streak of drying coffee.

"Really, I can handle nanny interviews. I've only got two this afternoon." She sipped, then set the cup down when Evie kicked and almost spilled it.

"You didn't let me in on the last ones. You met them at a coffee shop."

"I didn't want you to scare them off."

"I'm not scary!" He stuck his tongue out at Evie to prove his point. Evie tried to kick him too.

She rolled her eyes. "You know what I mean. When it comes to your daughter, you get this 'don't you dare fuck with her' look."

Morrison frowned, but he pulled Shannon close and put his other hand on Evie's back. She was right. He'd have spent all his time cross-examining the potential candidates and scared the good ones off. Interrogating them. Petrosky would have been proud. Shannon would have been pissed.

"I love that you love her, Morrison."

She had never called him "Curt"—he'd been "Morrison" when she'd fallen in love with him. "I love you too, you know," he said.

"I do." She kissed his neck, the highest she could reach. He brushed his lips against her cheek, then over Evie's downy head, inhaling talcum and milk and something sour and ripe that he should maybe take care of before he left. But even if he offered, Shannon would yell at him to get out anyway. And no one in their right mind started the day fighting with a lawyer.

"Go to work," Shannon said. "I've got shit to take care of." She pulled herself from his arms and peeked at Evie's bottom. "Liter-ally. Besides, you know you miss Petrosky. Might as well stop and grab him some donuts. He's going to make you go later anyway."

"Already got him a granola bar."

Shannon smirked. "Oh, he'll love that." She glanced at the clock. "I have to get ready too. Meeting Lillian at the park for an hour early this morning since she's going to meet Isaac for lunch." Isaac Valentine was a good cop and an even better friend with more goofy jokes than Morrison and a brand-new scar on his cheekbone after a run-in with an agitated burglary suspect. Valentine was also married to Shannon's friend Lillian. Even their kids were besties—Valentine was convinced Evie and his son Mason were going to get married one day and officially make them "one big milk chocolate family."

Morrison grabbed the stainless-steel coffee cups off the counter before he could convince himself to call in sick. "Whether he loves the granola or not, Petrosky will eat it. He's probably too swamped at the precinct to get any food at all." He opened the front door, and the still-damp air from last night's storm stuck to his skin.

"Yeah, right. He's probably busy shoving all the paperwork to the side for you." Shannon slapped his ass. "Now stop stalling and get out."

He forced himself not to look back as he headed to his Fusion, struggling with the coffee cups and his keys and the pressure in his chest that was urging him to stay home.

2

THE BULLPEN SMELLED like old coffee, older paperwork, and dry perspiration, same as it always had. It felt the same, too, the dynamic energy of cops running on caffeine and sugar and a rage that always simmered just under the surface. It was anger at the bad guys, probably, or maybe indignation at the cases they hadn't managed to solve. For every arrest, there was at least one cold case—some douchebag walking free. He gripped the stainless-steel coffee mugs tighter like they were the wrists of an elusive, and definitely guilty, perp.

Morrison cut down the center of the room, a dozen desks on either side of him, a giant post in the middle, making the usable sitting space more L-shaped. He nodded to a pair of plainclothes in suits and ties, one of whom looked familiar—*homicide detective*—the other with the nervous eyes of a cornered opossum. *New guy.* Morrison smiled at him, and the guy smiled back, though his eye twitched.

As Morrison approached his desk, someone clapped him on the shoulder, and he turned to see Detective Oliver Decantor—broad face, broader smile.

"Heard you were coming back today!" Decantor's smile was infectious, though Morrison's chest remained tight, a subtle pressure, but persistent. "I knew you'd eventually get sick of sitting around watching people drool." He crossed his arms over his barrel chest and winked.

Morrison snorted, glancing across the room at Decantor's desk, where he kept his files and his celebrity crush of the week. "You're right; I can always come watch you guys drool over Jennifer Lopez." But he let the grin creep onto his face. "You're not nearly as cute as Evelyn, though."

Decantor rubbed his chin. "Can't argue with that."

They both turned at Petrosky's cough, more of a bark. Petrosky didn't turn toward them, but the set of his shoulders was stiff like he was listening to their conversation. He was probably just anxious to get his hands on Morrison's coffee—the precinct coffee was shit.

"Catch you later, Morrison," Decantor said, his smile suddenly at half-mast. He stared across the bullpen at Petrosky.

Morrison nodded to Decantor's back, then headed for their desks, smack in the middle of the bullpen at the crook of the L. "What's up, Boss?"

"Who you yammering with over there?" Petrosky looked like he'd gained a few pounds in the months since he'd walked Shannon down the aisle in place of her absent father. The zipper on his jacket strained over his belly, and his jowly face had filled out. Morrison hadn't noticed it when Petrosky had visited the house, but at work, everything came into sharper focus. Life: constructed of the details you paid attention to.

"Decantor just stopped by to say hi," Morrison said.

Petrosky raised an eyebrow. "Decantor?"

"I know what you're thinking. Decantor, like the thing you put mimosas in for brunch. But he spells it differently."

"Decant...what the fuck are you talking about? I just thought he was on vacation this week." Petrosky shook his head. "Brunch. I don't know what you've been doing this month, but I don't want to hear any more shit about mimosas."

"You got it, Boss." Morrison suppressed a smile, tossed the cereal bar onto the desktop, and peered into Petrosky's empty Styrofoam cup. The coffee dregs were thick and oily. Typical. "Looks like I got back here just in time."

Petrosky side-eyed the granola bar. "You trying to get me

back on your hippie diet?" He rubbed a hand over his belly. "Don't need it. I've just got a little winter padding."

That's what happens when you replace whiskey and beer with cookies and jelly beans. Hopefully, Petrosky's heart was holding out along with his sobriety. Morrison set one of the cups on the desk. "It's not winter, Boss, it's May. You been to a doc lately?"

"Fuck off, California," Petrosky said, but his eyes crinkled, and his mouth turned up at the corners. He grabbed the mug.

"Miss me, did you?"

"With every bullet so far. Not that I'm aiming too hard."

It was more than Petrosky would say for most people.

"We've got a lot to catch up on." Petrosky gestured to the three stacks of file folders on his desk. The police department was perpetually overworked and understaffed, though probably more so in recent years. No surprise. Ash Park itself shared the police department's undercurrent of agitation—a quiet but desperate despondence that seemed to permeate the air, the water, the citizens who would leave—if they had the means. But understaffed or no, it didn't look like Petrosky had filed a single report since Morrison left.

"Your paperwork skills are atrocious," Morrison said.

"You're the English Lit major—thought your guys loved that paperwork bullshit as much as your fancy-ass words." He snorted and shook his head, muttering: "Atrocious."

"Figured if I confused you, you'd forget about making me write the reports." Morrison pulled up a chair from his own adjacent desk and gestured to the shortest stack of file folders. "So, what've we got?"

Petrosky grunted and pulled the manila stack closer. "The usual. One missing persons, thirteen-year-old girl, turned homicide. Davis thinks sex trafficking, which is why we ended up with it."

Morrison squinted at Petrosky, watching for signs of distress. Petrosky's daughter, Julie, had been raped and murdered before her fifteenth birthday, and his marriage had dissolved soon after.

Petrosky's eyes betrayed nothing. "We've also got two domestic violence cases, one with a stabbing, the other with sexual assault history, both almost wrapped except for the paper-work. Valentine's got one guy in holding now, picked him up on a routine traffic stop. Though you might already know that."

Petrosky peered at the side tabs, slid a folder from the center of the pile, and laid it in front of Morrison. "Then, we have this one."

Morrison opened the folder to the crime scene photos. A dark-haired man, burly, face down in a storm drain. Messy tribal tattoos covered his shoulders, though the stains might just as easily have been grease—or maybe they *were* grease. No pants. Blood pooled under his groin.

"Rape?"

"Nope. Someone took his dick as a souvenir."

Morrison winced, trying not to imagine the searing pain of amputation. He crossed his legs.

"Keep it in check, California," Petrosky said, but his voice had lost the hard edge of condescension.

Morrison passed the folder back. "Any promising leads?"

"Ex-girlfriend. Melanie Shiffer, got a place over on Wild-shire. She's probably home now."

Morrison's mouth dropped open. "You know who she is? Why haven't you gotten her yet?"

"Waiting for you."

Morrison stared until Petrosky sighed.

"Fine. I picked the victim up several years back for molesting Shiffer's two-year-old daughter. He took a deal for seventy months, only served four years. Got out last week." He stood. "Maybe we can convince the prosecutor's office to plead her down on the murder the way they did on his charges."

"Not sure the prosecution will go for it unless this guy went after mother or daughter," Morrison said. "She intentionally severed his junk." *And I probably would have done the same.*

"Maybe she didn't mean to kill him." But the look on Petrosky's face told Morrison he didn't believe that either. "They can plea molestation down, might as well see if they'll plea vengeance."

Morrison nodded, but he didn't believe it'd happen, even

though Roger McFadden—lead prosecutor and Shannon's dick of an ex-husband—did have a rather impressive history of dreaming up plea deals. In the past, Roger had taken cash for it, too—or so Morrison believed. He'd never had enough evidence to do anything about it, and an internal investigation the year before hadn't turned up a thing.

"What time do you have to be home to pick out nannies?"

"Around noon." Morrison raised the coffee mug but stopped it halfway to his lips. "How'd you know about that?"

"Fucking detective, remember? Like you used to be." Petrosky grabbed the folder and stood. "Let's get Shiffer squared away so you can get back to your own manhood—Shannon keeps it on the kitchen counter, right?"

"In the bathroom next to the mouthwash."

Petrosky half grinned. "Good to have you back, Surfer Boy."

MELANIE SHIFFER LIVED in a whitewashed townhouse with a tattered broom leaning in a corner on the front porch and a doormat that read "Beware of Attack Cat." No one answered the first knock, but the front curtain flipped—a finger, nothing more—and went still. Petrosky put his hand on his gun.

Morrison's mind flashed to the man in the storm drain, and he squared his shoulders, hand on his own gun, as an edgy heat rose into his chest. He'd nearly forgotten that feeling—dirty diapers were slightly less stressful than approaching the home of a killer. "She got weapons registered?"

"Nope." Petrosky tried the handle. It turned. "Ma'am?" No answer from inside, just a subtle shuffling to the left of the foyer, like a rat scuttling through tissue paper. Petrosky disappeared into the hazy dimness of the house, and Morrison followed, alert for the source of the sound. He saw her as they emerged into the next room.

Shiffer sat on a green rocking chair in the front room, her hair disheveled, staring down at a photo album in her lap. She did not look up as they entered, just flipped a page, then another

—a family vacation somewhere, a little girl playing in the water, another picture of the girl on Shiffer's shoulders.

Morrison's gaze darted around the room, looking for any other person, the little girl, signs of disturbance…or a weapon. But everything was orderly, almost inexplicably so. There were fresh vacuum tracks on the beige carpet.

Petrosky stepped closer to the chair. "Ms. Shiffer?"

She looked up slowly, as if awakening from a dream or perhaps a nightmare, her glassy eyes punctuated by starbursts of broken blood vessels. "I remember you," she said to Petrosky. Her voice was barely a whisper as if she was trying not to wake a sleeping child. Morrison might as well have been invisible.

Petrosky said nothing.

"She still cries at night, you know," she said. A single tear trailed down her cheek.

Morrison approached her and laid a hand on her shoulder, half for comfort, half to prevent her from reaching for a weapon, though nothing in her manner suggested aggression. Just bone-crushing sadness. His own heart ached for the little girl, abused, still fearful of the man who had hurt her, and for a moment, his ears filled with Evie's cries. Something hot and vile bloomed in his gut. He pictured the heat draining from his chest, and his body cooled accordingly. "Is she home now, ma'am?"

She shook her head. "At school." She looked at Morrison, set the album aside, and stood. "I'll never regret it. Not for one second." Her eyes were dull.

Neither of them reached for their cuffs. She came willingly to the car, the crisp, blue sky overhead heavy and oppressive as if they were all bearing the weight of injustice on their backs.

3

MORRISON LEFT the precinct in a haze of discontent. Reading the details in the reports had drained him. Sex crimes had been bad enough before he'd become a father, but now it was like every kid was Evie—with every story of an injured, raped, murdered child, he could almost see her face staring at him from the files.

As he crossed the lot to his car, Morrison turned to the courthouse steps to see someone watching him. Karen…something. Her red hair seemed darker than it used to be, and her belt was cinched tight around a barely-there waist. Karen waved, one quick, nervous jerk of the wrist, then averted her eyes and bounded up the courthouse steps, probably late for a case.

She worked at the local rehab center and had been the girlfriend of Frank Griffen, an old college buddy of Shannon's. Morrison's fist clenched involuntarily. Last year, Griffen had suddenly gone off the deep end and bludgeoned two people to death. He'd killed Shannon's niece's kitten, too, then framed an innocent woman along with Morrison himself for the murders. Then he'd attacked Shannon, murdered his own ex-girlfriend, and headed to the courthouse to blow more people away. Petrosky had put a bullet in Griffen's very fucked-up brain, maybe right through the tumor that had caused the hallucinations and aggression, though Morrison hadn't asked. Petrosky and Shannon never spoke of The Incident. But afterward, Karen seemed to be around all the more.

Poor girl. Had to be hard watching someone you love unravel.

Morrison waved back, but she was already gone, leaving him with an uneasy feeling in his belly. Griffen's journal entries were full of references to voices, and the way they'd plagued the man was all too familiar. Morrison had his own mysterious voices, some memories, some surely imagined, and even for him, the line between imagination and reality was hazy at best. Was it the far reaches of his past still whispering as he awoke, or a simple trick of the mind, mere remnants of a dream? And what happened if the ramblings in his head became like Griffen's— sinister and murderous and barbaric? Not that a mere voice could get you to act, but…

Morrison got into his car and headed out, mindful of the steering wheel, the pressure of his foot on the gas, the leather against his back as he sped home, each green light surely the universe's way of telling him he should be with his family instead of at work. He turned into his neighborhood. On either side, two-story brick houses passed along with the occasional stone ranch, some with pools, though he'd be damned if Evie played at any of those houses before she knew how to swim. He'd gotten called on a child drowning case last year. Though the child had been injured and unconscious before being thrown into the water, every whiff of chlorine recalled the memory of that baby's purple face.

He pushed the thoughts aside, forced a smile, and waved to his neighbor, Mr. Hensen, an eighty-two-year-old chatterbox who still wore his purple heart on Veteran's Day.

Shannon met Morrison at the door. "Hey! Welcome home!" Her smile faltered when she saw his face. "Bad first day?"

He put his hand against the small of her back and leaned over to kiss her on the mouth. She tasted like Cheetos and coffee— probably skipped lunch caring for Evie. He'd make her something to eat before he left.

"Not a bad day, really. Just the usual." He followed her into the kitchen. The usual was brutal and distressing, but Petrosky would have slapped the shit out of him if he'd said those thoughts out loud. *You can't let it get to you. Go in and do your job and fuck everything else.* Morrison hoped he would never see the day where he wasn't affected by someone abusing children. Killing children. That ache in his gut was the least he could do for a tiny life so violently snuffed out.

"You can call me if you need to, you know," she said.

"I know." But they'd never been that couple, the kind who chitchatted about nothing over the phone. Shannon had always stared at a ringing phone like it was a boil on the ass of humanity, and after the baby, their phone communication all but ceased. She'd said she was busy. He'd worried she was lonely.

He kissed the top of her head, happy that her hair smelled like lemon shampoo and that Dr. McCallum had given her the shrinky go-ahead to go back to work after she returned from visiting her brother-in-law and niece in Atlanta. He knew the loss of her brother, Jerry, to cancer last year still weighed on her, but the look on her face when she talked about the trip—excited and resolute—showed him that his take-no-prisoners wife was back. Though he still wasn't sure how he'd sleep without the constant hum of the baby monitor at night. Even now, the silence of the house wrapped around them like a fog, muffling everything but Shannon's breath. Was Evie asleep? Must be.

"So…" Shannon drew close to him. "We had one scheduling conflict, Alyson Kennedy had to come earlier."

"What? But I wanted to meet—"

"Shh. We've got twenty minutes before anyone else gets here…wanna get me out of these pants?"

He pulled back from her and ran a finger over her cheek, down the front of her throat. Her mouth was warm, her tongue fervent against his own. She pressed herself against him, her soft skin a stark contrast to the determined grasp of her fingertips against his belt.

He lifted her onto the counter, and she leaned back so he could undo the button on her jeans, every movement a frenzied dance of need. He pulled her face to his with one hand, the other at the waistband of her panties. Then his thumb was on her clit, his fingers inside her and she was already wet, ready for him, and she moaned into his mouth—

Evie's wail sliced through the sound of their heavy breathing.

Every time. He released his wife, pulling his fingers from her, and she arched against him, then let him go.

"Fuck." She jumped from the counter, buttoning her pants. "Maybe tonight," she called over her shoulder as she padded through the kitchen and toward Evie's bedroom. He stared after her, betting she'd be too exhausted later on. With the way his morning was going, maybe they'd both be ready to fall asleep come nightfall.

From the driveway came the whisper of tires on concrete. Their first nanny candidate was early. Sometimes Evie got it right. Not usually but…sometimes.

Morrison washed his hands and thought about baseball. Paperwork. Then he pictured the guy in the sewer drain, blood pouring from his crotch, and Morrison's body wilted like a flower in frost.

NANNY NUMBER ONE, Patricia Weeks, was old as time and stocky as a bull. She had cold eyes that reminded him of a thousand mug shots. Her square jaw and bulbous nose didn't help either, though he knew it was superficial to think that way—what wasn't superficial was the white hair and the musty smell that clung to her. *How old is she?* This woman could die while watching Evie, and neither he nor Shannon would know until after they got off work. And she was so stern. He tickled Evie's chin, watching for the slightest glimmer of warmth in Weeks's eyes, something that would hint at grandmotherly affection, but the woman just answered curtly as Shannon rattled off the questions they'd written up and only smiled halfheartedly when Evie let out a fart that sounded like it might rip straight through her onesie.

"You're doing it again," Shannon told Morrison after Weeks had disappeared down the drive.

"What?"

"That stare."

"She didn't seem bothered," Morrison said, harsher than he'd intended. He took a breath and tried to lighten his tone. "Not that she'd be bothered by much other than the grim reaper and kids playing on her damn lawn."

"She's not that old—"

"She's got at least twenty years on Alice from *The Brady Bunch*."

"She's younger than Petrosky. And he can still chase bad guys."

"If they're running slowly."

She cocked an eyebrow.

"I mean…" He exhaled the tension from his body. "Really, she just didn't seem that interested."

"She might have been bored—I asked her the same questions on the phone last week. And she came highly recommended. I've called every reference on her list."

"Like she'd give references for people who'd say she has all the personality of a dead fish."

Shannon pressed her lips to his, then stepped back. "Morrison, you're pouting."

Between them, Evie farted again.

4

HE LOOKED LIKE A BOY. But he was no boy. And someday he'd show them all.

His heart hammered as she pulled up in front of the house, the sun heating the still-damp walk under his feet and turning the metal of his bicycle into a scalding implement of torture against his bare leg. But he did not shift his calf away from the bar—he could withstand far worse.

Happy, happy, happy.

The red streaks in her hair blew in the breeze like every finger of wind desired her, wanted to touch her, the air itself crackling with the tense energy of unrequited possession. She knew it too, knew she was desirable, powerful, just like every bitch he'd ever met. They all thought they were better. Too good for the likes of him, no matter how many times he did their homework, carried their bags, told them jokes. Just once, he'd wanted to show them the man he was on the inside. He'd wanted to parade one of those girls on his arm. Show the jocks, those self-proclaimed masters of the universe, that he was one of them. To prove he was better. Just once.

But they'd never given him a chance. He knew he deserved more from them, and yet, as the woman raised her eyes to him and nodded, his mouth went dry. That old familiar itch began on the side of his face, on the back of his neck, and he pulled the visor of his ball cap down. The stance he'd taken to hold the bike upright faltered, and he almost crashed to the pavement.

The girl looked up and down the road. Opened her car door to retrieve something—a purse.

He watched. That was what he was supposed to do, though here he was too vulnerable, too exposed. Then again, Frank Griffen had been hiding in plain sight, buddying up to Petrosky, talking to Shannon, all the while planning to kill her. But Griffen had failed. *Weak.*

He was more of a man than Griffen ever was. He was definitely stronger than his so-called buddy from this morning who'd wept like a little cunt just because that stupid kid was dead. He had hoped he could learn from the fucker, but things hadn't quite turned out that way. But he would learn nonetheless.

He was the bigger man. The better man. And someday everyone would know it.

The red-haired bitch finally reached the front door, and as she rang the doorbell, he lowered his gaze to the sidewalk, pushed off from the road, and pedaled up the street, an unassuming streak of metal and gangly limbs.

But his boot left a bloody smear on the pavement, delicious and dark and unquestionably masculine.

5

THE DOORBELL RANG. Morrison tried to beat Shannon to it, but she sidestepped around him, shoved him back, laughing, and opened the front door to reveal a tiny woman who might've been there selling Girl Scout cookies if it weren't for the fine lines around her eyes. She was right around thirty, maybe—sparkling brown eyes and platinum blond hair with red streaks underneath that were too light to be punk. A smiling mouth full of bright, white teeth, too exuberant to be genuine. Across the street, a lanky high school boy on a bicycle had stopped, probably watching her from under his ball cap, though when Morrison approached the door, the boy lowered his gaze to the sidewalk and hit the bricks. *Move it along, son.*

"Natalie Bell." The woman offered her hand. "So nice to meet you in person." Her hand was cold, thin, breakable, and Morrison felt like a bear trying to capture a bird as they shook. She would be no assistance against an intruder—any eighteen-year-old tweaker like the kid out front could throw her into a wall and barge right on in. They'd need to get a dog. A big one. He should have gotten one already.

Bell bent to Evie as Shannon closed the door. "Well, good afternoon, Miss Evie. How are you today?"

Evie kicked her feet and whined. Bell tickled her toes.

Shannon led them to the couch and settled Evie to nurse.

Morrison sank onto the sofa next to her, making his face placid and blank, trying to save his intimidation for suspects instead of aiming it at potential caregivers. But despite his efforts, Bell shifted uneasily on the chair across from them, her plastered smile faltering.

"So tell me, Ms. Bell, how long have you been in this business?" he asked. "You were a nanny previously, yes?"

She straightened, her smile returning. "I started when I was eighteen, officially, though I babysat before that."

Evie farted again. Bell laughed. "Sounds like someone ate too many beans."

"And the ages of the children in your charge?" It came out of him more bark than question. Like Petrosky. He was turning into the old man.

Shannon elbowed him and drew a finger across her throat. He shrugged at her, and they both turned back to see Bell staring at them, her eyes wide.

"Um…all ages," she said. "The last family, the Harrises, I started out with one six-week-old, a two-year-old, and a five-year-old. I was there for three years until they moved." She grinned. All teeth. All smiles. But her gaze remained worried, almost…sad. "Now, I work mostly with infants at the gym daycare."

"You said that your previous employer moved out of state?" Shannon asked her.

"Out of the country," she said, fingers laced over one knee. "I think they're in Europe now." She locked eyes with Morrison, and his stomach soured at a twitch in the corner of her still-smiling mouth.

"And you don't have their contact information?" he asked.

Her face fell. "Well, no, I'm so sorry. I have the parents at the gym who can vouch for me, but I've only been there a short time. After the Harrises, I worked odd jobs. Got too attached to the kids, you know? It was hard when they left." Her eyes went glassy. She had all the right responses, but everything felt somehow disconnected, like a poor stage actor reading lines in a play.

Shannon glanced at the sheet. "I'll call the references you listed, Ms. Bell. I'm sure we can figure it out."

"The Harris family," Morrison began, peeking over Shannon's shoulder. "I'll need first names."

Bell's jaw dropped, but she recovered. Evie, still nursing, kicked her legs and tried to turn her head, yanking at Shannon's breast in the process. Shannon kicked him in the shin.

"Sam and uh...Fletcher," Bell said, and he had to lean toward her over the coffee table to hear her properly.

"Two men?"

"No, the mom was Sam. Samantha."

Morrison nodded. He was being a royal dick, as Petrosky would say. But why the hell would she put "the Harris Family" like it was a corporation instead of a person? What kind of psycho nonsense was that?

He'd been working the beat for too long.

Shannon passed him the baby, eyes narrowed in his direction, and walked Bell out. By the time his wife returned to the couch and sat down next to him, his distrust had mellowed, and it shrank further at the tightness around her mouth.

"I know you don't want to leave Evie, Morrison; I don't want to either. But I head to Alex's in two days, and we need the nanny ready to start when I get back. Not like we can keep asking Petrosky to help out so we can go to dinner."

"He doesn't mind. And he—"

"I know, Morrison, okay? But he's got his own issues."

But Evie helped Petrosky. Hell, just being needed helped Petrosky.

"We can't put it off anymore," she said, and her face was suddenly rebuilt in stone. *Don't argue with a lawyer.* "It's time. This girl is a good candidate. Name one thing wrong with her."

He touched Shannon's marble cheek, almost surprised by her warmth, a reminder that she was not hard and unmovable—she was his wife, she loved him, and she was here. Real. "Just let me check the candidates out first, Shanny. Okay?"

She crossed her arms. "You could have done that while you were off."

"I was busy." *I was stalling.*

"You were stalling."

He sighed. "You're right. I'm still not ready to leave her with a stranger. But I know we need to do it."

Her face softened, a chink in the wall of her stoicism. "Fine. I'll give you my top three to look up, but I knew this was coming. Which is why you've already met two of them."

"Weeks and Bell? But they—"

"No buts. They're my favorites based on their résumés, and their interviews didn't change that. Then there's Alyson Kennedy, the one who just beat you here this morning, recently out of Oaklawn."

"The hospital?"

"She used to be a nurse. Super sweet. Played with Evie on the floor throughout the whole interview this morning."

I should have been here. "She was a nurse?" He frowned, back muscles twitching as he leaned forward in the seat. "Why's she leaving the profession? She get caught doing something unscrupulous?"

Shannon rolled her eyes. "You'll find that out soon enough. Research away." She stuck her tongue out at him. He almost returned the gesture until he realized she was looking at Evie. Instead, he sank back in the chair and tickled Shannon's side. She shoved at his shoulders, and he cupped her chin and put his mouth on hers. Cheetos. Definitely Cheetos.

Evie kicked Shannon's arm from her perch on his leg.

Shannon pulled back, her face suddenly serious. "If you really want to know, Kennedy said she needed a change of pace, and I can't say I blame her. It's gotta be hard dealing with sick or dying kids all day. You of all people should know…"

A hook squirmed in his belly and caught the soft spot under his heart. She was right—seeing children in pain was horrible "Fine. But she better be good."

"Oh, she'll be good. Nurses always are. And if I come home and catch her in my nurse's uniform, you're in trouble." She winked and headed for the kitchen. "Just don't take too long to decide," she called over her shoulder. "If we lose all three because you're busy screwing around—"

"I'll look today, Shanny. Promise." He stood as she disappeared around the corner. "Wait, you really have a nurse's uniform?"

She poked her head back into the living room "I do if you can make this nanny thing happen."

He was opening his mouth to respond when his cell rang with the theme from *Miami Vice.* Shannon disappeared into the kitchen as Morrison pulled it from his pocket. "Hey, Boss."

"Fortieth and Shell. The middle school."

Hell. He looked at Evie, flapping her arms like an adorable, and extremely chubby, bird. Maybe he wasn't cut out for detective work anymore. "On my way."

Please don't let it be a kid.

6

IT SHOULDN'T HAVE BOTHERED her, but the sound of his car starting up in the drive started Shannon's own heart revving louder than his eco-friendly engine; the car door slamming was the muted thud of goodbye. *Alone.* The first full day in months that she'd been completely on her own. Not that Morrison had helped much when he was home today: the man was being irritating as all hell with this nanny thing, but she knew it was just because he loved her. Because he loved their daughter. But she would have been okay with any of these women…did that mean she didn't love Evie as much?

He deserves better than this. Evie deserves better than me. They deserved better than a wife and mother who would settle for any of the top three instead of fighting for the one perfect nanny for her little girl. Who was so damn fragile that she was terrified by the prospect of her own thoughts—of being alone with herself.

No, that was the depression talking; she was certain of that now. Most days, she squashed those thoughts like she was bringing a boulder down onto them, smashing them into useless pieces. It was a visual that she'd used to demolish negativity from her mother, her father, her ex-husband, every shitty bullshit defendant she'd put away. But every once in a while, these new thoughts bubbled up and reminded her that she wasn't quite…right yet.

Not that she was totally nuts, not like before. Just...stressed. This trip was wearing on her, the mere thought of it rendering her almost unable to think about anything else. Was she going to be okay for so many hours, alone in the car with Evie? Of course, she was. Could she even be trusted to be alone? Of course, she could. Dr. McCallum believed in her. Morrison believed in her—that's why he'd left her alone now. And goddammit, she knew she could do this. Alone? *Alone.* She'd never needed anyone else to hold her up. Why the fuck would she start now?

She squared her shoulders and turned from the door, toward the pack-n-play where Evie was gurgling happily, kicking at the empty air. Shannon's heart swelled at the sight of her. She was a good mother. This bullshit depression would not eat her alive. She would not give in.

But she *was* becoming too dependent on everyone else to keep her steady. Morrison had been back to work for a fucking day, and already, she felt like she might lose her shit. And every time she explained to him why they needed to hire a sitter *now*, she was really justifying it to herself. She'd never thought she'd be one of those women who wanted to stay home raising babies, but...she didn't want to go back to work. Or she did—she just didn't want to leave Evie.

Is that why Morrison was hesitant to hire the nanny? Because he thought she wasn't ready? She could feel it in every worried look he gave her, every concerned hug. Hear it in his voice each time he asked how her day was going. Even on the phone, it was like his concern was bubbling through her ear and into her brain, reminding her that maybe she was sick.

He didn't mean it that way. Her husband loved her. He worried. Fine. But she was going to kick depression in the balls. She could do this trip without his help—without anyone's help. And then she'd be back to kicking ass in the courtroom where she'd always belonged.

Without her daughter.

Below her, Evie gurgled, and Shannon blinked back tears.

7

THE SCHOOL WAS RED BRICK, scarred from continual sandblasting to remove graffiti, but still standing—more than Morrison could say for most of the other schools in Ash Park. Unlike the drab exterior, the signs on the doors were bright, and finger paintings lined the windows. Here and there, a tiny face grinned at him through the glass, little pockets of innocence, probably drawn to the flashing lights of the police cars or the news vans that were now parking in the lot. But the raw trust on those children's faces reminded him that someone on these grounds now understood how unsafe and cruel the world could be.

The earth, still wet from last night's rainstorm, sucked at his shoes. The grass pulsed with a vibrant energy that shuddered through the soles of his feet and up his legs, warning him to turn back toward the car before he had to see whatever waited for him behind the building. He strained his ears, but there was no wail of an ambulance siren, no shouts from an EMT pulling someone back into this world—just the ominous silence of a playground turned graveyard.

Beyond the trembling fingers of grass, swings moved back and forth as if of their own volition—touched, perhaps, by a murderous palm and now terrified of whatever evil lay hidden near the playground. He'd have the techs check for prints. On the far side of the swings, a low wooden fence marked the edge of the school property, and just past that, a few dozen ash and poplar trees waved in the breeze over low-hanging firs. Petrosky stood at the tree line, watching a man in white coveralls string crime tape between two birches. He glanced over as Morrison approached.

"What've we got, Boss?"

"Dylan Acosta. Eleven. Raped and murdered sometime during morning recess—about three hours ago."

A kid. Morrison followed Petrosky's gaze to the earth beneath the nearest fir boughs. Feet, socks. Sneakers, half the size of Morrison's own, heels to the sky.

Fuck. Morrison inhaled through his nose, trying to force the cool air into his burning lungs, trying to ignore the stink of gore and mud and what had to be feces. Trying to forget the fact that this pile of parts used to be a little boy. *Be placid. Cool. Ignore the heat.*

Morrison approached around the perimeter, staying out of the way of the techs who were scouring the ground for prints or bits of hair. His fingers felt numb, or maybe just cold, or maybe they weren't his at all—a collection of cold, random limbs like in the scene before him. He flexed his fingers, balled his hands into fists, and forced himself to look at the body.

Dylan Acosta. Skinny, shoulder blades prominent, face down in the dirt. Holes that looked like a series of small-caliber gunshot wounds marred the boy's bare back and buttocks. A T-shirt that the kid had probably been strangled with lay crumpled and limp above his shoulders like blue wings—a child turned to a broken angel. Morrison hissed in a breath through his teeth. The kid's pants were around his knees, his underwear…missing. If his clothing had been removed and replaced while the child was alive, the act was indicative of prolonged suffering. He hoped the killer had taken the undergarments as a souvenir after the boy was dead.

"Found his underwear in the bushes," Petrosky said, and Morrison swore he could feel the watchful eyes of the boy's spirit on his back. "All torn up. Ditto on his jacket."

So the killer had left the clothing, tossed it like rags. Probably still warm. Probably still smelled like boy.

Morrison let his eyes drift to where techs were bagging debris and cloth. The earth surrounding the dumping ground was muddy and creased in filthy waves. A struggle? He peered at the boy's feet, but the mud didn't cover his shoes as you'd expect if he'd been digging in his heels trying to escape. Instead, the dirt was speckled over the kid's skin, over his sneakered feet, over his legs and buttocks as if it had splashed up from the killer's heels only after the child had been incapacitated. But...there was more than one set of tracks. One appeared to be the shallow treads of a tennis shoe, small, but definitely bigger than the kid's. The other treads were deep, thick rectangles that looked like they'd been left by boots. One set from the killer and another from the person who'd found the kid or—

"We dealing with more than one suspect?"

Petrosky was still frowning at the techs in the bushes. "Appears that way. The teacher who found him came around from the other side—heels don't match these either." Petrosky dragged his gaze from the techs to the impressions in the mud. "From the size of the shoes and the depth of these depressions, the guy in the boots is probably five-nine, and slight—around a hundred and fifty, hundred and sixty tops. The other guy's shorter but heavier: five-eight-ish, a hundred and seventy pounds. Looks like they got into a scuffle."

A scuffle? What would make a couple of raping murderers go after one another? Unless...one of them wasn't a killer at all. Pedophiles didn't usually kill their victims—many genuinely believed that they adored children, that sexual abuse was an expression of love. So had the shorter perp tried to keep the other from murdering the kid? Had someone else been here trying to stop the rape to begin with? But if that were the case, they'd probably have another body.

Morrison followed Petrosky's gaze to the holes in the child's back. His stomach turned. He'd been wrong—the holes were round, but they weren't from a gun. Probably not from a blade, either. Unlike a routine stabbing, where the wounds varied in size and distance from one another, here, each set of round punctures on the boy's back was a uniform distance apart.

Between one set of punctures, four muddy rectangles,

smeared and bloody, ran between the round holes. Morrison swallowed hard and held his shudder in check. *Treads from the boot.* "The holes are from a sharp object," he began slowly. "But look at the patterns around the wounds. All the same. Like he strapped…spikes to his boot and…"

"Stomped him to death," Petrosky said. "This fucker didn't want to get his hands dirty."

Morrison could almost feel the sharp prick of a spike in his chest, and he inhaled over the pain until it subsided.

Petrosky walked around him and knelt beside the kid, lifting the boy's head with gloved fingers. When had he put on gloves?

"Lots of blood around the mouth," he said, quietly, almost as reverent as the hush that had fallen over the woods, as if every animal, including the techs working the grounds, felt the solemn emptiness in the air and were hiding from the evil that had caused it. "Punctured lungs, one or both. But we'll have to wait for the medical examiner to confirm."

Morrison avoided looking at the kid's face and squinted at the wounds instead. Middle back, either side of the spine—the kid had probably drowned in his own blood. He'd have been terrified. In agony. Strangulation would have been more humane.

Petrosky laid the boy's head—*Dylan's head, Dylan Acosta's head*—back into the dirt as gently as one might touch a butterfly's wing.

Morrison's eyes were still glued to Acosta's back, to a spot on the kid's side that he'd noticed when Petrosky had moved him. Scratches or maybe another stab wound. He could hear the kid's heartbeat—deep and fast—and was ready to crouch, check for a pulse when he felt the throb in his temples and realized the beat was his own. Morrison wiped his forehead on his sleeve and pointed. "What's there?"

Petrosky pulled the kid toward him, just a little onto his side. Along his rib cage, a few hash marks scored the skin to the left of one long, angry slice—like a crooked number one.

Morrison clenched his fist and released it before Petrosky saw. "You think the killer is saying this is the first?" It had been a few years since a serial killer had terrorized Ash Park, but

Morrison could still practically smell the blood from the crime scenes, see the dripping poems that sadistic asshole had left for the cops. They'd never found him. But this wasn't that killer's MO.

"There's no way this is his first," Petrosky said. "No one starts with this level of brutality." He gestured to the school, well within sight of the trees if one were to stand just a foot beyond the body. "Or this level of exposure."

"We'll look for others." Morrison stared at the school, tried to picture Acosta running, leaping for a football. He turned back to Petrosky to erase the image. "But how'd the killer get the" —*Dylan Acosta*—"victim to come back here?" It would have been hard to haul a kid away while he was playing with his friends unless the attacker was someone he knew.

Of course, those closest to a person were often the ones responsible for hurting them—Morrison knew that from experience, and not just his days with the Ash Park PD. Even years after the fact, a female voice from his past whispered in his ear late at night: *My turn! No, me next.* He could not recall who had said it or who was even there, only that he'd been alone when he'd awoken, blood covering his knuckles like he'd been in a brawl. And near the bed, his best friend, Danny, head gashed open, blood pooling on the floor, ants crawling over his face. *Crawling.* He scratched at his arm, the tickle of imaginary insects as real as the hint of blood in the air around him.

Morrison still didn't know if he'd killed Danny—he couldn't remember much of anything from that night—but he'd stopped using drugs after that day, tried to make his life right again. Still, the wrongness of that evening lurked in his memory like a malevolent fog. Sometimes he lay awake at night, trying to force his vision to clear, to let him *see* just once. During the day, he felt hunted, as if the memory had teeth that could eat him alive. Maybe better if he didn't let those images creep into his consciousness.

Behind Morrison, the clank of a gurney brought with it the sounds around him: the medical examiner giving orders, Petrosky's shoes, squelching as he backed up out of the way. And the boy was there—face down. Here, then gone. Just like Danny.

In the back of his brain, electricity crackled, bright and hot. *Me first. No, me.* Blood poured down the walls. *Come back. You can shoot it once; no one will ever know.* He forced himself to listen to the rustle of the body bag, the rattle of the metal gurney, the sharp hiss of the zipper, the keening squall of an obstinate bird overhead, and the gory walls disappeared along with the whispers. The boy in the bag receded across the playground. Morrison tensed his toes, trying to focus on the self-inflicted cramp in his foot, but he could still feel the incessant vibration of insanity, ready to drag him to hell.

8

THE NEXT MORNING started eerily white, the sun burning hot but unseen behind clouds like swollen mushroom caps. Morrison settled into the extra chair at Petrosky's desk.

The precinct hadn't missed him, and the feeling was mutual. By the time he had finished another stack of paperwork the night before, Shannon had been asleep. This morning she had slept through his alarm. But he hadn't missed the "Nannies" folder on her bedside table. On a Post-it note stuck to the top of the folder, she'd scribbled "Things to Do Before Alex's," and a list which included errands like grabbing her niece, Abby, a birthday present. Maybe he'd surprise her and take care of that at lunch.

Petrosky's mood had been as cloudy as the sky all morning as he pecked angrily at his keyboard—not that he was generally a ray of sunshine, but today felt especially bleak. Dylan Acosta's mother'd had to be sedated yesterday and would be in to see them this afternoon, but there was little else to go on until the medical examiner or the crime scene techs came back with some DNA or…something. They needed any little bit of evidence they could find.

Acosta was last seen playing on the swings. No one at the school had noticed him with anyone or seen him go into the woods. Had he been singled out purposefully? Had someone he'd known waved him over, or had Acosta gone back to the trees to play and become the victim of an opportunistic killer? Judging by the cigarettes and empty bottles the techs had found back there, the tree line was a popular place to get hammered, and two men fighting one another at the scene didn't scream premeditation. But there'd been no database matches on the fingerprints from the bottles, save a couple high schoolers previously arrested for burglary. And though the size of their suspects suggested they could be high school kids, both those boys had been in school at the time of the Acosta killing.

Morrison tilted his chair back and listened to Petrosky's agitated typing. At least they'd determined the brand of shoes and boots, though it hadn't helped much: middle price range, both readily available at several local shoe stores. The spikes on the boots—too far apart to be aeration shoes or cleats—had probably been added by the wearer. But Petrosky was looking into any place that might be in the business of altering footwear: shoe repair services and the like.

They'd already confirmed that the cause of death was punctured lungs. Morrison had really wanted to be wrong about that. The punctures were so clean, so resolute—the killer had stomped on the boy, then stood back and watched him choke. Enjoying the child's suffering. What kind of a sick fuck drowns a kid in their own blood?

He jumped at a cough near his ear. "What the fuck, Surfer Boy?" Petrosky's jowly face glowered down at him. "You got a bug in your ass? Probably from those cricket bars you eat."

Morrison forced a smile. "They're full of protein. You'd like them if you tried them, Boss."

"I don't give a fuck about protein unless it's bacon, and if you try to feed me a bug bar, I swear to god I'll shove it up your nose."

"Up my...nose?"

"Better than saying 'up your ass.' I'm cleaning shit up. You're a dad now." Petrosky flipped open a file and slapped it on the desk, and this time, Morrison managed to avoid startling. "I've found three other cases in the last two years that fit the pattern," Petrosky said. "Rapes in schools or the surrounding, victims left under trees or bushes, a couple with signs of strangulation. No stomping, though. No deaths, either. Trying to get the kids to review their statements, but apparently, teenage boys are reluctant to face their childhood attackers."

I can imagine. "Maybe at least one will come down, if only to see justice served."

"They don't give a fuck about justice. They just don't want to relive it."

Morrison closed the folder and slid it next to his final stack of paperwork. "We'll figure it out. Truth always comes out. Has to." But even as he said it, he hoped that wasn't true. Some secrets were best hidden lest they destroy you.

Petrosky stood. "Maybe you can do some of that fancy computer bullshit, see if there are any more vics. I'll go follow up with the ones I've got already."

"Want me to come with?"

"Nah, you see if you can find more." Petrosky hauled his coat over one fleshy shoulder. "I'll be back by noon."

THE BUSTLE of the precinct drowned out the images of Acosta's bloody back, and by lunchtime, Morrison had two more potential connections on the middle school rape-homicide, both cold cases fitting the same pattern: clothing around the neck to subdue, attacks occurring in or around the woods. Though in these files, the perp—or perps—had stopped short of the stomping and subsequent murder. The cases he'd found had children who were strangled to unconsciousness and had awoken traumatized—but they did wake up.

At lunch, Morrison hit up the toy store to grab a board game for Abby as well as a stuffed teddy for Evie—just because. The whir of the tires on his way to the park near the precinct was significantly brighter and calmer than it had been before he'd had a stuffed animal riding shotgun. But his peace wavered when he got out of the car. One dead tree stump in the middle of the park. A barren metal skeleton of a swing set to his right, not a single chain left to hint that it had once held swings. But such was the nature of socioeconomic decay—children, and those things that brought them happiness, always deteriorated first. Their voices were smaller, which made them more expendable to the powers that be.

It also made them more vulnerable.

He sat on the broken park bench—two boards missing, but still enough to hold his ass—with a sub sandwich and a folder full of horrible. Maybe Petrosky was already back at the precinct reading through the copy of the file Morrison had left on his desk. That'd save him from having to describe the brutality out loud.

Zachary Reynolds had been taken from his school five years ago, and, like Acosta, had been discovered in the woods that bordered the grounds. His mother had even been volunteering at the school that day. She'd been by the window, someone asked her a question, and *poof* little Zach was gone. Later he was found unconscious with a T-shirt still tied around his neck. Two years later, a seven-year-old girl, Kylie Miller, was taken during a field trip to the firehouse. The girl had been found in the wooded area behind the lot, brutalized and trembling. Not the same as the playground, and nothing around the neck, but she'd said someone had used her shirt to cover her face. Close enough.

Morrison had been in this job long enough to know that pedophiles weren't always choosy. Some male pedophiles even had normal relationships with women: marriage, kids, the works. Some exclusively targeted children. For others, gender was irrelevant, and the attraction was the innocence or the inability of a child to hurt them, common after sexual trauma in the perpetrator's childhood. He and Petrosky would talk to the department shrink, Dr. McCallum, to work up a suspect profile later this week. Or maybe tomorrow, since their perp in the firehouse abduction case was out already, probably roaming the streets for his next victim.

Fucking figured. If they waited long enough, maybe they'd find that guy in a sewer drain with his balls in his mouth.

PETROSKY DIDN'T LOOK up from the file as Morrison sat across from him. "How was your break, Cali?"

Morrison raised an eyebrow. "Cali?"

"Less letters, less effort."

Morrison eyed Petrosky's empty coffee cup. "You get comfortable with that lingo, and you'll be quoting rap lyrics before you know it."

Petrosky flipped a page. "I do that, and you need to take me to the hospital."

"To hide you away before someone younger and hipper slaps you?"

"No, because I've obviously had a fucking stroke, Surfer Boy." Petrosky shoved the open file across the desk, brows furrowed, a half-eaten granola bar in his other hand. "I checked out the cases you referenced," Petrosky said. "Got us an appointment with Dr. McCallum on Thursday, once we have little more for him."

Good. They were on the same page with the shrink.

"Also, the guy convicted on the Miller case…Nick Nolte–looking motherfucker, isn't he?"

"You say that about everyone."

"Give 'em enough crank, and everyone looks like Nolte. Best antidrug campaign there is."

Morrison peered at the mug shot. Pale, with flyaway blond hair and eyes so light they were almost purple. "Okay, so he's a little Nick Nolte. That should help us if anyone saw him around. I figured maybe we could haul him in for questioning. He doesn't have any housing registered, a definite no-no with his sex offender conviction."

Petrosky said nothing, just flipped a few more pages and grunted, his shoulders tight. Something had happened. Morrison opened his mouth to ask, but Petrosky cut him off.

"It was a good find, California. But this twat isn't our guy. Neither are the potentials I pulled this morning."

Morrison's cheeks heated, and he envisioned ice on his face, pushing the flush from his head. His skin cooled. "Twat? So much for cleaning up your language, Boss."

"Sometimes, you need the appropriate verbiage," Petrosky said.

Morrison cocked an eyebrow, and Petrosky shrugged.

"You're not the only one who knows words." He handed Morrison a sheet. "I spent lunch in the lab. Got Echols to rush the DNA."

Of course he had. Heather Echols had just started three weeks ago and couldn't seem to say no to Petrosky—or so Petrosky said. She was probably still scared of the old man, but that wouldn't last long.

"And?" Morrison prompted him.

"She told me this was the last time she was rushing shit for me, so it'd better be worth it."

That had taken less time than he'd thought.

"Found blood from one male suspect and semen from another man at the crime scene, but neither sample belongs to that Nolte-looking fuck from the Kylie Miller case. And there's no doubt that the scuffle happened after the murder and not beforehand: they found Acosta's blood and slivers of bone in the boot tracks. The killer stomped him hard enough to crack ribs." Petrosky grimaced. "Far as I can tell, the boot-wearing guy watched while his buddy raped the kid, then stomped Acosta to death. When the killer stepped back, the rapist went at him—or our killer tried to hurt the rapist too. And while they were scuffling, Acosta was gagging on his own blood."

"Jesus." Hearing it like that…

"That water-to-wine motherfucker abandoned us a long time ago, Surfer Boy. But you were right about Zachary Reynolds." He turned back to the paperwork. "DNA from the Reynolds case is a match to the guy who raped Dylan Acosta yesterday. If only they'd fucking caught him five years ago."

The sub sandwich rose in Morrison's esophagus.

Petrosky flipped the folder closed. "We'll head over to the Reynolds place after school. He'd be…what? Fifteen now?"

Morrison nodded, mute. He must have looked as ill as he felt because Petrosky squinted at him. "You think you can handle the trip, or you want research duty until you can pull your shit together?"

"I'm together, Boss."

Petrosky leaned toward him, his blue eyes softer now with

just a hint of irritation—the closest he got to genuine concern. "See that you stay that way, California. And for fuck's sake, figure out this nanny bullshit before you worry yourself into a goddamn heart attack."

"Not sure I'm the one in danger of a heart attack, Boss." The pile of crumbs near the granola bar wrapper on Petrosky's desk looked suspiciously like powdered sugar.

Petrosky grunted. "Not everyone wants to live to be a hundred, California. Some of us are happy just to make it through the day."

Wasn't that the truth.

PETROSKY MADE the phone calls about the case while Morrison pounded keys and called nanny references. Half the references on his list weren't home, though the background checks were coming up clean. *Progress.* He even checked the ones who weren't on Shannon's short list. Ms. Ackerman, whom he'd not met, was a former nanny for three families and a current psychology student, but Shannon had an x by her name with a note—*funny bone broken*—which made him smile. He did a check anyway, set her folder aside, and finally looked at one he'd met: Ms. Weeks, the grocery clerk who turned nanny after her children grew up and left home. Background check fine, lots of experience, but she was so…grouchy. And old. And he didn't like her. But she apparently had more clout with Shannon, who had not crossed her name off the list despite her humorless scowl.

Natalie Bell also checked out. No complaints. No weird social media activity, no one bitching on her Facebook wall about holding a grudge. No suggestion of an abusive boyfriend who'd show up at his house to grab her in front of his kid. Her life appeared perfectly normal—boring, even. He liked that in a nanny.

That left one more candidate, the nurse Shannon had tried to sell him on. Alyson Kennedy's boss at the hospital said all the right things, noting that Alyson had been a perfectly-perfect employee, but his voice grated on Morrison's ear as if the words themselves were made of sandpaper. He didn't like it. He also didn't like that he couldn't locate Natalie Bell's last employer, though there was something endearing about her. He'd rather have someone he'd met. Morrison didn't realize he was tapping his foot until Petrosky glared at him. He stilled.

Shannon was obviously having an easier time keeping her head straight about all this. He called her cell. "If you had to pick one—"

"Bell."

He smiled into the phone. "Fine."

"I'll call her. Love you."

It was much like the conversation they'd had about their wedding. Best friends for nearly four years, living together for almost one, and she'd just had his baby—he'd still been terrified when he proposed in the hospital with a onesie that said: "Will you marry my daddy?"

A month later, Shannon had chosen a dress and a spot on the beach for the ceremony.

"When should we do it?" he'd asked.

"Tomorrow," she'd said. "Call Petrosky."

And he'd responded with, "Love you," his heart as full as it had ever been, unaware of the demons she was fighting when he went off to work that first month. She was his lifeline. For the last four years, she'd been his everything. But if she could have it to do over, after the PPD had passed…would she still have married him? Would she do it again now? Unease twisted in his belly, deep but insistent as a writhing serpent. Yet another thing he really didn't want to know.

DYLAN ACOSTA'S MOTHER, Tara Lancaster, didn't look up when they entered the interrogation room. Her brown hair was still wet, damp strands plastered to her cheek under bloodshot brown eyes. Water speckled her gray blouse. The sight of those errant drops tightened Morrison's chest as if each one had purposefully escaped from her head, running from the heart-break, the pain. She kept her blank gaze fixed on the double-sided mirror as if waiting for someone to leap through it and tell her they'd made a mistake, that it was some other woman's child they'd found dead in the woods.

Shock did that to you, or maybe whatever the doc had prescribed her; the medications were the main reason they hadn't been able to see her earlier. A sedated witness, especially one numbed to the point of sleep, belonged in bed and not answering critical questions. Or perhaps her vacant look was denial. Her eye twitched, and Morrison wondered if she could already feel it trying to break through her composed façade: the thick heaviness of sorrow, the impending doom of a life where every day was just another in a new reality where a piece of you would forever be rubbed raw by grief.

Petrosky sat across from her at the metal table. When his chair squawked against the concrete floor, she finally turned to face him and sniffed.

Morrison brought his notepad to the corner and stood behind Petrosky, suddenly too antsy to sit across from Lancaster, or maybe he didn't want to look too deeply into her eyes, which surely held a glimpse of her future misery. His heart hurt enough already.

"I was at work," Lancaster said, closing her eyes a beat longer than a blink. "They told me to come to the station right away. I thought…I thought maybe his dad had taken him." She shuddered, though the temperature in the room was always a good five degrees warmer than was comfortable. Then again, Morrison's insides felt cold too.

"Is his father your ex-husband, ma'am?" Petrosky asked.

Slow nod. Then: "But he didn't do this."

Morrison flipped to a clean page and wrote, *ex-husband*.

"We'll need his address." Petrosky's voice was soft, but Morrison recognized the set of his shoulders—they'd investigate the ex. Most victims were abused by someone familiar to them, and it would have been easy for a father to get his son to walk off the playground.

He wasn't sure Lancaster had heard Petrosky until she nodded slowly.

"Any issues with your ex lately?" Petrosky shifted in his seat.

"Arguments about custody. He wanted more time with Dylan. I said no."

"How'd he take that?"

"Terribly. But—"

"What did he say?"

She lowered her gaze to her shaking hands. "That he'd see me in court. And he said he'd make sure Dylan knew what a bitch I was. That he'd drag me through the mud."

The mud. Literally what had happened to Dylan Acosta. But this didn't feel like an angry ex seeking revenge. The crimes committed against Acosta were vicious. And their killer hadn't started with Acosta—this type of rape-homicide was usually carried out by a sexual predator, escalating when the mere act of assault no longer thrilled him.

"How was your ex with Dylan?" Petrosky said. "Any changes in their relationship or Dylan's behavior?"

Morrison touched his pen to the notepad. He'd been in enough interrogations with Petrosky to know what he was getting at—whether her ex had been inappropriate.

"Once we divorced, Glen really started spending more time with Dylan."

Morrison wrote *Glen Acosta* next to *ex-husband* and waited.

"Dylan…loved him," she said to the table. "He never complained, ever." She looked up at Petrosky and blinked rapidly to clear the water from her eyes. "That actually pissed me off a little, that my ex was always the good guy."

"Inappropriate behavior toward Dylan or other boys?"

Her glassy eyes squinted at the ceiling, then settled on Petrosky. "Never. He even coaches Dylan's little league team. Coached." Her voice cracked, and Morrison could almost hear her heart breaking. "Glen's an asshole to me, but you're wasting your time. You find the bastard that did this."

"We'll do our best, ma'am." Petrosky leaned toward her, voice softer now. "Did your ex have any nicknames for Dylan? Maybe his number one kid, anything like that?"

The bloody *#1* carved into the child's side was seared on Morrison's brain too. He could almost feel the blade against his skin. He tightened his grip on his pen, hoping Acosta's mother knew something about the number—if she did, the killer probably knew the boy or his family.

"Nothing like that. My ex isn't very…creative."

Petrosky leaned back, hands clasped on the desktop. "What about other people who spent time with your son? Pastors, coaches, teachers? Anyone Dylan seemed uncomfortable around?"

"You think Dylan…knew the person who did this?"

In the other case they'd found—Zachary Reynolds—the victim hadn't known his attacker. But here there were two suspects instead of just one, and Acosta's killer would have a different pattern from the pedophile who'd raped the boys. Acosta probably knew at least one of them if the suspects lured him off the playground instead of waiting for him to wander into the woods of his own accord.

"We don't know, but those who hurt children often groom them for a period of time."

Petrosky didn't correct her assumption about "the person" who'd done this, and Morrison was thankful for that. She didn't need to find out today that a pair of men had brutalized her child.

"I always told him not to talk to strangers. I thought that'd be enough."

Kids were rarely attacked by strangers. Again, neither of them said a word to correct her.

"Does your son have a computer?" Petrosky asked.

"Of course. They need it for school." Her chest puffed up just slightly like her guilt was boiling over into defensiveness.

"We'll need access to it in case he was communicating with someone online."

"He wasn't communicating with anyone," she said. "I would have known."

"What about online gaming?" Morrison's own voice sounded oddly hollow against the concrete walls. Not every interaction would be saved as an email or readily available on a laptop or iPad, but if Acosta'd been using the web to communicate with the men who'd attacked him, Morrison would find it.

Petrosky glanced back, nodded, and turned back to Lancaster.

"No."

"None? At all?" Petrosky cocked his head.

"We don't let him play those grown-up games. There are kids in his class who were getting into trouble with that."

"Trouble like how?" Petrosky asked. "Strangers contacting them or—"

"No, just…there are some vile games out there."

Morrison leaned back against the wall and focused on the pad as Petrosky nodded his agreement about the video games, probably building rapport—he doubted Petrosky had ever actually played one.

When Petrosky stilled, she continued: "All he does is some block building game, but….well, he said you do have to be online. For some of it. And I guess…he did talk to his friends on there. But just his friends, I made sure."

Morrison made a note.

"We'll need those passwords too," Petrosky said. "Whatever user names he has."

"But it's just… I've read articles. Those games are good for his brain. *Were* good for…" Her breath came out rapidly, and the walls reflected it back like a shockwave of regret.

"Did you read about the six-year-old child who was lured from her home and kidnapped after playing a game like that?" Petrosky had obviously decided that Tara Lancaster wasn't providing him with answers fast enough—or that she was stonewalling him, even if she was in denial. Probably the latter, based on the harshness in his voice and the set of his shoulders.

Lancaster's jaw dropped, and she made no effort to close it.

Petrosky leaned across the table. "It's not the game itself," he said more softly. "The people who victimize children—these guys know how to find kids. They usually pretend to be other kids. There's no way you'd know. It's not your fault." Petrosky pulled out a photo from Zachary Reynolds's case file, a composite sketch of the guy who'd raped Reynolds. The guy whose semen was also found in Lancaster's son. "You ever seen him before?"

She squinted at it and shook her head. "I don't think so."

"Are you certain?"

"As certain as I can be about anything right now."

Petrosky shifted in the seat, grunting faintly with the effort. "Do you have a boyfriend? Babysitters? Anyone who had regular contact with Dylan?"

She shook her head again. "No boyfriend and no sitter. I work at the bank—I drop him off for school and pick him up after. No one else is around, usually. Just at baseball, but you'd have to ask Glen about that."

True, there wouldn't have been a lot of time for a predator to take Acosta aside during a game—let alone actually abuse him between innings. But to groom Acosta, to connect with him, a ballgame was prime abuser territory. Maybe an assistant coach. Another father. A man who wouldn't stick out at a little boy's baseball practice.

"Dylan does...did...spend time with friends. Sleepovers or mall trips with his friends' older siblings, that kind of thing. He was small, but he was almost twelve, so I guess he was...pulling away a little bit. Didn't tell me as much anymore." Her eyes filled, then dripped down her face onto the table. She sniffed.

"I'll need those names also, ma'am," Petrosky said.

"They wouldn't have hurt Dylan. They have kids too."

Half of their solved cases ended with the arrest of a family friend, one with children themselves. Morrison pressed his lips together. No reason to point it out—any correction would be taken as an accusation right now, and she'd already go home wracked with guilt. And if the agony that still tinted Petrosky's eyes like sorrowful watercolors was any indication, the heartbreak would never leave.

———

MORRISON AND PETROSKY left the interrogation room with a list of contacts from Tara Lancaster. Five stops to start with. Five times they'd have to see the anguish in Acosta's friends, in other parents who were overcome by horror thinking that it could just as easily have been their child. Though maybe in one, they'd see the twinkle of remorse or feel the niggling of guilt like goose-flesh on exposed legs. That'd be good—but it was hard to say whether it was likely. Not only did they have two perps, not typical for this type of case, but they had one rapist and one murderer—maybe. Acosta may have known one and not the other, or they both might have been strangers to the boy.

Outside the precinct, the sky was bright and blue and still, not even the hint of a breeze. Petrosky's car stunk of old grease and cigarettes. Gross, but somehow welcome, like coming home to a dirty house that was still comfortable because it belonged to you. Morrison rolled the window down anyway—even home needed to be aired out, especially since Petrosky was already pulling a smoke from the pack on the dash as he put the car in gear.

They'd start with Dylan's father. Petrosky had called him from the interrogation room after Lancaster left and agreed to meet him in a bar after work. Morrison's heart rate climbed at the prospect—Petrosky and liquor, addicts in their place of addiction. But when Petrosky caught Morrison's stare, he'd leveled a glare so fierce Morrison felt like an ass for even considering it.

Sobriety was a daily battle, but not necessarily a difficult one, at least not every day. Maybe Petrosky'd found a way to make his days easier while Morrison had been changing dirty diapers. He seemed fine, or as fine as he'd ever been. Petrosky had always worn his grouchiness like a badge of honor, possibly because he hated most people but more likely because he was protecting some soft spot inside from harm. God knew the man had been through enough.

They were halfway to the lot exit when a figure crossed the road from the neighboring prosecutor's office. As tall as Morrison himself at well over six feet, with broad shoulders and a blond crew cut, Roger McFadden—Shannon's ex-husband and lead prosecutor and incredible asshole—had a nose that would always be a touch crooked after connecting with Morrison's fist. Too bad his ego still wouldn't accept that he was less than perfect. Roger walked directly toward them, and Petrosky didn't slow—a game of douchebag chicken. Roger's suit was as impeccable as was his gold watch, probably the one Shannon had given him for their second anniversary. They hadn't made it to three. It shouldn't have annoyed him, but every hair on Morrison's arms stood up at the sight of the gold glinting in the morning sun.

Petrosky slammed on his brakes at the last possible moment, the front bumper practically kissing Roger's pants. A part of Morrison was disappointed that Petrosky hadn't mowed him down.

"Well, well, you're back," Roger said. His eyes bored through the windshield as he leaned toward them, hands on the hood, and Morrison immediately regretted rolling down the window. The corner of Roger's mouth turned up. "And how's my lovely wife?"

Roger would spend a lifetime seeking reinforcement, burning for Shannon to say: "I was wrong. You're worth it; you're better." And yet if that were ever to actually happen, he'd reject her as he had when he'd been married to her. Winning was all that mattered to Roger.

"Shannon's doing just fine." Morrison said, working to keep his voice even.

Petrosky puffed on his cigarette and grinned. "Better watch it, Rog, before he breaks your nose again."

The smug smile slid from Roger's face. "Not if he wants to keep providing for his lovely little family. Even if he is sloppy seconds."

Morrison's fists clenched, but he forced his face to remain placid. He could almost hear the ocean in his head, settling with each breath he took: stormy waves of rage and anger calming to a tumultuous lapping, easing to a gentle whoosh of salt on sand. Peaceful. He smiled and chuckled, making sure Roger saw it.

Roger's face twisted with anger—the man hated nothing more than to be the butt of someone's joke.

Petrosky stuck his head out the window. "Move, fuckhead!"

Roger squared his shoulders and held his ground.

Petrosky jerked the wheel to the right, and Roger leapt out of the way as Petrosky swung around him and sprayed his suit with gravel and dust. Morrison kept his eyes on the side-view mirror, watching Roger frantically brushing at his suit and muttering what were probably curse words under the squeal of the tires as Petrosky turned onto the main road.

"Once a dick, always a dick," Petrosky said.

Morrison dragged his eyes back to the front windshield, his smile still frozen on his lips. He itched with the desire to smash his knuckles into Roger's stupid face. Again.

"He's just pissed that Shannon's always loved you." Petrosky ashed his cigarette out the window and shoved it between his teeth again. "Even when she was married to him."

"I'm not sure that's true," Morrison said, but he felt suddenly lighter.

9

THE REYNOLDS FAMILY lived in Rochester, a forty-five-minute drive from Detroit, in a two-story colonial in a neighborhood where children still rode bikes without looking over their shoulders, and the stray dog wandering in your yard belonged to someone you knew so there was no need to be cautious about approaching it. Ironic that they were going to visit a kid who knew just how easily the illusion of safety could be shattered. It had been five years since Zachary Reynolds's attack, but hopefully, they'd get something they could use.

Mrs. Reynolds answered the door wearing a white turtleneck and a gold treble clef on a chain over her heart. Brown hair, brown eyes, brown freckles over the bridge of her nose. The living room was warm, with worn leather sofas and oak end tables, but there was nothing to indicate people actually lived here. No toys. No books. Just baubles and vases on the shelves flanking the fireplace.

She gestured to the couch. "So how can I help? You said you might have some new information about my son's...attack?" She smoothed down her pencil skirt and sat across from them. Feigning composure. But the subtle quiver in her hands gave her away. "I didn't know they were still looking at his case."

"We may have a related crime," Petrosky said, his face still and watchful as a lion sizing up prey.

"This is about that boy. The one they found…murdered behind the school playground." Not a question. Her mouth tightened—it could have been her kid dead on the ground. Almost had been. She wrung her hands.

Morrison set the case file in his lap and pulled his notebook from his back pocket: *Reynolds, mother.* The mere process of scratching ink on the pad relaxed his shoulders, though he had no real reason to be tense to begin with. Roger must have gotten to him more than he'd thought.

"Why do you think the cases are related, Detective? Because of the…rape at school thing?" She dropped her eyes.

"Yes."

And because of the DNA at the scene. Then there was the T-shirt around Acosta's neck, tied just like the one that had strangled Reynolds. But Petrosky didn't elaborate.

She clutched her necklace, stopping short of touching her throat. "You think he tried to kill my Zach, too?"

"I think he wanted Zach to be quiet," Petrosky said. "Or he managed to stop himself." But it wasn't the shirt around the throat that had killed Acosta. Leaping from rape to stomping a kid to death—or allowing it—was a stretch. And from the struggle at the scene…it didn't seem like this rapist had been ready to take that step. So who had? Morrison tried not to picture the gaping holes in Acosta's back, tried not to imagine the sound of his last breaths as they were reduced to a bloody gurgle.

"You think he's escalating?" she said.

Petrosky raised an eyebrow. "Ma'am?"

"My shrink, he tells me about this stuff. I mean, I ask, and he answers." She reached for a box of tissues on the end table, thought better of it, and smoothed her skirt again. "I read a lot too. Real crime. Books on these…pedophiles. Trying to understand what Zach went through. What he's still going through." She wrung her hands again, then looked Petrosky in the eye. "Ask your questions. It'll be easier for me before he gets here."

"Walk me through the day it happened."

She did, her eyes filling and overflowing. It had been a typical morning. They'd eaten breakfast and headed to the school like every other day. She'd even been working with Zach's homeroom teacher, putting together folders and supervising a class project on Abraham Lincoln.

"Do most parents volunteer like that?" Morrison asked, and Reynolds's eyes widened as if she'd forgotten he was there.

She recovered quickly and shook her head. "Not usually that much. Maybe an hour or two every quarter."

Morrison tapped the notepad with his pen, stopping when she frowned. "But you'd been there that whole week."

"Zach had just gotten out of the hospital, and I wanted to make sure he was…okay." She shuddered. "Leukemia. We almost lost him. And even now…I mean, the risk is there." She was trembling. "And he just keeps tempting fate."

Morrison made a note on his pad—*Acting out?*—while she grabbed a tissue and wiped her eyes like it was the fault of the Kleenex that her son's health had been shitty. He understood. Sometimes there was no one to blame.

"So after the homeroom project…" Petrosky said.

"I went to the office to make copies. The printer is right in front of the window that looks out to the playground. I never should have taken my eyes off him."

"Why did you?" Petrosky asked.

"This wasn't my fault!"

But she'd remember it every day for the rest of her life, that one moment of looking away from her child. And tomorrow, Evie would be gone for a week, away from his own watchful gaze. Morrison's gut clenched.

"Absolutely not your fault, ma'am," Petrosky said. "But the report said that someone asked you a question?"

Her shoulders relaxed. She nodded.

"Someone who worked there?"

"No. It was…just a guy. Came into the office." She furrowed her brows. "He asked whether there was school on President's Day, which I thought was weird because it was over a month away, but it wasn't really that strange of a question, I guess."

Same answer she'd given to the police five years ago— Morrison had looked through the witness statements. But he had yet to scour the atrociously-written and horribly-sorted police notes to see if the cops had actually located the question asker. They'd get on that next.

She glanced from Petrosky to Morrison and his pen and back again. "You think it was on purpose? That this guy asked me something just to get me to look away?"

"Probably not, ma'am. Just covering the bases."

"Then, did someone distract this new boy's teacher while they lured him off the playground?"

"Not that we know of."

"But you think he did it to…wait, was there more than one guy? With this new boy? Is that why you're asking about someone in the office?"

She was quick. Petrosky met her gaze and said nothing, but Morrison could see the wheels working behind her eyes. Petrosky inhaled to speak again, but she beat him to it.

"He was blond. Probably younger than I was then, but not by much. A few wrinkles around the eyes, you know."

"Eye color?"

She considered, then shook her head. "I used to think that every detail of that morning would be imprinted on my brain forever. But this…"

She hadn't known back when Zachary had been attacked—either Petrosky hadn't read the case file, or he was trying to catch her in a lie.

"Short or long hair?"

"Long. Ponytail, actually. I remember thinking that he looked like a hippie. The police must have interviewed him—they interviewed everyone in the school. But this guy was so…different looking. Definitely wasn't the one who attacked Zach—he looked nothing like the guy from the police sketch they did afterward."

"Any distinguishing marks? Scars?"

"No, I don't think." She swallowed hard. "I can't really remember. But like I said, I'm sure they talked to him. They talked to everyone."

"Is there anything else you recall from that day, anything you neglected to tell the officers?"

"I called every week for over a year. Everything I knew, they knew. Now it's been so long...I'm starting to forget details, I guess." Her eyes remained drawn, but there was a hopeful edge to her voice beneath the regret. It had to be rather promising that one *could* forget even small pieces of a day so awful. Perhaps one day, the other memories would fade as the good in life oozed in to crowd out the tragedy. Though the horror never fully disappeared.

"Does the number one mean anything to you? Even the symbol, the pound sign followed by the numeral?"

She shook her head, but the door interrupted her, a hearty slam punctuated by the throbbing beat of heavy soles approaching the doorway.

Zachary Reynolds had a dog collar around his neck and silver rings through his septum and eyebrow. He glared at Morrison and Petrosky, then at his mother. "I told you I didn't want to do this."

"It will just take a moment, honey and—"

"Fuck this." He pointed to Petrosky. "And fuck them."

"He did it to someone else." Petrosky stood abruptly, his eyes on the boy's boots. "Nice kicks. Where'd you get them?"

Kicks? Looked like someone had swapped the old man for a newer, hipper version. Morrison resisted the urge to tell Petrosky that the word might not mean what he thought it did.

The kid glared.

"I gave him the boots," Mrs. Reynolds said from the couch.

"You have more of 'em?" Petrosky asked, though why it mattered was beyond Morrison. It wasn't like Zachary Reynolds had teamed up with his rapist to attack and murder another child. And the boots didn't appear to have treads like those at the Acosta scene—too flat, and no sign of anything that would puncture the skin.

Zach squinted, and his mother answered again. "Just the one pair. For his birthday. Why are you—"

"I said I didn't want to do this," Zach repeated.

Petrosky stepped forward. "You may not give a fuck about this other kid—"

Mrs. Reynolds stood too, her eyes wide. "Detective—"

"It's my job to try to find this asshole," he said to Zach. "I'd like to fry the ever-loving shit out of the guy who hurt you. And if it's the same fellow, all the better when I hook his nipples to a car battery."

Mrs. Reynolds's mouth dropped in shock. "Maybe if you leave your questions, I can ask him later or..."

Zach appraised his mother, lips tight, then returned to Petrosky. "Let's talk outside."

Mrs. Reynolds reached out to touch the boy's arm, but he pulled away and stalked back out the front door. Petrosky followed, Mrs. Reynolds gasping objections behind them. Her cheeks flamed.

Morrison touched her elbow, expecting her to shove him off, but she stopped in the foyer and turned back slowly, her mouth drawn in acquiescence.

"Detective Petrosky might seem a little rough around the edges, but he knows what he's doing," he said quietly.

Her foot was tapping—like she was trying to decide whether to go tearing off after them. But from what he'd just witnessed, her presence would be enough to make the boy stop speaking altogether.

"Do we still have your consent, ma'am? To speak to your son?"

Her yes was barely audible through her heavy sigh.

ZACHARY REYNOLDS and Petrosky were already halfway down the street, twin trails of smoke wafting toward the sky above them. Mommy would love that. From down the block, Morrison heard a string of curse words erupt from the teen's mouth. *She'll love that too.*

Morrison caught up with them in time to hear Petrosky say: "—tone of voice? How about anything specific that he said?"

"No, he was kinda quiet. Smiled though, and he seemed so... nice. Gave me candy. Fucking cliché. I know it was stupid, following him, but..." Reynolds looked down. "He did look familiar, but I don't know where we'd met before. I tried for years to figure that out." He shook his head and pulled on the cigarette.

"You don't recall anyone else out there? Even just standing around?"

"Nope, no one."

"I read the report, Zach. Frizzy brownish hair. Scraggly, right?"

Slow nod.

"The report said you weren't sure on the eye color. Remember anything afterward? Not just on the eyes but on his appearance?"

Scars, facial hair, or acne could help them identify a suspect, but even recent eyewitness reports were often inaccurate. Five years ago? Petrosky was really reaching now.

Reynolds shook his head. "Seriously, I don't know. He was shorter than most adults, I guess, but he was old. Like…thirtysomething. And he was strong, and I couldn't…stop him."

Huh. It sounded like the pedophile who'd raped Reynolds five years ago had committed a crime of opportunity—if Reynolds had been groomed, he'd know where he'd met the guy. Would the rapist have stuck to that pattern? Had the *killer* known Dylan Acosta?

"Of course you couldn't stop him, Zach. No one doubts that. Right now, I'm just trying to find something we can use for identification. Stains on his jeans: paint or grease? Some other sign of where he worked? A name tag? The exact pattern on his T-shirt, an extra logo maybe?"

"He wasn't wearing a T-shirt. It was a button-down kinda thing, like a short-sleeved dress shirt. There wasn't anything on it…I don't think."

Petrosky stopped walking. "In the initial report, you told the officers he was wearing a clown shirt."

Reynolds's eyes narrowed as if he were trying to protect them from the smoke wafting from his nostrils. "Clown shirt?"

"That's what was in the file. A picture of a clown on his—"

"It wasn't on his shirt. It was on his stomach."

The pen in Morrison's hand jittered over the page more than

he wanted it to. He pressed the tip harder against the paper before Petrosky could notice.

"A tattoo?" Petrosky said it slowly as if worried he'd heard the boy incorrectly.

"I mean, maybe I said it weird. I was tired and scared and... confused. Or I might not have known the name for a tattoo back then." He fingered his eyebrow ring, and the metal glinted in the sun. "Maybe I told them he was wearing a picture? I was all fucked up in the head. I really can't remember what I said, but I know the picture was on his fucking gut, and I only saw it once I tore the buttons off his shirt, trying to get away. It moved when he—" Reynolds's lip quivered, and he covered it by jamming the cigarette between his teeth.

"Sounds like you remember it pretty well."

The kid's face disappeared behind an acrid cloud.

"Can you describe it?"

"Well...a clown, like I said. On a horse. But it was creepy, had fangs and stuff."

"Could you draw it?" Petrosky asked, his voice even. "Doesn't have to be perfect, just what you remember."

Reynolds took the notepad and sketched, his cigarette dangling from his lips. Ash dropped onto his boot, and he paused to shake it off before completing the sketch.

Morrison and Petrosky peered at the drawing: a vampire clown, carrying a rifle and riding a vampire horse, the animal's mouth full of foam and blood.

"You're a good artist," Morrison said.

Reynolds dragged at the smoke. "For all the good it'll do me." He turned to Petrosky. "You think he killed that other kid? My mom told me about it."

"Not sure yet."

"He probably should have killed me too," Reynolds whispered, his eyes on his boots as he toed the dirt. Silent. Probably waiting for them to challenge such a notion.

Petrosky shrugged. "Maybe he should have." Morrison balked, but Petrosky wasn't done. "Because if we get him based on what you said, he's going to be sorry as fuck that he left you alive." He inhaled sharply on the cigarette. "You know what they do to pedophiles in prison, Zach?"

The kid met Petrosky's eyes.

Smoke curled toward the pewter sky. "Use your imagination, before your mother files charges against me for corrupting you. But let's just say, he'll wish he was dead every goddamn day. And he'll never look at a broom the same way again."

Reynolds tossed his cigarette butt on the sidewalk, blew smoke at his shoes, and smiled.

"BUT AS IN ETHICS, EVIL IS A CONSEQUENCE OF GOOD, SO IN FACT,
OUT OF JOY IS SORROW BORN."
~EDGAR ALLAN POE, *BERENICE*

10

THE WORLD WHIPPED by the passenger window, but Morrison barely noticed. A search for scary-ass clowns had given him more results than he would have thought. On his smartphone screen, two men in clown costumes—more Stephen King's *It* than Bozo—screamed about slicing up their girlfriends and impaling them on fence posts outside a circus tent, all over the twang of a banjo. Clown Alley Freaks, a local band that appeared to be a combination of gangster rap and backwoods hillbilly. *Who listens to this stuff?* But he already knew the answer—he wished he knew less about all the sickness in the—

Morrison stopped scrolling through album covers on his cell and tapped one to enlarge.

The cover was purple and yellow, with a torn circus tent as the backdrop. In the foreground, a grisly clown atop a horse sneered at him over the top of a hunting rifle, blood dripping from its mouth, a severed leg in one hand like a club. A single arm was clamped between the horse's teeth, useless tendons stringing toward the ground like ghastly spaghetti. *Sick.* And these people were out there, walking around like normal folks, grocery shopping and hanging out at the park. With his wife. With his daughter. His stomach soured.

"Has to have something to do with these guys," he said,

glancing up as Petrosky maneuvered into the precinct parking lot.

Petrosky put the car in park. "Fucking hell. Kid's got a good memory."

"Guess some things you never forget." Morrison pocketed the phone. "Should we start with the east side tattoo parlors? I can pull up a list—"

"Go home."

"But we just got a break—"

"It's Tuesday night. They're not open now, California."

"How do you know?"

"You're worried."

Morrison balked. "What?"

"About Shannon. I can smell it on you." Petrosky chewed on the butt of the cigarette. "She's okay. A few scary post-pregnancy thoughts a few months back, but she's okay now. If thinking about suicide a few times made it happen, we'd all be dead."

"I don't think she's…unstable." Though anyone else she came across might be.

"Of course you don't. But I know you're thinking about how she was with Evie those first few weeks—how she struggled. And it's the first time she's been alone all day since then."

"Well, in just a few days, she'll be with Alex and Abby." But Petrosky was right. The nagging in Morrison's gut wasn't about how many crazy assholes Shannon might encounter on her way to Atlanta.

"If you're not home for dinner, Shannon is going to have your ass. And mine."

She'd still be up in a couple hours. "Nah, she'll—"

"This isn't a trial run where you get to check how she reacts when you stand her up." Petrosky yanked the keys from the ignition and pushed open the car door. "Catch you in the morning, California. And if I see you inside, I'm the one you'll need to worry about, not Shannon."

Morrison nodded, relieved, and pulled his car keys from his pocket. "Got it, Boss."

"I'VE CALLED Natalie Bell three times, but I can't get through." Shannon speared a bite of salad and frowned at the fork. "Maybe she already took another job."

Morrison glanced at Evie, who was nursing at Shannon's breast, dressing from Shannon's salad in her hair. He waited for a twinge of disappointment over the fact that they still hadn't hired a nanny, but felt no such irritation. Maybe he really wasn't ready to have a stranger caring for his daughter. "She got another position that fast?"

"I told you, the good ones get snapped up quickly."

"It's been a day."

"But a week from the first interview I did." She shoved a handful of blond hair off her face. Her curls fell right back down in a messy tangle.

Morrison suppressed a grin. "Maybe she just had something to do today. I'll try her after dinner."

"Oh, because you can make a phone call better than I can?"

"They call me The Master Dialer."

Shannon laughed and put her free hand up in mock surrender. Evie wiggled on her lap, only the top of her head visible under the table and one tiny, fleshy fist punching at Shannon's clothing as if Evie was personally oppressed by her mother's shirt. "Call away."

Movement at Morrison's ankle made him jump. The cat mewed at him, its dark fur glassy as an oil slick. "We need to get another dog."

"You love Slash."

"He hates me. Wakes me up at least four times a week to go outside." Already the cat had moved on to Shannon's side of the table, where his wife was dropping bits of salmon onto the tile floor.

"Install a cat door. And he doesn't hate you." Her eyes were on the animal. Evie's fist swung up again and almost connected with Shannon's chin.

"You tell her, Evie. Tell her Slash is a buttface."

"He's just an outside cat, Morrison. They're a little more...particular."

"He's a jerk."

"So's Petrosky, and we keep him around."

Morrison peered under the table and glowered at the cat, and Slash mewed back. Damn if he wasn't adorable. Morrison pursed his lips. "Don't look at me like that, you little furball."

"What's wrong?" Shannon sat the baby up and wiped salmon from Evie's forehead. Evie babbled in protest and scrunched up her face.

"Nothing."

"Stressed about work? Or the nannies?"

He pushed his own salmon around on his plate. "No. That took some figuring out today, but no." There was the case, but that was just the job. But Shannon was leaving tomorrow. With Evie. They'd be gone for a week and if Shannon started to have those dark thoughts again... No, he was probably just stressed. Or upset about...Roger's gold watch. Yes, just remembering the glint of sun on the watch's face, like Shannon's gift was happy to be on Roger's wrist, stoked an irrational fury deep in Morrison's gut. "I saw Roger today."

"Ah, that'll do it." She searched his face. "How did he seem?"

Why does she care? "Like himself."

"So, like a dickhead?"

Morrison's chest loosened a little, and the sudden lack of tension made him lean back in his chair. Had he really been holding onto that all day? "He was definitely a dickhead."

"I'm not looking forward to going back to work with him. Maybe one day you and I will just move away altogether. Start fresh."

"Yeah."

She furrowed her brows. "But?"

"You know I don't want to—"

"—leave Petrosky." She grabbed her fork. "He'll be okay, Morrison. I promise. We don't have to go far, just...far enough that I don't have to deal with Roger." She ran her fingers through her hair and blew out an exasperated breath. "Sorry. I'm a little stressed too. I've been thinking about getting a position in another city. I don't want to work too far from home, but I can't

9999

9999

9999

9999

9999

9999

9999

9999

9999

9999

9999

9999

9999

9999

9999

9999

9999

9999

9999

9999

9999

9999

9999

9999

9999

MEGHAN O'FLYNN

find much else in Southfield or anywhere within thirty minutes. I'm stuck."

Stuck. With him? *With the job.* The fork handle was digging into his palm, and he released his grip.

"I guess it's good. I can…heal a little more before making big changes. Get back to what I know. But it's been on my mind lately, and even Dr. McCallum seems to think it'd be a good move."

"You talked to McCallum before me?" Of course she'd talked to her shrink. Why wouldn't she? That was his job. But still, he was her best friend, her husband and—

"Well, no." Shannon switched Evie to the other breast, and the kid kicked her in the gut so hard that Shannon winced. "I mean, yeah, I talked to him, but I didn't want to bother you with it until I had it figured out in my own head."

God, he was a hypocrite. Dr. McCallum was the only person who knew—*really knew*—about Morrison's addiction and his missing memories. Now that Morrison was sober, McCallum thought the missing pieces would never come to light. "State-dependent memory requires you to be in a similar state for recall to the one you were in when the memory was formed," the shrink had said. So if you'd repressed a memory of an event that had happened, say, while drinking, you were more likely to retrieve that memory from your brain during an intoxicated state.

The gist, as Morrison understood it, was that he'd need to shoot up to fill in the gaps in his memory. And that wasn't worth one morning of traumatized reminiscing—withdrawal had been a beast. Though not as much of a beast as his emotions had been without the drug. He had never gotten to the sell-your-soul-to-the-devil stage of addiction, but heroin had been like a lover, the only thing that made him feel something besides the bitter emptiness from the deaths of his parents: his dad shot dead in a robbery when Morrison was still in primary school and his mother, beaten to death with a baseball bat by an abusive boyfriend Morrison's freshman year of college. And his best friend Danny, his glazed eyes, the blood on Morrison's hands…

68

Maybe the lack of memory was for the best. Most days, he sincerely didn't want to know what he'd forgotten.

Morrison watched Slash leap onto the extra chair at the dining table and curl into a purring ball. Shannon was right. If she'd asked him earlier about changing jobs, he probably would have asked if she thought big changes were a good idea while transitioning back into the working world. And he should trust her. He *needed* to trust her. Shannon was strong, intelligent—she wasn't one to tolerate being treated like an invalid. It was bad enough that she had doubted herself, but if she hadn't told him… she doubted his faith in her, too.

He touched her hand. "Whatever you want to do, Shanny, you know I'll support you." If they needed to move a little farther out, they would. The market wasn't great, but they'd figure it out. They'd—

Slash picked his head up as Morrison's cell rang. Probably Petrosky—maybe with a lead. Morrison dropped his fork and had raised the phone to his ear before he recognized that the ringtone itself was just the standard buzz and not Petrosky's *Miami Vice* jingle or the ringtone belonging to Valentine or the chief. Telemarketer? "Morrison."

"Hey, this is Natalie Bell." Her voice was hoarse, low. A cold?

"Ms. Bell. Good to hear from you." Across from him, Shannon straightened, and Evie fussed at the movement.

"I know you called about the job, but I took something else." Not sick. *Whispering.* Muffled like she was talking through a cloth or had a hand wrapped over the receiver.

"Oh, okay, thanks for letting us know." The line went dead before Morrison could say goodbye.

Shannon stared at him expectantly, eyebrows at her hairline. "So?"

"No-go on Bell. She found something else."

"Dammit! We should have just offered it to her when she was here. I know it's better to be thorough, but—" She frowned. "Why'd she call you? I left my number earlier."

"I gave her my business card yesterday. Besides, I told you, I'm The Master Dialer." He picked up his fork again.

"You didn't even have a chance to dial." Shannon looked at Slash. "Fuck."

"Indeed."

Shannon put her napkin on the table and stood, tugging her shirt down and shifting Evie to her hip. "You want to call Alyson Kennedy with your magical phone fingers while I take a bath?" She walked around the table and put Evie in his lap, then brushed his ear with her lips. "And if she says no, don't tell me until you've secured us another nanny, okay?"

He put his hand on the small of her back. "You sure Alyson is the one you—"

Her look stopped him. No arguing with lawyers.

"You'll love her," she said. "Trust me." Shannon kissed him again, on the lips this time, and her smell lingered in his nostrils like all that was right with the world was concentrated there in her scent.

"You got it, Shanny."

She headed for the door. "I just nursed Evie, so if you manage to get her down before I get out of the tub, join me. We're leaving for Alex's in the morning, and we won't see you for a week."

Morrison stared down at Evie's round face, at her wide eyes as blue as the sea, her Cupid bow lips grinning at him. "You're not going to let that happen, are you, beautiful?"

Evie just gurgled.

EVIE DIDN'T FALL asleep in his arms until well after Shannon had emerged from the bathtub, but the smell of Shannon's skin was all it took. Their lovemaking was patient, though faster than it had been in the days before Evie, when he used to spend hours stroking Shannon's skin, watching her writhe. Now she'd rather sleep—not that he could blame her. Parenthood was draining in a way he'd not expected—in a way he'd never have known about if he hadn't stayed home this last month. Afterward, he lay beside her and watched the moon cast shadows on her bare back, every familiar plane of her skin hazy beneath the soft glow. Somewhere in the night, a dog howled, loud and long, perhaps seeking another to share the moonlight with him. Seeking what Morrison had already found. The baby monitor crackled from the end table.

Morrison rolled toward the wall where the darkness was deep and quiet—a pleasant break from the harsh glare of day. He drifted off to sleep with his heart full and peaceful, the phantom voices of a repressed memory for once blissfully silent.

11

By the time Morrison woke up Wednesday morning, he'd almost acquiesced to the idea that Alyson Kennedy would make a damn fine nanny for Evie. When he'd called her the night before, she'd practically squealed with excitement. "I'm thrilled. I can't wait to meet you, Mr. Morrison. And I can't wait to care for Evie. She's a doll." Even Evie had seemed extra happy this morning, her pudgy cheeks shining, milk dribbling down her chin as he bounced her in one arm. But Evie didn't know that she and Shannon were leaving for a week.

Morrison's stomach was twisted in knots. He hefted Shannon's suitcase into the trunk alongside the pack-n-play she'd brought for Evie to sleep in, then grabbed the cooler and positioned it in the front seat so Shannon would have easy access when she got hungry. "Say hi to Roxy for me," he said lightly. He still missed the dog he'd given to Shannon's niece, though he wouldn't admit it. Nor would he admit how badly he wished the dog was there now—he'd have felt better knowing Roxy was riding shotgun, protecting his family in his absence.

He tried to smile, but his whole face felt tight, like the muscles in his cheeks were rubber bands stretched to a hair from snapping. "And say hi to Abby and Alex, of course."

"You know I will." Shannon slammed the trunk.

He kissed Evie's soft, downy head. "I'll miss you guys."

"I wish you could come. I wish you hadn't used up all your time off after Evie was born, but…I really needed you then." She wrapped her arms around him and squeezed. The spring air sent the branches crackling above them as if the atmosphere itself was irritated by the thought of their separation.

"And I'm fine now, Morrison. Really. I'm fine, and Evie will be fine." Her voice was tight, rushed, like she was trying to convince herself.

He pulled back. "I know you're fine. I didn't think for one moment you weren't." That might have been a lie, but he couldn't dwell on it. Some of the things she'd told him…

"I can do this. I've got this." He almost winced at the furious intensity in her gaze. Did she resent the mere idea that she'd needed him? He shook off the thought. Postpartum depression can mess with a person's head. But that was over now.

Evie snuggled her face against his chest, and he could almost feel half his own heart in her pulse. "It was my fault, too, running around trying to solve cases while you were here struggling with a new baby. I was…" He should never have gone back to work right after Evie's birth. He hadn't even taken the week off when they'd gotten married. Though the way she was looking at him now…

Her eyes bored into his.

"What?"

Her face softened. "This is the first time we've ever really talked about it. I mean, after it was over."

"I thought you didn't want to." He hadn't wanted to either. Just hearing that she'd fantasized about dropping Evie from an upper-floor window had been enough to keep him awake for weeks. He'd taken immediate vacation time until things had settled.

"I didn't. I just wanted to put it behind us." She reached for Evie, and he laid the baby in her arms. "But I'm glad we did, you know? It feels better, knowing that you don't think I'm nuts."

He ran his thumb over her cheek, memorizing the contours as he'd done so many times before. "I never thought you were nuts, and I don't think it now." *No more than the rest of us, anyway.* "If I was worried, I'd fight you about leaving."

"Instead, you'll just badger me with texts."

"Because I love you."

A subtle question remained in her eyes—was she worried about his thoughts on her craziness?—but she kissed him hard and turned to the car to strap Evie into her car seat. "When we get home, I'll be back to work, and we'll both be struggling to get on track. Enjoy this little reprieve from diapers and making dinner."

"I won't miss the diapers."

She hugged him again, her breath faster than usual. "Screw the diapers," she said, but there was a tremor in her voice he didn't like.

"Shannon?"

She met his eyes.

"I know you're nervous," he said, quietly enough that the breeze around them might have drowned out his voice.

Her gaze slid to her shoes and back up to him. "It's just hard, you know? After...how bad things got, sometimes I just feel... weird I guess." Her eyes were hard, determined, but her lip quivered almost imperceptibly.

"You're going to be fine, Shanny. You haven't had any of those thoughts in a long time." At least he hoped that was true. Then again, she had kept her desire to move from him—what else might she be hiding?

She nodded, but her silence unnerved him.

Don't beg her to stay. She'll think you don't trust her. McCallum was clear the last time they'd spoken—she needed to know she had his support, his trust. "I know how much this means to you to see Abby this weekend." Why wouldn't she be nervous about her first trip with a baby? He might have wished they were going somewhere else—there was still a part of Morrison that resented Dr. Alex Coleman. He had no logical reason for this disdain, only the image of Shannon's tear-stained face the day she found out Alex was leaving with Abby, her surrogate daughter. As if losing her brother to liver cancer hadn't been bad enough.

"I knew you'd understand." Shannon smiled, but her eyes stayed tight. "I'm nervous, but I *need* to do it. Maybe just to prove to myself that I can. I was always so headstrong, and to think that I needed a crutch, even if that crutch was just having you home with me—it's ridiculous, right?"

Shannon had called the medications a crutch too, but thankfully she'd taken the pills anyway. And she was damn right about being headstrong. Even at work, she had never met a defense attorney she couldn't take to the mat.

"You've got this, Shanny. You don't need the house to feel safe. You don't even need me. But I'll be here whenever you call."

One more hug and she was in the car, buckling her seatbelt, adjusting the rearview so she could see Evie. "I'll call when I get settled into the hotel."

"I'll be waiting by the phone."

She side-eyed him. "Maybe I'll wait until I get to Alex's to call, just to prove that I can make it there without sobbing on your shoulder." She smiled like she was joking. *Was* she kidding? Morrison appraised her as Shannon opened her mouth like she was going to say something else, then closed it.

"Drive safe, Shanny." He slammed the car door for her.

"I will. I love you."

He watched the taillights disappear down the drive and headed back inside to get ready for work. Every room felt empty, the silence stretching before him as though he'd lost them forever, but he knew that wasn't his real fear. It was what the absence of sound meant—the stinging blank in his eardrums screaming at him. *Idle time.* He'd never used it well. But this time, he had a case to work, so it shouldn't be too hard to find something to do.

He climbed into the shower, the rushing water filling his head with white noise. Better. Today would be a good day. Today he'd make headway on the Acosta case. Besides the reliable chaos of his family, there was nothing that silenced the whispers in his brain more effectively than catching a killer. And a killer this depraved would demand that much more of his energy.

He lathered his hair with shampoo and considered their most recent lead, the hideous clown tattoo. The image made his stomach turn, not because of the free tendons dangling from the horse's teeth, resembling bloody strands of yarn, but from what the pictures represented for someone who tattooed them onto their abdomen. Did this pedophile like fringe music, the sadism of the group? Or was he more into the images of creepy clowns, a child's nightmare come to fruition? Fear of clowns was pretty common, and if the guy liked scaring people, it would fit with the sadism. Or maybe...maybe he was into the circus shit because kids liked clowns—not that most kids would be impressed with the demonic variety. Would he have used friend-lier clowns to get closer to Acosta? To any child? To have a whole clown tattooed on your body, you'd have to be pretty into them, right? Unless you were a clown yourself. Or maybe the clowns had nothing to do with anything. Maybe it was just a stupid tattoo.

By the time Morrison shut the shower off, the silence was bearable. He whistled his way through toweling and dressing and shaving and shoes, shrugged on his jacket, and reached for his gun. He froze.

The dresser was clean except for a bottle of antidepressants —Shannon's name on the label.

SHANNON DIDN'T ANSWER the phone. Maybe she was trying to avoid using him as a crutch like she'd said, but more likely, she was just driving and couldn't hear it over some little kid nursery rhyme CD she'd put on for Evie. He tried again. Voice mail. Morrison resisted the urge to hit redial. She'd think he was stalking her, or worse, that he didn't trust her.

He slipped the phone into his pocket, got into his own car, and headed to the precinct. The neighborhood was still hushed, the birdsong muted in the morning fog. Morrison squinted through the haze, trying to see the creatures, but they were hidden in the gloom. He inhaled deeply and maneuvered onto the main road, then exhaled with such force he was half certain the birds would hear it and disappear for good.

This is ridiculous. He stopped at a light and sent a text.

"Just wanted to let you know you left your pills at home. But don't worry, I'm sure McCallum will call them in. Miss you already."

She'd call when she got free. And there was no point in having her turn back an hour into the trip since McCallum could call in a prescription for her to pick up near Alex's. He climbed the stairs to the bullpen, finding his calm, picturing ocean waves and practically tasting salt. Shannon would be fine. Evie would be fine. He arranged and rearranged his current files, ignoring the stack of delinquent paperwork in the corner.

Morrison had just opened the Acosta file for the second time when Petrosky appeared, pulling a fast-food sandwich from a paper bag.

"The guy at Zachary Reynolds's school was a dad of one of the other kids," Petrosky said. "Found it in the file. Ran him just in case, but he and the family left town last year for his job as a tech executive. Living in China now. He's clean as a goddamn whale fart."

Morrison paused, hand over the files. *Reynolds. Executive.* "Clean as a…what?"

"Also, that fuckstick clown group was popular in the early nineties. Now they all live up on the east coast. Two of them own some fucking auto-body repair shop. They all have alibis for Acosta and Reynolds, no clown tattoos on anyone's stomach, and none of them remember any particularly crazy letters or renegade fans. Nice enough people if you can believe that shit."

"You've been busy." Morrison watched the sandwich disappear incrementally. "Now, about the whales—"

"You got the nanny thing figured out?" Petrosky said around a bite of egg muffin. "When does Bell start?"

"How'd you—"

Petrosky set the paper sack on the desk, and Morrison eyed the grease stains seeping through the bag like blood through a gurney sheet. "Looked at your files," Petrosky said, digging into the sack and producing a hash brown patty.

"Bell was unavailable." Morrison watched Petrosky's face, but nothing changed.

"Alyson Kennedy's a good second."

No way Petrosky could know that one—Morrison hadn't marked it down anywhere. "You talked to Shannon."

"Shannon called a week ago just after she got Kennedy's application. Asked if I knew her from the hospital since I'm often over there harassing the shit out of people. Her words, not mine." Petrosky eyed his potatoes like they owed him money. "Before she switched to pediatrics, Kennedy worked in the morgue for a little bit. I remember her from that."

Autopsy nurse turned nanny. Interesting choices. Not that it was more interesting than his own life decisions. "And the verdict?"

"Met her a few times. Good at her job. Thorough. I'm sure she'll be good with Evie too."

So, Shannon had vetted her choices before she even gave them to him. Knowing he'd recheck. No wonder she had been so confident—not that he should have expected less. *Lawyers.* She really was back to her old self. The tension in Morrison's shoulders eased just a little.

"She left already?" Petrosky shoved the packet of fried hash browns into his mouth.

"Yeah."

Petrosky raised an eyebrow.

"I'm all right." But the pit in his chest told him that wasn't completely true. It would be about time for Evie to eat. If they were home, Shannon would be nursing her, and then he'd burp Evie and change her diaper, and she'd giggle and look at him with those excited baby blues like he was the most awesome person on earth.

Morrison nodded to the remains of the breakfast burger. "Those things will kill you."

"I've lived long enough."

"Give us a few more years, eh? Let Evie get old enough to call you Gramps."

Petrosky shoved the rest of the egg muffin into his mouth and wiped his greasy fingers on a takeout napkin. He was aiming at nonchalant, but the twinkle in his eye gave him away. "You want to drive in case my heart gives out on the way there? I hear you even get free leave if your partner bites it." Petrosky's keys jangled as he held them up. "But I'll see if I can hold out until we find this fucker. I want to be the one to leak his list of charges to his prison mates."

12

THE COLORFUL PICTURES that had been in the windows of
Acosta's school the day of the murder had been replaced with
children's art projects: crayon crosses and construction paper
cutouts with "Dylan" scrawled across the top. A shrine to the
dead boy. Inside, the halls were still buzzing with the same
nervous energy as the day they'd interviewed Acosta's class-
mates. But now, the gut-wrenching sadness in the air was
stronger still, wrapping him like a mournful blanket.

Petrosky sat across from the principal's desk, Morrison next
to him. They'd already spoken to Acosta's father and the families
of those the boy hung out with on a regular basis. All of them
were devastated. All of them were shocked. None of them had a
thing to tell them outside of Mr. Acosta, who apparently thought
that Dylan's mother should bear the blame for letting the kid
play video games. Petrosky figured the funeral would be a
fucking combat zone for Acosta's parents even after they found
that the online gaming accounts Acosta interacted with were
registered to his school buddies. Careful parents. But if his killer
was an older brother of one of those kids or another dad…

They'd look at everyone, like always: parents, teachers,
siblings, coaches. But that wasn't feeling right, not with the
manner of the killing, not with the rapist's DNA match on
Reynolds, and especially not with the place they'd chosen to

attack Acosta. If the attackers had known the kid, they'd have brought him somewhere more private, unless the exhibitionism was part of the draw. More likely, the killer had watched Acosta and attacked opportunistically as he'd done with Reynolds. A stranger, or close to. And to find him, they needed all the help they could get.

The principal answered Petrosky's questions with a drawn mouth. Her suit was pressed, her makeup neat, and her black hair was slicked back in a tight bun, but her eyes were bloodshot. Lack of sleep? Probably. Someone had just raped and murdered a little boy on her watch. She wasn't to blame, but it was better for media ratings to sensationalize the event and the media had done just that, thanks to a leak from one of the parents. They'd also leaked the fact that the boy had been sexually assaulted, something responsible news outlets generally didn't disclose. Morrison bristled. At least they'd managed to keep the stomping a secret. So far.

"You said one of your students saw a bike from the classroom window?" Petrosky said. "An adult bike not belonging to staff?"

The melancholy on her face hardened into resolve. "None of our staff bike to school, so it doesn't belong to any of us. And only one boy saw it. I've talked to every teacher here, students who were with Dylan earlier in the day, even the janitor. We are not taking this lightly, detectives, I can assure you." Her words were tight, defensive, but after the news reports claiming that the school allowed Acosta off the property to be attacked by a child killer… She had every right to be.

"No one suspects you're doing anything less than your due diligence, Dr. Goldstein," Petrosky said, and her shoulders relaxed some at the words. The media had definitely been getting to her unless it was just her own guilt. Morrison made a note.

She nodded. "Good. Hopefully, he'll be able to tell you something. I want to see this bastard brought to justice."

Before he does it again, Morrison thought, but no one had to say it. Behind Principal Goldstein, a child's squeal split the room, along with the muffled thunk of balls on pavement. Morrison peered out the window into the brilliant sun and watched a little girl run after a ball. Teachers paced the grounds, their heads jerking this way and that, watching for a monster in the shadows ready to claim someone else's baby. The girl just grabbed the ball and laughed. Probably around ten years old. But give Evie five years, and she'd be in school too, no more nanny, no more days at home, just his little girl flying off on her own to a place where any terrible thing could happen to her and there would be nothing he could do to stop it. Morrison touched his phone, felt the familiar weight in his pocket. Shannon couldn't magically transport herself from Detroit to Atlanta—it'd take her at least five or six hours to reach her halfway-point hotel in Kentucky. She'd call when she stopped for the night.

Petrosky opened the file folder, and Goldstein's eyes widened when she saw the glossy prints. He held out the composite drawn after the Zachary Reynolds attack. "Does he look familiar?"

"You have a mug shot? A suspect already?" She leaned toward them, squinting at the image, and her face fell. "No, I've never seen him."

Of course Goldstein wouldn't know him. No one had seen the suspect around Zachary Reynolds's school, either.

She glanced back into the folder as Petrosky flipped half a dozen pages from the file. He tapped the top sheet. "I've also got some pictures to help us identify the bike your student saw. Did he say where he noticed it?"

"The rack."

Morrison thought back to his initial trek around the school. He hadn't seen a bike when he'd arrived on the scene, and it wasn't in any of the crime scene photos. Their killer must have ridden off on it, maybe while Acosta lay dying. But they had two suspects—so had the men agreed to meet? Or had their bike-riding boot-wearing murderer happened upon Acosta's attack and decided to join the fun, much to the pedophile's chagrin? But no… what were the odds that some psycho would just accidentally come upon another crime, happen to have the tools in hand—or on his feet—and decide to kill someone? Impossible. Morrison shook the idea from his head as Petrosky tapped the bike photos and looked at Goldstein pointedly.

"You need Dimitri," Goldstein said. "I'll send the aide to get him out of class."

Four bicycle shops all had the same thing to say about the blue ten-speed bike Dimitri had identified: common, found everywhere from toy stores to big box stores to specialty shops. No way to track it, especially since he could have purchased it anytime. Unless the suspect decided to just brazenly ride by the school, it was another dead end.

Petrosky and Morrison spent lunch at a Thai restaurant, poring over the case files and calling professional and amateur clowns in the metro Detroit area. Neither Acosta's mother nor Mrs. Reynolds had been aware of clowns at any birthday parties that their children had attended, but the classified ads had given them a few hits and a list for follow-up, as had the party rental places.

Two dozen clowns later, and they were no closer to anything pertinent. Almost all of the clowns had alibis—turned out most worked day jobs, so their whereabouts could be easily verified.

Petrosky set the phone aside and shoveled spicy chicken into his mouth. "Goofy red-nosed motherfuckers."

At least they could say they'd been thorough. Past cases had been closed with crazier theories, but the birthday clown angle didn't feel right to him anyway—not that his gut had never been wrong. Morrison picked at his noodles and prawns and tried not to worry too much that Shannon still had not called him back.

13

THE FIRST TATTOO shop smelled like rubbing alcohol and reefer and someone's flop sweat. The reek was probably the skinny dude already sitting in the chair, wincing as another tattooed man ran a buzzing needle over his rib cage. The tattoo artists had nothing to share: no knowledge of the tattoo itself or the demonic clown group that had inspired the images. Morrison thought more highly of them for it. The second tattoo shop yielded more blank stares.

On the way to the third parlor, Morrison turned up his phone so that they could listen to the lyrics of *The Lion Tamer*, a song which glorified the dismemberment of a goat—tuneless rapping over a background of tinny circus bells and whistles. Morrison frowned, imagining the type of person who would listen to this garbage and be inspired. But had it inspired him to kill?

Petrosky flicked it off. "Shit's gross, but nothing on the kid angle. The murder thing, though...that's something."

Something, but not a direct link, not that he'd expected to find a song about stomping children to death. He winced, turning his face to the window so Petrosky couldn't see. "It's all like that—mostly just circus nonsense. Clowns as executioners, heavy on the violence. I printed the lyrics for the file, but this was the closest it got to the sexual assault angle because in verse two, they…uh…"

"They fuck the goat."

"Yeah." Morrison stared at Petrosky. "You listen to it, Boss?"

"Guessing. Probably the only way they get any ass. Kill it and take it. Force it. Fucking pussies."

Shannon hated the word pussy and would have flipped him off. *Fuck you, Petrosky.* Morrison coughed but held his tongue.

Petrosky kept his eyes on the windshield. "So call me a misogynist, Morrison. Go right ahead. I can already hear your wife in my brain."

"Glad I'm not the only one." But Morrison finally smiled.

"Tell her to get me a better word for shit like this, and I'll stop saying it."

"No way I'm getting in the middle of that. Tell her yourself."

Petrosky squinted out his side window and swung into a strip mall lot. "Fucking pussy," he muttered.

THE THIRD TATTOO shop had a door so white it looked like someone bleached it daily. Inside, the parlor was one large room with a cream-colored microsuede sofa near the door, the couch flanked by end tables made of clear glass. Along the right wall ran a long counter with a six-foot curtain of beads behind it, covering what was probably the back room or office. In the main area, half a dozen stations with black leather reclining chairs waited for clients, almost like a hair salon. Clean. Modern. Comfortable.

They sifted through the books on the glass coffee table: realistic drawings, pop art, some images that looked like watercolor paintings, everything in between. Lots of real art, too, not just cartoon knockoffs. Some of the pieces were utterly tragic, though he tried not to consider the circumstances that had led to their creation. Morrison was staring at a photographic memorial tattoo of a little girl when Petrosky grabbed the book, slammed it closed, and tossed it back onto the table with the others.

The beaded curtain rustled with a sound like a rain stick, and Morrison looked up to see a bald man covered neck to wrist in ink. "Can I help you guys?" He eyed the closed binders, then looked at each of them in turn, as if trying to guess who he'd be tattooing. "I can sketch you something original if you've got an idea."

"Nothing for us today." Petrosky flipped open his badge and approached the counter. The man appraised the shield with eyes as green as the dragon that snaked from wrist to forearm.

"What can I help you with, officers?"

"You are?"

"Randy. The hired help." His lip ring glinted when he smiled.

Petrosky pocketed his badge. "Looking for a guy with a tattoo."

"Well, that narrows it down."

Petrosky dealt him a withering glare. Randy's smile fell.

"He's a bad, bad man." Petrosky pulled out Zachary Reynolds's drawing of the tattoo and slid it across the counter, along with a copy of the album cover. Morrison looked away from the gory image.

"You seen a tat like this?"

Randy glanced at it, and his eyes lit up, hot and wild. "Hey, Drake!" he called to the curtain. A burly man with a dark ponytail and intelligent brown eyes sauntered out toward them. T-shirt, but no ink on his arms. Or neck. Or anywhere else Morrison could see. Odd. Maybe he was new.

Drake studied the photo. "That guy. Been years though." He shook his head. "That fucking guy."

"Want to tell us about that fucking guy?" Petrosky said.

Drake shrugged. "Not a lot to tell. He was kinda quiet, didn't talk much to me. He liked Jenny's work over mine. She said that he was nice—used to tell her jokes and shit."

"So he's a regular," Petrosky said.

"Was." Drake nodded along with Randy, the dragon boy, and Petrosky put the pictures away.

"Any distinguishing characteristics outside of the tat?"

"Not really." Drake shrugged a shoulder, and the muscles in

his arm coiled, then stilled. "Skinny. Kinda dorky, but in a way that seemed like he didn't really know it. More awkward—bland. Not really someone you'd notice walking down the street."

Awkward. Unassuming. Bland. They'd said almost the same about Jeffery Dahmer, and that guy kept his victim's severed body parts in his freezer in case he got hungry.

"Eye color?" Petrosky said.

"Can't recall."

"Hair?"

"Brown? Lighter than mine, though, and kinda scraggly. Over the ears but above the shoulders."

That might be useful if he hadn't dyed it. Or shaved it. Across the counter, Randy's head shone in the fluorescents.

"How tall was he?"

"Shorter than me for sure. Just a few inches taller than Jenny."

Petrosky's eyes narrowed for a beat, then relaxed. Drake's description was confirmation that their shorter, sneakered suspect, the man who had raped Zachary Reynolds and Dylan Acosta, had always been a scraggly, weird-looking dude. But why the rapist was fighting with the killer at the scene—that was eating at Morrison. Unrest between the suspects meant the killer could just as easily have murdered the rapist too. Maybe he already had.

Petrosky produced the composite sketch of Zachary Reynolds's attacker, and Drake nodded.

"Yep, that's him." He studied the ceiling. "Been a while. Two, three years, maybe."

If their rapist was still alive, they could flip him on the murderer, but... They could be searching for another corpse. Not that dead rapists were a bad thing. Morrison noted Drake's statement, and the pen tore a hole in the sheet. He flipped to a new page.

Petrosky nodded to the credit card machine on the counter. "How'd he pay?"

"Cash, I think." Drake squinted. "We just really started taking cards in the last year or so."

"Keep records? Consent forms? Maybe a copy of a driver's license?"

"No consent forms from that far back. And we just check their license to make sure they're over eighteen."

"You get his name from the license?"

"Sorry, man, can't remember his real name. We called him Mr. Magoo, on account of he couldn't look me in the face, stared everywhere else. Seemed to see Jenny just fine, though." He bristled on the last sentence.

Petrosky leaned an elbow against the counter. "Jenny your girl, Drake?"

"She's a girl who married me, yeah." Drake's chest puffed up as he straightened his shoulders. Proud. Morrison pushed an image of Shannon's face from his mind—she'd surely call soon.

"I hear you." Petrosky pulled a photo of the bike from the folder. "Any idea who this belongs to? What'd your Magoo drive?"

Randy shook his head.

Drake gestured to the door, where little of the street was visible beyond the sidewalk immediately in front. "Never saw a car or bike, but that doesn't mean much. Unless we went outside or took a break, we wouldn't have seen a bike or a car anyway, and even then, we wouldn't necessarily know whose it was. Lots of traffic out there." He tapped the photo and leaned toward Petrosky. "So, what'd he do?"

"Not at liberty to say."

"Shit, that's bad, ain't it?" Drake straightened. "He was here, in my shop every couple months. Four times or so, total. If he was a bad guy, really bad, talking to Jenny…"

"I'm going to need a list of his tattoos. Anything you recall."

Drake bent behind the counter, pulled out a few sheets of white paper, and started sketching. "The last one Jenny did was a three-D piece on his back. A hand clawing out of his skin. He said it was for his kid. I figured it was a euphemism, you know? Flesh of my flesh kinda thing, a part of him escaping?"

"So it was a child's hand." Though Petrosky's face didn't change, Morrison could feel the tension radiating from his corded muscles.

A kid's hand. Morrison's stomach turned. Sick bastard wanted a child's fingertips touching him at all times.

"How about a number one?"

Drake stopped sketching. "No, don't recall that. I do remember a few other clowns. And a tent, yellow and purple. Kinda in the background here on his chest." His pencil scratched away. "I know this here still needed more work, but I can't really remember—"

"He had that weird Mr. Ed one too, right?" Randy interjected.

"Oh, yeah." He sketched another line, then another. A horse appeared in front of the tent, and in a moment, it was clear it was dead, blood leaking from its eyes. Macabre. Sadistic. Maybe the rapist *had* taken part in Acosta's killing, even if he'd just encouraged it. But if he was on board, why fight with his murderous spiked boot-wearing partner?

"Creepy," Petrosky said. The dead horse glared at them, bloody eyes dilated and aggressive as if ready to pull any passerby with him to the depths of hell.

"Totally. But some people like that. The...dark stuff. And honestly, Jenny does it better, probably remembers more about his ink than I can." He shook his head. "She won't be back from Florida until Friday morning—down there for a friend's funeral. Damn shame."

"We'll come back."

It wouldn't stand up in court, a composite so many years after the fact, but maybe Jenny would recall something that Zachary Reynolds hadn't. What they really needed from Jenny was a closer copy of artwork she'd needled onto his gut in case there was an image even more telling than the clowns. Another picture that might give them a hint as to where he'd spend his time. Maybe he'd told Jenny something that would help. Maybe Jenny even had some insight into why he hadn't finished his tattoos here—had something happened to spook him? Did he have a weakness they could exploit?

Petrosky peered at the corner of the ceiling, then at another corner. "You guys have security tapes?"

"Nothing like that. Sorry." Drake passed Petrosky the page

he'd been working on, and Petrosky slipped it into the folder. "Should I be worried? About Jenny?"

Petrosky shook his head. "I think she's a little old for him."

"She's only…" Drake's eyes widened. "Oh fuck. My daughter, she… You think—"

"How old?"

"Seven."

So she would have been four or five back when their suspect was frequenting this place.

"He show interest in her?" Petrosky asked with a subtle, aggravated twitch of his eye.

"I…" Drake grimaced, almost snarled. "She came up after preschool one day when Jenny was inking him. Sat behind the counter with me. He looked a little too long, got me all upset. But I thought I was just overreacting, that he probably was trying to forget the pain and the needle. If I'd thought he was… well, looking like *that,* I would have fucking killed him myself." He swallowed hard, face reddening to a shade deeper than the rose on Randy's neck. "Not literally… You know what I mean."

Common. Ignore what you don't expect—or what you fear the most. Morrison touched the cell in his pocket.

"I would have felt the same," Petrosky said. "Just watch your daughter close, sir, and enjoy her while you can. Time flies."

Morrison pictured Evie's chubby cheeks, her smiling eyes. He should call Shannon again.

Petrosky turned to head out but stopped short at the door and gestured to Drake's nude arms. "Where're your tattoos?"

"I've always been afraid of needles."

"Interesting career choice."

Drake looked down. "I guess I thought it would help."

———

THEY CANVASSED the street and interviewed other business owners, but none had been there longer than two years. Dead end—just like the other four tattoo parlors nearby. Reynolds's rapist had gotten his tattoos finished somewhere else—if he finished them at all.

By the time Petrosky pulled into the precinct parking lot, Morrison's head was throbbing. He massaged his aching temple. "Want to grab dinner? We can come back here and—"

"You go home, California. I'll pull the names and addresses of the folks who were in that strip mall around the time Mr. Magoo was getting his work done. Maybe one of them will recall something. Tomorrow we'll see what other places one might go to get inked since that dickhead probably got the work done somewhere else."

"Like the slang, Petrosky."

"You would." Petrosky shut off the car. "And with the sheer number of tats, the tattoo shit itself might have become an addiction, the pain, the endorphins. And I think we've established that he has a hard time controlling his drives."

True enough. They'd talk to McCallum about it. "We've got time with the shrink tomorrow, right?" Maybe Morrison could even sneak in a few minutes, if he got there early, to ask about Shannon. Or get McCallum to call in a prescription for Shannon if she hadn't called the doctor already. Hell, she probably had— she might flake on a phone call, but not on her medications.

"We've got McCallum's four-thirty. Plenty of time to run around beforehand. Maybe we'll have more leads by the time we get there."

"Maybe." Morrison leaned his head against the seat.

"Get out," Petrosky barked so harshly that Morrison nearly jumped.

"What?"

"Go home, Cali." Petrosky nodded to Morrison's car next to them in the parking lot. Had Petrosky parked next to his Fusion on purpose?

Morrison reached for the door handle. Petrosky of all people should understand what it was like to just be…alone. Alone with your demons, the pain in your head, the kind that consumes you. The kind that takes bites out of you just when you thought you had a moment's reprieve.

"I don't need—"

"Go home and take a goddamn nap and just be happy you can sleep." Petrosky pulled out his cigarettes and a lighter but paused with his finger on the flint. "Everyone needs time to recharge, even do-gooders." His eyes were far away, flickering with agitation and pain and a grief so intense it tore at Morrison's gut, not the sharpness of a sudden stabbing, but a dull, old wound healed over but not gone. A wound as poignant as his own.

MORRISON DROVE HOME, preoccupied with the haunted look in Petrosky's eyes. He'd hoped things were getting better—that Petrosky had found some new meaning in his life. God knows having Shannon and Evie had helped Morrison, and now with them away…

Morrison inhaled and blew the breath out sharply as if to clear the thoughts. They would be fine—they *were* fine. But was Petrosky? There remained a nagging in the back of Morrison's head that he was looking at someone just shy of relapse when he saw his partner, just shy of self-abuse, despite the fact that he'd surely deny it—addicts didn't share easily. Morrison never shared at all.

Morrison shut the car off in his driveway and let himself into the kitchen, the silence thick with foreboding. The cat was probably asleep somewhere. They should get another dog—a year already, and he still missed that old girl. And though it hadn't even been a day, he definitely missed his family.

14

THE FIRST THREE hours at home crawled by doing laundry, installing a cat door for Slash, taking a bath. And reading Edgar Allan Poe. He'd read hundreds of books, maybe thousands over the course of his studies as an English major, but there was something about Poe that filled some empty place inside him with an almost tangible serenity. The darkness on those pages made him feel almost normal, not alone, like another soul was there in his head with him. When he got to *The Tell-Tale Heart,* he relished the obsession—the madness. At least he could reasonably tell himself, "Hey, I'm not *that* crazy" when he worried about his wife for the umpteenth time.

But by the time the bathwater had cooled, the apprehensive whispers in his mind had grown to a dull roar. Why hadn't she called back yet? It was well past time for her to have settled into a hotel.

I can do this, Morrison. And to think that I needed a crutch, even if that crutch was just having you home with me, is ridiculous...

She didn't need him checking up on her, didn't want his help. He should have taken her at her word. But goddammit, she could call just to ease his mind, just to squash the thoughts running through his brain.

Has she been in an accident?

Have the meds worn off and left her with horrible fantasies on a dark road somewhere?

No, antidepressants can't wear off that quickly.

Maybe she'd taken Evie and leapt from an overpass.

His heart frantic, he tried her cell again. Again, no answer. He tossed the phone on the bed and closed his eyes.

She's showing herself that she doesn't need me.

He moved on to distraction. It should have been easier, but playing the guitar without Evie on his lap or on the bed beside him made the experience feel empty—like he'd never played before her birth as if every song he'd ever strummed had always been meant for her. He tried to embrace this and accept his preoccupation—turn it into a new song—but his heart was still jerking around in his chest, choking his voice. Sit-ups, pull-ups, nothing took away his agitation. And when he closed his eyes to meditate, he saw the memorial tattoo at Drake's shop, and it suddenly looked like Evie. He saw himself getting her face needled into his forearm, like Petrosky might want to do for Julie, and his stomach turned so that he almost wanted to vomit the idea—and the quinoa he'd eaten. Evie wasn't a memorial. She was fine. Shannon was fine.

And then Shannon came to him, shaky but louder, the panicked tears evident in her voice: *Sometimes I just want to drop her to see what will happen. Or toss her out the car window. I went to the pediatrician this week, and I crossed an overpass and thought for too long about what it might be like to drive over the guardrail.*

He felt half fucking insane. And more than that, he was being obsessive, more so with every hour that passed.

In the tumultuous quiet, the whispers began: *They're not home. No one will ever know. Just this once. You'll be happy.*

The habit was latent but not silent. It would never be completely gone.

He checked his phone again. No missed calls. No texts. No Shannon. No Evie. He dropped the phone onto the bed before he could dial. He trusted her; she had to know that. And she should be at the hotel any minute. Maybe it was taking extra long because she had to stop and nurse the baby. He wouldn't know. He wasn't there.

Just like he hadn't been there when she was considering tossing their child from the second-story window.

A vein in the crook of his leg throbbed wetly, remembering. *It will make you forget about her. It will take away the worry. And no one will ever find out.*

I'll know. I'll never forget.

He pulled out his journal and scribbled everything down: every thought, every whisper, every concern. Every desire, regret. Half an hour later, he was sweating, and his hand was shaking, but it was better. He ripped the pages from the notebook, walked to the kitchen, and shoved them into the garbage disposal. This was not about his family. This was about him looking for an excuse to use.

The motor in the bottom of the sink choked and sputtered like the heart of a man waking up the day after a bender with no spoon, no needle, and no drug. Morrison turned his back on the sink and stared at his shoes by the front door.

Never too late to literally run away.

THE NEIGHBORHOOD STREETS pulsed with the reticent energy of an impending storm, though that surely was just him—the stars above shimmered clear and white, untainted by the murk of amorphous clouds. His breath echoed in his ears, hissing through his chest and into his lungs, and a discarded napkin skittered across his path, reminding him that even perfect things —like a moonlit run—were imperfect. Life was a struggle, perfect in its imperfection. It was a thought that Shannon would have called "zen bullshit," but it helped.

The tightness in his stomach eased along with his thoughts of Shannon, and the case came into clearer focus. *The case.* What were they missing? The punctures, possibly from boots— nothing like that existed in the rape case they knew to be related, and they hadn't found other murders with similar MOs. The rapist seemed to have a pattern—same type of victim, same T-shirt around the neck—but where the hell did this other guy come from? Was he a pedophile too? Or just a voyeur who got off on watching? They'd ask McCallum about that too—a profile should help.

McCallum. Shannon. Morrison's heart beat faster, and he didn't think it was from his pace. He checked his phone again as he ran, then again. Oily sweat from his finger streaked the glass.

Nothing.

A breeze chilled the dew on his brow and rustled through the leaves like the whisper of waves against a shore. He inhaled and exhaled to the rhythm of the wind. His chest cooled, and the film of concern cleared from his mind.

The case. *Think.* He focused on his feet thumping against the pavement.

The clowns were definitely weird. Savage shit. A guy who enjoyed feeling pain? Causing pain? That would explain the punctures, but the killer was a different guy. A night bird startled by his footfalls fluttered through the branches, and something bigger leapt from one tree to another with the crackle of snapping twigs.

He checked his phone again.

Nothing.

Sweat ran down his back and soaked his T-shirt. He ran harder over sidewalk and grass and pavement and tried to ignore the silent cell by listening to the treads of his shoes thumping against the earth. Rhythmic, measured. Grounded. By the time he circled the last block, he'd managed to brush aside the urge to check the phone.

She was fine. She was okay. And everything was as it should be.

As he rounded the final corner to his house, his breath caught in his throat. Headlights flashed in the drive—his drive—and the porch lights caught the reds and blues, turning the front lawn into a lewd and gruesome display, like the reflections of fireworks on a corpse.

She was dead. They were both dead.

He ran.

15

He met Decantor halfway up the drive—Decantor's arm out in front, a proverbial *whoa boy.* Morrison's heart did not slow, but he brought his feet to a halt.

"Is it Shannon? Evie?" He almost vomited the words onto Decantor's shoes.

"Shannon?" Decantor's eyes widened. "Dear god, man, of course not. I wondered why you were tearing up here like someone was chasing you."

She was okay. They were okay. She probably would have slapped him for the horrible thoughts he was having. He gulped in a breath.

The tightness in his chest remained.

Decantor lowered his hand, slower than seemed natural. Was Decantor trying to calm him down? Police training at its finest, maybe, but Morrison was unnerved by it, and he tensed and released his toes to make sure the digits were still there, that he was still there.

"Got a homicide out at Row and Luther, need to chat with you about her."

"Consultation?" Morrison and Petrosky primarily worked special cases—sex crimes and the like—but sometimes he talked through profiles with other detectives. But Decantor's posture was hardly the relaxed shoulders of the guy he'd spoken to earlier that week, someone just interested in a chat. And Decantor had never come to the house about a case. Not once.

"Not exactly a consultation," Decantor said. "Can we go inside? It's fucking cold tonight."

Morrison flexed his fingers. The spring breeze hadn't seemed all that cold, but his hands were tingly and numb. "Yeah, of course. I'll make coffee."

Decantor said nothing, just followed Morrison in through the unlocked front door, and Morrison suddenly regretted leaving the house open. *Had* he left the house open? Must have. He grabbed a dry dish towel from the drawer, green—Shannon's favorite—and mopped the sweat from his face. Decantor didn't move from his spot next to the counter.

"So, what's the deal?" Morrison asked as he poured grounds into a filter, fighting to keep his voice low and steady.

"Got a few questions about Natalie Bell."

Morrison paused, finger over the start button. *The nanny? Fuck.* Had Decantor said…homicide? Bell was dead?

"You knew her, right?"

"She interviewed here. We were looking for a nanny." Morrison punched the button on the coffeepot and turned away from the counter.

"When did you interview her?"

"Two days ago. Monday at lunchtime."

"You and Shannon were both here?"

"Yeah, you can give Shannon a call if you need a statement for the report." *Not that she'll answer her phone.* "She'll be in Atlanta until next Wednesday."

Decantor scribbled on his notepad, and Morrison eyed the book. He hadn't realized Decantor was taking notes. Was he being interrogated? Sweat popped out on the back of his already wet neck as he masked his face with nonchalance. "What have you got so far?" *They're going to lock me up. Again.*

"Found her in her apartment, chain lock cut. It wasn't a robbery—Bell had a gold bracelet lying on her dresser. Looks like the perp snuck in while she was sleeping. Shirt in her mouth, probably to keep her quiet. Some visible tearing in the genital region, and on her lower belly, all of it done with a round, sharp object like an ice pick, but bigger. Raped with the implement used to stab her. She bled out."

What the hell? Just like the wounds on Acosta's back. A couple attacks on little boys didn't fit with this case, and Acosta hadn't had any puncture wounds in the genital region. But that round shape was unusual, and they'd held that information back from the press. Then there was the shirt. Acosta's and Reynolds's shirts had been wrapped around their throats, but shoving it in the victim's mouth wouldn't be much of a stretch. "Sounds like a sex crimes case," he said slowly.

"Yeah, it does. But the chief said you guys were overloaded, and we didn't need specialized training to deal with a homicide —no living victim to assist. And there was no semen, no trace of spermicide, so the medical examiner doesn't think there was penetration by anything other than the spiked object."

Spiked object. It had to be related. Morrison jerked toward a sharp scratching sound just in time to see Slash poke his head through the cat door. The cat peered at Decantor, then yanked his face back through the hole to the outside.

"A jilted lover might fit," Decantor was saying. "Maybe she was out to get revenge on her boyfriend's other woman. Raped her with the knife or whatever for taking what she saw as hers. We did think about Acosta, with the size and shape of the holes, but—"

"How'd you know about the punctures? On Acosta?" Had the stabbing pattern gotten leaked too? Morrison ground his teeth.

"The ME. But he did say the rest didn't match—no rape in Bell's case, not enough force behind the wounds to be a stomping, different locations, vastly different victim. But he's double-checking as a precautionary measure because it is a weird weapon." He stopped writing and leaned against the counter. "Outside of Acosta, what other cases are you guys working on right now?"

Morrison kept his face blank. "Most were reassigned when we got Acosta, but the few remaining are about what you'd expect: some domestic violence, a few sexual assault cases. But they're all wrapped, just finishing up the final paperwork. Why?"

"Just curious because…well, you knew Bell. And"—Decantor

tapped the tip of his pen in the book—"someone went through her purse. Left the wallet, but pulled out a bunch of other shit, including your card. I thought maybe you were investigating her for something. Domestic violence incident, thought maybe she was an ex-hooker since that's Petrosky's specialty." He raised his eyebrow in Morrison's direction, maybe asking him to deny it.

"Nope, I just wanted to hire her as a nanny for Evie. But she turned down the job, said she took another position." The final hiss of the coffeepot drew Morrison's attention, but he didn't turn, just watched Decantor process the information.

Decantor's eyebrow sank to its usual position. Acceptance. "Did she say where she took that other job?"

Morrison turned to pour the coffee, swallowing hard over the knot that had taken root behind his Adam's apple. Some coffee splashed over the rim of the first cup, and he wiped it up with his face towel, then passed Decantor a mug. He left his own on the counter.

Decantor stilled—he must have noticed the panic on Morrison's face. "I'm just trying to track her movements," he said gently. "You know how it is. Not a single credit card hit, no ATM stops, nothing. You saw her Monday, so you're the last to see her alive. No one thinks it was…you know…you." Decantor, and the whole Ash Park PD, had seen Morrison's imprisonment last spring, had watched as the incident unfolded in court: the false arrest for Griffen's crimes, the way Shannon's ex-husband had gone after him tooth and nail, trying to keep him locked up, the evidence planted at Morrison's house that would have convicted him if Shannon and Petrosky hadn't uncovered the real killer. Thinking about it still made Morrison nauseous, and he'd only been locked up a week before Shannon and Petrosky had managed to clear him. "It was just an interview," Morrison said. "I'll get you her résumé, but we didn't cover anything except her job history." He went to retrieve Bell's file from the stack still on Shannon's night table and returned to Decantor, who squinted at the fat folder in surprise.

"Really checked the babysitters out, didn't you?"

More than he should have. He probably looked guilty as hell, even though he couldn't imagine another cop who wouldn't do that for his kid. Valentine sure as shit would. Decantor just didn't understand; he was still a bachelor.

"Just background checks." Morrison passed him the folder with a tightness in his throat that he covered with a smile. "Just do me a favor and pretend you did the research yourself, all right?"

Decantor nodded and tucked the folder under his arm. "Absolutely. And I'll give Shannon a call for follow-up, just to have her statement on record."

Morrison recited her cell, and Decantor's pen flew over the page, jotting other notes apparently, maybe about Shannon being out of town. Maybe not.

Morrison cleared his throat. "Seems like there'd be someone else at her apartment building who would have seen her after she came here."

"Yep, and nothing. Doesn't look like anyone noticed her missing."

"Then how'd you—"

"Fluke. Building superintendent went to see her because her car was getting towed—she'd parked in a reserved spot. He got worried when she didn't answer the door because she had a diabetic seizure in the lobby last year—he figured better safe than sorry."

Bell hadn't mentioned anything about being diabetic when she was interviewing for the nanny position. *She should have told us.* And if Bell had withheld something so critical, how could he know whether the nanny they'd actually hired had been forthcoming?

Decantor was still talking, and Morrison had to force himself to tune back in: "—closet full of books, no heels or going-out clothes like you'd expect. Lucky we got the call before she started to smell. Or before a friend or family member found her."

"Lucky."

Decantor nodded. "So you interviewed her on Monday. What time did you call to offer her the position?"

"Shannon called her Tuesday, earlier in the day. She rang me back that night, around…seven or so."

Decantor stopped writing. "Tuesday night?" Worry etched itself into the lines around his tight mouth. "She was dead by then, Morrison. The medical examiner says she died on Monday."

Morrison froze. *Impossible.* The ME had to be wrong. Morrison pulled his phone from his pocket, handed it to Decantor. "The number she called from matched the number on her résumé." He paused. "Though it was weird that she called me and not Shannon—Bell had my card, but Shannon was the one who had called her. Shannon interviewed her initially, too. And the voice on the phone was...a little off, deeper, but I thought she had a cold."

"No cell found at the scene."

Someone had taken it. *And they called me.* It was just a phone call, but he felt almost...violated. His stomach churned, and he turned to the kitchen window, half expecting to see someone watching them. His fist clenched. He stared hard at it until it went slack.

"Why kill someone and call back random numbers the next day?" Decantor said, frowning. "You think he was trying to make it look like she was still alive?"

"Maybe. But why bother to do that?" He met Decantor's eyes. No one would have found her for days without that tow truck, he'd said.

"Maybe he wanted to make sure no one got worried so that he could have his...way. After she was dead and cold." Decantor grimaced. "He probably creamed his pants before he could take it out the first time."

Who the hell called me?

"Gotta be someone she knows," Morrison said. "Someone who stalked her at least, and knew how to get in and out of her apartment. Who knew she'd interviewed with us." The implication tugged at a soft spot in his stomach. "And the voice on the phone was female, so you're looking for a woman, too. Or someone with one of those electronic voice changers." What the fuck was going on? Had they badgered Bell about why she had a cop's card in her wallet? Were they fucking with him? But...the weapon. So similar to the one used on Acosta.

Then again, it wasn't hard to get hold of an ice pick. The press leaks were probably behind this bullshit, too, someone who knew more than they should. Later this week, there'd surely be a big story out about the weapon and the stomping, and everyone and their mother would be wasting the department's time with nonsense tips.

"Maybe Shannon will have some insight since she interviewed Bell initially. You think she'll be up now?"

"Not sure. Haven't talked to her today." She was trying to prove to herself that she could do this alone. That she didn't need him as a crutch. She was driving and trying to be safe. *But she forgot her medication.* "I'll call her now."

He got Shannon's voice mail three times in a row, and in that time, Decantor finished his coffee and moved into the living room, stepping on Shannon's favorite rug with his heavy boots. Though Decantor left no mark, Morrison winced at the intrusion.

"I'm sure she's driving." The phone echoed with the last line of her voice mail, Shannon's voice, and his stomach twisted and turned, the knot in his throat expanding, trying to cut off his air supply. And the needle of panic in the back of his brain wriggling its way free, struggling against his self-restraint and Decantor's worried stare. She'd planned to stop halfway to Atlanta, stay in a hotel, but if Evie was sleeping, she might have kept driving. And there was no telling whether she'd be in a good cell zone, right? Or maybe her phone battery had died.

He forced a smile. "When she calls back, I'll have her call you, okay?" His chest was hot and sweaty, and it had nothing to do with his run. "I'll write out a statement about what happened on Tuesday, too, what the caller said and all that. And I'll email you my phone records so that you can follow-up on the Bell case."

"Okay, man, sounds good. I appreciate it." Decantor nodded. "And I'm sure whoever called was fucking with you. Found a cop's number at the scene, wanted to be an asshole."

With a voice changer?

"I'll walk you out," Morrison said to the dead screen, willing it to ring.

WHEN THE TAILLIGHTS from Decantor's car finally receded, panic wrapped around Morrison's heart like a skeletal hand and crushed the last remnants of calm. She was okay. Had to be. But why wouldn't she call him, dammit? It had been…what? A day? No, not even. Twelve hours. No, fifteen. They could surely go a few hours without talking—she fucking hated talking on the phone. He was being paranoid. He was freaked about being away from them.

But something weird was going on here.

He grabbed his keys to go back to the precinct. He'd run down her credit cards and goddammit he'd drive out to Alex's himself if he had to, just to put his nerves to rest. And to tell her he missed her. That he missed Evie. That this really wasn't about her—it was just his own need for them and nothing more. She'd surely be able to see that. *Hopefully.*

His cell rang. No, not rang—text. Shannon. *Oh, thank fucking god.*

"Sorry, horrible reception. I'll call tomorrow, ok?"

He responded:

"Ok. Love you."

He waited for a response, but none came, and finally, he pocketed the cell.

Of course the reception is bad. Of course it was. Had he really thought the miles of freeway were replete with cell towers? But the silent phone seemed to amplify the quiet of the house—too quiet—and every nerve in his body sang with anxiety and agitation and acute panic. He would have felt so much better just hearing her voice.

Then suddenly, every shadow was an invitation to go back,

every creak of the house settling a whisper to return to a life he'd left behind. *I can make the pain stop,* the voice whispered. And it could. Just one hit would soothe his frayed nerves, make sleep come fast and hard, and he could start again tomorrow, refreshed. It was the drug, an emotion more than actual words, but he could feel each syllable echoing in his head, through his chest, and prying into those tiny glorious places of exquisite loveliness that could only be reached with the needle. He hadn't touched those quiet places in years.

Stress. It was always the stress that tried to drag him back. But if Shannon could be strong, avoid her own crutches, then goddammit, he could too. And if he couldn't…he'd never tell her.

No.

He yanked at the doorknob, and his hand slipped, slick with his own sweat. He tried again, felt the click of the latch giving way, and escaped into the night.

16

PETROSKY'S WINDOWS glowed yellow with murky lamplight. There were no other cars in the driveway, but the tinkle of female laughter wafted through the open window and over the porch. Petrosky had picked someone up. Probably someone he shouldn't have, like always. Never for sex, he didn't think, just for company—and because Petrosky wanted to get them off the street, if only for the night.

When Petrosky let him in the front door, the women at the table eyed Morrison suspiciously. One dark, one light; one tall, one short; both thin as rails. One wore shorts so brief only the fringe was visible underneath the hem of a sweatshirt reading "Ash Park PD."

"Am I interrupting something?" Morrison asked.

Petrosky ignored the question and turned to the women, raising his voice so that they could hear him across the room. "Ladies, this is Detective Morrison. Morrison, June and Rita."

Morrison raised a hand in greeting, not trusting his voice enough to speak, and Petrosky gestured to the table. "Now that we have four players...how about some spades? You in, California?"

Anything to distract him from Shannon and her terrible reception. Anything to distract him from the case and the fact that a killer had possibly called him, though surely it was a sick prank or they'd have made some type of demand, right? He should bring up Decantor's visit, almost wanted to, but the thought of having to rehash it right now while the drug was still whispering softly at the back of his mind no matter how he tried to forget—he needed to be distracted from that, too. He needed to forget all of it before he lost his shit. "Yeah, I'll play." He leaned close to Petrosky's ear and lowered his voice. "Did you pull them off the street tonight?"

"Mind your business, California. Nothing illegal about this. Just a couple of people playing cards."

"Yeah, okay, I know." He tried to keep his voice even, hiding his anxiety, his addiction, his past, beneath a grin. "Wouldn't be fair to avoid people based on profession anyway."

"Well fuck, you think they want to avoid us because we're cops? I hadn't even considered that." Petrosky headed for the table and plopped into a chair.

Morrison took the seat across from Rita and her hazel eyes shifted to Petrosky, who grinned at her. She smiled back with teeth so white and clean they could have been featured in a toothpaste commercial. Morrison peered into the plastic cups on the table.

Please don't let him be off the wagon.

Of course he's off. No point even trying to stay clean. We all fall eventually. We'll go down together.

He resisted the urge to smell the cup.

Petrosky saw him looking and frowned. "Shirley Temples." Almost defensive. "Want one?"

Morrison glanced at the counter—bottles of 7up and orange juice sat with a jar of cherries in the glow of the pink princess night-light that had belonged to Petrosky's daughter. No liquor, at least not out in the open.

"You can just make OJ too, straight up," Petrosky said.

"Too bad you got nothing to go with it." June's voice was raspy as sandpaper. She pouted as she dealt the cards, and Petrosky shot her a narrow "stop giving me shit" look, but he lost his scowl when she winked at him. Then she smiled. There was no way these girls were here for free, which was sketchy at best, but at least Petrosky was sober.

"Shirley Temples sound great," Morrison said. Rita stood, but he waved her back down. "No, I'll make it."

"She's been playing bartender all night," Petrosky said. "Rita makes a damn fine drink—she's a professional now, too. I called in a favor over at The Lounge."

"The place Crazy Mark runs? I thought we arrested him."

"We did. He's on probation. Good deeds will help him stay that way." Petrosky winked at Rita, and she beamed.

June picked up her cards. "Eddie got me an interview tomorrow too," she said, not to be outdone. She smiled at Petrosky, then down at her hand while she arranged her cards. "Three."

Morrison exchanged his own cards and waited while June and Petrosky made their plays. They were halfway through the hand before Morrison realized his heart had slowed, and the back of his neck was dry.

The needle in his brain was gone.

"IT WAS NIGHT, AND THE RAIN FELL; AND FALLING, IT WAS RAIN,
BUT, HAVING FALLEN, IT WAS BLOOD."
EDGAR ALLAN POE, *SILENCE - A FABLE*

17

THERE WAS NO LIGHT, only the blackness of fear that pulsed in time to her throbbing head. Her breath came in heavy gasps, thick and muffled, echoing in her ears like she had a hood over her face. But there was no hood, only the dark—the cloudy thunderstorm gray of a tomb. Stifling. And all was silent. How long had she been here?

Shannon raised her head, and pain shot through her neck and down to where her shoulder connected with the floor.

The *floor*. Cold, hard. Concrete? No, it was smoother than that, but she couldn't tell much more through the coat she had on. Wood floors? Was she inside a house? And…she hadn't had a jacket on when she left the house, but she was certain she did now.

And Evie. She'd had Evie. Her breath quickened to a frenzied panting in the dark. She flexed her legs, and pain shot from her knee to her hip, white and hot, but nothing moved. Her ankles and shins were bound together, her toes numb. How had she gotten here? She gritted her teeth until the pain settled, but the thick numbness in her limbs remained.

She had tried to kick him; she remembered that. She'd stopped to feed Evie, parked in the back of the gas station lot, and he'd come down fast and hard with something, maybe brass knuckles, against her temple. She winked tentatively—felt the tightness of what was probably dried blood on her cheek. At least the gash had stopped oozing.

Would Morrison know she was gone yet? If he didn't, he'd know soon when she didn't call. Though she had specifically told him she was going to avoid him—to prove she was fucking *strong* as if you could prove such a thing by ignoring the people you loved. The panic rose, and she let it in, let it build into a fire stoked by fury and indignation. This motherfucker would pay. But then fear wrapped around her throat like a noose. She didn't believe in God, didn't believe in much of anything outside of hard work and grit, but she prayed now:

God, please don't let him hurt Evie.

She tried to move her arms, but they were also bound, or rather, stuck in front of her in the coat. Not a coat—a straitjacket, and stiff, much harder than cotton. The rough stitches rubbed her arms raw as she struggled. Leather? She flexed her wrists, but her bonds stuck fast, and her fingers cramped from the position of her palms, each held flat against the opposite hip.

She heard her then, a tiny whimper. *Evie.* The noise wasn't a cry, yet it sounded more ominous, more urgent, than the subtle giggles or mewls that trickled through the baby monitor every night. And even the grainy black and white of the monitor was less distorted than the profound darkness around her now.

Where are you, baby? Shannon held her breath, trying to locate her daughter, but her right ear was muffled, probably thick with her own blood unless he'd hit her hard enough to deafen her. *Come on, sweetheart, just a little louder.* Her abdominals cried out as she heaved her head off the floor, wrenching her neck and—

Electricity zapped through her, from one ear to the other, and she caught herself on her elbow. Concussion? But the stinging sensation wasn't coming from the side where she'd been struck. And she wasn't lying on a power grid...she didn't think.

More muffled whimpering came to her through the gloom, and she tried again, throwing herself forward, ignoring the rigidity in her neck, her stomach, her wrists. And saw her. To her right, about six feet from the bottom of Shannon's toes, Evie lay on the floor, her legs already kicking air, her fists balled and working in the manufactured dusk. Evie—healthy and vibrant and *furious*. But deep within Shannon's chest, dread blossomed and grew teeth and gnashed at her lungs.

Shh, honey, shh. She didn't dare say it aloud. She wormed her way toward the sound of Evie's breath, the sound crescendoing with each passing second—here another whimper, there a whine. She squirmed more quickly, the floor bruising her elbows, her hips. Then Evie cried out, long and high, and Shannon's heart skipped a beat. Her breasts tingled, heavy with milk.

Please, baby, hush.

Her abdominals trembled in the half-sit-up position, every muscle screaming with exertion until she collapsed against the floor. Evie could not understand the danger, could not feel the horror in the room around them. Or perhaps she did and knew only to beg her mother to save her.

But Shannon couldn't save her. She was failing. Her worst fear: that she'd hurt Evie, that she'd leave Evie to be hurt, all coming to fruition, and she couldn't do anything to stop it.

Don't think about that. It isn't true. I'm going to get her and get the fuck out of here.

Evie squalled, but softly, the way she sometimes did when she was putting herself back to sleep, and Shannon wrenched her body toward the sound of Evie's shuffling, toward the soft whisper of her cotton footie pajamas, until she could see her daughter, face to face. Four feet away, but it might have been light-years. An impassable void. Shannon whispered across the expanse: "Shh, honey, it's okay." Shannon strained against the shirt, yanking one way, then the other. She'd be out of this contraption before Evie fully awoke.

Then footsteps—heavy and slow, deliberate, somewhere behind her. No squeal of door hinges or clack of a latch. He'd been there the whole time, watching her struggle. *Oh, fuck.* Her heart shuddered, then froze.

Shannon moved faster away from him, her ribs aching, her wrists and knuckles grinding painfully against the floor. She couldn't roll toward the intruder—it would be like leaving Evie alone.

"Now, now, girl, that won't do at all." His voice cracked on the "girl," but the tone was low and hollow, reverberating in her ears like the heady thrum of a plucked cello string. Yet there was nothing melodic about it: each syllable drove icicles of fear into her throat until she feared she'd faint, leaving her limp and powerless to help Evie. Or herself.

Another thunk of foot on floor, then a shuffle, then a stomp as he stepped over her body, his foot next to her ear. The clank of something metal rang from his shoe, which was strange—unless her hearing was off. Her head throbbed. He took one more step over to Evie. *Definitely metal.* And close, too close to her daughter's face like he was moments from smashing her head with his boot. Then he was at the wall, but not far enough from Evie—one step backward, and he'd crush her. He flicked on the light, reducing the room to him, only him, and the contrast of his back against the sudden blinding glare.

Adjust. See. I need to use this shit.

As he retreated, she rolled onto her back to track his movement. In front of her, a wall. White paint, but not clean—scuffed and dirty, and a single window, or what used to be a window if the unused curtain hooks on the ceiling were any indication. The rest of the wall was covered by insulation and thick black plastic—an exterior wall, then. *Escape.* And the plastic itself could be a weapon if she could get a piece over this asshole's face. Above them, metal spines from a small, iron chandelier cast agitated shadows on the walls. Actual metal or just painted to look like iron? Either way, it would hurt if it connected with his fucking skull.

Evie whined again, softly as if she were still dreaming, and the tightness in Shannon's breasts intensified as her milk let down. She turned her head toward Evie, and it hurt—*God, my head*—and her temple felt damp like it might be bleeding again. Evie, so close, on her back. One arm moved, reaching, looking for her momma. "It's okay, baby, Mommy's here. It's okay." Evie's legs kicked the air futilely, then stopped.

Shannon's chest tingled with fear and rage and oily hatred. Milk soaked her shirt. She wrested her face to where he stood hidden in shadow in a corner where the light of the barbed chandelier did not reach. Average-sized, even smaller than, judging from the position of the ceiling, but he seemed huge, and she had to force breath into her lungs. *Fix this, Mommy. Get yourself together.*

Evie fussed again, not yet fully awake, but getting there. Soon she'd be wailing.

"Let me feed her." *Be nice to the big bad asshole, Shannon.* "Please let me feed her, sir." *Give him what he wants.* But what was that? "I don't know what you want, but if it's money, I'll get it."

He stepped forward, the overhead light glinting against something in his hand—a long and pointed thing, metal, with a spear at the top covered with spiky protrusions like thorns and a thick hook glinting on one side. An ax on the other side. Shannon's heart stopped. Evie squalled again, and Shannon's brain, her nerves, her heart, everything went into hyperdrive, panic racing like electrical currents over her chest and into her legs. Her baby's front was exposed, her soft underbelly vulnerable to the hooked blade, but on her side, Shannon couldn't see them both at once, and his face…

The whole front of his head was covered by a mask, leathery like the straitjacket she wore and with heavy stitching on either side of an enormous beak-like nose, as thick as a toucan's. The eyes were covered with what looked like round aviator glasses. From the top of the mask, additional triangles of red metal protruded in different directions, like a bloody porcupine. The entire thing was painted: large red joker's lips, smiling and sinister, and a firework of black around each aviator eye. A circle of garish red stained each cheekbone.

Below the mask, his neck was white, as if he hadn't seen the sun all year, and his collarbone, visible at the neck of his black tunic, was sunken, everything sunken, wasting but in a sharp-featured way. He was skinny, gangly, too awkward like a child trying to get used to his growing limbs. Was he very young? Or maybe sick? He had a sore on his neck, no…several of them, but the shadow under the mask made them hard to see. Measles? Lesions? AIDS? Her eyes flicked to the weapon again. *Please, not that. Focus, find something I can use.* Maybe the marks were burns. Or abscesses from drug use. She never could tell that kind of stuff the way Morrison could—he had a sixth sense from working with the Ash Park PD. She had never missed him so much as in this moment. Hell, it was probably just a shaving cut or an infected fucking pimple. *Stop looking at it and think, Shannon!*

Tears burned behind her lids, but she blinked before they could fill her eyes. *Don't give him the satisfaction. One thing at a time.* "Please." Shannon glanced at the bed against one wall, black sheets shimmering like they were wet. On the end table sat a heavy-looking lamp, cord severed halfway to the plug. "Just let me take care of her before we draw attention to you. Then you can tell me what it is you want, and I'll—"

The rap of his boots silenced her as the sound echoed through her head: the thunk of rubber soles but something else, a click of... It *was* metal. Orange tinged with green, copper formed in spiked ridges along the back of his shoe, longer than the actual boot treads, making him taller—high heels on crack. But he wasn't stomping; his steps were tentative. Quiet. Almost...secretive. He took a step over to Evie, and the metal tool seemed to shudder in his hand, though it might have been her vision blurring. Every cell in her body vibrated with the desire to tear her child away from the weapon, from this maniac.

"We already have what I want," he said. "Happy, happy, happy."

We, who's we? Her gaze darted around the room again, but there were only walls, yellowed by the light. Then he was moving away from Evie— *thank you, God*—but instead of retreating to his shadowed corner, he marched toward Shannon again. The scrape of metal on wood ground through her eardrums until he stopped just beyond her toes. A breath of air whooshed by her legs as a sound like the squeal of hinges cut the silence—but she would have noticed an exterior door. A closet?

She couldn't breathe, every beat of her heart, forcing the oxygen from her lungs. Sweat-soaked hair matted itself to her cheek as she craned her neck toward her feet, toward the man in the mask, but she could only make out the top of the door: thickly padded. Soundproofed. *Oh, Jesus, he's going to lock me in the closet...* Though it wasn't a closet, but a bleak, black room, an enormous beam across the middle. *A dungeon.* She coughed, choked, as vomit rose in her throat and cut off her air with acid.

He turned back to her. *Get out, run! Run!* She strained again and finally looked down at her own body, at her jacket: mismatched cowhide pieces roughly sewn with upholstery thread. And at the base of one of her wrists, an evil-looking metal lock, rusty and thick, attached to a metal hook sewn into the leather jacket itself. No escape.

Get him talking. Or she was dead, Evie was dead.

"Do we know each other?"

He snorted in response. "You'd never know someone like me." No cracking in his baritone this time, just rage. Had he been snubbed? Humiliated?

"I'm sure I would." She hated that her voice was shaking, but it felt like her bones were trying to vibrate their way out of her body. "You don't need the mask."

"I don't want to smell your stink." As she watched, the air from each breath he took broadened his back, inflating him, steadying him until he was tall, straight—emboldened. He was composing himself. But for what?

Evie screamed, and his shoulders tensed. The tip of the beaked nose caught the light –metal too. Everything so sharp. Shannon's chest dampened her shirt to her belly, still soft from childbirth.

Shh, Evie. She heaved herself over, floundering like a beached whale.

She could feel his eyes on the back of her neck, but she lay still, staring at Evie, wanting to pick her up, desperate to pick her up. She was failing. *No, I am not.* "Please," she whispered, aiming for hopeless, helpless, but in that moment, the fire in her belly burned stronger than her terror, flaming into her face, blistering her insides with incredulous fury. *Just let my arms go. Give me an inch, motherfucker, and I will destroy you.*

He stepped in front of her, away from the padded closet, one heavy boot so close to her face that she could see the mud on the copper spines on the bottom. But no—the hue was far too crimson, not nearly the right shade of brown to be dirt. And the smell: not only the copper of the metal but the cloying wet of a wound not yet healed. Blood? On his boots? She squinted at his feet, at the spikes that could only be weapons—sharp enough to kill.

Her breath caught again as the other boot fell heavy in front of her, close enough to her belly that it snagged the straitjacket. He pulled it free, cursing under his breath, and bent to her, leaning his beaked mask so close she could smell his sweat, setting the metal hook of his bladed tool hard against her shoulder, the coolness of it reaching her skin even through the leather straitjacket. This time, the blade did not shake. He leaned closer, closer, until his breath echoed in her ears louder than her own, amplified by the hollow mask and her own sheer terror.

He peered at her through the mask, with eyes hard and dark and emotionless behind the strange bubble lenses. Looking for something. *He wants to see my fear.* She allowed her lower lip to tremble. Allowed the tears to spring into her eyes.

Please let that be enough.

He cocked his head.

Evie was still wailing, but Shannon could barely hear—like he was sucking the sound waves from the room and swallowing them with his beaked mouth.

Then he straightened, stepped heavily over her, and she hauled herself back to look toward Evie, following his steps. When one taloned boot narrowly missed Evie's head, Shannon cried out, shrill and harsh against the hiss of his breath, jerking so hard against the straitjacket that he turned back to her. His sharp, metal beak was aimed right at her as if he might use it to impale her.

"Please," she whispered. He held the tool out in front of him, the points, the barbs, the hooked, spiked top glinting darkly, consuming her attention, every sliver of the instrument standing out in ominous detail.

"Happy, happy, happy," he growled. And still, he watched her. Showed the weapon to her. She bit her lip.

He bent to one knee in front of Evie.

Shannon screamed.

The man in the mask tipped his face toward the ceiling and laughed.

18

SHE'D BE ANGRY, maybe. But by the next morning, Morrison didn't care. He'd dialed Shannon's number again—twice—and she still wasn't answering. But she had surely hit the road early to take advantage of Evie's happy time; she had to be somewhere with reception by now. So he'd run their credit cards. Last used yesterday near Toledo, only an hour from Ash Park, but she'd get a good six hours of drive time out of that one tank of gas. And she hadn't needed to stop for food—she'd brought a cooler with her because eating out with an infant was a pain in the ass. He'd tried to check on the hotel, too, but she had planned to use their points to book it from the lot, and it would still be another day before it showed on the credit card statement—the company could tell him nothing. *Nothing.* He put a hold on their credit and debit cards. Regardless of her determination to make it to Alex's without his support, she was being selfish, and that fucking pissed him off. But the anger sat on his chest, on the surface, while deeper, more primal fears lurked in his gut, and if he breathed too hard, he felt them swell up and try to consume him.

I've lost them. They're never coming home. The worst was that he was alone—if Morrison called on his fellow officers to look for his wife it made this…real. His girls might be gone. His life might be over. And if Shannon really was gone, Roger would wrongfully throw him in jail again, and he'd be helpless to save his family.

Goddammit, Shannon.

He dialed again—no answer, not then, and not on the five more attempts on his way to work. And all the while, his fears fought with the logical part of his brain, the one that reminded him that Shannon had flat-out told him she was going to wait to call him. That she didn't want him to be her crutch. That this was only the second day—she wouldn't even be at Alex's yet, not when she had to stop to feed Evie every couple hours. And she had texted him. If he waited a little longer, she might call.

BY THE TIME lunch rolled around, his agitation had morphed into relentless anxiety; panic seized his innards every time a new thought seared through his brain. He tried to tell himself it was the case. They'd spent the morning ascertaining that none of the prior occupants of the strip mall had seen the bike or Mr. Magoo.

"Not even coffee today?" Petrosky asked him.

Morrison shook his head, his stomach tying itself in knots at the mere scent of food.

"Worried about Shannon?"

"Yeah. But she did text me." His voice was almost defensive. Forcing himself to believe it was okay. Morrison looked away, trying to avoid Petrosky's piercing stare.

"So, what's the problem?"

Morrison sipped at his water but set it down when his stomach rebelled. "Decantor came by last night."

"After my house?"

"Before."

Petrosky narrowed his eyes and dipped a fry in ketchup. Said nothing. But he just glared at the fry instead of eating it.

"I didn't want to say anything in front of your friends." Morrison looked at him pointedly. "And because I was…thinking." *No, I was trying not to think.* He cleared his throat. "Our first-choice nanny, Natalie Bell, was found murdered in her apartment, stabbed in the abdomen and groin."

Petrosky tossed the fry onto his plate, where it landed in a pool of ketchup. "What the fuck, Surfer Boy? Why the hell wouldn't you tell me?"

"Like I said, I was trying—"

"How'd Decantor catch that, anyway?" He drummed his fingers on the table. "Sounds like more than a standard homicide. Should have come through us."

"They figured we had enough to do?"

Petrosky stared at the fry like he wanted to slap the shit out of it. "What else, California?"

Morrison looked at his water glass and grimaced. "Bell died on Monday of wounds just like those on Acosta's back. And the killer took my card from her wallet and used Bell's phone to call me Tuesday night to tell me she wasn't taking the job." *They'd used Bell's phone.* Maybe they'd also used Shannon's to text him. Was she dead too? Morrison tried to shake the thought from his head, but it stuck.

Petrosky's fingertips beat frantically against the table. Morrison half expected the spoon to start vibrating and work its way to the floor where the clatter would surely alert everyone to his predicament—his sanity was hanging by a thread as thin as spider silk.

"You're certain they called you after she was dead?" Petrosky asked.

"I'm sure…or rather Decantor is. He thinks they were just fucking with me." The question was *why*.

"How the hell would they know about Bell's job offer? You think that just randomly came up while she was being stabbed to death?" Petrosky pulled his hands from the tabletop, and the silence was more nerve-racking than his incessant tapping. "Maybe they're coming after you because you're investigating the Acosta case. Hence the similar wounds."

The thought had occurred to Morrison, and he'd pushed it from his head before it had eaten him alive. "But if they wanted to threaten me, they would have. They didn't ask for anything. Just said Bell wouldn't be in to work. Either they didn't want people looking for her because they planned to come back and… mess with the body, or it's a prank." *Even though it doesn't feel like one.*

"Mm-hmm." Petrosky picked up the fry again and shoved it into his mouth. "How many times did Shannon call her?"

"Two. I think. No one answered."

Petrosky shook his head. "She probably called at least three or four times; she's persistent as fuck. Maybe they just called back because they wanted the phone to stop ringing."

They could have turned it off. Petrosky still hated his smartphone—one day, he'd probably put it through the wall before he found the ignore button.

Maybe Shannon's pushing ignore on my calls. His finger twitched with the desire to hit redial, but if she hadn't picked up by now, she wasn't going to. And there was surely a logical reason. Had to be.

Petrosky was drumming on the tabletop again, his pork sandwich getting cold and soggy with coleslaw. "I know there's more, Surfer Boy."

Morrison pushed his water glass away. Someone had called him and pretended to be Bell, and they'd had enough information to know what to say to him. He should have recognized that the voice was disguised—that it hadn't been Bell at all. Some fucking detective he was. "I don't like it, Boss. I can't figure out any reason for them to call me at all. And the way Decantor described the wounds… I mean, there are clearly differences in the crimes, but this isn't right." He ran a hand through his hair.

"And?"

And I need to find her. Now. We need backup. "It's driving me crazy that I can't get ahold of Shannon. I put a block on our credit cards. She's texted me but—"

"I'll call Valentine, put out an APB on her car." Petrosky gestured for the check, practically ripping his wallet from his pocket.

He's worried. And if Petrosky was worried—

"You call Alex first, just to make sure she didn't drive all night and then pass out when she got there. Then we'll keep on this case because if it's the same person who did Acosta, we need to follow what leads we have."

"We don't know that Bell and Acosta are connected. And Shannon doesn't have enough gas to make it there; she hasn't filled up since—"

"Unless she paid cash at some rinky-dink station. Just fucking call Alex." Alex. The man who'd moved away and made Shannon's postpartum period with Evie that much more horrible, like she'd lost everything important to her all at once.

She still had me.

I wasn't enough to make her happy. Morrison followed Petrosky out to the car, tapping his phone. The car felt like a prison cell.

She won't even call me back.

Alex answered on the first ring, and Morrison tried to keep his voice even as Petrosky pulled from the lot and headed toward the home of their last potential contact—a guy who had owned a nail studio next to the tattoo place back during the time their rapist had been there. "Hey, Alex. I was just wondering... did Shannon make it there yet?"

"Not yet, but I wasn't expecting her until later this evening. Figured she'd need lots of breaks with the baby." Alex was quiet a beat, then said, "Why, did she leave earlier or something?"

She's not there. But he'd known it would be a long shot. "Nah, I've just been trying to get through on her cell. Figured I'd ask if she'd called."

Another pause. A sound like a crinkling candy bar wrapper. "Something wrong?"

Morrison didn't answer. He didn't want to lie. Petrosky pulled down a side street.

"Should I be worried?" Alex asked, his voice a touch higher than usual.

Yes. "No, of course not. I just got some bad news on one of the nannies we were considering hiring. Thought she'd want to know."

"Hope you had a backup choice." His voice was back to normal, though Morrison's heart rate climbed with every word. He fought for control.

"Yeah, we have a backup—I just wanted to tell her. But if you talk to her first, maybe leave out the part about it being bad news. You know she'll want all the details, and she'll have a laundry list of questions all set before she even calls back." He tried to force a laugh, but it came out strangled.

"Yeah, she sure will." Alex said, and Morrison could hear his smile over the phone. "I'll have her call as soon as I see her, okay?"

"Deal."

Petrosky pulled out his phone, keeping one eye on the road. His jaw was tight. "Calling in the APB. I'll take the fall on it. She won't think it was you."

"Because it wasn't me." But he didn't care if she thought it was him, not anymore. His heart was beating a thousand times faster than it should, almost whirring at the speed of the tires on the road.

She's dead.

She just left yesterday.

Evie's dead.

Shannon texted me.

Someone took them, stomped them to death in a field.

Shannon told me she wasn't going to use me as a crutch.

His heart slowed, but the thoughts remained, fighting, screaming at one another in his brain.

"Valentine will tell her it was me anyway. Or his wife will." Petrosky stopped at a light and pushed a button on the phone. "And I don't give a fuck if she hates me."

"Yes you do," Morrison muttered as Petrosky put the phone to his ear.

"Valentine. Need an APB on a white Enclave. Yes. Shannon Morrison."

Valentine's exclamation of surprise emanated from the phone, but Petrosky shut him down. "Just do it, Valentine. And call me back." Morrison listened numbly to Petrosky's side of the conversation, trying to focus on something else. Anything else. Anything but the nausea in his gut and the knot throbbing between his shoulder blades. He raised his hand to massage the knot, but his limbs felt weak—shaky. He lowered his arm.

Petrosky shoved his phone into the console and sighed, the

sound raising Morrison's hackles more than anything his partner could have said. "Let's toss the Acosta case at Detective Young, maybe even Decantor—if they are connected, he'll solve them both at once. Then we'll drive down to Alex's place to visit your niece. See Roxy. You know you miss that mutt, and she is kinda cute."

"You hate that dog." Morrison still couldn't believe he'd given Roxy away last year, but Abby had felt unsafe after Griffen had stomped her kitten to death. *Stomped.* An image of Dylan Acosta's body sprouted in his brain, and he shoved it away before it could take root.

"How do you know I hate Roxy?" Petrosky half grinned, but it looked forced.

Stop changing the subject. "We can't just leave now—Acosta's murderer is still out there, and we don't know these cases are connected in the first place. And our best shot at finding who did Bell, and who called me, is to follow these leads." The APB was probably a better way to go about finding Shannon anyway. If she had made it to Alex's fine, she'd be pissed when Morrison showed up, and if she was in trouble, he wasn't going to find out just by going Alex's; he'd still have no idea where to look for her, and in Atlanta, he might be a lot farther from Shannon and from his little girl. Which meant he might as well stay here, which meant he needed…a distraction.

"I bet she calls soon. She's probably just trying to prove to herself that she can handle the trip all on her own."

"Sounds like her." Petrosky didn't turn from the windshield, but the muscles in his jaw were working overtime in his fleshy face. "We'll wait on the APB before we head out there."

"Plus, she always says I'm overprotective."

"That's a dad's job, California," Petrosky said, and the pain was apparent in the creases around his eyes, the tightening of his jowls. He pulled into a drive, checked the address, and shut the car off. "Let's meet Mr. Xu."

THE OWNER of the nail salon had answered their questions with frantic little hand movements that belonged to a twittering sparrow, not a grown man. But they didn't come away empty-handed. Xu swore that he'd seen their rape suspect with another man—skinny with a buzz cut—exchanging a large paper sack for an envelope. But whether it had a bearing on the case remained to be seen. Despite Xu's vehemence about what he'd witnessed, this many years after the fact and the distance from the tattoo parlor to the nail salon made it just as likely that he'd seen another man with scraggly hair selling something to a friend. All the same, they'd look on local buying and selling websites, but it was doubtful they'd find anything of value.

By the time they left Xu's, Morrison was actively listening for Petrosky's phone, a buzzing to tell them where Shannon's car might be. But if she was on her way to Alex's, and already out of state, no one would have seen her yet. Not like she'd be likely to get pulled over.

Petrosky slammed his car door and lit a cigarette. "Let's pretend Xu did see our guy. Thoughts on the exchange?"

"Not sure. Something worth cash, if that's what was in the envelope."

"Right. And they wouldn't be so careless if it was porn." Petrosky checked his phone. Watching for Shannon too? For information to come back on her car?

Morrison's scalp itched, but he balled his fist instead of picking at it. *Focus on Xu. The package.* He couldn't make the APB go faster by fucking up his case. "The boots?" He squinted out his window, hating the tightness in his voice. Whatever these men had exchanged in the daytime had to be something less overtly threatening—less illegal—but still something they didn't want others to see. "But that'd mean our tattooed suspect made the boots for the man he eventually tried to stop from using them. And if these guys got together that long ago, you'd think we'd have seen other victims pop up well before now."

"You'd think so, but—"

Morrison's phone buzzed, and he ripped it from his pocket with enough force that he nearly tossed it through the front windshield. *Shannon.*

No, not Shannon. His heart rate quickened, liquefying his insides, pulsing faster and hotter within his chest.

That number—he'd seen it just yesterday when Decantor had come by his house.

Natalie Bell's cell.

He put the phone to his ear, the world around him slowing to a crawl, even the persistent whisper of the tires disappearing into some imperceptible void. "Morrison."

"How's the pig, Curt? Not the food, your partner." Female voice, alto, same as before. Breathy, but clear now and laced with venom.

Bolts of panic slithered up Morrison's back. "Miss Bell?" The world around him returned, and he eased his notepad from his pants pocket, positioning the pen so that he wouldn't miss some crucial bit of information. She wanted something. From him? Or was he merely convenient because they had his private number?

Petrosky jerked his face to Morrison, eyes wide, then back to the street, unable to stop the car as he merged onto the freeway.

"You know very well this isn't Natalie. I hear she was a pretty girl, Curt. Were you going to hire her, get a little strange on the side?"

Petrosky hit the gas, glancing at Morrison out of the corner of his eye. From the phone, there was a rumble like laughter, but not of the amusement variety—this was more like a ripple of madness.

Morrison's mouth was too dry to speak, not that he would have said anything anyway. You don't push crazy.

"I bet you were," the voice said. "You always were a whore."

That was a new one. "If you're not Natalie, then who am I talking to?"

"Tsk tsk, Curt. Don't ask, don't tell."

Curt. She knew his name. It wasn't on his business card—even Shannon didn't call him that.

"I rather think you might enjoy this, Curt. It has to do with everyone's favorite prosecutor."

Shannon. No, not—

"Roger McFadden." Tires squealed as Petrosky skidded past

the right-hand lane onto the shoulder and slammed the car into park.

Morrison's heart descended from his throat back into his chest, where it fluttered weakly, trying to pulse within the tightness of his ribs.

"Roger's been a very bad boy. Which I suspect you know already."

Roger. This was about Roger? Probably someone he'd prosecuted, pissed off—career criminal, angry at Roger for putting him away? A criminal's lover? But why kill Bell? Why harass Morrison? Unless...they'd just seen Morrison's card in Bell's wallet, did a little research, and only later decided to bring him into the game. But that seemed too haphazard, too coincidental.

"Roger is an asshole; I'll give you that," Morrison said.

"He's dirty too. How would you like to take down your wife's ex? Cathartic, yes?"

His chest constricted. This woman knew a lot about him. But then, Shannon's former marriage to Roger was public record; the caller didn't need much to find out that information. Just motivation enough to mess with the police.

"I'd love to put Roger away. But I need a reason. Evidence." Too bad—anything he got from this woman was probably moot or a flat-out lie. "I'm more interested in Natalie Bell."

"I'm sure you are." That laugh again. Almost manic. "Roger's got a book in his safe deposit box. A log. Bribes. He needs to go to jail, Curt. And you need to get him locked up in the next twenty-four hours."

Morrison had long suspected Roger of taking bribes, of dropping reasonable charges for a price—though, he'd never been able to prove it. But this... How would this woman know about Roger's safe deposit box? Lucky guess? Either she was full of shit, or she actually knew Roger. Or...he knew Roger; the higher register could still be the trick of a voice-over contraption if this caller really was the same person who'd killed Dylan Acosta.

"Investigations like this take time," Morrison said slowly. "Weeks to uncover evidence, scour bank accounts. I can't exactly walk into a bank and get into his deposit box without hard evidence. Sounds like you've done your homework, so surely you know that."

"He'll give you the book. Then you can go to your chief."

"There's no way—"

"Be persuasive and arrest him. Or kill him. It doesn't matter to me. One way or another, he needs to be punished."

Kill him. The silence stretched on as Morrison jotted notes on the pad: *Natalie Bell's relationship to Roger? Bribery? Notes in safe? Or bullshit?* The buzz of other motorists on the freeway approaching, and then whipping by with the hiss of tires, made him suddenly claustrophobic. He circled "bullshit." The caller was fucking with him because she could. Opportunity, right? Sociopaths took what they could get. Unless she was just a normal—albeit impulsive—person who was really fucking pissed at Roger. He could see that happening too.

But this person wasn't normal. Whoever had Bell's cell had murdered her, tortured her—or at least knew about it. At least the caller wasn't after Shannon. He hadn't even recognized how worried he'd been until he felt the relief at the absence of a ransom demand. Shannon was just driving. Busy. And okay.

"So...what does Natalie Bell's murder have to do with Roger?" he asked.

Silence. "We've got a lot to work through, you and I." The woman's voice was hard, angry, and the words sounded personal —and not at all about Roger.

"I'm not sure I follow." Something about the voice suddenly nagged at him, the lilt of it tugging a memory from somewhere, a memory he couldn't quite retrieve. "Why don't you tell me how we know each other, so I can make sure I don't mess up again?"

"You still don't get it, do you? You see me, but you don't. But you'll figure it out—you'll remember me. And once you do, you'll know exactly how to find me." Her words felt less like a promise and more like a threat. Was she stalking him? He tried to place her voice, but the timbre did not call to mind anyone he knew.

"I'll call back when you're alone. But keep this to yourself,

Curt. Keep your appointments. Work your cases. Wouldn't want your boss to get suspicious. And don't fuck it up."

The line went dead.

"What the hell was that about?"

Morrison stared at the phone like it was going to wake up and bite his hand. *Damn crackpots.* Had to be. Right? "Roger."

"What the fuck does that dickbrain have to do with anything?" Petrosky put the car into drive and eased back onto the freeway.

"Long story." Morrison related the details as best he could, starting with the cell call the day after Bell's murder and ending with the caller's suspicions that Roger was taking bribes for pleading cases out. But Bell…the caller hadn't seemed concerned with her at all. Was she just collateral damage, or was she connected to Roger somehow?

"Nothing that fucker does would surprise me. But the call… interesting." Petrosky tapped his knuckles against the console. "When we get back to the precinct, we'll look into it," he said finally. "We've got a few minutes before we need to see the doc, so we can do a trace on the call with that triangulation bullshit, yeah?"

Morrison nodded, but an urgent disquiet rose in his belly. He was just a bystander here, his number stolen and used in a killer's game of intimidation, probably against Roger, the prosecutor who'd done…something to this asshole. So what kind of person were they looking for? If the caller had benefitted from a plea deal with Roger—if the accusations about bribes were even true—they wouldn't be trying to expose Roger now. So maybe Roger had fucked this killer over, maybe jailed her—or him— despite a bribe, or…had Roger refused to take a bribe altogether? Then the killer gets out of jail, finds Roger, and kills someone to make sure the cops pay attention. But…

Morrison sucked air into his lungs as Petrosky pulled off the freeway and stopped at a red light that suddenly looked like an evil eye. *You still don't get it, do you? You see me, but you don't. But you'll figure it out—you'll remember me. And once you do, you'll know exactly how to find me.* Trusting his memory was dubious at best, and for the life of him, he could think of no one who would threaten Roger like this, who would kill an innocent girl. No one who would know the intimate details of Roger's life, well, no one except...

But Shannon had nothing to do with this—the only thing that was keeping Morrison sane. The killer wanted Roger. Why, he wasn't sure, but who didn't want to fuck Roger up?

Petrosky pulled into the precinct parking lot, but Morrison couldn't shake the uneasy feeling in his gut, or the flicker of electricity running over his spine.

19

TRIANGULATION WASN'T DIFFICULT. He clicked the mouse, entered Bell's number, listened to the clack of the keyboard. *Click click click.* There was a time when the focus would have helped—mindfulness quieted voices and memories and cravings far more effectively than talking about those things, dwelling on a jaded past. But today, his thoughts pressed in on him, loud and insistent over the sound of the keyboard. Why was he being dragged into this, and what did Roger have to do with Bell? Was the Acosta case connected? And, at the back of his mind, eclipsing all other thought like the remnants of a disturbing dream you were desperate to forget: *Where the fuck is Shannon?*

He pulled his fingers from the keyboard and tried Shannon's cell. Voice mail. He tried again, each buzz of the ringer more ominous than the last. Voice mail. He slammed the phone onto the desk, checked that it hadn't broken, and opened another computer screen to check her cell records. Why hadn't he thought of that yesterday? He was a fucking idiot. Morrison was hovering over the *locate* button when his cell pinged with a text, and he flipped it over, heart hammering.

Shannon:

"Sorry, just got your message. Love you too."

Morrison:

"Call me."

The phone stayed silent. On the screen, the towers blinked. He clicked back and forth, from Bell's cell to Shannon's and back again, drumming his fingers on the desk as the first, and then the second, cell tower blinked onto Bell's screen and stayed steady. If only they had better department funding and more up-to-date location equipment. Even 9-1-1 operators had a hard time locating callers with their outdated tracking systems.

The third tower blinked once more and solidified.

"Petrosky…"

The caller using Bell's cell was…there. Within a block of the precinct.

Petrosky wheeled over from his desk and peered at the screen.

"What do you make of that?" The disquiet in Morrison's belly was spreading, wrapping around his chest. They'd called *from* the precinct. Was the caller watching him? Or Roger?

"Fucking insider bullshit," Petrosky said. "I don't like it." He grimaced, and Morrison's fist clenched.

Insider bullshit—probably a reference to Shannon's old buddy Griffen. But he was dead. "Griffen was delusional," Morrison said. "Not likely it'd happen again, not like that."

Petrosky stood and shoved his chair toward his desk. It banged into the side, and Morrison jumped, his pulse hammering in his chest so violently he might as well have been running a marathon.

Petrosky raised an eyebrow, then lowered it. "Come on, kid, it's time to visit McCallum."

"Hang on…" On Shannon's screen, the second tower blinked. "Shannon texted me a minute ago." *If it is Shannon.* He turned to Petrosky, trying to keep his voice slow and even. "Any news on the APB?"

No reply.

"Petrosky?"

The boss's eyes were glued to the screen. Morrison turned back to the computer. The last tower was blinking, and like the droning of every ring on Shannon's unanswered cell, each pulse brought with it a sharper, fiercer pang of dread. Then it was up.

Her cell was at the precinct too.

20

Maybe the system wasn't working—it wouldn't be the first time. Once it had traced all the anonymous 9-1-1 calls to an apartment on the east side, and the residents had almost sued the city for harassment when the cops kept showing up. But the cramp in Morrison's belly crept higher through his chest, into his shoulders, into his neck.

His entire body was stiff by the time Morrison emerged in the parking lot, Petrosky at his heels. *Come on, Shannon, call.* The air outside was electric with an impending storm, and Morrison had to concentrate on the breath in his lungs to make sure they inflated. In, out. In, out. The sky had darkened, and the thick, gray clouds had turned the lot into an apocalyptic sea of ash, stark against the neon green of the grass. Every car in the parking lot was empty, as was the lot itself, save for one wrinkled woman with a shock of white curls, creeping slowly toward the courthouse on a metal cane, wind plastering her hair to one withered cheek.

The breeze scattered leaves and the occasional plastic bottle in an ominous soundtrack. Morrison whipped out his cell as they strode across the lot. Shannon was fine—had to be fine. Evie too. But he didn't feel fine, every gust of wind from the heavens a whisper that his life was about to collapse. *We're looking for her. We'll find her.* And in the meantime... Morrison followed Petrosky's gaze around the lot, up to the windows of the courthouse. No prying eyes watching to see if he went to visit Roger's office.

Fucking Roger. But he'd have to go up there and at least let Roger know someone was trying to get his stupid ass arrested.

"Who you calling, Cali?"

"Decantor. Figured I'd let him know about the call on Roger. Maybe by the time we get out of our meeting with McCallum, he'll have something else on the caller." *Or maybe he'll have something on the APB.*

Voice mail. Morrison clicked off. The muted thuds of their shoes on pavement vibrated through his body, a steady metronome to the frantic beat of his heart as they approached the door to Dr. McCallum's office.

"Morrison!"

He turned to see Valentine running from the precinct, waving one beefy hand over his head. With every step he took, the apprehension in Valentine's eyes became more apparent—even the scar on his cheek seemed agitated.

Petrosky's breathing had increased. He shouldn't be winded. He shouldn't be. Was it his heart, or was it…

"I just ran into Decantor." Valentine had reached them, panting. "He's looking for you."

Stay calm. Morrison nodded, the muscles in his neck corded with nervous energy "I just tried to call him. I'll run over after McCallum…unless it's urgent?"

Valentine didn't respond, just stared at him with the hollow look of a Holocaust survivor. "Decantor said you guys have the same killer. For sure."

Petrosky stilled beside him.

"He just came from the ME's office." Valentine averted his eyes, looking almost guilty, but of course, he couldn't feel guilty—there was nothing to feel bad about. No, not guilt. His friend felt awful. *Distressed.*

Morrison's heart seized.

Valentine looked back up and met Morrison's gaze. "Found a single hair at the Bell scene—blond at the root, black at the tip. Got a DNA match to the blood at the Acosta scene. And that spike thing…uh…that she was…penetrated with? Lab results concluded that it was the same object in both cases, or at least from the same batch of metal—there were patina fragments." He wrung his hands. "And he scraped a number one on Bell too…on that spot between…you know. The taint." He winced. "Before she died."

Morrison swallowed hard, trying to keep his breath even. It was about their case. Not about his wife. *The case.* Dylan Acosta. Natalie Bell. "We've got a few leads on ours too. We'll be heading back to the east side after profiling with McCallum. Tell Decantor we can reconvene afterward, go over everything."

"Oh, okay, yeah, sure that sounds good." But Valentine's eyes were on the building, on his shoes, glancing back at the precinct —everywhere but Petrosky and Morrison. He looked like he wanted to run.

Petrosky coughed and moved to Morrison's side. "Spit it out, Valentine."

Valentine stared at them, his mouth working. Morrison couldn't feel his chest. His legs were numb.

Petrosky clapped twice in front of the man's face. "Valentine!"

"You need to talk to Decantor."

"You said that already," Morrison said, softly, almost whispering because his throat was too tight to do more.

"Goddammit, just—"

"We found Shannon's car."

He said you guys have the same killer. And the killer had called him. Bile rose in his throat, blocking his airway. What if…

"An hour ago. Gas station near Toledo, just over the Ohio border."

She'd barely made it out of state—an hour from the house, two tops. She'd been missing for all of yesterday. He glanced at the sky, the low-hanging clouds, the weak hint of late afternoon illumination. Nearly all of today too.

Missing. But without a struggle? She'd have fought a kidnapper. Maybe she'd leapt from an overpass, thrown Evie into the river. No. *What the hell am I thinking?* No way. She had just texted him—she was fine. She had to be fine. She was fine, completely fine, and probably pissed at him for not trusting her.

Texted him from the precinct. And he hadn't heard her voice.

A glance at Petrosky's face turned his insides to water, the apprehension he saw reaching for him with panicked fingers as tangible as his own. Petrosky had probably told himself it would be fine all the way to identify his daughter's body. And then it wasn't fine. Nothing had ever been fine again.

If their killer had taken Shannon, she was in for a lot worse than a leap off a bridge. And his little girl—no. *No.* He faced Valentine. "You found her car. Did you find my wife?"

Valentine's eyes were glassy. He shook his head.

Dylan Acosta and Natalie Bell—they'd been killed by the same sadistic fuck. The same sadistic fuck who had called Morrison. The vicious monster who had killed both his victims within an hour of first attacking them.

A murderer had his family, and he had no idea where they were.

Or if they were already dead.

21

PETROSKY LIT A CIGARETTE WITH QUICK, jerky movements as Valentine headed back into the precinct under the guise of getting the file. "They probably followed her until she stopped for gas, or to feed Evelyn, then grabbed her."

Morrison watched Petrosky's acrid cloud appear and fly sharply away in the breeze like his own happiness—here, then gone. And again. Every time the wind whipped the cloud away, he saw it taking pieces of his tenuous grasp on sanity.

Petrosky coughed. "We're heading over to—"

"What? They were here! She's here!"

"She's not, Morrison. You think this guy's hiding Shannon at the courthouse? A screaming baby at the prosecutor's office?"

Screaming. God, they'd make her scream. Until they killed her. "I don't know where the fuck he's hiding her, goddammit!"

Petrosky did not respond to his outburst, just said, "And that text you got...anything weird about it?"

The smoke above Petrosky's head was the embodiment of Morrison's own boiling insides—fear, pain, bubbling in his belly and rising through his throat and escaping out his nostrils. But when Morrison exhaled, he saw no plume to indicate the existence of his terror.

"You're the tech genius. Couldn't they just be shooting the signal around? Saying the phone is here when really it's in butt-fuck Egypt?" Petrosky squinted at the sky as if the answer might be written in the indignant clouds.

"I... Maybe. Yeah." They could be scrambling the signal, or they might have used one of those cards that puts any number on a caller ID. Which meant Shannon's actual phone could be anywhere. Fuck.

Petrosky cocked an eyebrow and blew smoke at the sky. "Our best leads are on the Reynolds case—we have a DNA match on the semen, so we know we're looking for the same rapist. And that sick pedophile knows who the killer is. The object used to stab Acosta and Bell is unique—there has to be a way to trace it. I'll talk to the ME, see if he can trace the metal itself."

"When's the DNA back? The rest of the crime scene labs?" Morrison's heart felt like it had stopped beating, but it was beating—had to be.

"Ours is due by tomorrow." Petrosky grimaced. "I'll make it fucking sooner on both ours and Bell's."

Morrison scanned the lot. Along the back, the upper boughs of the ash trees twisted in the wind, though he felt no breeze. In one corner, a maroon Suburban pulled into a parking spot, and a twentysomething white guy in a backward cap leaped out and started toward the sidewalk, hitching up his pants. The man gave them a cursory glance as he removed his ball cap, then disappeared up the stairs and into the courthouse next door.

The world was starkly focused, but Morrison could not seem to attach his thoughts to his body—his brain felt disconnected and fuzzy and wrong. The wind howled and silenced itself just as abruptly, leaving him with the emptiness ringing in his ears. Where did he need to go? What could he do?

"We should talk to Roger." Morrison turned to the building and glanced up at the third floor. Because the caller had threatened Roger. Because whoever had Shannon had a vendetta against Roger. Was Roger the reason Shannon had been taken in the first place? They were aware that Shannon wasn't married to Roger any longer, but no one could mistake the way Roger had lusted after her from the moment she'd left him. If they were watching him, maybe they'd know that. So did Shannon know them too, get out of her vehicle willingly? Know them through Roger? From the prosecutor's office? Shannon was stronger than she looked, though Evie would have slowed her down if she'd been forced from the car.

Morrison's chest burned. Evie. Shannon. *Fuck*. He couldn't breathe. Maybe it was a misunderstanding: someone had swapped her plates in a parking lot, and any moment now, she'd call from Alex's. But he felt the wrongness of that deep in his belly. And if Valentine was right and it was Shannon's car at that gas station—there might be something in the vehicle to help them find her. "We'll go look at the car first." He pulled out his phone to text Decantor.

"Heading to Toledo. Meet back on the cases in a couple hours."

Petrosky ground the cigarette under the heel of his shoe, and they walked across the lot, the ash trees leering at them. Maybe someone *was* watching, lurking behind a pine or a clump of brush. He could feel the rain spitting on his skin, but distantly, each drop merely a subtle pressure devoid of cold or wet. His shoes made a sickly squashing sound, like sucking a brain through a straw.

Someone was trying to scare him. Probably used software like Trickster to fake a caller ID number. Maybe they'd done that to Bell's phone too.

Maybe they didn't have Shannon after all.

He felt the tug of denial and the hope it provided, but hope could be a sickness just as much as a godsend.

If they had her… The world wavered, disappeared, returned, but this time he could no longer feel the thumping in his chest.

They'd start with her car. If they drove fast, they could get there before the coming storm obliterated the evidence.

PETROSKY'S CAR smelled the same as it always did, but everything felt heavier, dank, gluey in the back of his throat like the stale stench of cigarettes was going to drown him in a river of tobacco and confusion.

He couldn't call the police. He *was* the fucking police.

It's up to you, Curt, old boy.

A shock, an electric buzzing jolted through his right hip. Morrison jumped and hit his head on the car window, and his phone buzzed again in his back pocket. He jerked it out. Text message from Shannon. Or Shannon's number.

"Don't miss your appointment. And keep your mouth shut."

Petrosky was staring at him, keys in hand, car still in park. Morrison looked frantically around the lot, but there was no one, only the silvery threads of rain on the window and the thunderheads obscuring his view of the sun. How did they know he was leaving? Petrosky was staring at him, but he couldn't speak, couldn't answer the question written in the lines on Petrosky's forehead.

Breathe. He felt the rain as if it were thrumming through his veins. *Breathe.* But he was drowning in the downpour, every drop that hit the windshield trying to wash away his family and send everything that mattered out to sea. He typed:

"I need to talk to her."

The phone buzzed:

"No."

Nothing else, no instructions, no ransom demands, nothing. Just "no": the severing of hope.

They had her. She was dead. Evie was dead. They were dead already.

Morrison:

"Please."

Shannon:

"You'll do what you're told, or I'll take it out on her. I'll save your baby girl for when you get here if she doesn't starve to death first. Be the same selfish asshole you've always been, and I'll take pleasure in watching them bleed."

Evie. *Starving.* They weren't feeding her? Panic and fury and helplessness roiled in his abdomen.
Morrison:

"Please don't hurt them."

Shannon:

"Fuck off, Curt. Let me know when Roger's taken care of. Then you can talk to your lovely wife. I'll call tomorrow night for a progress report."

Morrison:

"Give me time. Please let them go, and I'll help you with whatever you want."

He stared at the phone, waiting for another reply, another answer, but none came. How'd they know he had decided to skip McCallum's to head to Toledo? He had texted Decantor, but...they must have tapped Morrison's phone. Or bugged the car.

Petrosky was frozen, keys in his palm. "What's up?"

Keep your mouth shut. Morrison felt the weight of the phone in his palm. "Nothing." But he rested his cell on the console and turned it so Petrosky could see.

"You're a fucking liar." But there was no anger in Petrosky's voice as he read the texts, just the whisper of helpless apology and a panic that mirrored Morrison's own.

"We should go see McCallum." Morrison's voice wavered. They wanted him here, so this was the last place he should be. Yet without any idea where Shannon and Evie were, he was helpless to get to them. He needed time. Needed to buy that time by doing what these fuckers wanted… But killing Roger? He pictured Natalie Bell, her smile when she played with Evie, then later, nude, bloody, disfigured by something sharp, the same object used to kill Acosta. They'd done that to her. They'd do that to his wife. *To his child.*

Everything vibrated, and Morrison flung the door wide and vomited bile onto the pavement. When his stomach was empty, he hauled himself onto the seat again and leaned back against the headrest. *They took my family.* Shannon might be dying, carved up like Acosta, like Bell. Evie might be—

"Buy that tiger for Evie yet?" Petrosky snapped, the harshness in his voice betraying his fear. "She'll be happy to see it when they get back."

Morrison balked, but when he met Petrosky's eyes, he saw the earnest question. *Tiger. Tiger.* Then it clicked. Tiger kidnapping: an abduction carried out to coerce another into committing a crime on the kidnapper's behalf. While putting Roger away wasn't illegal, killing him most certainly would be, and there was no way Roger was going down for anything as long as he had a breath in his body.

Morrison's breath shivered through his lungs. "Yeah, she'll like the tiger."

"Shouldn't take too long here with the doc. Ten to thirteen minutes? What do you think?"

McCallum liked to talk—they'd never been there less than half an hour. *Focus. Think.* The way Petrosky was talking now, he seemed to think his car was bugged. So…ten-thirteen, that meant civilians were present and listening. Were they, or was it a ruse? Their suspect had been aware how they'd spent the morning, and they'd known Morrison was planning on canceling the appointment with McCallum even before McCallum did. Morrison nodded again, trying to think, but every thought seemed to run through his brain like sand through a sieve.

His baby.

His wife.

These monsters had his whole world.

Petrosky pulled out his cigarettes, glared into the rearview, mouthed *fuck,* and lit up.

Morrison wiped his lips on the back of his hand, inhaled through his nose, and climbed from the car on shaky legs. He started for the building, the echo of someone else's footfalls in his ears though each thunk matched the beat of his own shoes— marching to his own execution. Maybe he was. If he lost his family, he might as well be dead.

"THE BOUNDARIES WHICH DIVIDE LIFE FROM DEATH ARE AT BEST SHADOWY AND VAGUE. WHO SHALL SAY WHERE THE ONE ENDS, AND WHERE THE OTHER BEGINS?"
~EDGAR ALLAN POE, *THE PREMATURE BURIAL*

22

FIND BELL'S KILLER. Acosta's killer. Find their killer, and he'd find his family.

This was how you solved cases, caught the bad guys. But every fiber of his being wanted him to tear out of the building, leap into his car, head to Toledo and blast through the streets, gun drawn, until he found his wife and baby girl. Here he was impotent, helpless, and he was well aware of the fact that most kids are murdered within three hours of the abduction. Was Evie dead already? Was Shannon? Even if he got them back, they'd know—for the rest of their lives—that he couldn't keep them safe.

He'd known safety was tenuous at best—even an illusion. But he hadn't wanted Evie to know.

Please let them come home.

Dr. Stephen McCallum met them in the outer office. He led them to the back room where he squeezed his three hundred pounds of shrink and sweater vest behind the desk and watched them with the penetrating eyes of one used to uncovering secrets. Morrison's already turbulent belly squeezed like a sponge, forcing bile up his esophagus so that he had to gulp it back down. His throat burned from the acid he'd vomited onto the parking lot.

Petrosky nodded at him, almost imperceptibly. *Act normal. Do the job. Work this case.*

But he couldn't speak. He couldn't breathe. If McCallum figured out what was going on and alerted anyone, Shannon would die. Right? And Evie…he couldn't even consider it. *No.* He inhaled harsh, stale office air through his nostrils and tried not to retch again.

Petrosky cleared his throat. "Let's get right into it. Looking for two attackers."

"I read the reports," McCallum said. "You have one definite rapist, a pedophile with a distinct pattern—from his previous attack on Zachary Reynolds, he rapes, he strangles, he leaves. That attack was carried out alone. Here, he followed the same pattern: rape, strangulation with the T-shirt, and leaving the boy alive. But you have another man at the Acosta scene—most likely the one who killed the child. If Acosta had died of strangulation, I'd say it was an accident or escalation of your pedophile's normal MO. But you have a totally different pattern here." McCallum tapped a pen against the desktop, and Morrison struggled to remember the doctor picking up the ballpoint. "Combined with the indications of struggle at the scene, I'd say your murderer is the other man, the one with the spiked boots and a penchant for stomping or stabbing, though how or why he was there is another question."

Petrosky had the notepad. When had he taken the notepad? Suddenly unsure what to do with his hands, Morrison dug his fists into the chair on either side of his hips.

"We thought as much," Petrosky said. "And now we have an additional killing: Natalie Bell, twenty-nine, stabbed in the lower belly and groin, penetrated vaginally with the same object. Bled to death. The weapon was distinct—likely of the same batch of metal as the one used on Acosta. Might even be home-made." Petrosky's voice did not waver. How could he sound so normal? Nothing was normal. Nothing would ever be normal again.

McCallum furrowed his brows. "I suspect you have one stan-dard pedophile, and one with piquerism, a fetish that involves penetration. They tend to be sexually sadistic, brutal, and often stab areas of the body related to sex, like what happened to Natalie Bell. In these cases, the stabbing object essentially becomes an extension of his body and the source of sexual excitement. Many notorious serial killers like Albert Fish and Jack the Ripper are thought to have had piqueristic tendencies."

Jack the Ripper. Shit. His lungs were too small. Morrison sucked in a ragged breath, trying not to imagine what it had been like for Acosta as the air left him, trying not to think that his baby girl was wheezing her last, face down in the dirt somewhere.

McCallum's eyes swung to Morrison's. "You okay, son?"

"He's fine. Bad sushi." Petrosky's leg bounced a steady rhythm, but his knuckles were white around his knee—the only indication that something was amiss, different, horrible.

McCallum cleared his throat and glanced at the file. Nodded as if this wasn't the worst fucking thing he'd ever seen, as if Shannon and Evie were just hanging out at home. "Your murder suspect went after Bell right away. The scuffle with the other suspect at the Acosta scene might have dampened the excitement of the killing itself, leading your murderer to attack soon afterward to release that frustrated energy."

"Our pedophile is sick too—has some creepy clown tattoos. Sadistic stuff even if he wasn't the one who killed Acosta."

McCallum nodded knowingly.

Petrosky scribbled a note on the pad. "We might have a woman present as well or someone with a higher voice. Could be using something to alter their voices, though."

A woman. A woman who hated Roger. But there had been no trace of a woman anywhere at either crime scene… Where did she fit into all this? Morrison's stomach lurched, but McCallum was already answering: "It's also possible that either of your suspects is effeminate. If this is the case, he's likely triggered by any challenges to his masculinity—maybe afraid of women if he believes they'll reject him—and that may beget rage. If it's your piquerist, he might be expressing his masculinity through the stabbing. Enough sexual rejection for being effeminate, and he might have begun to enjoy punishing those who reject him; he might even enjoy it more than penetrating them with his penis."

McCallum leaned toward them. "He's clearly still angry. He wants to punish someone for perceived slights and rejections."

Morrison could hear the words but was having trouble sorting them—as if each sentence crumbled apart as it hit his ear, rearranging itself like the nonsensical ramblings of a schizophrenic. *Focus.* Who had Shannon? The killer who had gone after Bell, stolen Bell's phone? As McCallum said, their suspects had widely different patterns—and this was definitely more in line with that of the killer. But what if both killer and pedophile were a part of this? Maybe they'd rape Shannon too. They'd rape her and rape Evie. Maybe they'd even taken Shannon for the killer and Evie for the pedophile, and his whole fucking world was already gone.

Petrosky wrote something on the notepad, but his scrawl was unreadable, or maybe it was just Morrison's eyes—everything seemed blurry and unfocused, even Petrosky's hand.

"Individuals with this fetish tend to have a type, just like other rapists. Do you have other female victims or just Bell?"

"Nothing yet."

"What's her type, physically? Small? Vulnerable?"

Morrison nodded, picturing Natalie Bell: her hand had been tiny in his own, and the tension in her eyes could be perceived as vulnerability. She'd worn clothes that could probably have fit a fifteen-year-old. Was she chosen because she looked like a kid? If so, Shannon wouldn't do it for this guy. She was thin, but no one would mistake the gleam in her eyes for that of a child.

"You mentioned our suspect having to kill again to release energy." Petrosky shifted in the chair. "This guy—our stabby bastard, the killer—must have watched his buddy rape the kid. Why would he watch if he's only in it for the stabbing?"

"He might have gotten excited and surprised them both by killing the child. I'm more concerned that he was watching because they're feeding off one another. Your pedophile got off on the voyeuristic elements of being watched, and your killer enjoyed the pain of the child so much he couldn't restrain himself. Or your killer might be…learning, especially if he has a strong history of rejection and emotional shutdown."

Rejection. Had the killer been slighted by Roger specifically?

Maybe he'd been pushed aside by a woman who preferred the affections of Shannon's ex over some maniac.

"Your killer might be thinking, watching, considering why people are attracted to his friend. Trying to figure out how to attract meaningful others and avoid rejection, or how to lure them in, specifically to cause pain." He shrugged. "It's just a theory, mind you, but an interesting one."

Interesting, his ass. Was McCallum some kind of psycho? How could he not see that the world was collapsing around them? *Because we didn't tell him.*

Morrison was wasting time. But he had to listen. Work the case. Ask something. Shannon wasn't a target for pedophiles or an opportunistic abduction. She'd had been taken because… Why the fuck did they take her? All the caller had demanded was Roger's suffering—retribution.

But Roger wouldn't get that close to another guy—Shannon had said Roger kept his friends at arm's length. It had to be someone Roger knew intimately. Forget McCallum—they weren't looking for an effeminate man unless he'd tucked his dick back and tricked Roger too. And transsexuals were almost never perpetrators in sex crime cases—victims, yes, perpetrators, no.

Morrison cleared his throat. "If there is a woman involved… what would we be looking for?"

Petrosky was staring at him. McCallum was staring at him. Morrison dropped his eyes to his knuckles.

"Opportunity is the biggest precursor to abuse. Women often have an easier time gaining access to kids, and it is common to see female pedophiles in positions of power over children. Teachers, babysitters, nannies, and the like. But your crimes don't fit what we typically see in those cases."

Teachers. Someone at Acosta's school? Morrison'd had a whole bunch of babysitters and nannies cycling through his own house in the last month, but that didn't mesh. If a sitter were seeking an opportunity, she'd have waited until she was hired and alone with Evie. She'd have waited until—

"Obviously, a profile is tricky because you have more than one suspect; you may have a mastermind and one along for the ride. But one of them is cunning. They staked out the play-ground beforehand so that they would know exactly where to take the child to avoid being seen from the school itself." McCallum cleared his throat. "Now, I didn't see much evidence that Acosta was singled out ahead of time, but the number one scored into Acosta's skin, carved along his rib cage—it feels inti-mate. If he'd been chosen earlier, you'd expect grooming for weeks or months: gifts, kindnesses."

Acosta's parents and friends had denied any such attention being paid to the child, and it hadn't been present in the Reynolds case either.

"The T-shirt could indicate a need for silence, a fear of being caught, or perhaps even not wanting to hurt the boy, maybe letting him sleep through the attack itself if your pedophile convinced himself that he loved the child, as many do. He might even see it as part of the romance."

"Romance?" The word was out of Morrison's mouth before he could stop it, and more words kept tumbling, louder and faster. "It's fucking rape, not dinner and a goddamn movie."

McCallum's eyes widened, and he stilled, though his training was probably preventing him from expressing much surprise at the outburst. More than that—he was fucking *calm.* They all were.

They were liars.

"Some see it as seduction," McCallum began, his voice slow and even as if talking to a rabid dog he feared might bite. "You know that. Some believe they're in love. Some convince them-selves of this because they don't want to accept the guilt that they did something horribly, atrociously wrong."

"What the hell kind of delusional—"

Petrosky stiffened too. "Easy, Morrison. We're dealing with tigers."

Tigers. Morrison's shirt had adhered to his back with sweat. The woman on the phone had told him...*he'd remember her.* That he'd know where to find her. Was she going to tell him where his family was if he did as she asked and locked Roger up—or killed him? He'd trade Roger's life for the safety of his family in a heartbeat.

McCallum was watching him, fingers laced on the desk, eyebrow cocked. Waiting. *Or...examining.* Morrison wiped away the sweat beading on his forehead. He had to go. Had to leave. Every muscle screamed with the need to act, to save the people he loved.

But there was nowhere to go. Not yet. The killer had texted him about going to this meeting.

How could he just sit here?

Did he have any other choice?

"Delusional might not be far off," McCallum said, and Morrison scoured his brain trying to recall what question the doctor was responding to. "Some even manage to convince themselves that everyone has these same fantasies, though at first, most are genuinely upset that they are sexually attracted to children. Of course, with the advent of online communities and chatrooms, camaraderie spreads, and eventually, it becomes normalized, acceptable, even just within the group. And that in and of itself can trigger escalation."

Escalation. Murder was sometimes intentional, sometimes accidental; he knew that much. But Shannon and Evie's kidnapping was purposeful—premeditated. Stealing a cop's kid and his prosecutor wife meant you knew what you were doing—had to if you thought you were going to get away with it. Right? And killing Acosta...was that purposeful too, or was it a fetish that got out of control? A tornado waged war inside his brain, tearing snippets of thought from their foundations and mixing them up until all he could make out were disjointed words as they were carried away on the wind.

Escalation. They were killing his wife and his baby *right now.*

Romance. Did they romance Acosta?

No one romanced Reynolds.

Rape.

Kidnapping.

Stabbing.

Murder.

But with Acosta and Bell, it wasn't just escalation or an attack gone wrong in the moment. They'd brought an *object* with them, an object that was used to stab the victims. That required forethought—planning. At least one of the perps had always intended to kill.

McCallum was still speaking, but his voice was far away as if Morrison were listening through a tunnel. "It's safe to say these men have done it before, probably more than just the few times you've found out about. It's unlikely that they'd go right to murder after five years of silence."

Silence. Did they want Roger silenced? They did want Roger locked up, but why? To get to the point where you would kidnap a woman and her child, you had to be desperate.

There was no air. He tried to feel the chair on his back, his feet on the floor, the hot wheezing of the heat vent. Why did McCallum have the heat on?

McCallum must have been talking, probably still about the cases, but now they were all standing, and the walk to the front door took five times as long as usual—his world hyper-focused, every air molecule biting his skin. At the outer exit, he hung back and let Petrosky head through, then leaned toward McCallum's ear, a new, separate concern bubbling to the top of his consciousness.

Shannon was the only one Evie could count on at this moment. She might be incapacitated, but if missing her medications made her more helpless, more hopeless…

"Are there side effects to the medication Shannon's on if she suddenly stopped taking it?"

The worry lines around McCallum's mouth deepened. "There would be some side effects. Though I'd be more concerned about the depression returning. Postpartum depression needs longer-term assistance, and I think in her case—"

"What would happen?"

"She might have some irritability. Brain zaps, like little electric currents in her head. Nausea, too. And of course, anxiety and what we call rebound depression, which can be significantly worse than the original episode." He narrowed his eyes at Morrison. "I strongly advise that she come in before stopping the meds, even if she feels okay."

From outside the door, Petrosky peeked in, appraised Morrison, and left again.

"Morrison?"

"I was just worried that she left her medications on the dresser when she headed off to her brother-in-law's. How hard is it to call in a prescription somewhere out of state?"

McCallum's Santa Claus face softened, and a hint of a smile touched his face. "That's why you're upset, son?"

Morrison nodded, and McCallum patted his shoulder. "I know how much she's struggled, but she'll be fine. Just get me a pharmacy number, and I'll call a script over. She should be able to pick them up within a few hours, and missing one dose won't trigger any unwanted symptoms. I'd advise her to find a pharmacy soon, though. Don't want her to miss more than a couple doses."

It was going on two days. She'd already missed four.

23

YOU CAN'T FUCKING GO. Petrosky's scrawl on the notepad was barely legible. Shaky. Maybe because Petrosky was writing on the steering wheel. Maybe because one or both of them was shaking—not that Morrison could tell anything about Petrosky's state. His own insides were quaking so violently a roller coaster would have seemed stable.

They hadn't needed to discuss whether Morrison's cell was being tapped. Had their suspects hacked the cell, or added a listening device to the car itself? That was another question, but if the suspects were watching, they'd be pissed if Morrison went out to see Shannon's car instead of speaking to Roger. Hostage takers didn't respond well to being ignored.

Morrison's jaw was clenched so hard his teeth hurt.

Get the fuck up to Roger's office, Petrosky wrote.

You might miss something, Morrison scrawled, not because Petrosky was inept by any stretch but because she was his wife, goddammit, his baby, and he knew what they had with them, what they might have dropped. If one of their toys, a bottle, *a bobby pin,* were left in the lot, he'd find it. He knew their smell so vividly he could almost taste it.

Petrosky was still writing: *I'll take pictures. Tell you everything. We don't know what's going on here. Don't have time to wait on Roger.*

Divide and conquer. It was logical. But it felt wrong.

Can't risk her, Petrosky wrote.

If they'd threatened Petrosky, the old man would have walked into the lot with a bunch of officers, guns blazing, "fuck it, kill me" stamped on his face. But…

Can't risk her.

Petrosky had walked Shannon down the aisle. He'd been there with her after the birth when Morrison went to the nursery with Evie. Though Petrosky could be a crotchety bastard—with everyone—he truly loved Shannon. And he wouldn't take any chances—he'd already lost a daughter once. If there were evidence to find, Petrosky would find it.

Roger was the one the caller had been after. There had to be a reason the killer hated the prosecutor, just like there had to be a reason Morrison had been chosen to go after Roger in the first place.

He pushed aside the desire to run, to drive, to find her car and touch the last place she had been, to feel her energy as if it would convince him she was still alive and calm the thundering in his chest. He grabbed the case file and threw the car door open.

Petrosky squeezed his shoulder once and let him go.

MORRISON RUSHED into the stairwell leading to the prosecutor's office, trying to focus, trying to avoid thinking about anything but the task before him. He'd taken this trip numerous times to see Shannon—to bring her lunch. Coffee. Just to see her face. And, later, flowers or personalized stationery or little baby shoes that made her smile through her tears as her belly grew and her depression worsened.

Now she was gone.

So was the secretary, her desk empty as the hole in his gut. The butterfly photographs along the tawny walls felt less like they were fluttering and more like they were trying to escape their glass prison. If panic had a voice, it would be his breath against the walls, his shoes against the carpet, and his heart, muted but frantic and heavy and pressured like an elephant stampeding toward a hunter—a battle from which one or the other would not emerge.

What was he going to do? Ask Roger to turn himself in? Morrison had had no proof of wrongdoing, and no guarantees that his actions here would get Shannon back. But he had no choice, either, just the stinging, frenzied horror, the prospect of a life lived without… He couldn't even think it. Couldn't think at all. Every time he blinked, he saw red behind his eyelids.

This is why we don't let the hostage's family make decisions.

Behind Roger's door, Shannon's asshole ex laughed, low and long and…eerily gleeful. Morrison glanced down the hall at the door that had always been Shannon's. His chest pinched, and his breath came faster. He cleared his throat and knocked.

There was some scuttling in the room, and Roger opened the door, his cell phone to his ear. His eyes narrowed when he saw Morrison, and he touched his nose, as if by reflex, like he couldn't help but recall the time they'd come to blows. Morrison had never regretted the way Roger's nose had felt under his fist —the way it had crunched.

Until now.

"I'll call you back." Roger pocketed the phone and glared at Morrison. "What do you want? I swear if Shannon's not back by—"

"This isn't about her maternity leave." Morrison put his shoe against the doorframe before Roger could slam the door in his face. "We need to talk. It's about a case." *A case. My family.* "It's about you."

Roger appraised him, his mouth a smirk that made Morrison want to hit him again, but he wouldn't—couldn't. "You have two minutes. I'm busy."

Morrison closed the door behind them and sat across from Roger in a short wooden chair, not nearly as plush as the leather one Roger eased himself into. A power play—typical for Shannon's ex. But equal seating was a trivial concern compared to what he needed from Roger now.

"I—" The words stuck in his mouth. *Someone kidnapped Shannon and Evie.* It still felt unreal, a dream he'd awaken from. And Roger might not care, even if he did still love Shannon as a conquest—the one who escaped. Escaped to Morrison, who had failed to keep her safe while Roger had kept her intact.

Intact. Emotionally scarred, perhaps, but alive. And Evie, his poor, sweet baby girl…

Roger cocked his head. "What the fuck's wrong with you?"

Keep it on him. Let Roger be the hero. "I need your help."

An arrogant smile plastered itself across Roger's face. "I don't see why I should do you any fucking favors."

Strike one. "It's not a favor, Roger. I got a call this morning. You're taking bribes, and someone knows it."

"Someone who?"

Shit. Morrison swallowed his hatred, his fear. *Be a cop.* "If you turn everything over, I can help you. We can—"

Roger crossed his arms, haughty and indignant. "I haven't done anything wrong."

"You have, Roger." *Please let that be true.* There had to be a way out of this—had to be.

"There's no evidence of that." No change in his face.

"Roger, think. Who knew about it?"

Recognition flashed in Roger's eyes and disappeared into the mask again. "No one." Another flash of white teeth, almost a snarl.

Morrison's heart leapt. "Someone," he said. "Please."

"Get out."

"Roger, listen to me, if you tell me who knows, I can find them." He inhaled sharply. "They called this morning, they—"

"There's nothing to know." Roger touched the head of a glass figurine on the desk, Lady Justice holding scales half as large as herself. But Morrison knew just how easily those scales could be persuaded to tip to one side or the other—they all knew.

Justice was rarely the point.

"They have Shannon," Morrison said. "Someone took her."

"Sure they did."

He stared back, stunned. Of all the possible outcomes, Roger disbelieving the situation had not occurred to him. Roger was erring on the side that put Shannon and Evie in danger. "Roger—"

"And they'll let her go if I just destroy my career? My life? Seems rather convenient. If you wanted to get rid of me, I'd have thought you'd be more creative. At least make it less obvious that you want me locked up the way you think I did to you."

He didn't think it—Morrison *knew* his arrest had been intentional, and that Roger had been behind the whole thing. But Roger was right—he'd never gotten over it.

He never would.

Rage burned in his chest, mingling with white-hot desperation. What was he going to do?

Kill him.

Can't. If he was locked up and the killer decided to keep his family…

"They're not going to stop here, Roger. If someone… If you can just tell me who might want to hurt you, who might want to see you locked up, I'll have a place to start. Better if they have reason to believe that you did something…wrong."

"Every perp I've put away in the last fifteen years wants me gone."

Morrison glanced at the file in his hands. *Every perp.* He'd forgotten about the composite from the Reynolds case. "This guy look familiar?" He flipped open the folder and thrust it at Roger.

"He looks like a fucking goon. And no."

"He's got a partner, around five-nine, thin, blond hair, black at the tips."

Roger snorted, shaking his head like he felt sorry for Morrison now.

"What about someone personally connected to you, someone you've been in a relationship with? Anyone who might want to hurt you?"

"Your wife, maybe. You."

"Roger—"

"Exes always go away a little pissy, don't they? This isn't about me."

Yes it is. The only thing the caller had asked him for was Roger's fucking head.

"Whoever has Shannon already killed someone else. Natalie Bell, found raped and murd—"

"The Bell case, huh? So now Shannon's been gone all week?" He raised his eyebrows as if he'd caught Morrison in a lie.

"No, Shannon was still here when—" Morrison stopped. "How do you know about the Bell case?"

"Maybe you told your good friend Decantor that if he acted like the Bell case had something to do with me that you'd get me fired. Decantor and I have gone toe to toe three times in the last six months over stupid shit. He hasn't won once." Roger sneered again. Predatory.

Morrison rubbed his temples where the rage and fear mingled, whirring painfully through his brain. "Roger, whoever's doing this, whoever knows about what you've done, won't keep it secret. All that will happen is...Shannon will die. Evie will..." His voice cracked on the last word, and he didn't fucking care, not now.

Roger paused, keeping his eyes on the figurine. "And why should I care what happens to my ex-wife? You're the one who has her now. You're the one who's supposed to be taking care of her, not me. Hell, you probably took care of her while we were married."

While they were— "Goddammit, this isn't about you and me, Roger!"

"Ah, but it is. You can't ask a man a favor after you've stolen his wife." He chuckled. "Besides, if you're involved in a kidnapping situation, you know as well as I do that giving them what they want isn't all that likely to help you. Do your job and find out who did it and stop coming in here fucking with me."

"Who knows about your safe deposit box?"

The crinkle at the corners of Roger's eyes died, but his mouth stayed even, his shoulders back. "No one."

"Roger, someone does."

"So some ex-girlfriend or a one-night stand went through my drawers and assumed something that wasn't true. Did they give you the name of the bank?"

They hadn't. He shook his head.

Roger's face relaxed. "Well, there you go. They don't know anything. It's just someone trying to get even."

"You think one of your exes would murder another woman to get back at you?"

"What can I say?" The smile was back.

"This isn't a fucking joke!"

"You're full of shit, Morrison. I know Shannon was going to Alex's this week because she told me when she called with her work-return date. And you know about the box because Shannon knows about it. Even kept her wedding ring there until she sold it." He flattened his palms against the desk and pushed himself to standing. "Convenient that they grabbed her just before she was supposed to be coming back to work. Maybe you're threatened, knowing she'll be here every day with me. That was how you got her in the first place, right? Pulled her away little by little, a CrossFit class here, a dinner after work there."

"This isn't about us, goddammit!"

Roger leaned across the desk, his crooked nose, all the more sinister from above, like a deadly, hooked beak. "Then why are you here, Morrison? Why aren't you out there trying to find who did this?"

Hatred burned in Morrison's chest, a thick, scalding rage. And *fear.* "They have Evie. Please, Roger. I need time to find them. I need your help to buy that time."

"Fuck you, Morrison."

"Roger—"

"Get the hell out of my office."

The Lady Justice figurine was the last thing Morrison saw before he backed from the office and took the stairs two at a time. He'd find another way to expose Roger. He'd find out what Roger had done, and why the kidnapper wanted Roger dead. He'd get his family back before the killer took them away from him—from this world. *No.* He'd get them back, or he'd die trying. And if Roger got them hurt, he was a fucking dead man.

Morrison's phone buzzed, and he ripped it from his back pocket in time to see Shannon's name. She was back. She was fine. Just texting to tell him that it had all been a bad practical joke, that her phone had been stolen and—

"You know what your asshole partner's doing right now?"

He didn't. But he had a feeling his family was going to be punished for it.

24

As the nighttime hours went on, a fuzzy warmth overtook him, and at some point before dawn, Morrison almost felt a cooling breath against the back of his neck as his nerve endings quieted to a painless hush. He wasn't there. None of them were. A dream, only a dream. He sat at his desk and stared at his fingers. They were someone else's, surely. But with the numbness, the logic seeped back in. And the logic was all he had.

Morrison had responded to the kidnapper's text, insisting that he wasn't sure what Petrosky was doing, but there had been no reply. When he'd triangulated the location, the system claimed the texts coming from Shannon's number were originating somewhere in Nevada—no way could they have traveled that distance in half a day. Whoever had his wife was scrambling the cell signals, maybe had even uploaded a virus into one of the cell companies' databases to assign the numbers to random towers. Maybe. Or maybe he was wrong. Decantor was already researching IT guys and spyware places since their phone scrambler and possible voice-over artist clearly had a penchant for electronics. It was possible—and easy—to get your phone to show one number on a caller ID regardless of where you actually called from. There could no guarantee that the phone was even Shannon's to begin with. That was the cold logic severed from the frenzied heat of terror, and it sustained him for a moment.

But the terror knew the phone was Shannon's. The panic knew they'd taken his baby, his wife. The frenzied energy in the air knew he was helpless to save them.

His muscles twitched involuntarily, first a leg, then an arm, electricity with nowhere to go. He stood and paced the bullpen, empty this time of night—back and forth, back and forth. He knew what would make the cool stay.

He knew what would make him remember.

You see me, but you don't. But you'll figure it out—you'll remember me. And once you do, you'll know exactly how to find me.

He should have known who she was. But where—how? McCallum's words echoed through his head: "Maybe it's for the best that you can't remember everything. Not all memories are useful." But this woman, the memory of her, that was the key to finding Shannon and Evie; he could feel it, and yet he could think of no specific person with a vendetta against him outside of an angry perp or the family member of someone he'd arrested. He didn't have a history of sordid love affairs, hadn't even dated for years before he met Shannon—too much trouble. Too many triggers. Anything questionable he'd left behind him in California. And the caller had a vendetta against Roger, so was it someone local: someone he'd arrested and Roger had put away? But that'd be hundreds of cases. He had no time.

You'll do what you're told, or I'll take it out on her. I'll save your baby girl for when you get here if she doesn't starve to death first.

Daddy's coming, Evie. He needed to figure out how to get to Roger. Fast.

Morrison ran a hand through his hair, ignoring the blond that stuck to his fingers, ignoring an old track mark that throbbed and stilled and pulsed again. *Heroin will make it worse.*

Heroin is bliss—euphoria. The purest love I've ever known.

But that wasn't true, not anymore. Shannon's love was real. And when he looked at Evie...was there anything more pure than the adoration in her eyes? And now they were starving her. *Starving.*

He sat, letting someone else's fingers type for him on the keyboard. Letting his mind wander to the case, to the logic, to the things that would help. Hacking, working around the number blocks, the scrambled signals…a plan. He needed a plan. He kept typing, code after code after code, but he didn't know what the kidnapper had used, where they were scrambling the signals from. He had no idea where to look.

Solve the case. Catch the killer. Find his wife.

You'll remember me. And once you do, you'll know exactly how to find me.

The case files on his desk whispered to him, and he ripped the top one from the stack and devoured the words as if he could tear out the throat of the kidnapper by attacking the page. Decantor's file on the Bell case—there wasn't much to it. Decantor had interviewed a dozen people at her apartment building, none of whom had seen anything suspicious. He tried to ignore the fire building inside him as he squinted at the notes in the margins: *Stabbed in lower abdomen/genitals with rounded object, spike-like, same as Acosta case, ME says copper.* Unusual for a weapon. Then came the reports from people who knew Bell personally. But this wasn't a date rape or an acquaintance killing. If someone had killed her purposefully to get at Roger— and he had to assume so based on the phone call—they had taken Shannon with the same goal in mind: get Roger put away by forcing Morrison's hand. But why did Bell have to die? Why her specifically? Just because she'd interviewed for the nanny position? What was he missing?

Petrosky would be back soon. He'd have something from Shannon's car—a fingerprint from their perp, maybe. But Morrison couldn't sit there and do nothing until Petrosky got back. Already it felt like his brain was sizzling, every rational thought boiling and escaping like steam before it could fully form. He flipped open the Acosta file and scanned the crime scene notes, the teacher interviews, the bike information. He paused on the sheets about the tattoo parlor, the demon horse staring at him, bloodthirsty and horrid. *The psychopathic circus.* He'd research the band.

Morrison pulled the keyboard closer and started with the tattoo. Websites full of Clown Alley Freaks song lyrics, fringe groups claiming to be fan clubs, and chat rooms catering to people steeped in all manner of depravity. On one message board, he found a convoluted discussion of what the "artists" really meant when they sang about disemboweling a circus elephant. "It's clearly a renouncement of the establishment, specifically of the republican right that makes things so difficult for the working class," proclaimed one man identified as Goober15. But eating raw, bloody elephant tripe seemed far less poetic and far more aggressive than any of these individuals could see. He compared IP addresses, hoping to find a clown-loving pedophile living near Acosta's school, but none of the commenters showed up on the sex offender database in any state, and even fewer had addresses within six hundred miles. Not that this meant much—sex offenders often ran to avoid having to register and tell the neighbors that they were sick fucks, and Morrison knew from the DNA that their guy wasn't in the system. But that didn't mean some other pedophile wouldn't know him, especially if they'd met over a mutual love of clowns and carnage.

Facebook pages and Instagram stalking gave him some photos of the commenters on the Clown Alley Freaks websites, and he pulled the ones with tattoos and printed the likenesses—most so damn normal looking. He pulled the fans with dyed hair too—blond at the root, black at the tip. He'd take them back to the tattoo parlor in case one of them had made a trip to visit their pedophile at Drake's shop, maybe to swoon over his clown ink. If they got lucky, one of these guys would be their killer.

Through the side window, a stormy dawn was creeping through the room. He abandoned the clowns and pulled up a chat room for pedophiles. Then another. Three. Looking for clown references, mentions of spiked boots, discussions about Acosta, or the #1 symbol that had been carved into Acosta's and Bell's skin. But was this even what he wanted? If one of their suspects wasn't a pedophile at all, they wouldn't have met in a pedophile chat room. Maybe…fringe sexual interests? Fetishes?

A hand on his shoulder made Morrison jump. "Anything?" Petrosky's eyes were heavy with lost sleep and…anguish.

"No, Boss." The world shifted, tilted, and his bodily sensations crashed back to him with the force of being hit by a truck. His stomach, painfully clenched, forced bile into his mouth. His bladder spasmed—he had to pee. His neck was as wet as the storm-drenched window. But his thoughts were suddenly stilled, frozen, as though every ounce of logic had been consumed by terror. He sucked in a shuddering breath and held onto the side of the desk. "What did the scene look like?"

"Like a gas station." Petrosky ran a hand over his face, and Morrison could see the dew at his hairline, a subtle darkening. "Got there before the rain. Collected every fucking thing."

"What about her car?" It came out more like a wheeze than a question, and he pulled the chill air into his lungs and held it there, imagining the waves against the shore, the shush of the ocean in his ears, the taste of salt instead of vomit.

"A bunch of prints on the car itself, but they'll have to sort out which are hers, which are yours and which are from friends whose prints are supposed to be there. I've got the lab putting a rush on it now."

Morrison nodded, mute. Petrosky's eyes were drawn, his jowly face sagging as if he'd aged ten years since he went out there last night.

"What else?" Morrison said slowly, prolonging the moment when he'd have to hear whatever was making Petrosky's mouth so tight. But he could feel his composure slipping away with every terrified beat of his heart, every moment one step closer to insanity.

Petrosky met his eyes. "Blood."

His vision tunneled, and tingling began in his fingertips—crept up his arm. *Calm. Cool. Pacific.* A wave of electricity passed through him, and he didn't respond to it, just let it go like the tide going out to sea. His vision opened again, but the tingling remained. "How much?"

"Not much. Some spatter on the headrest. Probably hit her with something to subdue her."

Fuck.

"Not enough to really hurt her."

"Doesn't take much with a head injury." And she'd already had a concussion last year from Griffen, and there was always a chance for a brain bleed or—

"Shannon's tough as nails, kid. And there was nothing in the back—no blood, no signs of struggle around the car seat."

No, because they weren't bleeding Evie. Their pedophile strangled his victims with a T-shirt. And they were…starving her. Were they really? Or had they just told him that to fuck with him? He inhaled low and long imagining the ocean, blue as Evie's eyes, and the air stabbed at his lungs, his belly as if he were imbibing shards of glass.

Petrosky peered at the screen. "Show me what you found. Then we'll swing by to see Jenny at the tattoo shop and get another composite sketch out. Got nothing on the first."

Morrison ran Petrosky through the websites and the utter lack of useful information he'd discovered while Petrosky had been staring at his wife's blood.

"It's something," Petrosky said finally.

"It's nothing."

"Simmer, California."

"Is that all you did, Petrosky? Just look at the car?"

Petrosky cocked his head.

"They texted again." As the words came out, he immediately wished he could take them back. Maybe the killers had heard him. But Petrosky didn't seem bothered, didn't seem upset, and the heat crept into Morrison's cheeks.

"Let's take a look, and we'll—"

"How can you be so *fucking calm?*" Morrison hissed.

Petrosky punched the desk, and across the room, another cop stood—when had he even gotten there?— but the guy turned away again because it was Petrosky, and of course, he was pissed: Petrosky was always pissed about something. But not like this. The tension in Petrosky's jowls was more than agitation. *Fear.* And if Petrosky was scared, Morrison sure as hell better be.

"We need to...work the Acosta case," Petrosky said, almost panting.

Morrison cleared his throat, fighting to keep his voice steady —to keep his heart steady.

"There was a print in the grass just behind her car," Petrosky whispered. "Just one, but enough."

Prints? But they hadn't found fingerprints at the other crime scenes, so why—

Realization dawned, slow and painful in his chest as if his heart were only now awakening to the idea that Shannon had truly been taken by a killer. "Prints from the boots." *Like Acosta.* But they had killed Acosta. They'd killed Bell. And they were saving Evie for when he got there. The words rolled around in his head and settled like marbles in a dish.

Petrosky nodded.

Work your case. They wanted him looking. The kidnapper wanted him to remember something. And if he did, he'd find his family—the caller had said that, right? But she'd given him no other clues. Unless...the kidnapper wanted him to fail, so they'd have an excuse to hurt Shannon. An excuse to take Evie and stab her and watch her bleed.

Morrison swallowed hard, pushing down the warm ooze, trying to creep up his throat. *This is about Roger. All they want is Roger.*

Petrosky glanced at the screen. "This is your call, California. Your family. We can call in the chief. The Feds."

And Shannon's blood would be on his hands. Evie's. He pictured Dylan Acosta's body, the punctures still wet and seeping, and Shannon, begging for her life, for Evie's life. He didn't know what to do. Nothing felt right. His gut instincts were betraying him—he couldn't even trust himself.

"They'll kill her," he whispered. "We need to buy time."

"Drake's wife should be home now, so I'll have them meet us at his tattoo shop this morning," Petrosky said, his voice louder than it needed to be, though perhaps that wasn't for Morrison's benefit—the room was filling now, all officers with families at home. Safe.

Morrison nodded, still numb, wishing he was at home with Shannon, with Evie. He'd never leave them alone again. But he *had* left them alone. He'd not been there when they needed him most, and there was no fixing that. His only consolation would be to see the kidnappers' fucking faces. Look into their eyes. Breathe their foulness, their insanity, right before he ripped them apart.

25

MAYBE THE TATTOO parlor was the same, but it could have been the first time he'd ever seen it. The white door that had seemed so clean yesterday was now blank and dead, the pale face of a corpse when the blood pooled on the underside of the body. The bright and cheery pictures of potential tattoos now seemed sullen and morose, offended at his gaze. Even the yin-yang, white and black surrounded in vibrant blues and greens, burst forth with such rage that Morrison half expected it to leap from the wall, teeth bared.

Drake paced behind the counter, his hands clasped behind his back. From the couch inside the door, a woman with green hair and arms sleeved in wildflower tattoos appraised them. When Petrosky flashed his badge, she stood and extended her hand.

"I'm Jenny."

"Detective Petrosky." She looked at Morrison, but he couldn't find his tongue—he was watching a freckle-faced little girl coming through the back curtain to stand next to Drake, rubbing her eyes. Bib overalls. Blond hair, maybe what Jenny's hair would look like without the dye.

"I've got some things for you to look at," Jenny said and moved with the light steps of a dancer to stand beside her husband and the girl. "Go finish your homework, baby," she said and patted the girl's shoulder, so kind. The girl scampered off.

Morrison watched her go, heart wrenching, and when he pictured Evie as she might look at that age, the wound in his heart expanded like a black hole, widening as if each and every breath he took enhanced its emptiness.

Jenny reached beneath the front counter and produced a folder, manila like jaundiced skin, containing a photograph-quality sketch: a man with scraggly brown hair and a thin mouth. Squirrelly. Despite the light hue of his beady eyes, the man's gaze was blank—dead, vile. Zachary Reynolds's attacker. Their pedophile. But Drake was right—it was far better quality than the composite.

Petrosky pulled the sheet closer to him, and Morrison laid his folder on the counter, showing her the photos of the Clown Alley Freaks fans. Drake and Jenny both leaned close to examine them, eyebrows furrowed. Petrosky did too, glancing back and forth from the mug shots to the picture Jenny had drawn. Heads shook. They flipped through the entire stack.

"Nothing?" Morrison asked.

"Sorry, I don't see anyone familiar," Jenny said. Drake nodded agreement, shrugging his shoulders like it was no big fucking deal that Morrison was no closer to finding his starving baby girl while Drake's own daughter was happy and safe in the back room.

Morrison tossed the sheets back into the folder, stepped back, and dumped the whole mess into the trash can with enough force that the wire basket shook, stuttering and rocking, before settling with a clang. He clenched his fist, trying not to kick the thing over.

"Sorry, man," Drake said, and Morrison could hear the tension in his voice. Petrosky stood like a bulldog, ready to block the path to the counter if Morrison should prove to be unstable.

He *was* unstable.

"Do you recall anything about his voice?" Petrosky asked the couple over his shoulder. "Anything strange? Higher than normal?"

Petrosky was asking whether their suspect sounded like a little bitch.

"Nope, just…normal." *Normal.* Their perp fit in, walking among them, raping children, kidnapping families, starving babies. And passersby never saw the evil in his stare.

"What about badges, name tags, anything he said about interests, or how he spent his time?"

She pursed her lips, then shook her head. "No, nothing about himself. Sometimes he told stories about his…daughter."

Daughter? This guy had a *daughter*? If he did, she was in trouble.

"What'd he say about her, ma'am?" Petrosky said quickly, his shoulders high and rigid.

"Oh, well, I think it was his stepdaughter, actually. And it was nothing strange—just that she was really smart, that he was planning on having her take up the flute. Asked if I ever took music lessons—you know, normal things parents say. I remember thinking it was nice that he was taking such an interest in her." She winced.

"He give a name? An age?"

She shook her head again. "He played everything close to the vest. I guess now I know why, but I wish…"

A daughter. Morrison took out his phone and held it over Jenny's sketch on the counter. They needed to get the photo out on the streets, on the news, find this fuck. But Petrosky's hand on his wrist stopped him just shy of snapping the picture. Petrosky shook his head and pointed to the phone.

Right. Someone might have his phone tapped, and they didn't want the kidnappers to know that they had this asshole's picture until absolutely necessary—or to know they'd connected the Zachary Reynolds case. Morrison would have just fucked them all, maybe killed the people he loved. But…they'd asked him to keep investigating, right? *Do your job.*

And that was why Petrosky hadn't called him from Toledo; he must have thought Morrison's phone was tapped too. But if Morrison shut it down, maybe tried to track the bug inside it… they probably had a safeguard. They'd know. He was good at cracking codes, but not perfect, and the stakes were too high.

"They want an excuse," Petrosky whispered. An excuse—to hurt Shannon and Evie.

"Do you have a fax machine?" Petrosky said to Drake, but he dug his fingers into Morrison's wrist until Morrison registered the pressure, took his hand back, and dropped the phone into his pocket.

"Of course." Jenny gestured to the picture. "Does this help?"

Petrosky nodded. "Yes, ma'am. Better than our sketch artist did."

She smiled. "Well, if you're ever in the market for some ink…"

Petrosky's left eye twitched. Ashes and ink—*in memoriam.* Morrison grabbed the counter and held on as the room wavered, and his breath hitched and stopped.

"If I'm ever in the market, I'll be back here," Petrosky said, and Morrison straightened at the sudden gruffness in Petrosky's voice. "Now…the fax?"

The machine was modern and had more features than the one at the precinct. They faxed the photos to Decantor and used the email feature on the fax machine itself to send it to the contacts they had made when they'd scoured the neighborhood—those who had owned a place in the strip mall back when their suspect was getting his ink. But follow-up calls from Drake's landline yielded a series of "Sorry" and "Nope, never seen him" and "Wish I could help." Only one man was unaccounted for, Mr. Xu, the guy who had owned the nail shop across the road. And he'd already admitted seeing the guy—he'd just never gotten close enough to be more helpful.

Petrosky drove back to the precinct while Morrison held onto the door handle like it was a life preserver in a stormy sea. They'd find their killer. They would. And he'd get Evie back. He'd get them both back.

He took rapid breaths through his nose and stared at the ash trees, at the few leafy branches clawing the clouds—half barren even in the height of spring. Ash Park. Where everything went to die.

Everything. *Everyone.*

Petrosky pulled up at the precinct and opened his door. "You coming, California?" Voice tight. Strained. Morrison nodded. Petrosky appraised him for a moment, then slammed the door and headed across the lot, his back receding, then going fuzzy as he left Morrison's line of focus.

Disappearing. Where did one find a person who didn't want to be found? If there'd been victims before Zachary Reynolds... maybe he'd done it to his own daughter. But his DNA wasn't in the system; if he'd abused his daughter, it hadn't been reported. Had they missed something at the school? Bell's apartment building? Zachary Reynolds's neighborhood? But they'd already taken the composite of Reynolds's attacker to those places— nothing. Jenny's drawing was better but not so much better that it'd get them a different answer from the same people, and they'd proven as much asking the neighbors around the tattoo shop. It'd be a waste of time—and Shannon and Evie didn't have time to spare. So what else did he know? Decantor had already ruled out connections between Bell and the other victims, outside of the person who'd killed them. No common acquaintances, no similar hangouts, no foreseeable opportunities for them to have met the same person—not that he'd expect a twenty-nine-year-old woman to chill at the park with a bunch of ten-year-olds. In fact, Decantor hadn't found any activities for Bell at all in the days before her death outside of her interview for the nanny position. Morrison's house had been her last known outing.

He'd been the last one to see her alive.

Morrison sat straighter in the seat. Had their killer seen Bell at his house and followed her home? Thus far, he'd assumed that someone was after Roger alone, that he and Shannon had become pawns in a game. But someone had to have known when Shannon left Ash Park. Someone had been watching his house. Watching Shannon. Was Bell dead because she'd been there? Were the other nanny candidates in danger? Then, suddenly, it clicked—the kid on the bike, the one he'd seen watching Bell the day she interviewed for the nanny position. Morrison had never seen the kid before in the neighborhood, and the teen could have matched the description of their thin, taller killer—the one in the boots. The guy had been wearing a hat that day, and he'd been too far away for Morrison to see clearly, but the bike... Someone had reported a bike at Dylan Acosta's school the day he died. They'd presumed an adult killer, but teenagers were very similar in stature. They could be looking for a kid—an impulsive, murderous, psychopathic kid. And if he'd been watching Shannon, watching Bell...he might have been watching the other candidates too. Maybe one of them had seen him.

Morrison got out and closed the gap between Petrosky's car and his own. Maybe Alyson Kennedy could help him nail this fucker to the wall.

If she was still alive.

26

ALYSON KENNEDY'S eyes widened when he introduced himself. "Mr. Morrison?" She clapped a hand over her mouth. "I wasn't supposed to start this week, was I? Oh my god, I thought—"

"No, no, you're fine. Next week."

"Well…um…" She peered behind him at the street where his car was parked half on half off the lawn at the curb.

"I'm not here about the job. There was an"—*our first choice nanny was brutally murdered, and I thought he'd killed you too*—"an incident. Near our home the day you interviewed. I thought I'd come by and ask you a few questions. Routine."

"Oh." Her eyes remained tight, but she stepped aside so he could enter the apartment. The hallway smelled like coconut. She didn't invite him inside farther. Did she think he was there for…what had the caller said? A little side action? *No…strange. A little strange on the side.*

He backed up a step and kept his voice brusque. "When you arrived for your interview, did you notice any other vehicles in the area? A bike?"

Her brows knit together. "Uh…no, I don't think so. Just your car in the driveway."

That had been Shannon's car in the driveway—he hadn't even been home yet, something Kennedy'd surely noticed. Either Kennedy was unobservant or lying. Probably the first.

But…what had McCallum said? That female pedophiles are…*babysitters. Nannies.* Maybe she'd purposefully come before Morrison arrived—then he wouldn't have recognized her voice when she called pretending to be Bell. But there was something slightly nasal in her register that didn't fit. Not her, of course, it wasn't her. Had he really expected her voice to match? That he'd walk in here and find Shannon tied up in the living room? What was wrong with him?

He cleared his throat. "How about this guy?" He held out Jenny's rendition of the tattooed man and Reynolds's composite sketch.

Kennedy shook her head, nostrils flaring as if the photos themselves were distasteful. "Nope. He looks kinda…dirty, so I feel like I might have noticed that. You live in a nice neighborhood."

A nice neighborhood. Where bad things didn't happen—unless the bad weaseled its way in.

Morrison watched her face, the set of her shoulders: uncomfortable, but she seemed confident that she didn't know the suspect. He put the pictures back into the file and tucked it under his arm. He didn't like the way she was clenching her jaw. Nervous? Maybe she was ready to toss him out along with his troubling questions before the wrong word shattered her illusion of safety.

"What about anyone else outside?" he asked. "Someone walking a dog or looking out from a window?"

"A window?"

"A house window. A car. Anyone." The kidnapper could have planned everything from a distance, but maybe the man who'd taken Shannon looked like he belonged there. "A kid in a ball cap?"

She shook her head. "No. I was kinda nervous about the interview, so I wasn't really looking." She shrugged one slender shoulder, and Morrison narrowed his eyes. Pretty, lithe—Kennedy was Roger's type. And they might have met when she worked at the hospital morgue. Unlikely, but—she might know Roger enough to hate him.

"Where were you on Monday night?"

"Oh, uh…" Her face reddened and she crossed her arms. "I went dancing with friends. Stayed at my fiancé's after with another girlfriend who didn't want to drive home." A little defensive maybe, yet Kennedy didn't seem worried. Her alibi was easily verifiable. But had Kennedy mentioned that she was getting married?

"I'll need those names. From Monday night."

"No problem." She gave him the information while her index finger tapped a steady rhythm on her elbow. No hesitation. She wasn't a suspect. He was being an idiot. But the paralyzing waves of fear were washing his brain clean of all thought, rendering him ineffectual, useless against a kidnapper. Against a killer.

"Do you know Roger McFadden?" he blurted.

"I know who he is. But we've never met." It rang true. And he'd come here to get information and protect Kennedy, not accuse her… Were they watching her the way they'd watched Bell, the way they'd watched Shannon? Had he just signed Kennedy's death certificate by showing up here? *Did I kill my wife?*

Her face had hardened. Was there really anything else to ask? "Thank you for your time, Ms. Kennedy."

"Oh, sure. And um…I'll see you next week?" Her arms stayed crossed. He knew by her posture that she wasn't coming next week or the week after.

Not that it mattered. He might not have a child for her to watch.

THE HOUR after he left Kennedy's passed by in a numb haze, the street signs approaching impossibly slow, road and cars in front of him wavering like a mirage, only blackness in his peripheral vision. Patricia Weeks wasn't home. Morrison didn't recognize what he was doing until he was pulling into his own driveway, the file with the drawings of their suspects held against his chest.

He strode to Mr. Hensen's porch on autopilot as if the nerves that tied the actions to his brain had been severed. He glanced back at his car, registering that he'd left the door open, but not able to manufacture a reaction. Even the cool breeze elicited no goose bumps. Morrison grabbed Hensen's door knocker and let it drop. The first time he'd met Hensen, the man had said, "Good work, son, you do good work," though he probably had no idea what Morrison's job entailed.

He'd find out today. At the very least, he'd have something else to gossip about.

The spider veins on Hensen's nose glared at him, purple and red streaks that screamed the truth: bodies eventually give out, and no one gets through it alive. When Hensen smiled, Morrison's agitation spiked as sharp as the fine points on the man's canines. "How are you today, son?"

"Fine, Mr. Hensen." If the dead could speak, they'd sound like Morrison: voices a mere shadow of what they once were, every utterance strange and flat and hollow. "Just wondering if you'd seen anything strange around lately. A car that didn't belong. Maybe a teenage boy on a bicycle Monday morning?"

Hensen cocked his head, and the lines spiderwebbing their way across his nose went from horizontal to vertical. "No, but my days aren't spent by the window. I been seeing that nice woman you set me up with from a block over. Ms.—"

"Mayfield."

"That's the one." He furrowed his brows. "There some kind of trouble?"

"No, no trouble. Just trying to find someone."

"Someone who was at your house?"

"No, just…" *This is a mistake.* "How about him?" He opened the folder and showed Hensen the photos.

Hensen shook his head. "No, can't say I've seen him. I don't like his look, though."

Me neither. "Okay, well, thanks for your time."

"Son?"

Morrison turned back on the top stair.

"Thank your wife for the soup the other day. She sure makes a mean chicken noodle."

He swallowed hard. "I will."

Eight more houses on that side yielded nothing better. He was considering heading for the precinct when he saw Kathryn Welks on the stoop across the street, blowing bubbles for her two-year-old son, Shane. Shane's dark hair blew in the breeze as he giggled and leaped, the bubbles floating above his head and out of reach. Morrison dragged his eyes to his own vacant lawn, straining his ears as if he might catch Evie's laugh on the breeze.

Kathryn was waving when he turned back to them, using her hand as a visor to block out the afternoon sun. "Hey! How's Shannon's trip going?"

He'd nearly forgotten Shannon was supposed to be gone. "Oh…good." Something sharp stabbed at Morrison's gut, and he inhaled, inflating lungs that couldn't seem to recall how to breathe. "Listen, question for you."

She smiled. "Shoot."

"You seen anyone strange around our place lately?"

Her almond eyes widened, and she glanced up and down the street. "Strange? Like how?"

"Anyone you didn't recognize? Maybe a teenager on a bike?"

"I see people all the time while I'm out front with Shane. No one that looked suspicious or anything." She shrugged. "Why, has there been another one of those car break-in things going on like last summer?"

"Nothing like that." He opened the folder for her and held the pictures in front of his chest.

She bent closer, squinted, and when she straightened, her easy smile had fallen. "Haven't seen him, but I know the cases you work. You'd tell me if I should be worried, right?"

"I'd tell you."

"Are you sure? Another neighbor was over here last week asking if it was a safe place to live. I feel like I'm missing something."

"Neighbor?"

"I don't think she's bought the house yet. Just looking at the area. She asked…" Her mouth stopped moving as if she'd realized something critical. "She asked if there were any cops in the neighborhood, like patrols. And I…I said one lived right across the street, so we didn't need patrols." She looked back at the photos but shook her head.

"What, Kathryn? What else did she say?"

"She asked what the going rate was per square foot. If it was a good neighborhood for children. If there were bus stops."

That sounded like a homebuyer—not abnormal. But it wasn't like their suspects would walk through the streets, sneering, waving around someone's severed dick.

"She did mention liking your place," Kathryn said slowly. "Asked whether I thought you'd sell it."

That was strange. They'd had no sign in the yard, despite their conversations about moving. Yet someone had been asking about their house. Watching.

"I said I didn't think you were putting it on the market, but that I knew a realtor if they needed one." Her eyes were saucers. "They didn't want the name. Said they had one."

They. "What'd they look like?"

"She was our age, pale, thin. Reddish hair, kind of big eyes. Really pretty. Her husband was in the car, too, but I couldn't see him as well."

"You're sure this isn't him?"

"Positive. He was bald, not like that guy. But he had on sunglasses, kept his eyes out the other window, so I didn't really get a look at him."

So he wasn't the pedophile who had raped Acosta and Reynolds. But they still had the booted man who had killed Acosta and Bell, and the woman who had called Morrison from Bell's cell phone. Three killers. He'd considered the possibility before, but confirmation that there were three people wandering around stomping kids to death and stealing others for sport—it was unheard of. Ridiculous. What was this, some kind of fucking cult?

His heart quickened. "Tell me more about him. Tall? Short?"

"Just average. He was thin, though." She frowned. "I do remember being worried because of his neck. Looked like he had chicken pox or something, and I didn't want Shane exposed, but it was probably just acne."

Thin. Acne. That did sound like a teenager. Maybe the same one he'd seen on a bike the morning of the nanny interviews.

"What day was that, Kathryn?"

"Last Thursday, maybe?"

Thursday. Before he'd even gone back to work, they'd been watching.

"I mentioned it to Shannon, but she didn't seem to think much of it. Just laughed about selling, what with the market like it is right now."

Of course she hadn't thought much about it. Asking about housing prices wasn't threatening—but it did give you an awful lot of information if you asked the right questions. Acting normal made you invisible. Unless…they really were just a couple looking for a house.

"Any way you might come to the station, give me a sketch?"

Her mouth dropped. "What's all this—"

"Missing persons case. Nothing to do with us, just thought she might have been seen in the area. I'll explain later. Promise."

She looked at her son, who was spinning in circles in the yard, and back to Morrison. "Okay, I'll head out in ten."

He glanced up and down the empty road. "I'll follow you."

Kathryn bit her lip, grabbed Shane off the lawn, and disappeared into the house, leaving Morrison staring down the street, waiting for a man with a bald head and covered eyes to appear with Shannon's corpse.

27

AT THE PRECINCT, Morrison led Kathryn into the conference room and used the main line to call Crystal Irving, local artist and their resident sketcher. He took Kathryn a drink of water, barely registering the worry lines on her forehead, her frown, and the way Shane was already rubbing his eyes. *Does Evie need a nap too?* But the thought belonged to another man entirely, a stranger concerned with sleep schedules and diaper changes instead of starvation and death. He closed the door on his way out with a shaking hand.

Petrosky ambushed Morrison just outside the room, his breath fast, eyes blazing. "Where the fuck have you been all afternoon? I thought you went rogue or some shit. Not that I'd have blamed you, but..." He swiped a hand across his beet-red face.

Rogue. If only Morrison knew where to find these bastards, maybe he would have hunted them down himself. Morrison filled Petrosky in on interviewing Alyson Kennedy and the neighbors, realizing just how little he had to go on besides Kathryn's memory. If only he'd been there to see the suspects in that car. "Most of the neighbors weren't home," he finished.

"I'll go back later." Petrosky's face had returned to its normal color. His fists unclenched. "Better if it's someone else, so they don't assume it has to do with you."

It's too late for that. He'd already spooked Kathryn. Had he put his family in danger?

"Heard back from forensics about the copper," Petrosky was saying. "Too common to trace the weapon to a source."

Were they using that weapon on his wife? His daughter?

"Still no hits on our photos either," Petrosky continued, and Morrison imagined the suspects' car in his neighborhood, a killer taking photos of his house, of his family. Were they still watching his place? No…they had what they wanted. They had his whole world.

Petrosky coughed once, pointedly, and Morrison focused on his partner's troubled gaze. "The entire city's out looking, Cali. Including Decantor and your buddy Valentine."

Decantor. Valentine. *Fuck.* "Decantor say anything about Shannon? I mean, he already knows that her car's been found and—"

"I told him we had it under control, nothing to worry about. That Alex went to get her, and it was all a big misunderstanding. Unless he actually calls Toledo and talks to the techs over there, Decantor won't know any different until they show up here to investigate. And I made sure the Toledo PD has my name as their go-to."

"And Valentine?" Valentine and Lillian would be all over Morrison and Petrosky if they thought something was wrong.

"Told Valentine the same. He might call out of concern, but he'd talk to you about it before he acts. And I gave him The Face."

Morrison nodded. The Face was usually reserved for perps, but it was just as effective for getting other cops to walk away. He'd call Valentine later if the man didn't come to him first.

"Detective?" Crystal. Curly black hair, eyes like midnight, sketchpad in hand.

"Thanks for coming," Morrison said.

She smiled—"Anytime"—and brushed past him into the room with Kathryn and closed the door.

Petrosky gestured in the direction of the bullpen. "You know the FR software best. Get that going on all three sketches, see what you come up with."

FR. The facial recognition software, the one thing the chief had made sure they had a budget for. He'd start with Zachary Reynolds's rapist—but he really needed to ID the people Kathryn had seen in front of his house. *Please let us get a hit.* "Might just be people trying to find a house to buy," Morrison said.

"You don't believe that."

"No, I don't."

"Call if you get something." Petrosky headed for the stairs.

Morrison hovered outside the room, willing Crystal to hurry, rubbing a throbbing nodule in the crook of his arm. *Find the killer. Find the woman. Find my family.*

WITH THEIR FACIAL RECOGNITION SOFTWARE, each photo came back with a list of the top fifty potential matches. Not the best program, but it was what the powers that be said they could afford. Usually, half of the matches were dubious at best or just felt wrong. The closest to Jenny's picture was a man who'd been killed in a car wreck two years back, so he hadn't attacked Acosta—and even with that one, the nose was a touch too pointy. Either the guy they were looking for hadn't ever been in trouble, or he'd been in trouble somewhere that the database wasn't active.

Morrison tossed aside the sketch and headed for the conference room in time to see Crystal emerge, shoving a pencil into her handbag.

"Thanks again for coming." His words sounded insincere even to him, though he thought he meant them.

"Sure thing." She handed him two pages and took off down the hallway as Morrison peeked into the room to see Kathryn, still at the conference table, Shane asleep on her shoulder. Comfortable. Safe.

He backed away from the door before the clenching in his gut became an ache and glanced at the first picture—the man. Nose too thin for his round face, skinny shoulders, fragile-looking jaw. Sunglasses that covered half his cheeks. And the rash on his neck: not chicken pox…acne. Were they really looking for a kid, or did he only look like one from afar? If he was the kid Morrison had seen on the bike Monday morning, then the guy would have had to kill Acosta and hightail it all the way over to Morrison's place immediately. Was he watching to see if Morrison caught the homicide call? Or just watching? Did that mean Natalie Bell was in the wrong place at the wrong time —an impulse decision when the killer saw her get out of her car?

He flipped the page and frowned at the black-and-white image of the woman Kathryn had seen: wide, light eyes, freckles over the bridge of her nose, and a tiny crescent scar on her chin, though that might have been a shadow or a dimple.

Something about the photo niggled at the back of his brain. He tried to picture this woman with the reddish hair Kathryn mentioned. He imagined her with glasses, with darker eyes. Imagined her without the scar. None of these mental pictures seemed quite right, but still, an insistent awareness was creeping up the back of his neck like ghostly fingers trying to break through to the living's plane of existence.

I know her.

Kathryn exited the conference room with Shane on her hip, his head lolling on her shoulder, and he felt a pang of jealousy. Her eyes were tight, mouth drawn. "Listen, I thought of one other thing. The woman…she said something about our neighborhood being close to her job, said that was the reason she wanted to move there. If she has a job around there, it'll be easier to find her, right?"

If she worked nearby, there was a good chance someone knew her. Maybe that was why she looked so damn familiar. But if she was scoping out his house with intent to harm, she wouldn't have told Kathryn the truth. *Hey, just stopping in to stalk a woman so that I can kidnap her and her child someday. And, by the way, let me tell you about my job.*

"Yeah, that helps. Thanks so much for coming down."

She nodded, said nothing. Morrison left her standing in front of the door to the interrogation room, cradling Shane to her chest.

Back at his desk, he loaded Crystal's rendition of man

number two into the system. Their pedophile's slightly taller buddy yielded another fifty photos. He pulled the top ten, then ruled out half due to stature because of the footprint indentations left at the crime scene—their killer was only five-nine at best, and thin. Probably why he went after Bell and not Patricia Weeks: that stocky old broad would have kicked his ass.

Morrison ruled out another set of suspects due to incarceration and one due to death. But the remaining two—either could have been their guy. He pulled up birth certificates, driving records, last known addresses. One, Walter Gomez, had been given a ticket three days ago, the day of Natalie Bell's murder, in Arizona.

And then there was one.

Richard Carleson stared back at him with beady eyes and a grin too easy for someone having their mug shot taken. His face wasn't a perfect match—he looked too old, for one thing—but he'd been arrested twice for fraud, once for identity theft, and once for assault and battery during a bar fight. Last known address was in Florida, nearly ten years ago, so he could easily have moved here and committed the attacks while flying under the radar. Didn't need much else if you had cash—just don't get arrested for anything. With his identity theft history, it wasn't unreasonable to think he was living here under an assumed name.

Which meant he'd be hard to find unless someone recognized his photo.

Morrison watched Carleson's information print achingly slowly and stared again at the woman's image. Even if she'd told Kathryn the truth, she could work pretty much anywhere. He'd get her loaded into the computer, check for any hits, and then start showing her picture to local businesses, maybe near his house again. But how long would that take? *I'm grasping at straws.*

He needed help. He needed more cops to canvass. But even Decantor and Valentine would want to call in the Feds. He couldn't get assistance without admitting what was going on and putting his family in more danger—by the time they had anything to go on, Shannon and Evie could be dead. He ripped the sheets from the printer, headed back to his desk, and loaded the woman's photo into the facial recognition database.

Nothing fit well; the pictures weren't quite right. If she'd been arrested, she'd have been in the database, so she couldn't be a perp Roger had put away. How did she know him? He squinted at the photo. Different hair? Skin tone? He looked back at the screen. She seemed familiar in a way that neither of the men had. Then he changed the brightness on the screen, and something snagged inside him, jolted his memory. He bolted upright in his seat.

No. *No way.*

Karen? The nose was different—too wide here—and he didn't recall her having freckles, but maybe she wore makeup. Did she have a scar on her chin? He'd seen her numerous times over the last year, outside the courthouse, at the restaurants near the precinct, and once in a dark bar, back when she was still dating Griffen.

He traced the line of her jaw on the screen. Probably her. But…*why?*

Griffen had been sick, obsessed with Shannon to the point of hurting her and those around her, but he'd had a brain tumor. Delusions. He'd heard voices, and his actions were a desperate cry for help. What were the odds that his girlfriend was just as crazy? And Griffen had never hurt a child. If Karen had taken Shannon and Evie… Maybe she was more ruthless than Griffen had ever been.

"What've you got?" Petrosky's voice didn't jar him as it had earlier, and Morrison tapped the screen. *Unreal…*

"Griffen's girlfriend, maybe? It isn't the best rendition, but—"

"Now, wouldn't that be something?" Petrosky's jaw worked overtime in his fleshy face. "Can't imagine that she just happened to pick up where Griffen left off."

"Maybe she snapped."

"Or maybe she was the voice in Griffen's journals."

Morrison tried to conjure images from the notebooks Griffen had left behind. Griffen had mentioned hearing voices. Doing things…for *her.* Said that *her voice* was stronger than all the others. They'd assumed it was nothing but hallucinations, all of it, but what if some of it had been real? What if *her voice* had actually been— "You think Karen manipulated him? To go after Shannon?"

"I can't imagine why that would be true. Just throwing out ideas, California."

But there'd been no trace of her at Acosta's rape-homicide, nor at Bell's house. The men were the ones who'd killed, who'd raped. Not Karen. Had she become involved with one of them inadvertently? Morrison flipped to Carleson's picture. Or maybe she'd sought them out on purpose, knowing they were as sick as she needed them to be. Knowing that she could mold them. Maybe she'd wanted someone harder, more psychopathic than Griffen, since he wasn't able to pull off what she wanted—since he hadn't been able to kill Shannon. But why?

Feeding people ideas. Something she'd know how to do from years of working in the rehab center. But what did she want now? To hurt Roger, but—

"I'll grab Griffen's file. Wish I could remember Karen's last name." Petrosky already had his phone to his ear. He headed for the stairs, and Morrison threw the papers together and followed him through the bullpen. "Good afternoon, I'm looking for Karen," Petrosky said. "I believe she's one of your therapists?" He paused. "Oh, really? That's too bad. Thank you." He turned to Morrison. "She doesn't work there anymore."

But Morrison had seen her at the courthouse. He saw her all the time. Maybe she was only there because he was. His heart shuddered to life.

Once you remember me, you'll know exactly how to find me.

Petrosky shoved the phone into his pocket. "Looks like we'll be grabbing that file—see what we have on Karen. Then we'll pay a little visit to the rehab center's HR."

THE RECEPTIONIST at the rehab center had a sore on her lip, a dour expression, and skin nearly as sallow as the Formica countertops. She grimaced when Petrosky flashed his badge, but called her boss and gestured to a waiting room outfitted with vinyl chairs and green linoleum. They stood against the wall beside a framed print of a pasture.

"Some shrink probably said, 'You know what would calm these addicts down? Pictures of fucking meadows,'" Petrosky muttered as the head of HR emerged from the back. Black suit. White blouse. Straight, fifties-style bangs.

Marie Silva's office was decked out with the same green floor, though some effort had been made to pretty the place up with an Aztec wall covering. "So, what can I help you with?"

"Looking for a Karen Palmer."

"Oh. Well…" Her gaze darted around the room. "What's this regarding?"

"We just have some questions for her in an ongoing investigation," Petrosky said. "No bearing on the facility, mind you, but without your assistance, we might be forced to look more deeply into your organization to rule out culpability."

Her lips formed a tight line as she appraised them. "Her reasons for dismissal are not protected by law. But I must say that—"

"Sorry, ma'am, but time is of the essence. We're on the same side here." But Petrosky's tone was more confrontational than friendly.

She crossed her arms. "She was let go for a violation of ethics."

"The Griffen case."

"She was dating a patient during the course of treatment." Her words were clipped. "Clearly a violation of ethical boundaries and contradictory to the agreements she signed at the outset of her employment."

Petrosky nodded noncommittally and opened the file. "Can you take a look at these photos? Tell us if any of these individuals have been in treatment here?"

Silva shook her head and pursed her lips. "Now that I cannot do. Patients are protected heavily by HIPAA laws. I'd lose my job and my license."

Petrosky pulled the male suspects' pictures out anyway and set them on the desk side by side, but she pushed them back toward him without so much as a glance.

"You can help us, or we can come back with a court order."

They didn't have time for a court order.

She leveled a hard stare at Petrosky. "Do that."

Fuck.

"Can you tell us whether they've ever worked here?"

"Half the people who work here have been in treatment. Peer support is great for addiction centers, and our programs push rehabilitation and job seeking as a part of continuing sobriety." Her back straightened, proud. "We practice what we preach, which means we pay now-sober ex-patients to provide mentoring and to help with groups. That makes what you're asking a gray area for us, and ethically I cannot—"

"What about the basics? Recent terminations? Anyone else that Karen took a special interest in?"

Her eyes narrowed. "No. If I'd seen her taking an *interest* in anyone else, I would have put a stop to it immediately."

Petrosky leaned in and spoke quietly. "Ma'am, we all have the same goal here."

She sighed. "Listen, I can give you dates of employment, titles, and salaries, but I'm not comfortable giving out every employee's confidential information without a warrant."

"A list of employees for the last year. I'll get those before we leave, and we can come back with follow-up questions."

She glared at Petrosky like she wanted to slap him.

"For now, let's stick to Karen Palmer," Petrosky said.

Her mouth stayed tight, but she leaned back in her chair as he slid the pictures back into the folder.

"How did Karen meet Frank Griffen?"

"I can't comment on Griffen."

"He's dead, ma'am."

"That doesn't mean he has fewer rights, Detective."

Petrosky's jaw was as hard as the stone crushing Morrison's chest. Petrosky was trying not to push her—trying to get what they needed without losing his shit. But the boss was getting angry. The next words from Petrosky's lips would probably get them thrown out, and they needed to ask about Karen anyway, not patients.

"What did Karen do here?" Morrison's voice sounded strange

to him as if it had come from someone else. Silva seemed equally surprised to hear him speak, her head jerking his way as if she'd forgotten he was there in the presence of Petrosky's bluster.

"Mostly intake," she said.

"Was she a clinical therapist?"

"No. She was in her last year of school for her bachelor's in social work, some online program. Had me fill out forms saying she was here as part of an internship." *Probably for a school that didn't exist.* "All she did was the initial contact and the first set of paperwork: financials, legal issues, basics on what they came in for. Shortly after Mr. Griffen's...uh...death, an act unrelated to this institution, our investigation found that she had been dating him. Which was quite surprising to those of us who knew her and not only because of her position with the center."

"Why was that, ma'am?" Morrison asked.

She leaned over her clasped hands. "Because, last we knew, she was dating Roger McFadden."

28

EVERY BUMP in the road sang through Morrison's body like a voltaic jolt. Behind him, the sun sank into the blackening troposphere, and dusk crept over the road now washed in amber from the streetlights.

You'd better be home, you fucker.

He tried to calm the heat in his chest as he pulled up. Roger's lakefront property was more ostentatious than it should have been for a public servant's salary. Red brick columns flanked a deep front porch with floor-to-ceiling windows on either side of an oak door. Above, the second story balconies provided cover for the porch, reaching from one side of the home to the other. Trees lined the edges of his property, their trunks silent and gray as prison bars in the gloom. And so quiet. Even the water behind Roger's house had ceased to lap the shore, though it still shimmered red and orange like fire under the setting sun.

No one would know Morrison had been there.

Roger answered the bell still dressed in his suit, though he'd loosened his tie. It lay against his button-down like a failed hangman's knot. "Back again?" Smug as hell. "Ready to apolog—"

"Do you remember Karen Palmer?"

Roger's eye twitched almost imperceptibly, but enough that Morrison knew the answer before he said it. "Vaguely."

Bullshit. Morrison sucked a breath through his nose. "You dated her last year. At the same time Griffen was dating her."

His mouth tightened.

"Why didn't you tell anyone, Roger?"

Roger paused, then sighed and backed into the house. Morrison followed him into the living room across light oak hardwood floors. A deer's head glared at him from over the fireplace, though Shannon had once told him Roger didn't hunt.

Roger made himself a drink from a bar cart in the corner: scotch on the rocks. He didn't offer one to Morrison. "Dating Karen wasn't relevant," he said finally. "I date lots of people. And so did she. Obviously." But the last word was laced with malice.

"Not relevant?" Morrison snapped, but he inhaled sharply and leveled his voice. "She was feeding you information about me, telling you that I was taking advantage of those in rehab, lying to you about people under her care." And Roger had bought it all, not thinking for a moment that she might have been covering for Griffen or even egging him on.

"So what?" Roger jerked back hard enough that scotch splashed over the rim of his glass. "She was crazy, but she wasn't a killer. He was the whack job."

"If she was so crazy, why didn't you give a statement after you found out about Griffen? You could have mentioned she seemed unhinged."

Roger slugged back half the drink and pointed at Morrison. "What happened with Griffen wasn't my fault."

"Shannon was attacked while I was in jail. If you knew your girlfriend was messing around with an unstable guy who was close to Shannon during that time, you had an obligation—"

"I didn't know Karen was with...him." He spat the last word, eyes tight as he downed the rest of the drink and poured another. "Not until it was all over. And once he was dead..." He shrugged.

Based on the journal entries, Griffen had no idea about Roger—your girlfriend banging someone else was worth writing about. Had Karen manipulated them both? If she'd convinced Roger of Morrison's guilt when she and Griffen were the ones involved in the crimes, maybe she'd even been the one to plant the murder weapon at Morrison's home. And Shannon—

"Did she ask you to hurt my wife?" The last words escaped Morrison's lips with an intensity beyond his control. He tried to calm his shuddering insides, but it felt as if his entire being were trapped in an earthquake.

Roger balked at the accusation, or maybe at the reminder of what he'd lost. "Don't be ridiculous. I wouldn't have let that slide."

But just this week, Roger had refused to even listen when Morrison told him Shannon had been kidnapped. "How could you not know Karen was dating Griffen?"

"It wasn't like we were in an exclusive relationship. She was young. And…flexible." The smirk was back for only a fraction of a moment, and then it was gone. Roger's eyes went as fiery as the lake behind his house. "I had no reason to think she was seeing anyone else."

Maybe Roger really hadn't known. If he'd been aware, he would have cut it off. "Roger, I think she manipulated Griffen. Sent him after Shannon. Now she's after you. And she was in my neighborhood the other day, just before Shannon was…taken."

"If you're trying to fuck with me, you're doing a—"

"Call the Central District Station in Toledo and ask about Shannon's car."

"What?"

"Found abandoned. Blood on the headrest. No leads yet."

Roger still didn't look convinced, but the heat in his eyes had mellowed. "A prosecutor, kidnapped? That's big news."

"The people who know about the car think it was a misunderstanding." Morrison stood and took a step toward Roger and the bastard flinched. "Goddammit, Roger, I'm not making this up. There's no way in hell I'd be speaking to you if it wasn't necessary. And I swear to god I wish it was my life on the line. I'd gladly give it to get my family back."

"Karen was just a piece of ass." Roger's face did not change, but his voice almost sounded…remorseful. Maybe he'd figured out why this woman was pissed at him. Maybe she had a good reason.

"Did she know about the safe deposit box, Roger?"

"Everyone has a safe deposit box."

"Does she have reason to think you had something question-able inside?"

Roger's lips were nearly white from pressing them together so hard. "No."

The hairs on the back of Morrison's neck stood, but he had expected nothing less than a lie. "I have a list of questionable activity taken from your accounts, much of it in the form of irregular deposits." Morrison nearly whispered the accusation, but Roger reeled back as if it had been shouted at him.

"You didn't have a warrant for that."

"No, I didn't. It was acquired over the course of the Griffen investigation when we considered you a suspect. And now with the knowledge that your girlfriend was also Griffen's—"

"That's a fucking illegal search, and you know it. I should have you—"

Rage flamed through his chest, and his vision went red. "Have me *what*, you entitled fuck? You want to charge me with getting this information illegally? Just a rumor would spell the end of your career, and you know it. I'm not going to hold my fucking breath."

Roger sat heavily on the couch, the scotch slopping over the side of his glass and darkening the oak floor. His face hardened into a stony mask. Morrison was losing him.

"Griffen's journal entries," Morrison said in a calm, measured tone. "He wrote about a woman's voice, telling him to do things, and comforting him after he killed Johnson. We assumed that voice was a hallucination, maybe even Frieda Burke, the social worker he dated before Karen. But...what if it was *her*? What if Karen is pulling the strings now, but with a more dangerous crew?"

"That waif of a woman? You're out of your mind." But Roger's confidence seemed to have cracked. His voice was tenu-ous, his gaze exploring the ceiling as if he was considering something.

"Roger? What?"

"She asked about you. A few times. I thought it was because

of her work, the rumors she said she heard about you during the Griffen case." Roger set his glass on the end table, and it clattered briefly like his hand was shaking. "She was nuts. Intense. But I didn't think she was lying."

"You found out afterward, didn't you?"

"I couldn't verify what she said, but that didn't mean she was wrong. And by then, Griffen was already dead, and the case was over."

Know your opponent. Know your killer. "What did she do that was so intense?"

"She was a good fuck, did everything I wanted her to do. Threw herself at me the night we met, all over me in the parking lot after we'd talked for like twenty minutes. Begged me to take her back to my place, all glassy-eyed like she'd lose her shit if I refused."

Maybe Shannon had done that too. Morrison averted his gaze before he puked all over Roger's lap. *Don't think about her in his bed. Focus.* Morrison's fist clenched, and he tried to relax his grip as he asked: "What'd you do?"

"What the fuck do you mean? I took her back to my place. Figured it'd be a one-time thing."

"But it wasn't," Morrison said, muscles taut, ready to throttle the asshole. "You did something to make her angry. She isn't after you for nothing."

Roger shifted in his seat. "The next day, she seemed to think we were together. I didn't call her for a few weeks, but she kept showing up places where I was, and eventually, I took her out. That first night at dinner, she waited until I ordered, then asked me to order her the same." He snorted, and it was a derisive sound. "When it came, she said she was allergic to shellfish and refused to get anything else. Weird shit. And the next week, I saw her in court, and she asked if I liked to ski, suggested we go onto the slopes. She had no idea what she was doing, almost broke her fucking leg. Two dates later, and she started accusing me of bullshit, and I broke it off. Wasn't like we had an actual relationship."

"What'd she accuse you of?"

"The usual. Looking at other women."

"That doesn't seem that strange." Morrison's voice was colder than he'd intended, but he couldn't seem to connect himself to it. And Roger probably *had* been looking at other women: his continuous infidelity was one of the reasons Shannon had left him.

Something flashed in Roger's eyes—angry, incredulous—and disappeared. "She tried to kill herself when I broke it off, screaming and threatening me on my voice mail, and then just hung up, like that's supposed to make me want to call her. How's that for crazy?"

Morrison glared at him. *How fucking stupid is he?* "Why wouldn't you say something about that before? We're talking about her being unstab—"

"I didn't think that much of it, I guess. Not the first woman ever to go stalker on me."

"What did you do when she threatened suicide?" But he already knew the answer—he'd have known if Roger had called the police.

Roger shrugged. "Told her to fuck off. Put a block on my phone."

Blocked. That must have pissed her off, especially if she'd planned to use him for more than just a fling. But...that didn't make sense. This wasn't just a fatal attraction. She hadn't kidnapped Shannon for being Roger's ex, or she would have done that long ago. She wanted to hurt Roger, but...he was a bonus. Instead of going after Roger when he'd hurt her, Karen had just kept dating Griffen. And continued to pursue Shannon.

And Shannon had been Griffen's ultimate target, and maybe Karen's too—she'd spent a lot of time filling Griffen's messed-up head with hatred if the notes in his journals were any indication. Shannon had been the one in danger then, and she was the one in danger now. Maybe Karen had given Morrison this futile mission because she wanted a reason to kill Shannon—to do what Griffen couldn't.

But why?

He was missing something. Something big.

"Where does Karen live, Roger?" They hadn't been able to find a recent address.

Roger glanced at the mantel—at the framed photo of himself and Shannon on their wedding day.

Morrison's heart seized, and his body seemed to come back to life, every nerve ending alight and singing with desperation. "Please, Roger. Don't let Karen kill Shannon."

When Roger turned back, his eyes were glassy, mouth hard. *He loves her.* For all his narcissistic bullshit, Roger really did love Shannon. He always would. If Karen, unstable as she was, had sensed Roger's devotion to his ex, she would have had ample reason to hurt Morrison's family.

Roger blinked rapidly and lurched to his feet so fast Morrison jumped. "I'll go with you," he growled. "I want to talk to that bitch myself."

THE ADDRESS ROGER had for Karen was a handsome colonial on the outskirts of Berkley, a place not listed in her employee file. The couple who answered the door had bought the home six months before. They didn't know Karen and had no idea who the previous tenant might have been. He'd look into that.

But if Karen was hiding, she probably hadn't left a forwarding address.

Roger stared out the side window on the way back to his house. "You're not fucking with me? She's really gone?"

Morrison kept his eyes on the road in front of him, avoiding Roger's face.

"She is." But not forever. *Please, not forever.*

"Why don't you call in the FBI?"

Petrosky had found no bugs in the car, and the killers couldn't hear him with the phone off, even if they had it tapped. Still, he shoved his cell deeper into his back pocket and leaned his weight against it. "I don't want her to get hurt. And I think Karen...wants *me* to find them." On the phone, Karen had said they were waiting for him, saving Evie for when he got there. If the FBI came barging in, everyone was dead. If he went alone... hope burgeoned in his belly.

"Why would anyone want Shannon?" Roger said, slowly but

pained as if he still couldn't accept the truth of it. "She doesn't have much of a past."

No, she didn't. A dead brother. Alcoholic parents, deceased. But nothing about this case was normal. Had Shannon prosecuted someone close to Karen? Convicted one of Karen's family members, maybe another lover? Morrison shook his head. That theory was what Petrosky called "Maury Povich shit," but it might make sense here. Karen was calculating. Ruthless. She'd killed Abby's kitten last year for fuck's sake—or rather encouraged Griffen to do it. She had wanted to make Shannon suffer. This was personal.

Roger cleared his throat. "But you do."

What was Roger talking about? "I do what?"

"You have a past. I investigated you, too, remember?"

Morrison clenched his jaw and drew his eyes back to the road. "Not a past that most would be interested in."

"Come off it, asshole. You and your fucking partner do all kinds of shady shit. Petrosky's known for being a loose cannon —picking up hookers, paying their bills."

"How do you—"

"I get around too." Roger raised an eyebrow. "Maybe some of their pimps don't fucking like that. And anyone watching him would know he's close to your family. He's probably into other things too, that drug-addicted—"

"No." Rage bubbled in Morrison's belly. "Petrosky isn't on drugs."

Roger snorted. "No one tried to take her when she was married to me, *Curt.* No one but you. And you didn't get over your past. No one gets over their past. We all are a certain way. Just because you go around convincing everybody that you're better doesn't mean you are."

"I've never—"

"No, but you think it, don't you? Every time I saw you with Shannon, it was all, 'Hey, Roger, how's it going, Roger?' Showing me, you didn't care how pissed I was about you hanging around her. Showing me, you thought you were better. Challenging me all the time. And you know what? Congratulations. You provoked me until I got angry. And I scared her off and gave her to you with a fucking bow on her ass." Roger grunted as if that had all been part of his master plan. "And the second you saw the opportunity, you took it. You took her."

"That wasn't about you, Roger. Shannon and I were friends."

"Of course you'd say that now. But you saw her, and you wanted her, and you couldn't go about it the reasonable way, the honorable way. Like I did. I didn't have to steal her to get her to marry me."

Morrison's wife, his baby, had been *kidnapped,* and Roger was trying to make this about himself? *He's fucking with me.* Shannon had told him many times about the way Roger could turn things around, make everything about him. And right now…it was. He needed Roger no matter how much he wished that weren't true. Roger might be the key to getting Shannon and Evie back.

"You wanted her, and you figured you'd try to hurt me." In the space of that sentence, Roger's tone went from vulnerable to acidic. From victim to aggressor. "But you can fucking have her, especially now that you have someone else pissed at you. Tell me, how many other women have you taken? Who else might want to get back at you?"

I don't steal women. And no one but Roger would think he had, of that, he was quite certain. But Morrison couldn't leave things this way—he needed Roger's help. "The better man doesn't always win."

Roger said nothing, but Morrison could almost hear him smirking. He swallowed his pride and the lump in his throat and headed over the amber streets toward Roger's house by the lake. The house that would have been Shannon's now if she'd stayed married to Roger. Maybe Roger was right. Maybe this was all his fault. Maybe he should have looked out for her better. Protected her.

If only she'd never met Roger.

If only she'd never married me.

BY THE TIME Morrison returned to the precinct, the bustle of the early morning hours had been replaced by a solemn nighttime shuffle of people disappearing one by one back to their families. Because they still had families. Even Petrosky was gone, and Morrison felt the absence of his own family as vividly as if he'd been boiled alive, his skin raw and exposed and utterly defenseless.

He needed to talk to Shannon. To hear her voice. To prove to himself, there was something there for him to fight for. To prove they weren't dead already. *Find her.*

Roger'd already checked social media—all traces of Karen gone—so Morrison sat at the desk and searched for Karen Palmer's driver's license from the state of Michigan. *Strange.* She should at least have a photo ID, but according to state records... nothing. No records at any nearby university, despite her employer's claim that she'd been in school. He flipped open her employee folder from the rehab center—nothing but a state ID from New York. Forged? Wouldn't the center have double-checked?

He grabbed the phone, and a quick call to the rehab center told him that while they ran the names for background checks, they just ensured the licenses were valid. The out-of-state license wouldn't have been an issue unless it had been suspended. Not unusual, but...

The New York State database, then. This time he got a hit. The address, the date of birth, everything matched the license photocopy in the file...except for the picture. Dark hair. Wide nose. No freckles.

It wasn't her.

Heart in his throat, he clicked through to the national data-bases and on to birth certificates. Using the New York driver's license, he found her: Karen Palmer, born in 1985 in California, in a city ten minutes away from Morrison's hometown. And died...no, that couldn't be right.

Karen Palmer had died eight years ago in New York, the records said. Cause of death: suicide. Maybe she'd faked her death? Gotten plastic surgery? No, that was real Maury Povich shit. And Karen Palmer's information had been out of circulation after she died—until the kidnapper had resurrected her four years later.

Which meant Griffen's girlfriend had been someone else until a few years ago. And she probably hadn't known Shannon until she'd arrived here—otherwise, his wife would have remembered Karen when she met the woman again as Griffen's girlfriend, especially if "Karen" was someone with a reason to be angry.

So Shannon hadn't known her, but this was no new wound. It was something deep and primal and feral. Based on old hurt. Not something Shannon had done in connection to Griffen or Roger or anyone else. Maybe not even something Roger had done since she hadn't gone after him until now. Was Roger just a bonus too? But Karen had definitely gone after Shannon. And she'd gone after…Morrison. Had him arrested.

He stared at the state of birth.

California.

Karen Palmer had been born in California. The kidnapper had taken her place. Had the kidnapper known the real Karen Palmer? Had she known…him? And if so…

Shannon's kidnapper had come to Michigan for him. And he couldn't for the life of him remember why.

"IN OUR ENDEAVORS TO RECALL TO MEMORY
SOMETHING LONG FORGOTTEN, WE OFTEN FIND OURSELVES UPON
THE VERY VERGE OF REMEMBRANCE, WITHOUT BEING ABLE, IN THE
END, TO REMEMBER."
~EDGAR ALLAN POE, *LIGEIA*

29

SHANNON'S ARMS ACHED, every muscle burning from the position she'd had to take, balled in the corner of what used to be a closet. No straitjacket now. Her breasts throbbed with unexpressed milk, nipples itchy and raw from letdown, and the dried fluids on the inside of her shirt.

Panic came and went in waves, and more often than not, she felt the tug of depression: the desperation, the hopelessness. Like now.

She hadn't fed Evie in what had to be days. Sometimes she heard her baby crying through the wall when they opened the door to toss in a bottle of water. Her own stomach was gnarled with anxiety and hunger, and her nerves were so frayed that it felt like she was brushing up against raw wires in the walls. But she could perceive nothing with her fingertips even when she scratched so ceaselessly at the concrete she swore she was exposing the bones in her hands. And sometimes the shocks seemed to originate inside her head, an electric pulse in her brain.

She was probably losing her mind. Maybe had already.

Shannon leaned her head against the back of the closet, the cement board cold and hard and surely insulated well enough to muffle the sound of her echoing sobs. The air reeked of vomit and shit from the bucket in the corner. She had never considered that she'd long for the cold, barren bedroom where she'd awoken. But every piece of her ached for that freedom…and for the ability to see her baby girl whether she could touch her or not. Was Evie alive? *Stop, don't think.*

In this dark chamber, time stretched and compressed and bent on itself—she couldn't be sure if it was day or night. But Karen came to see her regularly, her full lips whispering poisonous words into the dark. Always at the strike of a grandfather clock somewhere in the house, as if the woman had a planner and at seven and twelve and three o'clock each day she'd written "Fuck with Shannon" in scrawling red ink. Karen told her all kinds of things. That she was still angry at Shannon for breaking her collarbone the night she'd attacked Shannon by the lake. Shannon thought it was Griffen she'd fought off that night, but not according to Karen, and Shannon had no reason to disbelieve her. Nor did she disbelieve it when Karen hissed that she'd helped Griffen frame Morrison for murder last year. That Griffen had never set out to harm anyone, that he had flown off the handle and broken a man's head, but that he'd lacked the guts for premeditated murder. Griffen: Shannon's friend for more than a decade. Her friend that she'd *killed* because he'd been sick—he'd been a murderer. Though maybe he hadn't. And if that were true, what did that make her?

Karen was playing on the guilt that had been eating at her every day since she'd put a bullet through Griffen's eye socket. Maybe Karen had gotten into McCallum's files—besides Petrosky, who had taken the fall for Griffen's death, only the psychiatrist knew what she'd done. Even Morrison didn't realize she was a killer too. She'd have to tell him she was sorry. And he'd tell her there was no sorry, only love, but…she'd lied to him. He might not forgive that.

Even as Shannon rationalized each issue away, new ones were introduced. Karen whispered about hurting Morrison. She said Shannon's husband was a murderer—that she wanted him to suffer, to make him feel helpless too. But none of it made sense, not any of it.

Visit after visit, Karen asked her how it felt to be without Evie. Told her that her baby girl was starving as they spoke, as milk stained Shannon's clothes and soaked her front. Evie would be better off without her, Karen said, and maybe they'd kill her baby girl just to spare Shannon the trouble of doing it herself: "Isn't that what you want, Shannon?"

Maybe Karen was messing with her head, but Shannon felt the correctness of each lancing blow in the deepest parts of her soul because she'd said those words to herself. Every fear she'd ever had, every irrational thought embedded itself into her consciousness—as though these terrifying convictions were right in a way that McCallum and her husband couldn't see. Maybe Evie did deserve better than her. Evie might still be fine at home if she'd had a different mother. Shannon tried to tell herself it was the depression talking, but she was having trouble believing it. The days were bleeding into one another, the darkness and lack of life rhythm pulling at the edges of her thoughts until she feared it would drive her mad. Though insanity would surely have been preferable to the hopelessness encroaching on her like a malevolent fog, cocooning her in despair, imploring her to give up.

What kind of mother was she? She wasn't even *trying*.

She stared across the closet—the dungeon—but everything was just black. Above her, she knew, hung a huge wooden strut attached to either end of the closet with brackets. If she could loosen it, perhaps it'd make a good weapon, but it was at least a foot square and too cumbersome to swing at her jailers from the confines of the closet. And with any action she took, there was risk. She could not leave without her child. Would they kill Evie if she tried to escape?

She prayed Evie was asleep. Babies slept through worse in third world countries, right? And when the man in the boots had come to take Evie away, he'd seemed rather…uninterested. He hadn't hurt Evie, hadn't even looked at her daughter, just took her. If he wanted to hurt her, he'd have done it in the room, made Shannon watch, wasn't that what psychos did? She might be wrong. Maybe even now they were burying Evie out back, alive, her tiny body being slowly covered with dirt until it filled her lungs and—

Her empty stomach clenched, and she heaved, gagged, but nothing came up.

Evie. She could almost feel her baby's breath against her neck. Surely if they'd killed her child, she'd have felt it—a snapping of her own lifeline, deep in her gut like the very cord that had tethered them to one another for nearly a year before Evie's birth.

No, Evie was alive, Shannon was sure of that. But she was being hurt, traumatized, if only by her mother's absence. Her sweet baby girl! And Karen didn't give a shit. Nor did the man outside the closet.

The door was thick, but she knew he was there. She could feel him. Smell him.

Milk dripped onto her jeans from below the hem of her T-shirt, but she made no move to wipe it away. Even her body knew Evie was still alive. And Evie still needed her mother. "Please let me feed her," she called into the darkness. There was no response, not that she had expected one. He couldn't hear her through the padded walls, but she was almost certain that he felt her too—surely he must sense the rage that was growing in her belly like a demon ready to emerge and slash at her captors with razor-sharp teeth.

"Hello?" she cried out, louder this time, and again her plea went unanswered. "I know you're there!" Panic mingled with desperation, and then it was there, the fury, a storm brewing without means for release. Her arms and legs twitched with anticipation.

She clawed her way to standing along the wall, probably leaving more trails of red from her already weeping fingertips. Dizziness pulled at her, and she grabbed the beam, wrapping one shoulder over it. The fury burned, hotter and blacker until it cloaked her entire being in unbridled hatred. If they wanted to kill her, then god-fucking-dammit, they needed to just hurry up and do it. She wasn't about to starve to death in a tiny closet, wondering if her child was already dead.

Please don't let her be dead.

She kicked the door with her bare foot, a move gleaned from years of CrossFit and kickboxing, but the door wouldn't budge. She'd tried this before—the space wasn't large enough to get leverage. The sound of her kick thundered back at her, reverberating in her ears as her heel burned deliciously from the exertion.

"Fuck you!" she screamed, then kept screaming it over and over: "Fuck you, you piece of fucking shit!" She kicked the door again, the dull thud of the impact jittering through her leg bone and into her hip, a welcomed sensation after the black numbness of rotting on the closet floor. Again and again and again, she kicked, tears sprouting in her eyes at the pain of the impact. At the helpless fury writhing in her gut.

Then...something. A sound, a scrape, and the light came then, so glaringly bright that she was forced to squint into it or go blind. And a silhouette in the now open doorway: Karen, red hair engulfing her face like hellfire.

You fucking bitch. Shannon tried to lunge under the beam, but the world blackened at the edges, and she had to hold on to avoid falling. She couldn't fight Karen. Had they put something in the water? She shivered in her wet shirt.

"Why are you doing this?" Shannon whispered, straining to hear Evie—a cry, a coo, anything to hint that she was alive. But there was only Karen's breath, steady and soft above the frenzied throbbing of Shannon's heart.

"Your husband is an asshole."

Shannon tried to let go of the bar again, but her legs shook, and she tightened her grip.

Karen smirked, teeth yellowed by the dim light. "Let's call him, shall we?"

Shannon tried to nod, scanning the room behind Karen for something she could yell out to Morrison, any clues that might give him some idea of where she was, but there was just the black bed, its pillows dark as night. No sunlit window. Nothing to indicate direction or location or even the type of building they were in. For all she knew, she could be locked in a highrise.

Karen was holding her cell, tilting it back and forth like a snow globe. "Let's see if he killed your ex yet."

"Roger?"

Karen smiled, venomous, a look that Shannon had once

thought beautiful, but now it radiated malice—hatred. And then Karen froze, staring at—

He loomed just outside the closet doorway, terrifying with his bald head and thick boots, and the room felt heavier with his presence. And with that awful mask, more frightening than it had been the first time because she knew, she knew he'd keep her here, knew he didn't want her to see his face because he was going to do atrocious things to her. He was bare-chested today, thin, scrawny even, but wiry—probably stronger than she'd guessed from his height alone. The scars of what looked like small puncture wounds, maybe burns, maybe an ice pick, glared at her from his stomach, and in the trail of hair on his lower belly the wounds were deeper, larger: some old and healed, others fresh, gaping stains like drips of black oil across his torso.

It must be morning. He only showed up in the morning, or so she thought because he usually came with coffee and a bagel, watching to see if she'd beg for a bite of his meal. She never had. And he'd never given her any.

Karen smiled at him and straightened her shoulders.

Shannon eased her weight onto her jelly legs and tried not to wobble.

Karen whirled on Shannon, her eyes narrowed, lips still smiling, which was more unnerving than if she'd snarled. "You come at me, and I'll kill Evie in front of you."

"I won't. Please." Shannon eased her weight back onto the bar, her head spinning. Somewhere in the house, a clock chimed, again and again, but Shannon couldn't concentrate enough to count the hour.

"Why are you talking?" He spoke to Shannon, maybe, voice muffled under the leather, but it sounded oddly careful. One of his fingernails worried at the molding around the closet door, and he was staring at Karen from inside the mask. His angular shoulders were slumped like an old beaten dog, though he outweighed them by at least fifty pounds.

From the next room, a whine blossomed into a wail, one thin, long howl of exhausted hunger. *Evie. Alive.* Blood pumped into Shannon's legs, urging her to run to her daughter, to take her from this place. *Can't run. They'll kill us both.* She held the bar tighter as the man straightened, muscles corded. He glanced toward the door, toward Evie's screams.

"Please—I can make her quiet," Shannon said, hating that she sounded like she was begging, but she *was* begging. *God, please let me feed her.*

"I can make her quiet too." His voice was more menacing now as he dropped his hand from the wall and advanced. Unafraid of her, apparently, only wary of Karen. Because they were…together? Because she'd seen him without the mask?

"I'll get her quiet," he said, and he turned to the door.

No, oh Jesus, don't hurt her. "She's hungry, just let me—"

"Her agony is well-deserved."

Her agony. Was he enjoying watching Evie starve? He had laughed their first night here, laughed at Shannon's screams as he held his blade over her daughter. He wanted to see their misery. "Hurt me instead."

He turned to her and lowered his face so he could look into her eyes. His irises shone even in the dark of the mask as if madness could escape through his pupils. Where Morrison's pacific blue lenses were always so full of hope and promise and kindness; behind this man's eyes, lay only the glittering promise of pain.

"She doesn't understand what you want," Shannon said.

"Then she'll learn," he said with a lilt that made it sound like he was smiling.

"No, she won't," Karen said suddenly, her bottom lip between her teeth. There was something strange happening, a discontent, an aggression building between her captors—he took a step backward, away from Karen, shoulders tense like a kid being admonished by a parent. Was he…young? Was Karen his mom? *How can I use this to get us out of here?*

"Children don't learn from pain the same way adults do," Karen said. "Like that boy who *never should have happened.*" She glared at the man in the mask, and he shrank farther from her.

What boy? *There have been others.* This wasn't a new game to them; this was an old game, and Shannon and Evie were only new victims. Perhaps the boy was buried out back. Maybe he was in another room like hers, hanging by his ankles from his own wooden beam. And…this man's boots. They'd been covered in blood, hadn't they?

Karen stepped over to the masked man, and he flinched. Then she ran a hand over his abdomen, hooking a fingernail under a scab near his belly button and slicing it off. He grunted and righted himself, taller suddenly, muscles rippling as the wound welled and blood tricked toward his belt line.

Karen's face cleared—no longer angry, or perhaps she'd decided there was a better way to accomplish her goal. "The kid will just cry more. We'll never get her to shut up. But this one…" She gestured to Shannon, and Shannon's blood ran cold. "She'll never bother you again with her whiny bullshit." Karen's eyes were dead, stony, the beauty draining from her face as the blood drained from the masked man's wound.

He appraised Shannon, fingers practically vibrating with anticipation, and left the room.

Oh god. Shannon's heart throbbed, and each beat drove a spike of fear into her chest. Was he going to get that barbaric weapon with the hooked blade? Was he going to cut her open? Would he…cut Evie? *No, please, no.*

Her eyes darted around the room, peering at the doorway. "Please, Karen…" Could she overpower her? But in her weakened state, she could never take on both of them…and the masked man had her child. *Evie—*

She heard him then, his footsteps growing louder, returning, and every muscle in Shannon's body quivered. *Please let us go. Please don't hurt Evie.*

Then he was there, brandishing a small cloth bag in one hand. In his other hand, a collar, the inner part of it, the part that would touch the throat, glinting with what looked like razor blades.

Shannon's mouth filled with cotton, and her throat constricted painfully. The masked man stepped in front of her, his leather face turning this way, then that, the spines on top of the mask stabbing at the sky above him, the vicious beak sharp and deadly. One head butt and she'd be gone. Every panel of the mask seemed to leer at her of its own accord. *Fuck, fuck, fuck.*

I don't want to die.

He reached for her, and she stepped away, almost fell, but he wasn't after her, not yet. He attached the metal clamp to the front of the beam by threading a bolt through a small hole, securing the collar to the post.

"In."

She stared at the blades glinting evilly from the inside of the collar. "But it'll…" *Slit my throat.*

"In. And don't move."

Her eyes filled. Then she saw *her.*

She hadn't noticed Karen leaving, but now the woman walked into the room carrying Evie, her daughter barely struggling in Karen's arms. Evie cried weakly. Shannon's insides leapt and flipped, and she shook with the effort not to run to her.

The man turned his head to look at her daughter, then back. "In the collar, you can hold her, feed the bitch, whatever. You're going to make good on your promise."

Her promise. Shannon's lip quivered, but she stiffened it. *Fuck you.* She watched him set the bag on the beam next to the collar and open it. A sewing kit. Curved instruments glinting in the light, though dimmed by the closet's oppressive shadow. *What the hell is he going to—*

The thought froze in her brain as he produced an upholstery needle, the tip glistening like a shard of broken glass, and it felt as if he were going to stab her with a piece of her own shattered sanity. And…*would* he stab her? Would he shove it into her eyeball, blinding her? Every muscle in her body tightened in anticipation. *Run. Run!*

She dragged her gaze from the needle as Evie kicked one foot, weakly, her tiny mewl tugging at Shannon's gut more fervently than any instrument of torture he could dream up. She steeled herself, glanced once more at Evie, and stepped to the post. As carefully as she could, she leaned her neck against the back of the collar, where there were no blades.

He smiled. And clamped the thing around her neck.

One blade pierced her immediately, on the right side, just below her lymph node, not the fire of real injury, rather the sting of a paper cut. She adjusted a touch to the left, trying to avoid the blades on that side. She felt them, cold and sharp, but they didn't cut her. *Yet.*

His breath was faster, excited, and every exhale amplified by the mask like the hoarse rasp of a dying man. He moved aside, needle held up in front of his glass eyehole as Karen placed Evie in her arms.

Her baby's face was scrunched up. She was suffering—couldn't even raise her limbs to reach for her mother.

"Oh, baby," Shannon whispered. "Sweet girl."

Evie opened her mouth and wailed, but the sound was far smaller than it should have been. Careful to avoid jostling her own neck, Shannon lifted her shirt and pressed Evie to her breast, trying to do everything by feel since she couldn't look down.

Then he was there, staring into Shannon's eyes, running a finger over her lower lip, looking for her fear as he raised the needle. The thread was black like his fucking heart.

She stared back, eyes narrowed. But oh god, the needle. And he'd said…he wanted to keep her quiet. And as she watched his gaze lock on the lower part of her face, realization dawned with a wave of electric horror: he was going to sew her mouth closed. She'd feel every stitch, the blinding pain as he stabbed the needle into her. But if it kept Evie alive… *Come at me, fucker. Do it.* Just like getting your ears pierced. Except she'd not be able to speak.

To breathe.

Evie stirred. She clasped her daughter to her chest. "I love you, Evie, Evie."

He grabbed her face with one hand and stabbed the needle into her lower lip.

She wanted to cry out, but her air was gone as the needle rammed violently through her lower lip and pierced through to the top, the pain sharper and more vital than she'd imagined. *Stay still, keep quiet*—she had to keep her daughter from falling. She pressed her neck against the back of the collar and clutched Evie to her breast. The thread, bloody now, slid more easily than the needle, but it burned like a hot poker through her face. *No, please, no!* It stopped abruptly, a knot maybe and he was bringing it down to do another—*Fuck!* She wanted to scream, couldn't scream, she'd tear her lips apart and—she stared at his face, his mask, listened to his heavy breathing, tasted blood and salt on her tongue as the rage replaced the fear. He didn't deserve to have her cries to jack off to later.

Help me, please, someone, help. But there was no one else—only her. And…Evie. She inhaled deeply, shifted Evie to one arm, testing her strength, and raised the other hand to the beam.

He paused. "What are you doing?"

"Staying…steady." Talking from one corner of her mouth was painful, and she sounded like she was numb from a dentist visit. But he'd apparently understood and approved for he didn't respond, just stabbed the needle into her lip again, rougher this time. *Breathe, just breathe.* Tears welled in her eyes with the searing pain that radiated through her mouth into her cheeks, her ears, finding its way into every nerve ending in her body.

Her milk let down, and Evie was making tiny, sweet noises of contentment, and Shannon desperately wished she could see her face. *I'm a good mother god-fucking-dammit. I will get you out of here.*

Karen's eyes were alight with excitement—at Shannon's distress or maybe at the way the masked man was panting, every muscle in his arms twitching with anticipation. Karen approached behind him, ran her palms over the flat surface of his shoulder blades. *God, please let him stop, please let her take him away, please.*

Shannon snaked her hand toward the top of the beam. Karen didn't respond to the movement, fixated as she was on the stitches, or maybe the misery in Shannon's eyes or maybe on the man himself. His breath in the mask came faster, and she could smell it—hot and sour, though that could have been the smell of her own rank fear.

Another stitch. Panic seized her, a fresh wave ripping through her from toe to brain, begging her to run. *Run, Shannon! No. Not now, no!* She whimpered involuntarily, and it seemed to excite him further, his breath coming faster, hissing from behind that horrid mask as if the thing had come alive—a beaked monster of leather and metal. And then Karen was beside him, working his belt and his zipper—*not her son, defi-*

nitely not—and she knelt, out of Shannon's view, and he moaned into Shannon's face as he stabbed the needle into her lip again. And again, through the top, slower now but violent, the thread tugging not only through her flesh, but pulling her toward him as if she were a bull being led to slaughter by a ring in her mouth.

Don't move, Shannon. Almost finished. Don't move. She breathed heavily through her nose, fought the wave of dizziness. If she fainted, she'd be dead in minutes, her jugular shredded by the blades.

And Evie… Shannon tried to focus all her attention on Evie and the gentle pull of the baby at her breast. *Evie will be okay.* Tears stung her eyes.

Karen was standing, wiping her mouth, and he was growling into Shannon's face, the beak of the mask at her nose, and when it touched her, it sliced her right nostril, though that pain was dull compared to the stinging needle piercing her lips.

At the closet door, Karen pulled out the phone. Pushed buttons. Watched Shannon, practically panting. She put the phone to her ear. "Hello, Curt. The stakes have changed. Your partner's over at the rehab center. He's going to stay there."

Stay there? Why would they want Petrosky in rehab? But with the panic zinging through her body, her brain could only focus on the pain, could only scream inside as she watched the needle approach again. Her chin was wet, spit and blood dribbling down her chin, onto the arm that held Evie. Blood dripped onto her baby's head.

"What's to understand? Breckenridge Rehab has a reservation for one, Edward Petrosky. I'd hurry."

The man had paused, needle in hand, Shannon's blood on his fingertips, so much blood and was it hers or his or maybe both, and maybe she'd catch some crazy disease, *oh, fuck.* The dizziness pulled again until she feared she might not be able to hold herself up this time. He turned and stared at Karen, head cocked as if he were a student listening to a lecture.

"Please nothing," Karen snapped into the phone. "You're good at hooking people. Dragging them down to your level. Just be the same asshole you've always been. And they need a positive test for a same-day admission, so make sure your partner's good and dirty."

This bitch wanted Petrosky to—

The man turned back to her, peered into her eyes through the glass lenses of the mask as if he could see directly into her soul. His breathing turned everything inside her to ice.

"It's in your glovebox," Karen said. "Manila envelope. Get him to do it with you, or wait until he's asleep, then shoot him up and take him in. Do you understand?"

She couldn't think, couldn't focus. Something dripped onto her upper lip from the tip of her nose. More sweat. More blood.

Her torturer pulled his face back from Shannon's, and the air felt cooler, crisper. Then he chuckled like she'd told him something funny through her punctured lips. She ground her teeth together to keep from screaming.

"Roger taken care of?" Karen said into the receiver.

The masked man turned back to Karen again, and Shannon reached the corner of the sewing kit with her pinky finger. Ring finger. Then—

A sliver of metal, cool against her fingertips as the hooked beak swung her way again, but his eyes did not look at the beam or the kit, just at her as if trying to stare into her head. Sensing her pain. Enjoying it.

He made a noise like a groan, and for a moment, she feared he'd seen her hand in the sewing kit in his peripheral vision, but then his hand was flying toward her face, and he stabbed the needle deeper, higher, harder into her top lip; white-hot agony shot through her brain as he hit something, a nerve, a piece more crucial than before. He turned away. Done or waiting?

Don't move. Shit, don't move. Evie. Stay with Evie. Sweat rolled down her back and into the waistband of her pants.

A frown deepened on Karen's face. "Get the deposit box, his logbook. That's all you need. Or just shoot him in the face. But you better hurry. Women like your wife weaken fast—either we'll break her, or she'll break herself. Soon."

They would. They'd break her. Leave her in the dark, deprive her of her child, make her watch Evie weaken and succumb. *Come on, Morrison, come on.*

"I want to watch *you* suffer," Karen spat into the cell. "Like you watched Danny. Then I want you to watch the people you love die like you watched Danny die. And I'm going to love every second of it."

The man turned slowly, almost reverently, and her insides roiled, but oh god, she couldn't throw up, not anymore—she'd choke to death on her own vomit. And he was there at her mouth again, stabbing once more at the last remaining corner of her lips, and when he tugged the thread this time, it was as if he were trying to force her face into a grotesque joker's smile.

"I don't need rumors," Karen said. "I saw you."

The masked man cut the thread with the tip of his beak, and Shannon shuddered. The point of a blade from the collar pressed to her neck, and she felt the warm wet roll down to her collarbone. She'd cut herself. Hopefully, the wound wasn't too deep. *Or I'll die, I'll die, and Evie...* She forced her spine against the back of the beam again.

He snatched the sewing kit. Snatched Evie off her breast, the suction breaking and the sound slapping against the walls of the cell as Evie whimpered, then wailed.

"No, please, she's still hungry," Shannon wanted to say, but she couldn't say it, couldn't say anything. *Give her back to me!*

He put Evie on the floor outside the closet, roughly, as if she were a suitcase and not a living, breathing person, close enough to Shannon that she could only make out her daughter's kicking feet. He tossed the sewing kit beside Evie, his fingers still glistening red with Shannon's blood. The needles...so close to her daughter. *Oh god, not Evie, please don't hurt—*

"You've got a limited amount of time, Curt. She falls asleep, and she's done for," Karen told the cell. "And if she hasn't already killed herself, tomorrow night, I'll help her say goodbye."

If I fall asleep...oh, god...they weren't going to let her out of the collar. If she nodded off, she'd slit her own throat. No, shit no, she'd never make it through the—

But she couldn't tell them, not that they'd notice her trying to speak. Karen had dropped the phone, and the man was tearing at Karen's clothing, tossing her shirt and skirt aside as she grabbed his shoulders, wrapping her naked legs around his waist. He slammed Karen into the still-open door of the closet and entered her, thrusting into her again and again, right above Evie's head.

"Told you about the phone," he growled.

"You're good," Karen said. "We were made for each other."

"My number one girl." He shifted his weight, looked once more at Shannon, and hammered Karen into the wall. Shannon tried again to see Evie, but could only make out her baby's feet, no longer kicking so ferociously. Slowing down. Shutting down. Was it starvation? Trauma? *Oh, baby, please be okay.* On the floor lay the phone, still on, the time ticking away, upwards and onwards. And she knew Morrison was there too, listening to Evie scream, listening to the man's grunts and Karen's moans, hearing the sounds of sex and his screeching daughter and dear god, what he must think.

The man walked Karen to the bed and threw her off him, onto the black sheets. Then he returned to the closet, his erection at his belly, and there was…a tattoo. On his penis. A medieval sword, but terribly done, faded and pixelated like he'd done it himself. He paused at the doorway, and for one breathtaking moment, he studied the infant on the floor, his eyes behind the lenses wild with anticipation.

Please, no.

He pulled his eyes from Evie, and then the door was closing, encasing Shannon in perfect darkness, Evie's wails fading, and then gone completely, though she could still feel her daughter's frantic energy on the other side of the door. Shannon pressed her neck as far back as she could to avoid the blades. Blood trickled steadily down her chin. But in her palm, she tested the sharp point of the needle she'd stolen, hoping it'd be enough.

30

Karen's words echoed in his brain, mingling with Evie's screams and the sick grunts of pleasure. Morrison threw the phone to the floorboards like it was a ticking bomb. His baby girl. Not his baby.

Through the windshield, sunrise pinkened the bruised early morning clouds. One more day, two at most. And it was Saturday already: day four.

He'd run to his car when the call came in, his arm half-asleep from passing out at his desk, the remnants of a dream still thickening his mind.

Me first.

No, me.

A hallucination, or maybe a sliver of memory—girls laughing in his head, and Danny bleeding, and Shannon was bleeding too, covered in ants, just like—

He pounded the steering wheel with his fists.

Escalation.

These other assholes Karen was with had begun smaller—a rape, a little pressure on the neck. But Karen had started with murder in mind. His fist clenched, and he resisted the urge to punch the steering wheel. *Think.* What had driven Karen to embrace such savagery? If he knew her motive, would he be able to find her? To find Shannon? Was Evie still okay? Were they alive?

The cold. Keep the cold. But the fire and ice were fighting, sizzling, boiling, and he couldn't control it for much longer. He needed time. She wanted Roger punished, but he knew Roger wouldn't admit to anything. Fabrication of evidence? Frame him? He could do that. He could always clear Roger once his family was safe.

But Petrosky. Dragging him into the hell that was heroin…

The drugs were probably tainted. They were going to make him kill his best friend. Make him choose—Petrosky, or Shannon and Evie.

And with Petrosky gone… But why didn't Karen want him to drop the case? To clear her or whoever she was with for their other crimes? Instead, Karen had told him to keep going. Without Petrosky.

She wanted Morrison to find them. *Him.* No one else.

She wanted him there so he could watch Shannon die. So he could watch his child bleed.

She wanted to punish him.

Find the cold. Stay with the logic. Run from the heat.

The heat would kill them all.

He replayed the conversation. The voice wasn't familiar, but she seemed to know him. Had known him back when he was using to escape, when the only thing that made him happy, made him whole, was the needle.

I don't need rumors. I saw you. And she'd used Danny's name. Shannon didn't know about Danny. Not even Petrosky did. But Karen—she'd seemed familiar the first time they'd met, though he hadn't known her before, he could almost swear to it. Then again, the flashes of memory from the night Danny died told him next to nothing. Only that Danny was dead. That it was probably his fault.

Murderer.

He'd always suspected karma meant that mistakes simply repeated until you learned, and he hadn't needed a second chance to avoid repetition of that event. But perhaps karma was vengeful. Like a god. Like a jilted lover.

Think. What else did he know?

He had tried to start over. He'd tried to move on, to be better. To forget. But someone hadn't forgotten Danny, after all this time. Karen hadn't forgotten.

Maybe she'd been biding her time until he had something worth taking.

Evie's wails grew louder inside his head, and Morrison's heart threatened to implode. There was too much pressure in his chest. The world tilted and spun. Shannon and Evie couldn't pay for his mistakes—pay just for knowing him.

Unless that was all bullshit. Pretending to know him. Just part of the game.

You see me, but you don't. But you'll figure it out—you'll remember me. And once you do, you'll know exactly how to find me.

And she'd said Danny's *name.*

The phone on the floorboard buzzed. He shook as he collected it. Dropped it. Turned it over. Text: a picture.

No. Shannon. Fuck. His wife stood with her neck locked in some kind of collar, hands gripping a wooden bar on either side of her head. Shirt, stiff-looking, half of it riding high over her bare breast, the other half slumped to her waist. Blood coated her chin, had dripped down her neck from under the black collar. And her mouth—*oh god.* Ragged black stitches secured her lips together, her beautiful, perfect mouth swollen and angry and mangled and—

No Evie.

The air had disappeared entirely. And below the image, one word.

"Hurry."

Morrison hit his thigh on the wheel at the sudden thud against the driver's side glass. Petrosky's nose touched the window, hands cupped around his eyes as he peered inside. Morrison squinted at the sky, the bruised clouds solid now, the sun higher. How long had he been sitting there, staring into space?

You need to go into rehab, Boss. You need to become...an addict. He needed time. Petrosky would be an easier sell than Roger, but for someone already struggling with addiction, the pull of heroin would be strong. Morrison rolled down the window. For someone whose demons never went away…it would be an invitation to death.

Morrison shook his head, tried to refocus, tried to pull in the cold air that he couldn't taste or smell. He needed to ice the fire in his heart.

Tomorrow.

One way or another, by tomorrow night, this would all be over.

But he couldn't save them. Not like this.

He finally looked at Petrosky's face but couldn't discern individual features, only grainy beige fuzz and a pulsating movement where the boss's mouth should be.

"Nothing else at the center—she was a recluse, according to the staff. Morrison!" Petrosky clapped his hands, and Morrison blinked hard to clear his vision. The old man's brows were knitted together like they'd never come unstuck. *He knows.*

"What the fuck happened?"

How to buy the time he needed? Even if he could locate Karen, or whatever her name was, how could he find her in a day? Morrison swallowed hard, tried to ready himself to answer, but Petrosky was already hurrying around the car and sliding into the passenger side.

"Tell me, right the fuck now."

Morrison handed him the phone, open to Shannon's picture.

Petrosky froze. "They make more demands, or was this in response to Roger still being free?" His jaw was tight, every knuckle white and hard.

"Both." Morrison put the car in gear, certain that the hands gripping the wheel belonged to some other being put there to drive them away. There was no high road to take. This was life and death. Shannon's life. Evie's life. "We need to talk."

Morrison drove them to the edge of the river, where no one could approach without being seen. Few buildings to spy from, and before them, just the endless expanse of water until it butted up against the opposite shore in a haze of gray fog. He parked on the bank.

"So what's—"

Morrison pulled his phone from his pocket and tossed it into the console, then exited the car and headed for the water's edge.

"Morrison?"

No Surfer Boy. No California.

California was dead.

"I—" He'd rehearsed it all the way here. "I need you to check into Breckenridge."

No expression on Petrosky's face.

"Listen, I know you don't like the idea of—"

"I'm clean. Have been since the wedding. You see some fucking sign on my head that says 'user?'"

The air thickened around them until Petrosky's face softened with understanding. "She didn't like that I was at the rehab center, huh? Not that I found anything—no sex offenders, no violent offenses just a few burglary charges. No one that matches our descriptions."

What the hell was Petrosky babbling about? "Boss, they want you out of the way. They want you strung out. I figured maybe if you act the part, we can make it work. I'm just not sure what to do about the drug tests."

Karen probably still had access to the online medical records, so if they started switching up passwords, she'd know something was up. He could try social engineering…calling up there, tricking someone into coughing up their password, but either way, Karen had someone on the inside—someone who'd told her that Petrosky was there asking questions. "If I hacked their system, I could enter a positive drug screen," Morrison said. "But it's a newer system. One wrong move and the whole thing will shut down."

And Karen would know.

Then what next? They were already fondling Shannon, tearing at her clothes, sewing her fucking body parts together, and doing god only knew what to Evie. Had they raped her? Sewn her lips shut like they did to Shannon? He was panting through his nose, and Petrosky's hand on his arm brought him back.

The cold. Find the cold.

"Fucking technology." Petrosky's voice held not a trace of irony, only sad acceptance. "If she has someone on the inside instead of just online access to the medical files, I could sniff them out."

He'd thought the same. But he couldn't figure out a way around the screening tests. "Right, I know you'll find them. But you can't get in for a same-day admission if you're sober."

"Guess I better get un-sober. Liquor store around the corner, right?"

Morrison searched his face, trying to figure out a way around it, but he came up empty—there was no other choice that he could see, and he only had until tomorrow night. *I'm sorry, Boss.* "She…wants you doing more than that." Morrison gestured to the car, and Petrosky followed his gaze. "Glovebox," he said quietly, hoping that the package she'd mentioned wouldn't be there.

But it was. Petrosky returned with an unfamiliar envelope, a jagged construction paper *#1* taped to the cover. It looked like someone had carved it out with a kitchen knife instead of scissors. *Jagged cuts hurt more.*

"I'm number one, eh? Romantic." Petrosky opened it. Powder. A spoon. A syringe. A rubber band, not that the band would do much to assist with isolating a vein. Had she never used herself? And if that was the case…did they really know each other? The spaces in his memory were usually drug-induced voids: places where few, or any, sober people were hidden.

I don't need rumors, I saw you.

You see me, but you don't.

Petrosky opened the bag and poured half of the powder onto the spoon.

"What are you doing?"

"Checking. Don't need it all to get stoned. But if it's dirty, I'd rather know now." He handed Morrison the syringe, and it seemed to vibrate in his hand.

Checking. Not using it. *Checking.* He fought the urge to throw it into the river.

Petrosky pocketed the rest of the powder and pulled out his lighter, and they both watched as the mixture liquefied. Morrison's veins sang with electricity as if the drug were speaking to his cells directly, calling them to it.

"You know we can't get a warrant," Petrosky was saying. "And those fuckers at the center won't give up what we need without it. I might do better figuring this out on the inside anyway."

"Yeah, right." The vibration in Morrison's palm danced through his wrist, up his arm, spreading through his body. Warm. Enticing. Euphoric. Just one little prick, that's all it'd take, and he'd remember. *I don't need rumors, I saw you.* "State-dependent memory" McCallum had called it. He needed to be in the right state of mind to remember Karen. Then he'd be able to find his family.

Petrosky took the syringe from Morrison's hand. "Roger going to help?"

"If he won't, I'll force his hand. We both know he's dirty. There has to be a way to at least get him hauled in for questioning, which should buy us time." But Morrison didn't have enough evidence for that. There had even been an investigation last year, and Roger had come out ahead, all accusations deemed erroneous. But Morrison had to do better—frame him maybe. But that would take time Shannon and Evie didn't have.

"You'll find a way."

He didn't like the way Petrosky put it. *Just me? I'll find a way?* Morrison shook. This was all on him. His balled fists left tingling imprints on his thighs. They had her. Shannon. Shannon's lips. They were torturing her. Torturing his baby. He couldn't breathe.

Petrosky positioned the needle, drew half the liquid into the syringe, and held it up to the light, flicking it with his index finger: clear liquid tinged with brown. "This was your thing, California?"

Yes. "Not anymore, Boss."

"They know you. Knew you then."

"I assume she thought I'd go back, that I'd use again." She knew his weakness—there was a reason she'd chosen smack.

"You'd think she'd realize you wouldn't force this on anyone."

She had to know if she knew anything about him at all. But the more he played her words over in his mind, the more they branded themselves there along with the certainty that she had not been speaking in generalities. She knew something about him. Something he couldn't recall. *Be the same asshole you've always been.*

Morrison forced an inhale through his nose, noticing a slight vinegary tang. The scar at the crook of his thigh pulsed and shuddered. "Either they think I'm a…monster who will do whatever they want," he began slowly, "or they think I won't, and they want a reason to hurt Evie and Shannon…and me by default. To punish me." He ran his hand through his hair, and a few strands clung to his fingers as he pulled his hand away.

"What'd you do, California?"

Everything was hot, tight. "I hurt someone. At least I think I did. But I can't… I'm not sure who this woman is." He needed to remember. He had to find a way to remember, but the hurricane raging in his chest prevented any rational thought as if his abdomen were a vortex where the heat and the pain and the fear had collided with enough force to make his chest cave in.

My turn. No, me! And Danny's head, bloody and gaping to the bone, and the ants, everywhere, on his pants, crawling up his leg—

Cold. Feel the cold. He imagined the breeze off the water singing into his veins, flowing through him and calming the electric peal of panic, the desire for the drug. "If I can figure out where she is—"

"You don't need me to find her."

"I do." He couldn't do this. He didn't even know who she really was. But if he did everything she asked of him, maybe he wouldn't have to find her. *You'll remember me. And once you do, you'll know exactly how to find me.*

"You'll figure it out, Cali. And from the inside, I can help more than I can out here."

"That's not—"

"Decantor's a smart guy, Morrison. And he's on your side. You've got Valentine, too, if you need him. You know he'd do anything for you and Shannon." *Morrison.* The name sounded strange coming from Petrosky's lips, as did the compliments he was paying the other officers. And Morrison knew both Decantor and Valentine would be on the phone with the Feds the moment they found out Shannon and Evie had been kidnapped. Was he trying to tell him they *should* go to the Feds? He didn't need the Feds or Decantor or Valentine. He had a partner. Just not his family.

He gazed out at the water. "There has to be something else we can—"

Petrosky brought the needle up, stabbed it into his thigh, and emptied the syringe.

No.

The needle and the spoon with the remaining drug dropped to the earth.

"Petrosky!"

"You and Decantor will be fine. If the kidnappers want me in rehab, there's something there that I missed. I'll find it. And we'll find her. Now get me back to the car, Surfer Boy." He took a step and stumbled, one arm shooting out to steady himself as if his legs were turning to jelly, though it might have been a muscle spasm after the needle stick. Still better than the vein—shooting into the muscle tissue gave a more mellow buzz, less chance of overdosing. Had Petrosky known that when he'd shoved the needle into his thigh? He shook off the thought that Petrosky's addictions might be deeper and more varied than he'd realized. His boss was an addict, but there was nothing like heroin. *Nothing.* And Petrosky had many demons to silence.

Please let him make it. Morrison put his hand on Petrosky's arm, leading him, hoping he wouldn't have to carry him. Hoping Petrosky's heart wouldn't give out. Hoping—

"Aw, fuck." Petrosky reached the car and slumped against the door. "Get me to Breckenridge."

THE RECEPTIONIST'S eyes widened in surprise when Morrison walked into the rehab center, supporting Petrosky under the arm. Twenty minutes in and Petrosky was fully under heroin's spell, head lolling as if he'd been reduced to a sack of skin, his essence sucked from his marrow. A shadow of himself.

Another woman came out to take their basic information. Petrosky leaned heavily on the counter and gawked at her and the receptionist, who tapped diligently on her keyboard while Petrosky muttered half coherent responses.

The computer. Was the receptionist in on this? Was she the one who'd called Karen the moment they'd headed back with the HR director? Her squinty eyes danced over her screen. The boil on her lip was no longer as innocuous as it had been earlier—it stared at him like a third and horribly misshapen eyeball.

Petrosky listed Morrison as his emergency contact. Though Morrison had been the one to put him here in the first place.

Then there were no more questions. Orderlies, slim but strong, emerged through the door and took Petrosky's fleshy arms, one on either side. Neither looked suspicious with their sympathetic smiles, but smiles hid a great deal. He knew that all too well.

The younger, blonder one nodded to Morrison. "We'll take good care of him, sir," he said as he hooked his palm under Petrosky's elbow.

Petrosky tried to shrug them off, but as they started for the metal doors, he stumbled, and then the three men were heading back whether Petrosky was ready or not.

At the double doors, Petrosky turned and looked at Morrison one last time, eyes unfocused but wet. "Get 'em, Cali."

He had no choice. There was no time. Morrison walked away, convinced he'd just left his best friend in the care of a murderer.

31

THE DRIVE back to the precinct was unnaturally silent but blessedly short. Morrison headed through the bullpen and found Decantor at his desk, nose in a file, cell by his palm on the desktop. He looked up and grinned as Morrison approached.

"Hey, man! Glad you found Shannon! Women, huh?" He shook his head.

Morrison opened his mouth in shock. *Right.* They'd told Decantor that Alex had picked Shannon up—that she was safe. "Yeah. That was something else." He tried not to envision her in the collar; mouth sewed up like Frankenstein's monster. He rubbed at his temple hard enough to chafe the skin as he tried to push the images from his brain.

"Where's Petrosky? He finally take a Saturday off?"

It's Saturday? Morrison cleared his throat. "No. Just out looking into a few things."

Decantor cocked an eyebrow like he knew Morrison was lying. But there was no logical reason for the man to believe his suspicion was true, and as expected, Decantor's face softened. "Want to brainstorm in a few, then? Or should we wait for Petrosky to get back?"

No time. They'd taken his family. They'd taken his partner. Decantor didn't have what he needed anyway—it was locked in his head, hidden by sobriety. *You'll find a way.* And when

Morrison found these fuckers…he wasn't going to bring them in. He'd get his family back, and Karen and her fucked-up partners would die. "We'll wait for Petrosky," he said.

Again with the eyebrow, but Decantor recovered faster this time. "Sure. Just let me know when he gets here." He stood. "I need to grab a few sheets off the press."

"Sounds good. I'll be at my desk looking over your notes." As Decantor walked away, Morrison slid Decantor's phone off the desk, clicked it to vibrate, and dropped it into his pocket.

⸻

THERE WAS little new information in Decantor's case files, and the notes Petrosky had taken at the rehab center earlier didn't give Morrison anything he could use to jog his memory.

Once you remember, you'll know where to find me.

But he couldn't remember. He'd never remember if McCallum was right about the state-dependent memory. If he knew her when he was high, the memory was gone—while he was sober.

The woman who'd kidnapped Shannon had known Danny personally, maybe intimately. And though Morrison hadn't known everyone Danny had been with, she'd been insistent that he should remember her. They'd met. He'd thought hers might have been one of the disembodied voices he heard when he slept, keening to him from the night Danny died—*Me. No, me!*—but with the rubber band, he wasn't sure she'd ever been a druggie waiting for her turn. Maybe she'd been there in some other capacity the night Danny died. Maybe not. None of it helped him unless he got stoned, and his partner was already high enough for the both of them. Morrison couldn't afford to fuck it up. He couldn't take a chance on the needle.

I can't afford not to.

Something the kidnapper had said was irritating his brain. Something about…women like Shannon weakening fast. And the original Karen Palmer had killed herself—had she been driven to suicide? Or had she been murdered?

Who are you?

He'd start with the name she'd taken.

Karen Palmer, the real Karen Palmer, had been born to Hillary and Sherman Palmer. Her mother was easy to locate: address in upstate New York, listed phone number. According to her Facebook page, she headed an anti-bullying organization and was involved in another group dedicated to suicide prevention. On their own, either organization might not have struck him as profound—but together, they invoked the image of a harassed child, driven to escape the cruelty of the world by her own hand.

He put Decantor's phone to his ear.

"Hello, you've reached Hillary." Her voice was high, lilting, not weighed down by grief as he'd expected it to be. Not like Petrosky's. Maybe Petrosky had always sounded like that. "I can't come to the phone right now…"

He waited for the greeting to finish and left his name and credentials along with Decantor's number, and re-pocketed the phone.

Karen or whatever her real name was—she'd had a long time to plan. To disappear. She was calculating, too, like the psychopathic stab-fanatic who had brought a murder weapon to the Acosta scene and stalked and butchered Natalie Bell. But the pedophile who had raped Acosta and Reynolds was sloppier, leaving his DNA all over the place—and it was a lonely world for pedophiles. Decantor was chasing down leads on Bell. Petrosky was on the lookout at the rehab center. *Acosta.* Find the boy's rapist, he'd find his wife.

Morrison logged into the chat rooms one more time, scouring for clown-obsessed pedos, pedos discussing how to incapacitate their "lovers"—*victims*—particularly references to T-shirts or the woods or the *#1.* Though Reynolds had not received that brand, Acosta and Bell and Petrosky's drugs all had. Nothing. He dug deeper. Some websites were encrypted, and others needed passwords, but Morrison was better than that. Ten minutes to hack into one. Four to hack into another, twenty minutes the third. And as he read through each, the dread in his belly grew.

"The kid loves me, I know it…"
"I took him to a ball game…"
"Her parents seem upset, but we're in love. They of all people should understand that."

Morrison's breathing echoed long and loud in his ears, yogic breathing, the only way he was able to keep his shit together. He tried to tell himself that these sick bastards were not the ones holding his family prisoner, but it didn't help, not enough. The vein in his thigh throbbed once, and Morrison flashed to Petrosky on the shore, stabbing the needle into his leg, and he didn't feel guilt, didn't feel anger, just the searing burn of jealousy. His thigh. The one place no one ever thought to look. And they wouldn't start looking now.

He shifted his weight, letting his pants rub against that forever-tender spot in his leg. In the oblivion, he'd find his family. And if he didn't find them in time, he'd release himself into the oblivion, heaven or hell on the needle; it didn't really matter so long as he didn't have to consider the world without his family in it. Without Shannon. Without Evie.

He was almost panting now, the dizziness pulling at him, tunneling his vision until he sucked in a thick burst of oxygen. The agitation lessened. And then, there on the computer screen, large as life: The Juggler. Morrison's breath caught. Lots of child abusers. Fewer with a penchant for cult bands and bloody clowns. But with that name…

He scoured The Juggler's pages, poring over chatrooms, conversations.

"He was so sweet. I really think God made them adorable to tempt us—and that's not a bad thing. Even the priests get away with it. They know these boys were meant to be loved."

Translation: "I'm entitled to rape. It's their fault for being appealing." Morrison pictured Evie's beautiful little face and covered his retching with a choked grunt. Decantor turned and looked across the room. Morrison swallowed hard and went back to the computer.

He clicked on the bar to message users privately, picturing the man on the receiving end: scraggly hair, sneering at the screen, Shannon locked up in the background, lips mangled and swollen and bloody. He paused, his trembling fingers poised over the keys.

Finally, he typed:

"The jugglers were always my favorite at the circus."

Morrison consulted the song lyrics from his desk drawer and finished:

"Don't get under those knives, motherfucker."

He hit send.

Somewhere, a phone rang. Morrison jumped, touched his pocket where Decantor's phone rested—it wasn't buzzing. Nor was his own cell. The words on the computer screen were hypnotic, pulling his attention from all else.

He searched through more of The Juggler's pages, looking for IP addresses or anything else he could use to track him. But The Juggler was well protected. Firewalls. Encryptions. Rerouting mechanisms. This asshole wasn't living in Kazakhstan, that was for damn sure—he was craftier than Morrison had given him credit for. Even his profile picture gave nothing away: a mask like one from a Mardi Gras parade, white, porcelain maybe, with black checks around the eyes and fangs, much like the clown face on the cover of one of the CDs he'd seen. In one thread The Juggler had bragged:

"Made it myself."

The bag that Xu had mentioned seeing the guy handing off… had he made a mask for a friend and taken it to him? Morrison tried not to picture that hideous mask. He didn't want to imagine that mask being the last thing his daughter saw before she was stomped to death.

Focus on the clues. Find them.

Morrison went back to the private message screen and typed:

"Also, I love your profile picture. Do you make masks for other
people, too? If so, I'd love to buy one."

Cold. Find the cold. Too forward? Would he scare the guy
off? He squinted at the computer, willing a response. Nothing.
The words ran together on the page, swimming, then solidifying, wooziness pulling at him the more he stared. *I can't stop until
I find her. I'll never stop.*

And these bastards wanted to be found, didn't they? Karen
did, anyway. *Work your cases. You'll know where to find me.* That's
what she'd said. So Morrison was supposed to find them. He'd
be walking into an ambush, but he had no alternative.

Find him. Find them. Think, Surfer Boy.

Somewhere nearby, a phone rang again. Morrison eyed the
phone on his desk, patted his pockets. Not his. He rubbed his
eyes with his palms. He needed coffee. *No.*

He needed heroin.

One little prick and he'd finally remember how he knew
Karen. But it was an excuse. Or was it? He could stop again—
he'd done it before. And no one would ever have to know.

But Shannon's voice pealed through his head: "Evie needs
you. I need you." Could he do that high? *Yes,* the drug whispered.
No, he whispered back, less convincingly, his veins practically
trembling with the memory of the drug, craving it, begging
for it.

He was losing his mind. The phone rang again, and he looked
up. The phone. Petrosky's phone. He leapt from his seat, stumbled over Petrosky's chair, and threw the receiver to his ear.

"Detective Petrosky?" Music blared in the background over
the voice, a male voice, gruff and thick with what might have
been liquor.

"This is Detective Morrison. How can I help you?"

"This is Zach."

Zachary Reynolds. The Juggler's first victim that they knew
of and a connection to the kidnappers. A connection to his
little girl, to his wife. Morrison sat at Petrosky's desk and
opened the top drawer, rummaging for a pen and something to
write on. He snapped open the drawer on the other side and

found a nub of a pencil. No paper. "What can I do for you, Zach?"

"I found something. Or…maybe. I mean, I don't know if it's something, but Detective Petrosky asked me about that number."

"The number one." Morrison pulled a fast food bag from the first drawer and turned it inside out, throwing an old french fry to the floor and crushing it underfoot as if it were The Juggler he was stomping to death. The way Acosta had been stomped to death.

There was a sharp inhale on the line like the kid was smoking, and Morrison gritted his teeth against the pause, every synapse in his brain firing with impatience.

"Got this box in the closet. Shit I wanted to forget about. The scans and pictures of me in the hospital bed." Cancer. The kid had beat fucking *cancer* only to be raped and strangled. Some luck.

Another inhale on the line, this one longer, sharper. "Had some toys in there, things I forgot about. Cards and little teddy bears and shit. But one of them was this little brown bear with a Get Well Soon balloon sewed to his chest."

Morrison's nub of a pencil trembled over the bag.

"The balloon says 'You're number one.'"

Probably commercially produced, but… *Too much coincidence.* Morrison's heart palpitated, growing bigger with each beat, but his rib cage squeezed tighter and tighter around his lungs. "Zach, do you remember who gave it to you?"

This time the exhale was hard, as hard as if he were blowing up a balloon. "I don't know. I was out of it."

Morrison's stomach dropped. "Would your mom know?"

The music changed, and the bass vibrated through Morrison's hand and up to his elbow, rattling his already frayed nerves.

"Nah, she wasn't there all the time."

"Wasn't where?"

"At the hospital. Where I got it." Zach's voice was vaguely defensive.

Shit. He'd missed it. Hadn't Dylan Acosta's mother

mentioned him being in the hospital, too? If that was how their pedophile was choosing his victims, grooming the kids while they were sick and vulnerable… "Emerald Grace, right?"

"Yeah." The music stopped so abruptly that Morrison felt he'd been pulled into an alternate universe where the world was wrapped in cotton. "You think I'll go back?" Zach said, his voice so low that Morrison had to strain to hear him.

"Back to the hospital?"

Zach was silent on the other end. Then: "I'm just tired of being scared." The line went dead, and the pressure in Morrison's chest erupted with heat. The kid was going to fucking kill himself.

32

STRINGS of multicolored Christmas lights and the finger paintings strung from the hospital walls did little to mask the scent of rubbing alcohol and some kind of lemon cleaning fluid. Morrison kept his eyes on the center of the corridor, footsteps echoing back to him in time to his heart. Both too fast. At least a phone call had verified that Zachary Reynolds was not in immediate danger from himself or otherwise: his mother was home with him, and he was most certainly fine—physically, anyway.

The halls in the children's ward were empty. Maybe morning rounds. He peered into the nearest room at a little black-haired child, scrawny body wasting away under a thin sheet. Air hissed through a tube into a cannula held under his nostrils by a piece of clear tape. At the kid's bedside, his mother slept, face planted into the foot of the bed, one hand on the child's leg. Connected.

Shannon was stuck in a collar. And Evie was alone.

The next kid was just as asleep as the first, the gentle glow from a light in the corner glistening on her bald head. Maybe the stabby killer worked here and shaved his head as a way to connect with the kids. A doctor maybe. A nurse. An orderly. Or maybe their rapist had shaved his scraggly hair, which is why no one recognized him now.

"Can I help you?" A young nurse with butterfly-print scrubs and an afro approached him: L. Freeman, according to her name tag. "Visiting hours don't start until ten, but if you want to wait in the cafeteria downstairs for fifteen minutes—"

He flashed his badge. "I'm not visiting. Looking for information."

Surprise registered in her eyes. "On who?" she whispered. "Are you family?"

Zachary Reynolds had been there too long ago for most current staff to remember any pertinent details. But Acosta—they might get lucky. If he could get her to cooperate. "I'm looking for a killer."

Her mouth fell open. She closed it again.

"Dylan Acosta was a patient here a year ago. Did you know him?"

She crooked a finger, and he followed her to the main desk where another nurse—short, thin, brunette—was bustling around with files. Morrison startled when a buzzer sounded, and the other nurse glanced at him, then rushed off to attend to it. Freeman watched her go.

"I...saw on the news what happened to Dylan. Killed at school, right? Just horrible." Her voice shook with emotion. She *had* known him.

"I need to know who he would have been in contact with," Morrison said, as softly as he could manage. "His doctors. Staff who had access to him."

She shook her head, crossed her arms—preparing for battle. "I'm sorry, I can't give that kind of information out. I'm not even supposed to tell you if he was a patient here."

She was right. But he didn't have time to waste on a warrant or on a fucking release from Dylan's mother. So why the hell was he here? He could get all the information he needed on the doctors just by looking at the hospital website. Same for the nursing staff. Maybe if he hacked into the database—but no, hospital websites were notoriously tricky. One wrong move and he'd shut the whole thing down. He didn't want to give the killers a chance to sew any more of Shannon together or carve her up like they did to Bell.

"But..." the nurse began, glancing over her shoulder, "if you can give me a date, I can tell you who was on duty without discussing individual patients." She punched a few buttons and looked at him expectantly.

He opened his mouth to talk. He had no idea. But it wouldn't have been just one day. It would have been multiple days. Acosta and Reynolds had been admitted with cancer, not broken bones.

"Dylan Acosta was here for a few weeks." And in that time… had the pedophile given him a gift? Like he had with Zachary Reynolds? Other parts of The Juggler's pattern had remained consistent over time. "Specifically, ma'am, I'm looking for someone who gave Dylan a toy. A teddy bear, maybe."

"A teddy bear? Sounds pretty common. They sell them in the gift shop downstairs."

"Outside of parents, are there staff members who sometimes give toys to the kids?"

She squinted at him. "Sometimes? Most of the kids need a little distraction, so that wouldn't be out of the question."

"Anyone who does it routinely?"

She shook her head.

"What about someone who takes a special interest in certain children? In Dylan?"

She studied the ceiling, the wall, then her eyes widened, and Morrison's heart picked up. *She's got something.*

"Actually…nothing out of the ordinary, mind you. But we have people who come in to cheer the kids up, and those are the ones whose job it is to distract, to play. To take an interest. It's not that we don't, but we can't always take the time to play as much as we'd like."

"No one's accusing you of being inattentive."

Her shoulders relaxed, but her mouth stayed tight. "The people I'm thinking of are volunteers from a company called Winning with Grinning. Incredibly nice, all of them. So kind to the kids."

"How often do they come?"

"Once a week. Usually Mondays. Sometimes they do puppet shows here in front of the reception desk…or magic. And they always bring something for the kids who're here—books or toys or games."

These people wouldn't be protected by HIPAA—they weren't

patients. He had every right to their files. "Do you have records for the group? Names, addresses?"

She nodded slowly. "They would in HR. Anyone who has contact with our patients has to have a file. Background checks, vaccine records, all that. Especially with how ill some of our kids are."

Morrison glanced at the clock on the wall, ticking away precious seconds of his family's life. Felt the file under his arm. He'd almost forgotten.

He pulled out the photos and composite drawings and handed them to Freeman. "Any of these guys look familiar?"

She frowned at the bald man and shook her head. But slowly. "Are you certain?"

"I'm… No. There's something familiar about him, but I can't place where I know him from. Maybe he was here visiting someone? But we get lots of people in and out. He definitely wasn't here regularly." Freeman flipped to the second photo, the scraggly brown hair, squirrelly face, and her eyes lit up. "This one, I know. He's here like clockwork. Missed this Monday, though."

Because he was busy behind Dylan's school—he was busy raping an innocent child.

She shook her head again. "But you can't possibly be looking for him. He's amazing. So sweet and always makes everyone laugh." She beckoned him around the counter and over to a back wall with a bulletin board covered with photos. In one, a guy in dreadlocks and a magician's hat held up a deck of playing cards, his face every bit as animated as the children who sat in a circle around him. In another, a woman had a puppet on each hand, mouth open, apparently talking in what looked like a silly voice for the green caterpillar on her right fist.

And…*him*. Morrison's heart skipped a beat.

He was cleaner than he'd been in Jenny's rendition of him, and his thin brown hair was covered with a yellow wig, though a few strands had come loose and were plastered to his cheek. His light eyes were just the right shape. His mouth. But in this photo, his squirrelly nose was covered with a red foam ball.

The Juggler was an actual clown.

33

AN HOUR AND A HALF LATER, Morrison had a photocopy of a driver's license with Michael Hayes's face on it—a face that looked like their suspect. And Hayes was here. In the city. With Shannon. With Evie.

According to the volunteer records pulled by the harried head of HR, Hayes worked full-time at a plant that manufactured nuts and bolts for the auto industry. More telling was Hayes's website: Paraphernalia for Performers, which offered custom masks, shoes, boots, and even puppets, all made to order. Looks like they could guess what he was bringing to his buddy outside of Xu's nail shop. He'd been married and divorced in the same year about four years ago—maybe his ex-wife had discovered his little fetish. His sickness. He'd look for her too, just in case. But later.

Now he drove.

Every traffic light seemed to take extra long, and he flipped on his flashing red and blues and shot through the intersections in a blaze of angry horns despite the police lights.

Fuck them. Fuck everyone. When he found the kidnappers, he would stomp them to death with their own fucking boots.

Michael Hayes's neighborhood was good, not great, with smooth asphalt and adequate streetlights but noise pollution from the nearby freeway. The house was just another two-story colonial on a block with a hundred nearly identical colonials, but The Juggler's house was somehow more formidable than the rest, despite its white aluminum siding, brown shutters, and curtained bay window. It was the basketball hoop—probably there to tempt neighborhood children onto the property—that seemed to buzz with the energy of a thousand angry hornets. On the backboard was a painting of a clown, its fangs dripping green venom into a puddle just below the ring.

How many kids had Hayes taken? How many had he raped? Killed? Morrison glanced up and down the street as he drove by, but no one was out besides the brilliant midday sun searing the new growth on the lawns. His chest tightened. At Hayes's home, the grass was newly cut, though not edged. Bushes grew too tall against the house, but the sides had been trimmed back from the walk. Someone lived here. He looked again at the backboard clown. The Juggler lived here.

Morrison drove by the house twice, then parked in a neighbor's driveway where four newspapers sat piled on the porch. They were probably on vacation. He shut the car off and got out, then climbed into the back seat, so he could watch, hidden partially by the headrest and the shadow of the carport, looking for...what? He tamped down thoughts of the blood on Shannon's seat back. Her head. And then her mouth... *Oh, fuck, stop thinking.* He breathed in the cold, let it take the fire from his belly.

Karen had taken her time kidnapping his wife—she was patient. Calculating. It had been a year since her first attempt to harm Shannon during that bullshit with Griffen. And Karen was smart enough not to hold Shannon here, in the middle of suburbia, with a highly visible creepy clown in the driveway.

He shouldn't be here. This wasn't the place. His wife, his child...they were somewhere else. Had to be.

But he couldn't stop himself. He was being pulled by something deep and wild—the house called to him. And while Shannon might not be here, he'd get The Juggler—Michael Hayes—to tell him where she was. Unless...Hayes was with Karen, with Shannon, in another location. A storage facility. A warehouse. He'd never find them then.

But someone had cut the grass recently—if it had been a lawn service, they would have completed the edging too. Someone *lived* here. With another glance down the road, Morrison exited the car and crossed the street. The air was still heavy and wet with yesterday's storms. Had that been only yesterday? It seemed like an eternity had passed.

He hooked around the garage and pressed his body flush against the wall, creeping slowly past two garbage cans to the back of the property. The stink of rotting trash singed his nostrils. When was trash pickup? He wished he could see inside the garage, to know whether the car registered to Hayes was here. He'd find out soon enough.

Behind the cans, he scaled a chain-link fence and crossed a concrete patio to the first window. No noises came from inside —no scuffle of a shoe, and though he held his breath, he heard no cry that might have been Evie. Stomach twisting, he scanned the bottom of the building, seeking glass block windows, a vent, anything to indicate a basement. Nothing but a slab foundation. His family wasn't being held below.

Slowly, Morrison leaned his forehead against the glass and peered inside. He was looking into a laundry room, dim with drawn blinds. Plenty of grime on the window, but from what he could see through a gap near the sill, the room was empty. He strained his ears, squinted up at the second story. There'd be a couple of bedrooms up there, maybe a bath. But when he stepped back, he saw that the windows were open, just like those in front, curtains swaying softly in the warm breeze that was rotting the garbage. *They're not here.* It would be too easy to overhear the wails of a starving baby, the muffled screams of a woman having her mouth sewn—he retched, swallowed. No one would use this place as a dungeon.

He crept across the concrete, thankful for his stealthy Toms. On the other side of the patio, he could see into the kitchen, lit by the sun, see the bowl on the countertop, fruit flies and fat houseflies buzzing around something on a cutting board. Something…wet. Dark. *Please let it be animal meat.* Bile rose in his throat, and Morrison visualized the cold coming back in before the panic pulled him from what he needed to do.

He ducked under the window and around to the last section of the house, where the home protruded farther over the concrete. A glass door opened onto the patio, blue light flickering from a television inside. There were no other lights on inside that he could see. He peered around the corner, hearing only silence, and crept closer to the glass door. With one final inhale, he peeked into the living room and—

The phone in his pocket buzzed suddenly, and he snapped his head back so quickly he was certain that the sound of his temple cracking against the brick would rouse the man from the couch.

A mere six feet away. Michael Hayes. He looked exactly like Jenny, the tattoo artist, had drawn him.

Plan. You need a plan.

Making as little noise as possible, Morrison flew back along the patio on his tiptoes, then leapt the fence and ran around the garage to his car. They had cameras on this place. They knew he was there. Hayes's friends were killing his family now, were calling to tell him his family was dead.

The cell buzzed a third time.

But no, it was Decantor's phone, the caller ID blinking with a New York number. The phone Morrison had taken so anyone watching his cell would not know he'd contacted Karen Palmer's mother. He slammed the car into drive, trying desperately not to squeal the tires or call any attention to himself before he had a chance to think. He'd found the bastard. He'd go back to Hayes's while the man still lay on the couch. If he could do it without anyone knowing he was there, he wouldn't risk his family's life. He'd search to make sure the other suspects weren't there with Hayes, then look through cupboards, drawers, closets for clues to his family's whereabouts.

But if he found nothing, he'd need a bargaining chip. Could Roger help? It was the only card he had left to play, the only other thing she'd asked him for.

The phone. "Detective Morrison." He turned down another side street and headed toward the main drag where he could blend in with the other motorists.

"Yes, my name is Hilary Palmer, and I received a message from you earlier. Something about an identity theft case?"

"Thank you for calling back, Mrs. Palmer." *Don't sugar coat it. No time.* "I'm sure this seems a bit out of the blue, but I'm working on a homicide that seems to be linked to your daughter's identity."

Silence.

"Mrs. Palmer?"

"My Karen?"

"The woman I'm looking for is using your daughter's name. Has been for a few years. I believe she stole your daughter's identity after she died."

The silence stretched, amplifying the sounds around him. A car backfired somewhere up ahead, behind the shrill squawk of a bird. Had she hung up?

"I know who took her identity."

Morrison's hand cramped around the receiver. "Who?"

"Do you know why I got involved with Moms Against Bullying?" Her voice was cold, harder than before—and there was the longing, the grief that he heard every day in Petrosky's hello, in the way his partner asked about lunch. Palmer wasn't hiding it now, not like she was on her voice-mail recording.

Tell me who! He stopped at a red light and put on his blinker, looking for a parking lot where he could pull over inconspicuously. "No, ma'am, I don't know why you got involved with them." And it occurred to him that he should have known. He should have dug deeper. Which meant he'd missed something critical. *You see me, but you don't.* The light changed, and Morrison put his foot on the gas, resisting the urge to tell her to hurry up. To hurry because something terrible could be happening to *his* child right now.

"Karen was such a happy child," she said. "She played in the band, worked after school, had friends. Her best friend, though…she was something else. Got her involved in little petty trouble. I got a call one day that they'd been shoplifting. *Shoplifting.* Karen said Janey wanted to see if they could get away with it."

Janey. The name pinged a little memory somewhere in

Morrison's subconscious, but he couldn't place it. His brain was scrambled. *Think, or you might as well let them die.*

"Janey what?"

"Krantz."

His heart hammered against his ribs. Danny's last name. But Danny didn't have a sister, and she was too old to have come around after the fact. A niece? Cousin?

Palmer coughed, and it was a phlegmy sound as if she was swallowing tears, but when she spoke again, her voice was harder—angry. "I tried to keep them apart, but they gravitated toward one another. And then they started college. My husband and I were moving to New York, so Karen decided to come, go to college there. Janey stayed back in California. I thought that'd be the end of it."

The cell buzzed in his pants pocket, and it took him a moment to register that he had Decantor's phone in his hand already. His own cell phone was ringing. No…not a call. A text. *Shit.*

Palmer blew her nose. "Karen had a hard time; depression, anxiety, you name it. Then Janey cut her wrists, ended up in the hospital. And it seemed like"—her voice hitched—"like Karen blamed herself. After Karen died, I found messages from Janey to Karen. Awful things. A few little knocks here and there, but later, the texts were blatantly aggressive, encouraging her to hurt herself. And she listened. Karen took sleeping pills, but she never made it to the hospital like Janey did."

The phone buzzed again—*oh, fuck*—and he tried to grab it out, but the blare of a car horn made him swerve back into his lane. He fumbled his cell to the floor. *Fuck, fuck, fuck.* What if it was Shannon? Or the kidnapper? But this woman was telling him about the kidnapper. Palmer might hold the clue he needed to find her, to find his family.

"I tried to file charges against Janey," Palmer was saying, "but bullying isn't really a crime." She sniffed. "Janey should have to pay for what she did."

So what was he dealing with? Psychopaths didn't usually try to kill themselves—they didn't feel enough pain to merit escape. Narcissists didn't often commit suicide either; if a narcissist made a threat or slashed their wrists, it was probably to manipulate someone else, not because they truly wanted to die. But Karen—Janey—wanted him to suffer because Morrison had hurt someone she'd cared about. Narcissists might pretend to care, but they typically lacked the empathy for any meaningful bond to form. But this Janey woman—she felt. She felt everything too deeply.

Janey had manipulated people in the past, driven them to the edge, and pushed them off. And if she had emotionally tortured Karen from the opposite side of the continent, what was she doing to Shannon, right now? She knew how long it took to weaken people. How long it would take her to weaken Shannon.

Ahead, a driveway approached, a dry cleaners. He put on his blinker, resisting the urge to blare the horn at the driver in front of him. Shannon didn't deserve this pain. Evie didn't deserve to lose her mother. Evie didn't deserve to die.

But then again, neither had Danny. And Janey wanted to avenge his death. For years, the madness must have grown, festering like his dreams until she'd embraced the ferocity inside her, birthing cruelty and aggression until there was nothing left but revenge. She'd found Morrison, stalked him, taken her time planning her attack. She'd convinced Griffen to channel his rage into Shannon, into Morrison, to destroy their lives. And when Griffen failed to do it…

Now Janey had sought out men who really were capable of murder. Men who hurt others for the fun of it. And she'd turned these maniacs loose on his wife. She'd had them take his baby. His hand, wet with sweat, slipped, and he gripped the wheel so hard his knuckles ached. If he burst into Hayes's house, gun drawn, and hauled the man out—Janey would surely have a contingency plan. She'd take it out on his girls. He needed to find where they were before he—

"Detective?" Palmer's voice was tight, worried, but he couldn't find a way to respond. He screeched into a parking lot, slammed the car into park, and scrambled for the phone.

Text message:

"Roger's gone, or she's gone. You want them back, you do it tonight."

And below it a photo.

Oh, god, no.

Evie's onesie. Torn in half. Streaks of red covering the arm, the side, the neckline. Blood? They were going to kill his baby. Maybe she was already halfway there, the life ebbing from her drop by drop.

He felt it then, a swelling in his belly, the blistering fire that he'd hidden, the one he'd tried to keep dulled with drugs, the one he'd stomped out again and again and again since the day they'd found his father dead, shot by some asshole who just wanted the store register. The beast was waking up. But he had to keep going. Pretending. Pretending to be normal. Pretending he wasn't carrying a monster within him.

He needed more time. He needed to go see Roger.

"Detective?"

He hung up the phone.

Arrest him...or kill him. Janey didn't care, and as Shannon's bloodied mouth flashed in his mind's eye, as Evie's wails of pain lit up his eardrums, neither did he. *Work your cases.* She wanted to put him in an impossible position. Needing to fix it and being unable to do a fucking thing. He'd felt that same sense of help-lessness too, so many years ago, staring down at Danny's lifeless, broken body. And so had she.

But she would feel helpless again when he watched her bleed.

He would kill Karen, Janey, whatever the fuck her name was. And so help him, if they'd hurt his family, not a one of them would get out alive.

"I BECAME INSANE WITH LONG INTERVALS OF HORRIBLE SANITY."
~EDGAR ALLAN POE TO GEORGE W. EVELETH, JANUARY 4, 1848

34

JANEY DOWNED the rest of her wine and sank into the bathwater, listening to the footfalls in the next room, the telltale clack of the boots Adam always wore. The water suddenly felt too warm as if she were heating it with her fury.

The rage never went away, not anymore. She inhaled the scent of soap, trying to ground herself in the moment, but her back stayed rigid. *Fuck.* Danny had been perfect—the only one who'd ever understood her. He might as well have been her brother the way he patted her hand when something inside her snapped out of nowhere, and all the feelings burbled angrily to the surface like froth, seeking escape. And the depression that would follow those episodes, the ugly hole that would open inside her—every time, she saw it coming, knew it was coming, yet still couldn't avoid falling into the darkness. And he would just sit. Hold her hand. He was the only thing in her life worth clinging to.

And Curt had taken Danny from her.

Danny had said they were family, and his shining eyes had made her believe it. But the others—those who had loved Danny too—grieved him and ignored her, ostracized her, even. Everywhere she turned were such hateful people, trying to hurt her in one way or another. They said she was crazy. That she was broken. They left Danny's photos lying around just to taunt her, to make her cry.

And worse, they blamed her—for not acting sooner, for not calling an ambulance, for lying down beside his cooling body and falling asleep. It wouldn't have mattered. They hadn't seen his face. His blue lips. His body, broken on the floor of his bedroom, a few stray ants from the shattered tank still struggling in his blood. They hadn't seen the congealing gore clinging to the corner of the end table.

She had tried to become someone else so many times, altering every little snippet of her personality, every little quirk, convinced each was the cause of her misery—and every time, Danny held her hand when she realized she'd been wrong. Again. If Danny had lived, she'd have found peace by now, surely. She'd have been a better person. The day her last husband left her, she had decided: Curt had destroyed what she could have become by taking away her lifeline. Now he would pay.

She had moved to Ash Park. Gotten a job. And watched. Waited. Once, while following him, she'd come face to face with him in the grocery store, and there had not been even a flicker of recognition. He'd forgotten her, discarded her as completely as if she were a piece of trash. He'd destroyed her life and didn't even remember her. How it had stung.

But now he'd never forget—not as he had before when she was just Janey, useless to him, not even worth remembering. Now she had something of his that was just as dear to him as Danny had been to her. And now she had help, help more reliable than the insufferable Frank Griffen.

Somewhere in the other room, something shattered, and her heart rate climbed. Adam hadn't once tried to hurt her, but she'd seen signs of his rage simmering below the surface, seen the way he became silent and still when she tried to tell him how to do something, the way he froze and averted his eyes when she said anything, *anything* he didn't agree with.

She tried to make it up to him on those black sheets, but he closed his eyes there too—couldn't even get hard. The day he'd sewn Shannon's lips shut was the first time he'd actually responded to her sexual advances, stayed with her, looked at her when he came. Better than what Roger had done—he'd whispered Shannon's name once while they were fucking. Even if Curt had ended up marrying someone else, she would have killed Shannon anyway.

She rolled onto her side and submerged her face in the water, feeling the pressure of the liquid as her ears filled, the water muting the sounds in the house. Bubbles escaped from her mouth and crawled along her skin toward the water's surface like fingers tracing a path from her lips to her ear where the bubble burst above water.

Her lips. Blessedly untouched by a needle. But she had other scars, and her lover liked them. His eyes had lit up the day her sleeve had hiked a touch too high, and he'd seen the butterfly bandage on her wrist, though he hadn't said a thing. He'd been too timid.

He'd gotten over that, it seemed. She'd wanted help hurting Curtis Morrison, but he might no longer be there for the sole purpose of meeting her needs. He might be there for the blood. And if that were true, she would never be able to control him. And she didn't want to bear the brunt when the last of his anxiety melted, and the hostility in his eyes was stoked into an inferno.

He'd told her he had an errand Monday morning, that he was going to the store to get coffee. When she came home that evening, his boots had been in the bathtub, covered in mud. And there'd been no coffee. Just the newspaper the next day, the boy at the playground, found dead. But it didn't make any sense. The kid had nothing to do with her or with their goals, and the paper said they were looking for two killers—she didn't know anything about another guy. Was Adam working with someone else too? Or did he...like boys? Was his lack of sexual interest in her because he was a pedophile?

She couldn't even consider it. That wasn't in the plan.

Then there was the girl he'd told her about, whispered it like a confession while he picked at her lower back with his fingernails. Said he did it for her, but she didn't know the woman, only that he'd followed her home from Curt's. He'd insisted they needed the phone to punish Curt more, mess with him. And

Adam had looked so...concerned, practically begging for approval with those big puppy dog eyes. But she knew his motives were deeper than wanting to help her. The night after he'd killed that girl, she'd heard him moaning while he dreamed.

Had Adam fucked her? Rage simmered in her belly. She'd kill him if he had.

The mask stared at her from its stand on the sink, and her heart quickened. He'd told her it was a symbol of status, an updated replica of a doctor's mask that had been used during the black plague. But when he wore it, it was as if he became someone else. Without it, he chewed his fingernails. He couldn't meet her eyes. As soon as it was strapped onto his face, he stood straighter, as if the mask made him feel different, made him feel worthy.

Made him feel strong.

35

THEY HADN'T COME BACK, not once since they snapped her photo. Karen smiling over the smartphone screen, the beaked man—gone. Evie, gone. And Shannon felt herself creeping ever more quickly toward the brink of madness.

She could not hear her baby. She could not feel her baby. But she *could* feel. God, how she wished she couldn't.

Her lips throbbed, hot and painful with every beat of her heart, each pulse bringing with it the sweet, putrid stink of coming infection—though that might have been her imagination. Her legs were rigid with the strain of holding herself upright, frozen brittle with terror, and her arms ached from fruitlessly picking at the lock. For hours, maybe days, she had tried to free herself from the evil contraption on her neck, bloodying her shirt still more every time she shifted to pick at the lock from another angle.

The needle dug violently into her palm now, but she was unable to loosen her grip as if the sharp prick of pain would tether her to the closet, to this world—a lifeline, capable of keeping her awake and vertical. But so far, the needle hadn't helped her escape. And there was no way to hang from the collar unless she wanted to slit her own throat or strangle to death. No chance for reprieve even for a moment.

It would be so easy to take a step forward, neck against the blades, and just be done. Who knew what other atrocities they were capable of? Morrison should have been here by now, but they wouldn't keep her alive unless they knew they wouldn't be found. She was on her own. And whatever they had planned—it would surely be worse than death.

The air hissed through her nostrils, but it hitched occasionally as if trying to tell her to stop breathing, to just let go. The blackness in front of her eyes called to her, the quiet void of eternity, and she envisioned herself walking toward it, a sharp pang in the throat, warm, soft wetness, and then—

The sour reek of milk from her shirt called her back. Her daughter needed her. Evie could not escape without her. She gripped the needle still harder, the metal digging into the meat of her palm, and gritted her teeth against the scream that desperately wanted to escape her sutured lips. *Evie.* She imagined her daughter's face, her legs, her smile. Her tiny feet, barely kicking. Barely moving.

Shannon raised her aching arms and jammed the needle into the lock.

36

THE HOUSE WAS COLDER than it had been yesterday. Damper too. Morrison's cheeks were wet, though he wasn't entirely convinced they were his cheeks and not someone else's. His eyes watered feverishly. Aggression? Sadness? *Madness.* It was irrelevant. Nothing mattered, nothing but this.

He walked into the living room and opened a window. The screen was tight, but not stuck, and he removed it and set it on the floor. The couch Roger had sat on yesterday seemed smaller, or perhaps everything else just loomed larger now as if his world had shrunk with Evie's desperate wail. *She isn't dead yet; she isn't dead.* Morrison's ear was bruised and sore after that last call from Janey, from pressing the device so tight against his face that he feared he'd break it.

The photos on the mantel belonged to another life, another world—Shannon and Roger, both smiling with un-sutured lips and very much alive. Beside the photo, an angel holding the scales of justice. The one from Roger's office? Had he taken it home from work and stuck it there, or did he have one in every room, holding court over every place he was? Roger had probably always seen himself that way—not simply a purveyor of justice, but justice itself. But justice was dead. The deer above the mantel glared.

Morrison picked up the statue, leaving streaks of blood

across the figurine's white marble skirt, marring the mantel, too, with gore. He walked the statue to the body and dropped it. It rolled from chest to arm to floor, dully clicking as it caught the button on Roger's shirt. Justice was rarely clean, but the once pristine statue settling among the carnage—that was the last thing he wanted to see here tonight as if Lady Justice herself was admonishing him, condemning him for what he'd done, for the butchery. Not that it mattered.

He'd done it for Shannon. For Evie. And now he would find them.

He started at the back of the house with the gas can, fuel spreading in heady, oily snakes over tile, carpet, wood. The fumes turned his stomach, made him dizzy, but no more than anything else he'd seen and done that evening. He gagged. But the dizziness, the nausea, the burning in his gut, all of it belonged to someone else.

He could almost pretend that he wasn't really here. He could almost pretend that the deep crimson shimmering on his hands was just paint.

But it wasn't.

In the kitchen, he emptied the gasoline over boots, jeans, a button-down shirt. Roger's cufflinks glinted accusingly from the floor, just outside those dead wrists, but Morrison didn't look, just spilled, splashing the fuel over the floor, over the body, and onto the towel he'd used to conceal the man's face. For though Morrison was desperate, he could not bring himself to stare into those eyes—swollen and wide and dead. Just like Danny.

He turned his back on the body and grabbed the files from the deposit box, then set the packet on the floor beside the blood-soaked towels, pouring gasoline over all of it, watching as the papers absorbed it like they were thirsty enough to chug the poison, knowing it would be their end. A few renegade drops of fuel flitted through the air and struck the cabinets, streaking the cupboard doors. Leaving the finish in ruin. He tossed the empty can to the floor and walked out back.

The glass bottle was where he'd left it, filled with fuel, a rag protruding from its neck. Morrison lit it, waited a moment for it to catch, and then hurled it through the open window as he backed away down the walkway to the side yard and into the trees. He was parked one block over, well behind the lake where no one would see him.

Not loud, a subtle clank, a whoosh, a crackle. Soon it would roar, but he'd be gone before then. Shannon. Evie. *I'm coming, baby.*

Sometimes justice was nearly silent. Morrison took off across the yard, choking on unshed tears.

37

"It's done. What's the next step?"

HE SAT on the floor in his bedroom, guitar at his side, absently plucking at a single string. Waiting for them to call.

He texted again:

"Can I come to get them now?"

Nothing.

He tried calling next, but no one answered. Shannon's voice-mail greeting made tears prick in his eyes. Janey wanted to tell him where Shannon was, didn't she? But the phone stayed silent, save for Decantor's calls from his precinct extension—probably about brainstorming the case. He let them roll over to voice mail.

Janey had said to take care of Roger if he wanted his family back. But it had been hours now. He was no longer confident that she'd tell him where to find them, or whether she'd text him with other instructions. And was there anything at this point that he wouldn't do? He was already in too deep—whether he got his family back or not, he was in a lot of trouble. But Shannon and Evie were all that mattered. If he couldn't get them back safely, what happened to him was irrelevant.

The drug called to him now like a song in his heart. She'd said that once he knew who she was, he'd know where to find her, but all he knew was that she had cared about Danny. That she blamed him for Danny's death. He'd gone back to the hospital, in case, but no one recognized her photo. And Janey Krantz didn't come up in any birth certificate searches—she wasn't Danny's sister, and there were no other family members with that name. Had Janey always hidden her real name? Must have. But how? Why? She'd been a kid then. If she was adopted, her records might be sealed, but…

Janey had his family, and she was trying to punish him. And he couldn't even fucking remember her, other than a vague scratching in the back of his brain, an answer just out of reach. If only he could recall—

You can't get your family if you're all fucked up.

But the whisper of sweet relief had swelled to a dull roar, and every word had teeth, gripping him and pulling him in. He needed her name. Needed to know who she was. And if it helped him remember…

He had the remnants of the baggie, still had the syringe Petrosky had used. Sweat popped out on his forehead, and slices of memory teased at the edges of his consciousness. He leaned his head back against the bed. *You can do this. Remember her. And if you can't, if it doesn't help, you can go back out and keep investigating.*

He'd been sitting on the bed in Danny's bedroom. There was an ant farm on the end table. A few schoolbooks.

And they weren't alone. There were other voices, girls.

My turn!

No, I'm next.

Two meaningless lines, innocuous and on a continuous loop as if someone had broken a DVD and sent it spinning over this same swatch of memory again and again and again. But no new information, no images of family or friends or lovers. Where had Danny met them? Had he said?

One little prick of the needle.

He was rationalizing. Trying to find a reason why using would make sense.

And those reasons did exist, though he'd tried not to consider them. Tried and failed, oh so many times. State-dependent memory. Some people reported miraculous recoveries of memories long forgotten—once they were in the right state.

But he feared the blanks in his memory were far too wide. And were the blackouts due to trauma or the drug? He'd tried once before to recall that night, hopped up on booze. It hadn't been the same, though he hadn't been in the same panicked state as he had been the night Danny died.

He was plenty panicked now.

Outside his window, the night thickened with darkness, his hope dwindling as dawn crept toward him, the phone utterly silent. He only had one syringe—not that Petrosky was diseased. Hell, it probably didn't matter. *What's a little blood shared between friends?* They were all one step from the grave anyway.

Morrison's cell rang. He jumped at it, but it wasn't Shannon's number. It was one he didn't recognize.

He put the phone to his ear without saying hello.

"Need you over at Roger's, Morrison." Decantor. Borrowing someone else's cell to call him. "There's been an incident."

An *incident*. Not an *accident*.

Yes. There had.

THE REMAINS of Roger's home glistened under the street lamps and spotlights, each beam catching water droplets left behind by the firemen. The front door, once so thick and imposing, had been reduced to a blistered, splintered pile on the porch, blackened with char and water. While the brick columns and window frames were still intact—strong and sturdy behind the soot—the windows themselves lay in shards on the ground surrounding the house, and the vacant openings left by their absence were like eyes, glaring at Morrison, judging him for what he'd done.

He ducked under the remains of the entryway, ignoring the protests of the firefighters, and followed flashlights and voices into what was left of the kitchen, where the corpse was being loaded into a black body bag. A charred finger peeked out from

MEGHAN O'FLYNN

between the teeth of the zipper, accusing him. Morrison wasn't sure if he was sorry. He stared at the finger until the tech closed the bag and loaded it onto the gurney. The body moved with improbable lightness, and Morrison realized it was because the fat would have sizzled off in chunks and melted into the wood floor.

"Definitely arson," Decantor said. "Motive's unclear, but it isn't like Roger had no enemies."

"Was he dead before the fire?" Morrison asked, even though he knew the answer.

"Have to wait for the ME on that one."

Morrison toed the broken glass figurine and wondered how long he had before they figured out it was him. When he looked up, Decantor was eyeing him, an unlit cigarette perched between his lips. Since when did Decantor smoke?

"I can let you know when they have forensics back on it," Decantor said. "On him. Couple days. Hopefully, there'll be a trace of whoever did this."

There probably would be. But according to Janey, he only had one more day. And if he failed, nothing else mattered anyway.

Decantor was staring at him. Morrison nodded and turned to leave.

"Wait—"

Morrison's back stiffened.

"You get a hold of Shannon?"

No. "Yeah."

Decantor cleared his throat. "I never heard back from her. To get her statement about Natalie Bell." Decantor was scrutinizing him, and Morrison didn't like the look in his eyes.

"I'm sure she forgot," he said carefully. "Vacation and all." *And her lips are sewn shut.*

"Right." Decantor did not look convinced, just stared at Morrison as if the gaze could crack him. *He's suspicious.*

But Morrison was beyond that. He'd already cracked open, and the secret, brutal parts of himself had been unleashed. He glanced in the direction they'd taken the body bag.

"If you hear from her—"

264

"I'll have her call you. Until then, let's concentrate on Bell and Acosta. And now"—Morrison gestured to the charred remains around them—"this."

"Any progress on the case?" Decantor asked. "Missed you yesterday, I thought we were going to brainstorm. I called you a few times last night."

Yes, he had called. And Morrison had ignored him.

"I went to bed early," Morrison said. "I have a whole lot of nothing anyway." He paused at the smile lighting up Decantor's face. "Did you find something?"

"I got a hit on one of the sketches—our rapist. Guy at the automotive plant said he works with him over there. And get this—there's no record, but this guy from the plant said he heard a rumor that our suspect's wife divorced him because she caught him abusing her daughter, his stepchild. Elementary school age. Sick fuck."

Michael Hayes. The Juggler. Morrison's throat closed.

"Want to take a ride over there?"

He shook his head. He already knew what they'd find at the house. Morrison's phone hung, heavy and silent, in his pocket. *I did what the fuck you asked, why aren't you calling me?* He needed to think of a plan in case that call never came.

Decantor leaned close, away from the techs bustling around on what remained of the floor. "Listen, I heard a rumor. About Petrosky."

Of course he had. "You don't say."

"Hey man, what's going on with you?" Decantor squinted, his brows furrowed. "You're not…yourself."

None of them knew who he was. What he was.

Neither did he.

38

EDWARD PETROSKY STARTED the day with a shivering in his muscles, rancid liquid in his bowels, and bile streaming from his nose.

Fucking hell.

He'd told them that he'd used. Told them he needed help. He didn't—one use didn't do jack except make you want more of it.

And he did want more. There had been two blessed hours where he'd felt something other than the crushing despair which followed him every day like a shadow that had the ability to stab him in the fucking face. The heroin hadn't made him happy; it had made him better than happy. It had detached him from the pain that'd been wrapped around his throat since Julie died.

And the pain was back, especially now that they'd swiped his cigarettes. Since when was smoking forbidden in a rehab ward? If he wanted to kill himself slowly and perfectly legally, that was his own fucking business. When he got out, he was going to haul one of these twatweasels up on charges just for fucking fun.

The irritability was probably a side effect of withdrawal, but the pain in his chest was not. Walking Shannon down the aisle had been one of the happiest moments of his life since Julie was born and by far the best thing that had happened since Julie's death. When he'd held Evie the day she was born, still pink and warm from Shannon's body, he'd finally had a family again. And now that family was going to be taken away while he rotted inside this prison.

He hauled himself to the bathroom and did his business, his jaw clenched tight as his stomach lurched. Back by his bed, he drank the tepid piss they called coffee and nibbled a slice of dry toast. He never thought he'd miss Morrison's granola, but holy fuck did he ever. He'd keep that to himself once he got out of here.

And he could walk out. Sign himself out AMA. But if the kidnappers—murderers—wanted him here, then they surely had someone on the inside monitoring him. Probably enjoying the shitshow. But all the diarrhea and irritability in the world weren't going to keep him in his room while the day passed him by. Not while Shannon and Evie were in danger. Not while Morrison was in danger.

The common room was already bustling with residents as Petrosky settled onto a threadbare couch, probably riddled with dust mites and years' worth of imprints from other users' asses. Against the wall was some skinny twerp, maybe a coke head, sitting next to an overweight dude who was probably here as a function of probation, his cocky gaze showing everyone he didn't need no fucking help, though he was probably the one who'd end up needing it most in the end. It was always the ones who went down slow who seemed to forget that life existed somewhere else.

All the shuffling addicts were trapped there together, yet no one spoke. Three men in the corner stood close enough to strike up a conversation, but each merely stared in a different direction like some wholly depressing Renaissance painting. And none of them so much as glanced his way. If one of these guys was the informant, they'd at least have been interested in Petrosky's presence—after all, it was their fault he was here. Without his fucking cigarettes. He swallowed bile and headed to the nurses' station.

The on-duty nurse was young and pretty, with teeth that stood out brilliant white against her skin. But the bags under her eyes revealed her exhaustion. Watching people destroy themselves all goddamn day wasn't easy.

"Good morning, Mr. Petrosky."

"Detective."

Her smile faltered. "Of course, Detective. Did you need your pills?"

They wanted him to take some drug that would help with the tobacco cravings, but goddammit, they could kiss his ass. "No thanks."

"Sir, part of the program is—"

"I understand. You want compliance. But I don't want to take more drugs to get off the first ones, all right?"

"Detective, tobacco and heroin withdrawal can be—"

"I appreciate your position. But I'm okay. I'd have symptoms if I weren't." And he sure wasn't about to tell them how he really felt—the sick nastiness in his guts. "I'll let you check my blood pressure all day long." He leaned toward the window. "You could let me have a cigarette."

"Nice try." She shook her head and smiled kindly, probably trying like hell not to roll her eyes.

"Just one."

She looked past him into the room. Looked down. Wrote something on a piece of paper. Looked up again and met his eyes. "Oh, you're still here?" Now her smile was sarcastic. "Answer's the same." She waved him away, this time with her middle finger.

He liked her better every minute. Even better than he had yesterday when he'd sat in the back of the room trying to figure out how to get into the locked cubicle she was in now, where the computer was. She'd just sat there, pretending to ignore him but watching him out of the corner of her eye. He could always tell.

"How about a deck of cards?"

She appraised him. "Have you checked the table in the back?"

"I will now. Thank you."

He felt her eyes on his back, probably trying to tell if he was wobbly on his feet like he had been last night. Maybe wondering if he was about to have a heart attack or a goddamn seizure. He strode to the back of the room, taking extra care to walk square and stiff and probably looking like a fucking penguin, trying as he was not to shit himself.

The cards were on the back table right where she said they would be. He pulled them from the pack and shuffled, attempting to look nonchalant to conceal the fact that he was scoping out the other residents. There was a cocky-looking asshole in the back who didn't meet the description of any of their bad guys, and he was way too overtly jerky to be playing low-key. Petrosky turned his attention to the guys in the front corner, still all standing with slack expressions and pock-marked faces. Probably on heavy legal drugs, helping them come down from even heavier illegal ones. Not a good choice for an inside informant, but this Karen girl wasn't necessarily smart. Just manipulative. And patient as fuck.

He dealt solitaire.

He hated solitaire.

He fucking sucked at solitaire.

Three games. Four. Five. The nurse caught his eye, and he lifted the deck and nodded to her. She smiled and went back to her prescriptions or whatever she was doing behind the counter. Would she make a good informant? Probably.

Hell, probably not. She seemed too…genuine. He'd met a lot of perps, and he could see guilt like he'd be able to see a third nostril, knew whether they deserved to be handcuffed before he could tell you what they'd done. And the hairs on the back of his neck prickled now at the sound of another person breathing behind him. He resisted the impulse to turn around and look.

"One of my favorites." The voice was low, hoarse, the sound of someone who had damaged his vocal cords smoking bad crack or who'd had an unfortunate run-in with a kung fu master and got sucker punched in the trachea.

"Not mine," Petrosky said, dealing the cards again. "Turns out playing against myself, I can't win for shit." A steady *shh shh* crept into his awareness behind him, and he glanced down and saw the head of the broom, sweeping breakfast crumbs from under his seat into a messy pile next to the guy's shoes. No, not shoes. *Boots.* Like biker boots, but not—high from the outline through his taupe uniform pants, made of faux leather and adorned with buckles across the top of his foot. Treads bigger than were necessary for any self-respecting man. Not that this meant much—Morrison's hair was longer than any self-respecting man's should be, though at least his hair didn't look like it could leap from its owner and stomp you to death. Unlike this asshole's fucking boots.

Petrosky glanced up at the medication window and waved to the nurse again, who was now watching the pair of them from under a cocked eyebrow.

"No one likes to play alone if they don't have to, I guess." The man spoke softly, but there was a note of agitation to it. Irritation or fear? Their suspect had a fear of rejection, got worked up about challenges to his masculinity if McCallum was right. Petrosky stiffened and stared at his own feet again, keeping his face placid as he could manage. *I know what you are, fucker.* And soon as he was able, he was going to take this jerkwad down.

The man made no further effort to correct the mess on the floor but shuffled around the table toward the other chair. Petrosky squinted at the boots again. On the inside, near the heel, a set of hammered copper panels were sewn to the boot, mud or dog shit squished between the panel and the boot tread in the tiny, imperfect crevice. *Fucking fancy.* Looked homemade, too. Petrosky wondered if he knew how to make spikes. But surely, he did. He was flaunting it, teasing him. It was a slap in the goddamn face. He had to know Petrosky was aware of who he was, and the fact that he didn't seem concerned made Petrosky's heart rate climb. If this guy didn't care about getting caught—was the damage already done? Were Shannon and Evie already dead? Was the guy on a suicide mission? What?

Unless he was just there for Petrosky. Maybe he wanted to spill. From the sounds of his heavy breath, the guy was practically salivating with the thrill of *almost* discovery. Almost. This dude was a fucking idiot.

Dude? Now he was thinking like Morrison. His heart seized at the thought of Shannon and Evie, and he resisted the urge to grab the broom and shove it up the guy's ass for what he'd done to Shannon's face. Hopefully, this bastard hadn't done worse since that photo on Morrison's phone. And if he had... Petrosky's fist clenched, but he released it, sighed far more loudly than was necessary, and collected the cards into a pile. "Want to play? I can't do this shit anymore."

A *thunk* noise, wood on mortar, probably the broom being propped against the wall. "I suppose," the guy said softly. "I am due for a break."

Petrosky finally glanced up as the guy circled the table. Bald, shorter than Petrosky, thin— he'd fit the stats of the booted killer at the Acosta scene. No visible tattoos, but a stippling of pockmarks ran along his jaw. Some might have been pimples, even infected blackheads, but others were deeper as if he'd been digging for something in his face with a needle. Sicko had probably enjoyed that shit.

But his most striking feature was the lack of wrinkles—not a single age spot. This guy was *really* young, nineteen or twenty, especially with the acne. Just a fucking kid. He *had* been learning —McCallum's shrinky ass was right. He'd been watching the pedophile. Maybe watching Karen. His gaze was dead and dark, even when he smiled, but his black eyebrows had a touch of blond coming through at the corners like he'd done a shitty dye job. That explained the half-blond-half-black hair at the Bell crime scene, the one they'd used to type his DNA. The guy's gaze flicked to the nurses' station, and when the nurse looked their way, he sat quickly, averting his eyes though he could not hide the brief quiver in his jaw. Fearful. But as Petrosky watched, the man's face hardened—fear and *rage*. McCallum was fucking good.

A badge on his shirt said *Adam: Xtreme Clean Janitorial.* Fake name? Probably an independent cleaning company, unrelated to the rehab center. Looked like the center paid ex-patients for mentoring and not for cleaning up—or maybe they just hired out on the weekends. Still, if HR had been more forthcoming, maybe Petrosky would have been able to snag this bastard before he'd ended up in this shithole. Bunch of fuckheads, all of them.

Across from Petrosky at the table, Adam's eyes glittering darkly but still with a telltale tremble at the corners. "So, what are you in for?"

"Heroin."

"Mm-hmm." No shock. No surprise. He already knew.

Petrosky dealt out gin rummy. "What about you? Dabble a little on the side?" He leaned in conspiratorially and tried to wink, but his eyelid just twitched like he was hopped up on crank.

"I don't do drugs. Tried a few in my day, but…you know."

Yeah, he did know. This guy wasn't an addict. This guy had no demons that bothered him enough to drown them in liquor or drugs—inside, he was already numb. Some people were born that way.

To the left of the table, a tiny smear of mud from Adam's boot marred the linoleum. Petrosky nodded toward it. "Better wipe your shoes, or you'll be here all night cleaning up after yourself." He waited for a telltale grimace or a frown, and the guy didn't disappoint. His nostrils flared, and he kicked the mud with the toe of his boot. The walkways outside the rehab center were concrete. He must walk to work, or maybe he biked it through the park. Explained the mud. Forgoing car owner-ship would also mean one less thing to buy—one less record to have.

Petrosky picked up his cards, and the guy did the same.

"Looks like it's been a hard road for you, Detective." The guy's chest puffed out, almost in challenge.

Petrosky resisted the urge to remind the guy that he hadn't told him he was a detective, and instead chose a card, then laid another down. "You look a little tired yourself, Adam."

Adam did not respond to the use of his name—maybe not his name at all—just shrugged and played his turn, laying his discard down. Thin fingers, fidgety. Eyes darting all over the fucking place as if he was trying to decide how to act. At his temple…bumps—*hives?*—were appearing, swelling, working their way across his skin. Adam scratched the back of his neck.

"Bet it's hard, this line of work," Petrosky said. "All the bitches coming in and out every day, the nurses giving you shit. Having to *wait* on them like you don't even exist."

Adam's jaw worked, and his chin was suddenly pinker, angrier—definitely a rash. He clenched his fingers. What the fuck was wrong with this guy?

"Bet it keeps you up at night. You've got bags under your eyes: trouble sleeping, am I right?"

Adam's gaze darkened, but the corner of his mouth twitched almost imperceptibly. "Not really from this. More the cats. They claw the windows at night or fight on the lawn." He stared at the cards, perhaps unsure about his next move. "Any ideas for getting rid of them?"

If he had cats at his window, he probably had a one-story house. A one-story house within walking—or biking—distance. Petrosky wracked his brain. He'd lived in Ash Park for twenty-five years. He could think of two neighborhoods that were likely. But how to discern the exact property?

Petrosky pulled an ace and discarded it. "You got awnings? I'd think if you hung something from them, you'd make it uncomfortable for the furry fuckers. Strings of beads or something heavier that will sit against the sill. Block them out?"

Adam shook his head. "Nope. And the shutters are old as shit, and the worst piss-poor green you've ever seen."

Green shutters. This fucker was brutal but not smart—or maybe he was just too damn excited. The look on his face was closer to "come at me, bro" and less "holy shit, I'm about to get caught" like it should have been.

"Sounds like you need an upgrade."

"Or a better job," he spat.

Angry again. *Fuck.*

"And it's right across the road from some moron with an American flag that flaps all night long. Can you believe that? Not even sure how anyone can fly it all proud like that these days." His eyes flicked to the nurse and back. "What do you think, *Detective?*" His words dripped bitterness. He was telling him on purpose. If Petrosky hadn't asked a single question, this guy would have brought it up anyway. And if Petrosky hadn't been coming down off heroin, withdrawing from nicotine, and clenching his ass cheeks together, maybe he'd have noticed sooner.

He could find the place now. Probably rather quickly. In an hour's time, they could be walking Shannon out—so long as this guy was giving him the correct location, and Shannon wasn't locked in a storage shed somewhere, which was entirely possible. But the moment Petrosky checked himself out of this hellhole was the moment this fuckhead called his partner. Called Karen. And once that happened, Shannon and Evie were dead. Maybe he'd find their bodies full of holes like those in Dylan Acosta's back.

Adam smiled, but his eyes were menacing, not friendly. Adam was giving him this information because he wanted Petrosky to screw up. He wanted a reason to kill Shannon and Evie. Maybe he was tired of the game. Bored? But if Karen had another goal in mind—going after Morrison and Shannon both, as she had when she was with Griffen—she wouldn't be ready to give up yet. What had McCallum said? That their guy was afraid of women. That he'd been rejected. Maybe Adam was tired of playing the game, but he couldn't confront Karen directly, so he was forcing her hand by ending the game himself.

The guy was staring at him, not at the cards. He knew Petrosky was trapped. Phone calls were monitored here, and Petrosky was certain there'd be no home registered in this guy's name. Nothing to make the process faster. Even if the asshole weren't lying, they wouldn't be able to scout the neighborhood, let alone pinpoint to the correct house before Shannon and Evie got hurt.

Adam smiled at him. He'd been fucking with Petrosky the whole time.

Petrosky gritted his teeth and laid down his cards. "Gin."

39

Morrison turned the phone over and over in his hand as if that would make the text message different somehow. But every time the cell came to rest face up in his palm, the message was the same.

He had texted:

"It's done. Watch the news."

Janey's reply:

"Now to watch them suffer the way I watched Danny suffer."

The pictures she'd sent earlier practically leapt off the screen, and he couldn't stop looking. Shannon, the bottom half of her face covered in spit and gore, her lips surgically zipped together with blood-soaked sutures. Evie's onesie, drenched in blood. But no photos of his daughter. He could not allow himself to consider what that meant.

He had done everything he'd been asked to do, and he knew now what a grievous mistake that had been. This was the reason you didn't give in to demands. This was the reason no panicked spouse was allowed to decide whether to give kidnappers what they wanted.

He had settled some old drama she'd had with Roger. He had hurt his best friend—maybe irreparably. But the suffering wouldn't end there. He hadn't begun to suffer yet. That had been the point all along.

And after all of it, he still didn't know who Janey really was. *Once you remember me, you'll know exactly where to find me.* Was she full of shit? Didn't matter if she was—he had nothing else to go on and if he didn't do everything in his power…he'd never forgive himself. He was no longer concerned with the possibility that she was lying.

What if she wasn't *lying?*

Morrison leaned back against his pillow and dropped the cell to his side, picking up the photo of Evie they'd always kept beside the bed. Newborn, pink. Before she had known pain. Before she'd been taken. Before she'd been…abused.

His gut clenched, trying to force bile into his throat. He had to get her back.

I'm coming for you, baby, baby girl.

But what else could he do? He'd scoured all the newspaper clippings from around the time of Danny's death. Obits, headlines, every local high school yearbook that he could find online. No Janeys that matched the description he was looking for. And Danny had no family left that Morrison could ask—Danny's father had died before he'd met Morrison, and his mom'd had a heart attack nearly six years ago. No siblings. Even Mrs. Palmer had no idea who Janey's family had been, though she'd looked— had to be a runaway or adoption —and the cell Janey had used to text Karen Palmer was a throwaway. He'd looked at birth records from 1983 to 1987 for fuck's sake—no Janeys listed. Jenny? Janet? Jane? But there were too many. And he had no more time.

You see me, but you don't. Because she had been there that night. She'd watched Danny die. She blamed Morrison now, whether it was because he'd brought the drugs or left without getting help, or because she'd watched him beat Danny to death in a moment of drug-induced rage—he had no idea. He couldn't remember a fucking thing—or at least nothing that would make all of this click. But just because he couldn't recall it didn't mean he hadn't done it. And no matter how often he told himself he didn't want to know…he had to find out. Or he'd fail. He'd lose Shannon. He'd lose Evie.

He'd lose everything.

The needle called to him. There had been too much in that bag for Petrosky alone, way too much. And that was the point, wasn't it? That was why she had put him through all of this. To bring him to this place where the drug spoke louder than everything else, where the drug would talk, and he'd listen because he had nothing and no one else.

His wife was gone. His baby. Petrosky. All because of him. They'd never forgive him. And they shouldn't—he couldn't forgive himself.

The comforter, once so soft, so sweet, felt rough and full of sharp edges under his bare legs. No matter how slowly and purposefully he inhaled, the air did not restore his calm—it was a roaring ocean, trying to drown him. It had all been a carefully laid trap. She'd set out to destroy him from the very beginning.

And she would. Tears fell onto Evie's picture, still clutched in his hand. "I'm sorry. I'm sorry, I couldn't save you."

One last chance. One last shot.

The spoon, cooling now but not yet cold, sat next to him, staring accusingly. He palpated the vein in his thigh, and it sang with anticipation. *I'm ready*, it called. *No one will ever know.*

He'd always know.

Not that it mattered anymore.

He barely registered filling the syringe, but now it was loaded, liquid and sweet, and more vital than it had ever been. He leaned back on the bed, widening his legs, staring at the vein where his leg met his torso. The old mark could have been an ingrown hair or a little pimple, but now the scar appeared like a target—an evil eye. *Nothing to worry about, nothing at all.* He picked up the needle and brought the point to the center of the scar, but the tip wouldn't stay still; his hand shook with such force the needle scraped along his inner thigh, leaving a thin, angry line.

Just one little injection, and his head would clear. Just one prick, and he'd be ready to go back out and find them. He'd know who Janey was. Where Danny had met her. He'd know what to say to her. He'd know where to find her. Maybe.

He brought the needle back, pressing the pinky side of his palm against his thigh, trying to force his hand steady, but it was no use. His hand vibrated. The needle shook.

And if he missed…he had no more. One chance to do it right, that was all he had.

He brought the needle to his chest and laid it against his heart. The plastic was frighteningly cold next to his sweaty skin, though maybe not for long. Would the drug stop his heart on the first pull? Probably not, but it wasn't impossible, and he knew it. Had always known it. And it had never stopped him before, either.

Back then, it wasn't that he didn't care about death. More that he didn't care about life without the drug.

But now he did, didn't he? He gasped for air and held Evie's photo in front of his face. Her pudgy cheeks, her wide, innocent eyes so like his in color and shape. His baby girl. He could almost hear her laughing. She was why he had stayed clean. He'd been clean before her, but after, there was no greater reason in all the world than the remotest chance of looking into her eyes again. Even now, she was probably crying, needing him. He wasn't there.

Those fuckers. *That bitch.* Torturing his little girl.

He screamed at the ceiling, unleashing a string of profanities, resisting the urge to fling the needle across the room and watch the case splinter against the doorframe, soaking the carpet in the precious, vile liquid.

He would not let them win.

But if he didn't do this, he might lose.

He looked once more at Evie's picture, steadied the needle, and slid it into his vein.

40

THE COOL OF the liquid quickly morphed into a glow that spread through his legs, his belly, his chest, wrapping every part of his body in a pleasant tingly warmth. The world around him mellowed into pure love, and he could have kissed his creator the moment the euphoria flooded his brain. The nods came fast then, perfect and quiet, a heavy, peaceful sleepiness that drowned the pain, the helplessness, the terror. He felt his eyes flutter open—had he closed them?—almost of their own accord. He didn't want to miss anything of this glorious world. He was back with the family who'd been there for him when he had no one else. He was home.

His head dropped back against the pillow, and the ceiling was the purest, most perfect shade of white he'd ever seen, clear and clean and utterly devoid of color. Then his eyes were moving, his head lolling to the side, and he rejoiced, sure he'd see the window there, the awesome rays of light borne by a glorious midday sun.

But he didn't.

It was Evie. Evie's picture, crumpled in his fist on the other pillow, illuminated by the garish light. Her tiny face was creased and marred with hairline cracks, red drips coating her eyes like she was the devil incarnate. Blood? Had he hurt her? And in his leg, a sharp pain—the syringe had broken. He stared at it as if it were something entirely foreign to him. And smiled.

Until he remembered. Even as tears of joy sprang into his eyes, even as his chest vibrated with glee—he remembered. They were gone. Shannon and Evie were gone. And pain collided with the pleasure, euphoria slammed by panic so intense the buzz almost silenced itself. But only for a moment. Then it was nothing but a slight dampening around the edges of the blissful cloud he was riding, a storm under him that he'd surely have to acknowledge once he fell, but now—he was untouchable.

His eyes fluttered closed again, and he rode higher and higher, pleasure shutting out the world, and the blackness cocooned him in the deepest peace he'd ever felt. A name came from below his cloud, and one small whispered word carried on the breeze as if by angels: "Danny."

The dark around him began to gray at the edges, and then images shuddered to life: a curtain rustling in the breeze though he could see no window, a bedspread with a comforter as ice blue as Shannon's eyes. He could feel his wife there too, loving him, her presence wrapping around his heart and squeezing until he was certain the adoration would cause him to burst, and he'd finally succumb, leaving the world with her name on his joyous lips. The green walls pulsed, glowing with the vibrant energy of new spring buds. The wood floor was a sea of honey beneath him, sweet and ripe.

And…the ants. Ants all over, tiny, persistent soldiers forming impossibly ordered lines. They were trying to fix something, helpers, and he wanted to reach out to them, to help them too, for their nobility was like nothing he'd seen, each and every one of them a hero. Or a martyr. He smiled at them, and they seemed to smile back at him, and he felt their adoration as clearly as if they had whispered a collective, "We love you." And he smiled at Danny. At Danny's blood? Or maybe it was his own blood, running even now over Evie's picture.

Danny.

I killed him.

The room was alive, swelling and shrinking with violent gasps, the now heavy curtains whispering to him about the blood that snaked across the earth, vast and wet as the ocean, and each crimson wave murmured sounds of serenity in his ear. And Danny: a bump on his forehead, the center of the welt split open like a shattered egg, clear to the pure, peaceful white of his skull.

Danny's lips were bluer than the most beautiful cerulean sky, and Morrison rejoiced, for they too seemed to want nothing more than to wrap him in a glorious mist of everlasting unity. And he was so overcome by the elation at being near his friend that he wept. Wept for Danny's beautiful lips, for his pure alabaster skull, for every ant on his face, for the way he was looking at Morrison now, eyes glassy and so full of love that Morrison had to turn away lest he be blinded.

And behind him…voices. Girls.

"My turn!"

"No, me next."

It was like a VCR tape rewinding, scrambling backward over time and space, and all he could see was a screech of blur and color. But then part of him was outside himself, a conscious splitting as if someone had taken a divine ax and severed his soul from his physical being. The calm peace that had wrapped him remained thick and heavy in his body, but the other him, the one that walked away now—*his* heart was frantic. *He* was choking.

"My turn!"

"No, me next."

Morrison tried to see who was speaking, but the room was filled with fog and smoke. He twisted a little more and caught sight of them: they were laughing, their faces hidden behind dark, silky curtains of hair, and they were beautiful. And he saw himself, the other him, sitting on the bed, back against the headboard. Not looking. Maybe he'd never seen them—maybe he'd already been in the cloud when they arrived.

Morrison closed his eyes and let the cloud take him again, inhaling the mist into his core and releasing it.

"Goddammit, give it here!" A girl.

Danny: "Shut up, dicks, you'll wake up my cousin, and then we're all fucked." Morrison's eyes flew open, and there was Danny, standing at the foot of the bed, and there were no ants on him, and Morrison wanted to cry with relief. But the world was sideways. How had he gotten here? Was he lying down? Then came a scuffling sound, the swishing of fabric, and Danny approached the foot of the bed, by Morrison's feet, holding the syringe. Danny shoved it into his own arm, pulled it out and wavered, and she—long hair but she was all black and white and misty—grabbed the needle from Danny. Then Danny whipped around and faced Morrison, and here was the part where he'd get upset, where Morrison had surely beaten him to death, and Morrison wanted to stop it, but the heaviness in his arms and the calm in his chest kept him down. He just watched. Danny smiled, and his lips were moving—"Fucking A"—and then he was stumbling toward the bed, tripping, grabbing at the mattress where Morrison lay, but missing, crashing. His head connected with the end table, a book flipped up, the green ant farm tumbled, and Danny hit the floor with a hollow-sounding *thud*. Morrison giggled softly to himself, the crash and the thud and all that tinkling glass such an improbable, comical thing to happen, as if every hilarious thing he'd ever seen, ever done, ever felt, was multiplied a thousand times over.

And then his perspective changed again, and he was watching from across the room. Watching himself wake up on the bed. Other Him looked awkward and lonely, and decidedly not high—though This Him still felt really fucking high.

Danny. Other Him didn't say it, but Morrison heard it in the air as Other Him peered over the side of the bed at Danny's face, at Danny's closed eyes, that sleepy fuck. And then Other Him had the bedsheet—*what the fuck?*—and he leapt off the mattress and held it to Danny's head. Danny was going to be pissed about the sheet. Danny was going to punch Other Him in the nuts. And then something slammed into Morrison as if he'd been thrown into a wall and Other Him was gone, and it was just Morrison, staring at the floor, staring at the comforter, staring at Danny and his glassy eyes and the ants. Morrison's hands were wet. Why were his hands wet? And they were red…and the sheets were red…and he could smell it, stronger now, the iron in the air, thick at the back of his throat—rust, metal, death—but his body wasn't sure what to do. Laugh or cry, maybe, but neither seemed quite right even when the ants swarmed Morrison, crawling up his legs into his pants. And then they kept coming, pinching jaws attacking his flesh over and over again. He remained still, unable to move, unable to run, not even really wanting to, but his heart was seizing, throbbing with the panic that was slowly creeping in through the haze of the drug. He had to get out of there. Someone would come soon, and they'd see that he had done this, that he'd fallen asleep while his best friend bled to death on the floor.

Morrison looked at the ants. At his crimson palms. He ran to Danny's adjoining bathroom and let the water pour over his hands, icy and sharp, the sink turning first red, then pink. When the water ran clear, he wrenched a towel from the hook over the counter, twisting it around his hands as if it were a tourniquet, and he was the one bleeding. But the world was still foggy around him, and the panic pulsed and retreated as if it were merely a butterfly alighting on a flower, then fluttering off.

The girls were gone. He'd never known them, never seen them outside of their curtains of dark hair. Janey had to have been one of them, but he was no closer to an answer. *Find them.* He ran for the bedroom door—four feet away, three—then the knob twisted of its own accord, and the butterfly of panic returned, beating its iridescent wings until the air itself was alive with horror. The door squealed and came toward him before he could hide.

Her.

Tiny, twelve years old, maybe, red hair, freckles, eyes wide, smiling. "Dan?"

Morrison put his finger to his lips, shoved past her, and tore down the stairs, and he was tumbling, falling, head over heels over head, the world cartwheeling away from him in a perfect spiral of white and black and—

He opened his eyes. Evie's photo was stained a brilliant cardinal red. He could still smell the blood. Danny's blood? No. This time it was his.

Who was she?

Shut up, dick, you'll wake up my cousin, and then we're all fucked.

Cousin. Was Janey Danny's cousin? He'd already investigated

immediate family, anyone nearby he might have met, but maybe he hadn't gone far enough. He wanted to be angry about this, knew he ought to feel incensed by his own incompetence, but his limbs were too heavy and too loose, and he was just too fucking blissed-out to care about anything.

He could almost smell Evie's hair. Feel Shannon's hand on his arm, soft and warm and loving.

The cloud was still there, promising respite. Morrison breathed it into his lungs and walked into the mist, letting it consume him.

41

THE PHONE PULLED him from his nodding—insistent, a harsh and angry buzzing. Voice mail from Decantor. He'd missed three calls from Valentine, too. He touched the screen and put Decantor's message on speaker, his palm sticky and bright with injuries that were only now beginning to sting. He turned his hand over, appraising the hash marks on his palm.

"Morrison, we've gotta talk. I just got back from Michael Hayes's place. Someone filleted his ass. All we found were swaths of…flesh. Someone tried to skin him alive." Decantor coughed, gagged. Maybe he was still there, looking at the mess. "Fucking horrible. Listen, I'm going to head your way in a little bit. Hope you're around."

Fuck. Morrison headed for the living room on shaky legs, the wavering of the world pulling at him a little, but mostly he felt… dreamy. Sleepy. He'd been so stupid. And already, the promise of more pleasure was taking root in his head. He'd be good for a few days, and then he'd—

He punched the wall on his way down the stairs, letting the drywall crack and shower to the carpet as if he could obliterate his thoughts with a left hook. Photos of Shannon pregnant and Evie as an infant rattled in their frames as he pulled his hand free, knuckles smarting, but at least this time, it was his own blood on his hands. He squared his shoulders. He would get his fucking family back, and he'd move on like he always did. Shannon and Evie would be his bliss.

But not like heroin. Nothing was like heroin. *Nothing.*

Morrison almost tripped down the last of the stairs, caught himself on the railing, and stumbled into the kitchen. Coffee. Then research.

Janey. Danny's cousin. Danny's last name had been Krantz, and that was the name she'd given Palmer, but Janey Krantz didn't exist. He pulled Danny's parents and grandparents, but there'd been no adoptions, and Danny's father hadn't had brothers—no one to pass on the family name. He frowned into his coffee cup. No Krantz anywhere. He cross-checked birth certificates for each aunt and uncle, then cousins, then second cousins. No Janeys, but…

There she was. She'd been right there all along.

Janice Lynwood. Danny's cousin once removed. Parents deceased, automobile accident, the year before Danny died. Though she never was formally adopted, her school records indicated she'd lived at the Krantz house since the death of her parents—but she'd gone to a middle school and later a high school nearly an hour away. Problems in the nearby school? But there was no record of her enrollment there at all. Had Danny's parents tried to keep her with the friends she'd had before her parents died? Either way, it explained why she was able to use whatever name she wanted when she met Karen Palmer—if they went to different schools, Karen would have been none the wiser.

But…Janice had been a child when Danny died, and she'd only gone to be with his family the year prior. They were too far apart in age to share much more than blood. Though from Roger's description of her, Janey was prone to obsession and a self-righteous rage, as though she were intent on having someone else pay for the shitty hand she'd been dealt. He considered the suicide attempts, the threats she'd aimed at Roger. Maybe she was just terrified to be alone, to be abandoned. Under most bad behavior is fear.

Morrison understood loneliness well, and a tiny part of him just under his heart tightened with sympathy, but he crushed it, smothered it with the heat of fury when he pictured Shannon's skewered lips. After he'd lost his father, and years later, when he'd found his mother on the living room floor with her brains bashed in, he'd felt the same. Anger. Abandonment. Loneliness. And if he'd found the asshole who had done it, he'd have sent him to meet his maker just as quickly—back then, anyway. Over time, he'd been able to let the anger go and move on.

But Janice still blamed him. She had no one to blame for her parents careening off a rain-slicked road, but she did have someone who would pay for Danny's death: the man she'd seen that morning, and everyone he loved, innocent or not.

The doorbell rang. Morrison jerked his head toward the entry hall—woozy, he was so damn woozy—then kept typing. Searching. Janice Lynwood. No brothers, no sisters. The bell rang again.

Once you remember me, you'll know exactly how to find me.

Four marriages. All out of state. No children.

Pounding, incessant, on the front door.

He typed. The knocking stopped, but he could feel someone out there. Decantor—of course it was Decantor—could probably hear the clacking of the keyboard.

House deeds. Mortgages.

Morrison's cell buzzed. He took it from his pocket but didn't answer, just set it on the table.

A text came through:

"It's Decantor. Where you at?"

"Out to lunch. I'll meet you at the station."

Morrison searched property listings and deeds in the names of any of her immediate family. No current properties listed for any of the living family members within five hundred miles. *Click, click, click.* The cell pinged again.

"Who are you eating with?"

Morrison had left his car in the driveway. He should have put it in the garage.

He stabbed at the phone:

"Sister-in-law."

Did Decantor know Shannon didn't have a sister?

"K. An hour?"

"Sounds good."

Morrison wouldn't make that appointment either. Nor would he have his cell with him when Decantor called to ask where he was—not if he figured out where Janice was hiding. *Where is she?*

He tried Janice's mom's name. Nothing. Her dad—

Theodore Lynwood. He stared at the property listing, called up a map. The house was right in Ash Park. She could walk to it from the rehab center. And mortgages weren't kept up by dead men.

Morrison tore up the stairs to throw on a pair of boots and grab his gun.

He left his badge on the dresser.

THE SUNSET HAD STAINED the road with shapes like the splatter left behind by a gunshot wound. The adrenaline in his veins had burned off the dizziness, the nausea, or maybe he just couldn't feel anything beneath the ragged panic that even now scorched his insides. Perhaps there would have been a chance for recovery had the slightest hint of blue still streaked the sky, but as it was, the tree branches blackened all but the pattern of angry red gore.

The metal against his hip was a comfort. What would he do once he arrived?

He wasn't sure. Didn't know. But it felt right.

She wanted him alone. She wanted him to suffer. She wanted him to watch.

But she didn't know he was coming.

The house crawled by on his left, dark shutters of gray or green, a green door, a sparse garden in the front where haphazard tulips strained through overgrown grass. No vehicle in the driveway, but a one-car garage. The ripened sun turned the windows into blazing orange eyes.

His chest heaved as he lost sight of the house—like he was abandoning his family again. He parked around the corner, well out of sight of the place, just in case they looked from behind the smoldering windows to peer down the road. The pavement was still bloodied by the setting sun.

I'm coming, Shanny.

He switched the safety off his gun, climbed out of the car, and started around the block so that he could go in the back way.

Tonight, he wasn't a fucking cop.

He was a monster forged of rage and desperation and steel. A monster they had woken.

And Janice would pay.

42

PETROSKY SAT ON HIS BED, his stomach aching, his ass still half-numb from the rock-hard, torture device of a chair he'd been in all day. And while he'd sat in the common room, Adam, the agitated boy-man, had watched. When he'd left the table to take a shit, the perp was waiting outside. For every meal Petrosky ate, that asshole was there with his shiny, bulging forehead.

That was his job. Not the sweeping that he probably got paid some paltry amount for. His real job was to make sure Petrosky was stuck in here with critical information he was helpless to transmit—impotent to assist Morrison. Or Shannon. Or Evie.

He didn't want to think about the drug either. But he did. Jesus, he did. It was the happiest he'd been in as long as he could remember, and he had little to lose, if anything, once Shannon and Evie were safe.

He had been refused phone calls twice, thus far. Against the rules, they said—fearful he'd be contacting some dealer to hook him up when he got out. Inpatient rehab was meant to disconnect you from every aspect of your outside life. Old lives were ready triggers, old friends were eager enablers. They'd told him that in group therapy this morning, some sour-faced man with a cross around his neck wearing goddamn purple argyle. *Argyle.* Checkers were bad enough, but he didn't trust a man in fabrics with more depth than your average perp.

Petrosky shot to standing at a knock at the bedroom door—it'd be the therapist, or maybe the nurse. "Obstinate" and "uncooperative" they'd called him, respectively. Not that cooperation had been a prerequisite for this part he was meant to play; whoever had Shannon didn't give a flying fuck if he was actually recovering. They'd probably be happier if he weren't. They wanted him to hurt. They wanted to bring him down.

Karen…and *Adam*. But that couldn't be his real name; it was too easy. From the moment the name passed his lips, "Adam" seemed a little too confident like he figured once Petrosky got out of rehab, he'd seek him *only* by name.

They'll never find me! They think my name is Adam!

Fucking idiot. Though who knew, this might be part of his game. This fucker seemed to get off on giving away his hand, exposing critical information, and then…watching.

For now, Petrosky needed a better plan. The phones were locked in the nurses' station and in the main offices, but a few more hours and the majority of the staff would go home. Ghost staff overnight. He had a filed toothbrush that he could use as a pick, very prison-esque, but everything here was prison-esque. Not like he could throw a fit, pull his badge, and sign himself out —not if he wanted Shannon and Evie to live.

The doorknob turned, and Petrosky reached for the twentieth time for his holster but touched only cloth. Bullshit jailhouse pajamas. Scratchy and considerably less comforting than the cool heaviness of his Glock.

An orderly, skinny and irritatingly young—though still older than Adam—peeped his head into the room, then swung the door wider and took a few steps forward, holding a black plastic sack. Probably here to tell him it's therapy time, it's game night, or something equally asinine.

"Hope you're not here to get me for something stupid. I don't have time for that bullshit. But if you can get me a phone—"

"I have to take you out. Discharge."

Petrosky froze, not comprehending. "I'm in recovery here."

The orderly shrugged. "You've got to see the nurse." He handed Petrosky the bag. "I'll wait outside."

Petrosky opened the sack. His clothes. He was leaving. Was he supposed to be leaving? He had a sudden urge to take a shit.

But this had to be good news, right? Morrison had found them. Morrison was here to get him, and maybe Shannon and Evie were with him, or they were going to go together to the hospital. The girls would take some time to heal, but dammit, he'd be there to help them. They were okay.

Dressed in minutes in the sour duds he'd come in with, Petrosky followed the orderly to the nurses' station. Her smile was tight as she handed him prescriptions through the window.

"Why am I being discharged?"

Her smile went from tight to nonexistent. "I'm... You can speak to the gentleman outside."

The gentleman. Not "your friend."

"Listen, I'm not trying to be difficult here."

She pushed one last script through the slot. "Go talk to him. He can answer your questions."

But her eyes were narrowed—she was worried. They were trying to keep him calm. It wasn't his partner out there, ready to take him home, friendly and excited. Why would you try to keep someone from rehab calm? It wasn't like they'd be discharging him into the care of their psychopathic janitor. "I don't understand why—"

"It's not up to us." She sent a form through the slot. "Sign this, please."

Only so many things could upend recovery. The only time they released like this was...if someone was under arrest. If they thought the patient was dangerous. If it was an emergency. But who would be here? Decantor? And if it was Decantor...Shannon and Evie were probably dead. Morrison too.

He signed the sheet and shoved it back through the hole, heart hammering in his temples. It had to be good news. *Please let it be good news.* But when was the news ever good for him? It was over. If he was out, it was over one way or another.

He followed the orderly out of the common room and through the main hallway toward the exit. The orderly took forever fiddling with his keys, his badge, to get them the fuck out of there. The door finally swung open, and Petrosky bolted to the kid's agitated: "Hey wait, he said you're under arrest!"

The orderly's cry fell on deaf ears. Petrosky froze just outside the door, staring at the man who'd come to claim him.

Roger cocked his head. "What's up, Detective?"

Definitely not good.

"YOUR PARTNER ISN'T HOME," Roger said as he slid into the car and slammed the door.

Petrosky closed his own door, feeling like more of a prisoner than when he'd been trapped in his room filing toothbrushes into lock picks.

"He running?"

"Running?" What in the ever-loving hell? If Roger wasn't here to get him because it was over—"Wait, do they still have Shannon?"

Roger shrugged.

"What the fuck does that mean? Are you trying to get her fucking killed?" Petrosky's fist clenched, wanting desperately to drive it into Roger's already crooked nose. How long did they have before Adam found out and called his partner at the house?

Roger was appraising him—apparently, he didn't trust that Petrosky was actually dumbfounded. "Morrison and I had a deal," he said sharply. "He was taking care of something for me. Supposed to turn himself in this morning for arson."

Arson? "Taking care of what?"

"Don't worry about it."

Morrison had taken care of…incriminating evidence against Roger? But why would he do that when the assholes who had Shannon wanted Roger locked up? *Arson.* What the hell was going on?

"I went over there," Roger said. "Your boy's gone. Figured you'd know where." He narrowed his eyes. "And if you fuck with me, I'll make sure—"

"Shut the fuck up, Roger." Petrosky buckled his seat belt.

Roger froze, keys raised halfway to the ignition.

Petrosky punched the dash. "Drive, motherfucker. We don't have all day."

"We going to get Morrison?"

"We're going to get Shannon before they kill her."

Roger opened his mouth to say something else, but Petrosky put up a hand.

"We find her, and we'll find Morrison too." He reached over and took the keys and shoved them into the ignition. "Let's go."

THE DESIRE TO cut and run was strong, not because he had any intention of abandoning Morrison, but because Petrosky was certain Roger was a fucking twat. You don't go into battle with someone who doesn't know what the hell they're doing—you leave their sorry ass at home. But Roger refused to be left, even after a cruise through the first neighborhood seemed fruitless.

"I don't know how you can rule so many out," Roger grumbled.

"No flags."

"So what? You can't be sure that he even told you the truth."

But Petrosky felt it. The hairs on the back of his neck hadn't risen when that dickhead was telling him about the cats, bitching about the screen and his neighbor's patriotism. And Adam hadn't flinched once. Dangling the truth in front of Petrosky, taunting him with it—that had been part of the game. Part of the excitement. Adam probably *was* his real fucking name. "He told me the truth."

"I can do all the shit you guys do and better. I'd have found her three days ago."

"Then why didn't you?"

"If she wanted someone to get the job done, she'd have stayed with me."

But the edge in his voice betrayed his concern. God forbid someone got rid of her before she could fall into Roger's arms and tell him that he was clearly the superior model, that she'd made a huge mistake in leaving him. Petrosky appraised him.

His furrowed brows. His knuckles, white against the steering wheel.

Roger wasn't a prosecutor today. His interests might be selfish, but at least they were aligned with Petrosky's. With Morrison's.

And with Shannon's.

"There's that jackass's car," Roger said and went to pull beside it.

Petrosky shook his head. "For fuck's sake, Roger, drive around the block."

"But if he's here—"

"He didn't park in front of the house and go in rampaging. He's not an idiot." *Unlike you.* "But the place has to be close."

Roger's mouth tightened, and Petrosky gestured through the windshield at the road. "One block, two at the most." Morrison would have been in a hurry. "Drive around the right side first."

Roger ran a stop sign and hooked a right into the blinding sunset.

43

MORRISON'S BREATH was hot and fast, every sense acute, magnified by the thrumming of his anxiety. He could almost feel the sun being siphoned from the sky in measured increments like water sucked down a drain. The chirping of the crickets was deafening.

But still, he could hear.

The window was closed, and all he could see was a black curtain, yet muffled sounds came from within—more a feeling of movement than an actual noise. He brought his face closer to the window. The curtain was stiff, plastered against the glass. No one looking from the street would notice a difference, but there was no way the window covering was free and loose on the inside. Pressed to the window with cinderblocks? Spray insulation? Surely they had insulated the windows and the exterior walls. Unless…that was why they'd sewn Shannon's mouth closed.

The cold. It burned.

But he heard her. No, it wasn't Shannon, not the right timbre, just the tickle of a female voice, no discernible words.

Then the wail. A baby. His baby. Evie was surely screeching, but if he hadn't had his ear so close to the window, he wouldn't have heard her at all.

I'm coming, baby girl.

Every muscle ached with the desire to crash through the window and snatch Evie to him before he blew Karen—*Janice*—away. But he couldn't be sure of what was on the other side. Was it booby trapped? What if he knocked something over and hurt Evie instead? And if there was insulating foam, it might take him all day to saw through it and actually get inside, depending on how they'd secured it. Just the foam, cool. Bricks? Bad news.

He was still squinting at the corner of the window when he registered the sound of feet swishing through the grass, somewhere near the front of the property. The house was small, maybe thirteen hundred square feet. Was it Janice's sadistic partner? He pressed himself under the window, hoping they wouldn't come around. A dozen steps and they'd be on top of him.

Then the clack of shoes on the porch. So close.

Knocking echoed through the air, and he could feel the vibration in the house itself. The front door. Who was out there? Was Janice's accomplice insecure enough, afraid enough of Janice, that he'd knock every time he showed up?

In the room, the voice went silent. Evie continued to cry, but it was faint enough that it might have been his imagination. A door slammed, closer to him this time, but muffled, thick. Then no more cries.

The knocking came again, hard and fast, carrying through the air around the house, the shoes on the porch eerily silent. And a squeal of hinges, again from the front of the house, far more distinct than anything he could hear through this window.

"Hey, there." *Roger?* Morrison bolted upright, almost smashing his forehead on the exterior windowsill. *Shit.* Janice would know he lied about getting rid of him.

"I hope you don't mind me coming by, but I've been thinking about you lately. I've missed you."

Even from here, Morrison could hear the anxiety in her voice, though not her words, just a rapid stuttering of sounds. Had Roger spoken loudly on purpose? Did he know Morrison was there? Did Janice?

Morrison held his breath, the only sound a haunting moan of wind through the trees as if even the air could feel the gravity of that moment and was distressed by it. Roger could not let her go back inside. Could not let her get to Evie, to Shannon. Janice would hurt them.

Janice would die first.

He slid Petrosky's pocketknife from his back pocket—the one left on the passenger seat the day Morrison had driven him to the rehab center. From the front of the house came Roger's muffled voice, and hers too, not quite arguing with Roger, but raised higher than it had been moments ago. He took off for the back door. It was less likely they'd be watching that as closely as the rooms where they held captives. This door they'd need for escape.

It took mere seconds to reach his destination, and only seconds more to wedge the knife beside the jamb. A ray of orange sun clawed at his hands as he jimmied the back door, turned the knob, and pushed.

But...resistance. Not a deadbolt. A padlock? He couldn't crack a padlock from the outside, and if he broke the door down, he might not be fast enough to get to Shannon—he didn't even know where Shannon was, or if she was in a different room from Evie.

And then the yelling. Somewhere nearby, a thunk—sharp but muted. Not the front door closing shut, but maybe the door on Roger's shoe or against his shoulder if he was attempting to bully his way inside. Was he trying to be a hero? And if so... Oh shit, if he was, and Janice's partner was in there with his family—

He raced back to the window. He'd have only moments, but it had to be enough.

Had to be.

Janice was still talking, arguing now, louder than before. If there was someone else in the house, wouldn't he have come to her aid? Morrison heard no other sounds from within the home, and no other male voices save Roger's on the porch—though a man terrified of rejection might be cowering in the bedroom instead of assisting. There was no way to tell for certain. And Morrison was out of time.

The noise from the front was enough to cover Morrison

breaking the back window with an elbow wrapped in his jacket. Sound suppression goes both ways, and while they might have heard it from the front if they'd been quiet, Roger's voice kept booming over the splintering of glass and the tearing of Morrison's knife across the curtain and into whatever was behind it. Foam insulation. No bricks.

He sawed through it, the Styrofoam-like material squalling like nails on a chalkboard though the argument out front did not stop—so the noise couldn't have been as deafening as it was to him. The foam peeled from the window frame, and he tossed the pieces behind him into the grass, until he had an opening he could shove his hand through. There was pink fiberglass insulation behind the foam, but no resistance beyond that, and he sliced cleanly through the material, ripping chunks of foam and fiberglass from the window opening, each piece like a bit of hope he was stealing back.

Roger yelled something that sounded like "goddammit," and Morrison pulled himself halfway into the window, trying to see through the hole he'd made. Tight, but doable, and nothing below that he could see in the dim light, no child to be injured if he lost his balance and tumbled into the darkness.

From the front, something banged again. *Out of time.* He was up and over the sill in moments and had wiggled through the hole in even less, trying not to care when he heard the knife slide off the outside sill and into the grass. He heard another sound behind him, but didn't stop to think, didn't stop to see, just moved. Someone behind him. Someone after him. But if he could get to Evie and Shannon first…

The dimness of the room stretched around him, but the last blush of twilight through the torn window covering gave him enough light to see there was no crib in there, no mattress. Just a table against the far wall that held…bottles. A glass cup. A pet carrier crate in the corner of the room with a handle on top.

Did they have a guard dog? He had not considered coming up against an animal, but surely the beast would have heard him and growled by now or attacked Roger if it was in the front end of the house. In this room, he was the only beast. For now.

Evie had quieted, and for once, he wished she was crying—he

couldn't discern her silent breathing above the sound of his own heart and the muffled voices out front. Where would she be? Where would they keep her? In the picture Janice had sent of Shannon, she was in a room, attached to a beam, but behind a door. Like it used to be a—his eyes locked on the folding doors along the far wall.

He ran to the closet, the treads on his shoes soft and supple and above all else, silent. He paused as an image of Evie, suspended from the clothes rod, smashed into his brain: his baby girl hanging from a T-shirt around her throat, her skin blue and cold and dead. He inhaled sharply, reaching for the knob. And opened it.

The door creaked just a touch, but there was nothing inside that hinted at his family, only a few boxes of electronic equipment, empty bags, and a fast food-cup as if someone had gone shopping and deposited everything, including their snack.

But Evie had been here. He'd heard her. Janice hadn't taken her to the front door, had she? No, she wouldn't have let Roger see her. Morrison turned, scanned the walls, the floor, the—plastic pet crate.

Two steps and he was at the pet carrier. He gingerly lifted the crate, rushing back to the window as he did so that he could see inside it. She was there, barely moving, wearing only a diaper, one tiny fist opening and closing. "Baby. Oh, baby."

At the front of the house, a door slammed. Evie mewled weakly. *Fuck.* He tried to wrest the carrier door open, and only then did he see the padlock on the front. Opening the crate would take too long, and he'd risk hurting her if he smashed it.

A shadow fell over him from the window, and he shifted the crate into one hand, grabbing his gun with the other. *Die, motherfucker.* So help him, he'd—

"Give her here, Cali," the silhouette in the window whispered.

He didn't lower the gun.

"For fuck's sake, Morrison—"

He heard them then, the footsteps approaching the door. "I love you, baby. Daddy'll be right back." Morrison handed the crate to Petrosky and ran for the bedroom door.

44

JANICE DIDN'T HAVE Shannon with her—the padded sounds of her feet on the floor were too quick, too clean. Purposeful. And then the steps just…stopped. Morrison flattened himself against the doorframe, waiting, listening for one harsh inhale, a gasp to indicate her understanding that he was there for her ass. Nothing. He held the gun trained on the crack above the doorknob. If she opened the door, Janice wouldn't have time to speak.

But the knob did not turn. She knew he was there. She was listening, trying to hear him breathe even as he was trying to hear her. Perhaps she had a gun on the other side of the door, waiting for him to open it, ready to blow his face off too.

Perhaps she'd change her mind and go after Shannon instead.

He strained his ears for sounds of her feet on the wooden floor. If she stepped away from the door, he'd fling it open, go in low, and shoot for the knees, the belly. Even if he missed, a wild shot or two might throw her off balance so that he could cap her in the back of the head before she could get to Shannon.

And her ability to focus might be impaired—she'd be angry now. Angry that she might not be able to complete whatever sick goal she had in mind. Angry he hadn't killed Roger as he'd said. That she'd been tricked by the story in the paper—a story he'd leaked the day he'd carved the tattoos off the already dead pedophile and left him in Roger's house to burn.

But now, instead of the crackle of flaming wood and cloth, he heard only her breath. Whisper quiet, but there. Fast. *She knows.*

Then a step, just one, then another, and he yanked the door and fired into the hallway, low, so if he missed, it'd lodge in the floor and not ricochet into another room where he might accidentally murder his own wife with a stray bullet.

A scrambling, a thin squeal.

He got his head around the doorframe in time to see her foot, clad in a fuzzy yellow sock, disappearing into the next room. He leapt for the door, for her ankle, grabbing at her but coming away with only a few threads of yellow fuzz. He lunged again, trying to keep his head behind the frame, wanting to drag her out. His fist connected with ankle bone, and he gripped her foot so hard he thought he'd break it. He yanked her to him.

Pain, white and hot, shot from the side of his hand and up his arm, forcing him to release her as she swung the lamp again, the base heavy and metal and dented from the first blow to the back of his hand. He rolled in time to avoid it, clambering after her into the bedroom. She skittered back on her butt, and he reached again for her leg, but she was faster, scrambling for the closet on the far side of the room, pressing numbered buttons on a padlock.

He couldn't move his pinky finger. From the corner of his eye, he could see that it was bent at an unnatural angle. But he wouldn't need it to fucking kill her.

He leapt to standing at the same time she did. She threw the closet door open and ducked behind—

Shannon. *Oh, dear god.*

Her eyes were red-rimmed, her face haggard. Around her throat was the collar: heavy, metal, black like iron, bolted to an oiled wooden beam that ran horizontally through the closet five feet off the ground. Her hands appeared to be free. But she made no attempt to grab the woman—her fingers were locked around the beam on either side of her iron-clad neck. And her lips—*oh, baby, I'm so sorry*—angrier in person or maybe simply infected by now, congealed blood and yellowed pus clinging to the sutures, black thread piercing her lips from top to bottom like a huge, grisly zipper. Janice had done this to his wife. Put his baby in a cage. Hatred burned hotter than any flame. *I will fucking kill you.*

"Come closer, and she's dead. I'll slit her throat." Janice remained low, but shoved Shannon's legs from behind, just a touch. Blood trickled from somewhere behind the collar. Her neck had been sliced. *Shit, no, no, no.* Shannon whimpered, her eyes wide, moving her hands to the collar itself as if trying in vain to stop the bleeding from her neck.

The collar. Blades or something inside it. But it didn't matter what—he couldn't get near enough to free her, and as he peered closer, he could see the bolts and the lock attaching the collar securely to the beam. He'd have to coax Janice out, have to—

The collar swung open, and Shannon was free, and she stumbled forward against the closet door and pivoted, trapping Janice behind her near the beam.

Janice's jaw dropped, and she put her hands up, trying to block Shannon's knee as it connected with her chin. But Shannon was weak, off-balance, maybe she hadn't eaten or slept, and she fell to her knees, a piece of curved metal falling from her hand to the carpet.

Janice reeled forward, teeth bared, and punched Shannon in the belly.

Fucking bitch.

Morrison jumped in front of Shannon, hauling Janice from the closet before she could attack his wife again. He threw her against the wall, watched her mouth move, knew she was saying something, but he couldn't hear a word, couldn't hear anything but the ragged hiss of air through his teeth. Or maybe he was just far beyond listening.

He wrapped his hands around her throat. The broken bones behind his pinky and ring finger poked at the skin from the inside like spiked alien parasites. His tendons, swollen and bright with agony, screamed as he tightened his grip.

He didn't fucking care. He squeezed.

45

SHE FOUGHT HIM, slashing at his hands with her nails, every attempt to free herself, stoking the fire in his gut. *You fucking deserve this.* Streaks of bloody red welled on his fists and dripped onto the floor, but he did not relent. Nor did he stop when pain careened from his hand to his wrist and shot into his brain like lightning, an electricity composed of concentrated malice.

Her face reddened, then went purple, her eyes bulging. But her mouth… It wasn't the shocked *o* he'd expected. And though her survival instinct was kicking in, she was no longer pulling from him, pulling away—trying to escape.

She had expected to fight him. She'd invited him here. *Once you remember, you'll know where to find me.*

"You don't want this." Morrison heard the words but did not see the speaker, and though he knew it was Petrosky's baritone, it seemed to come from Shannon's mouth, and—*oh dear god*—she was on the floor, her lips unmoving, sewed together like a voodoo doll, and still, the voice came again: "Morrison, this is what she wants."

He squeezed harder, watching Janice's face as her lips turned blue, the veins in her temples bulging like fattening worms as she crept toward unconsciousness, toward death, the only fitting punishment for what she'd done.

"Morrison!" Now Petrosky was there, at Shannon's side,

tugging her shirt down, and Morrison caught a whiff of her, the harsh metallic tang of the collar, maybe Shannon's blood, maybe his own. He squeezed until he was sure he'd tear a muscle in his hand.

"You're not a killer. She wants you to be."

Shannon. Shannon's voice. He jerked back to her. Petrosky stepped away from her, a knife in his fist, and Shannon opened her mouth, her lips bleeding and swollen and cracked. Speaking —or whispering—but she might as well have been yelling at him, for her words were all he could hear.

Petrosky touched Morrison's elbow, not trying to impede him, just letting him know he was there, and then Janice was falling, this bitch who'd tried to take everything from him, who'd tried more than once to kill his wife, who had tortured her, who had taken his daughter. A woman who'd followed him, hunted him, plotted against him, with nothing but vengeance in her heart.

She hadn't won. But if he killed her, he was exactly what she believed him to be.

Janice was in a heap on the floor, unconscious, unable to stop herself from smacking her head on the boards, and then Petrosky was there, cuffing her arms behind her.

Morrison watched, dumbfounded. It was over. But no, it wasn't. They were missing one. "He here?"

Shannon's gaze darted to the door. He knelt beside her, and her hair smelled of grease and gore and the must of body odor and piss and rank, spoiled milk. And it was the most beautiful thing he'd ever smelled.

"Evie," she said into his chest, her voice trembling with terror that the news was bad, that she'd lost her daughter.

"She's okay. She's okay." Morrison jerked his head toward Petrosky.

"Roger has her," Petrosky said. "He's driving her to the hospital with a police escort. Figured it was safer than staying here, in case there was any...trouble." He hauled Janice to her feet, and her eyes rolled around, but she stood, wavering ever so slightly. Her face was returning to a furious shade of pink.

"Your asshole boyfriend on his way here?" Petrosky asked

Janice. When she didn't answer, he jerked her arm, and she stumbled, almost fell, and caught herself against the wall with one shoulder.

"Fuck you." Janice's voice was hoarse, but she could still speak. Morrison should have squeezed her throat harder. Or sewn her goddamn mouth closed. He glanced at Shannon, who was running her tongue over the sutures, the ends of the severed threads poking from her torn lips.

"I sent Decantor over to the rehab center," Petrosky said. "That's where these douchebags met, where Adam still works. If he's there, Decantor has him."

Morrison eyed the door behind them, straining his ears, listening for the telltale sound of the latch on the front doorknob, a boot in the hall, the clink of spikes ripe with purpose and violence. Morrison would show him fucking violence—he'd ram those spikes down his throat. But there was no noise besides the far-off clang of a grandfather clock striking a quarter past the hour.

"We'll get his ass, Morrison. Now let's get Shannon to the hospital. Put your family back together."

Relief shuddered through Morrison in waves, one after another. He wrapped his arms around Shannon again, trying to be gentle. She was so weak, so beat up, so bruised. She'd suffered because of him.

"I'm so sorry," he whispered into her hair.

"You didn't do anything wrong," she said. "There is no sorry here."

"Only love," he finished. But he felt the guilt, tearing through his gut, that heavy aching sorrow he feared would never disappear. And one day she'd resent him for it—for all of it. She'd leave him. Take Evie.

And then he'd only have the drug. The vein in his thigh throbbed, one slow, deep pulse, then stilled. But when she put her injured lips to his neck and kissed his throat though it must have hurt like hell, he knew he'd endure.

"Only love," she said. "You didn't cause this. But you did save us."

His heart swelled and throbbed, harder than the vein.
The drug could kiss his ass.

46

THE ROOM WAS dim when Petrosky awoke. Not the mellow dusk of a day's end, but that brassy half-dark of another day trying to creep in when you're not yet ready for it. He rolled over and tried to push himself to seated, his tongue rank and sour from last night's vomit, shoulder still tender from the tattoo he'd had Jenny ink on him last week. Julie's face, memorialized. Maybe it would always hurt.

And that was difficult to take.

Each day he drew closer to an unknown conclusion. But he didn't want to get there. He eyed the gun in its holster, hanging innocently over the chair as if it had no intention of luring him with that quick, easy path to peace. Petrosky reached for it, comforted by the hardness of it, wondering if he'd register the moment he died as a flash of light, a deafening crack of lead as his soul left his body, or if it would be only silence and floating. He wasn't much for religion and the afterlife. If he'd believed in a heaven where Julie waited for him with open arms, he'd have put a bullet in his brain a long time ago.

He put his feet on the floor and heaved his doughy body off the bed. The room shuddered violently around him, the edges wavering, then solidifying like he was exiting a tunnel or a horrible nightmare. He might as well have been.

Another day, another dollar. Another day of wondering: *Will today be the day someone shoots me?*

Like he'd be that fucking lucky.

———

HE MET Morrison and Shannon at their house, the leaves already falling to their deaths on the front lawn. Helicoptering red and orange skittered across the driveway, and he kicked them aside on his way to the stoop.

Everything died, and today just happened to be their day. Petrosky envied them.

Morrison greeted him with a warm smile and a worried look, though he said nothing. He never did. Petrosky was thankful for his silence, though perhaps Morrison simply knew that the moment he opened his mouth, Petrosky would cut his ass out of his life. Not like Morrison and his family needed Petrosky's bullshit.

Shannon was already at the table, their newest addition at her heel, his ears pricked and alert. The dog appeared to relax when it saw Petrosky, but he knew it was from the gentle command Shannon had whispered. One word and the German shepherd would rip his fucking throat out, as would the other two who were probably in the backyard now, patrolling.

Shannon spooned eggs off her plate with a pink plastic spoon and grinned at Petrosky as he entered the kitchen. Petrosky tried to smile back.

Her mouth turned down, and the tiny marks where her lips had been sewn together dimpled just a touch. Almost healed now, but still a little pink, a little angry. "You look like shit," she said.

No wonder they'd sewn her mouth closed. "Nice to see you, too."

Evie gurgled and waved her arms, spraying eggs across the highchair tray and into Shannon's hair. Shannon ignored it, just frowned at him. She'd gone from tough to fucking badass after the kidnapping. Maybe being locked in a closet for a week made you realize what was important. Maybe she was on guard in case

Adam Norton came back for her, though he was surely long gone by now.

And Janice had been little help. She'd met Norton at the rehab center, and swore she'd never met Michael Hayes, the guy who raped Acosta and Reynolds. Further investigation had determined that Norton and Hayes had met at the hospital, Norton working with the cleaning service and Hayes volunteering as a clown. Both of those jackoffs seemed so fucking fragile he couldn't begin to determine who had approached whom, though from everything they had found online, Michael Hayes seemed the less violent one—creepy tattoos, and a rapist, though not a killer.

But Adam Norton—that motherfucker was vicious. Dangerous. And impulsive, possibly because of how young he was. At least Norton's DNA information was in the computer now, so they'd find him when he did it again—it wasn't like he'd be able to stop himself.

And he could be anywhere. The trail had dried up. They'd chased down every futile lead, and, through it all, Morrison had kept that stoic, cool-collected façade, as if this shit had never happened. Like it didn't bother him.

But Morrison had bought the dogs.

Petrosky squinted back at Shannon's narrowed eyes. Still watching him, possibly for tremors or looking for needle scars. His ankle twitched, and Petrosky shifted his weight. At least she didn't look scared. Maybe it was the canine unit.

Maybe she'd stopped giving a fuck too.

Petrosky waited for her to say something else, but she turned back to Evie and offered her another bite of eggs.

Morrison approached with two stainless-steel coffee mugs and handed one to Petrosky. "What the hell is this?" Petrosky said, frowning at the garish blue peace sign on his mug.

"Present." Morrison smiled.

"Liar. You just wanted a new mug and were afraid your wife would say no." He cast a sidelong glance at Shannon, who raised an eyebrow and went back to feeding Evie. "Give me the other one, Surfer Boy. Then we can swing by the donut shop and get a few crullers."

Morrison exchanged cups with him. "You sure you need all that sugar, Boss?"

Speaking of not giving a fuck… "Damn sissy beach boys and their peace signs and their *kale*."

"If we go, maybe we can bring some to Roger."

That asshole. He had come in handy even if he was a lying sack of shit. Even if he'd just done it for the headlines that came out right afterward: *Lead Prosecutor Rescues Ex-Wife from Homicidal Kidnapper.* No mention of the fire. And before the press got wind of Morrison's role, coercion and duress had cleared Morrison as well, though it had been touch and go for a few weeks: he'd found Michael Hayes dead in his home, suicide by pills according to the ME, probably guilt over Acosta's death. But filleting the tattoos from his dead body to purposefully mislead police was something the taxpayers would have been pissed about—it would have been a public relations disaster. In the end, Morrison had walked away with five thousand dollars in fines and some restitution to Roger. Insurance had rebuilt the house. And the extenuating circumstances were enough to keep Morrison out of jail, off probation, and still on the force.

Roger had applauded Morrison publicly for finding Shannon, which, for Roger, must have fucking hurt. But it was surely worth it—all the critical information Morrison had on Roger, everything in the safe deposit box, was gone along with his dining room table and the last of Roger's goddamn dignity. Fucking shmuck. Maybe he'd stay on the up and up. If he didn't, Petrosky had no intention of giving him another chance, regardless of his partner's opinion.

Morrison was still looking at him expectantly.

"Fine, goddammit, we can bring some breakfast to your new best buddy."

"Not exactly best"—Morrison winked—"but I figured we'd butter him up before Shannon goes back next week."

Petrosky gaped at her.

She smiled. "You look like you've seen a ghost, Petrosky."

"I thought you were going to wait an extra month or so."

"I thought so too, but even McCallum says I'm doing awesome. I think I'm ready." She drew her shoulders up, proud maybe, or maybe trying to seem stronger than she felt. "And Lillian, Valentine's wife, is going to take Evie during the day to play with her little one. Starting tomorrow, actually. Get her adjusted before I really have to leave."

"Is he going with you?" Petrosky gestured to the dog.

"I'll have Ozzy with me, and Floyd and Prince will be at Valentine's. At my husband's insistence." Shannon rolled her eyes, but she was still smiling. "Don't look so worried. You're as bad as Morrison."

Morrison shrugged one shoulder. "I thought she'd wait longer too. But you know...prosecutors."

"Fucking lawyers," Petrosky agreed.

"Evie's going to be talking soon," Shannon said. "Watch your mouth."

Morrison was gazing at his wife with that adoration thing he did. Shannon ate that shit up, and she looked at Morrison the same way. He was glad for them, he really was. Or as glad as he was capable of being.

His ankle itched again, reminding him that the bliss never lasted long enough. And every morning, awakening felt worse than it had the day before—more desperate. The world was tightening around him like a tourniquet.

"Lawyer or no, there's no stopping Shanny when she gets something in her head," Morrison said.

"Women, am I right? Always doing crazy shit...stuff," he amended when he saw Shannon's raised eyebrows. Petrosky headed for the door.

"Screw you, Petrosky," Shannon called as Petrosky touched the knob.

Screw him indeed.

"THIS STORY IS TOLD THROUGH THE EYES OF A MADMAN, WHO, LIKE
ALL OF US, BELIEVED HE WAS SANE."
~EDGAR ALLAN POE, *THE TELL-TALE HEART*

EPILOGUE

THE LAST STONE brick went in more easily than the one before as if each new support was begging to be a part of something great. And great it would be, now that he was free of Janice—of her *restraints*—though he'd been too cowardly to take care of her himself. He'd left that to the police. They might still be looking for him, but they'd not find him here. *Happy, happy, happy.*

He adjusted the fiber optic camera behind the brick and applied mortar to the last section of wall. He was tired of being afraid. He was also tired of being invisible, but he wouldn't be for much longer—at least, not to his number one girl.

He'd paid his dues, lying low under the radar, mopping up the puke of degenerates. He was capable of more. He deserved more. And now he knew how to get it.

The mortar complete, he dropped the trowel and turned to the back wall of the room, a checkerboard of heavy iron bars from floor to ceiling, and shackles practically begging to be filled. He inhaled the steely scent deep into his lungs. None of that plastic zip-tie bullshit: this equipment was harsh, substantial, from back when they used to make things that lasted. Before people had the luxury of escape. Shannon had stolen from him, gotten out using his own needle, but he'd have no more surprises, not here. He'd watch every movement. The house upstairs held enough food for months, if not years.

In the corner of the room, the dress waited, satin of a vibrant red, the color of wealth and status. A belt of gold ovals circled its waist. Every stitch of cotton puckered ever so slightly, bringing with it the memories of the night he'd sewn it. It was all his. He'd built this. He'd built her.

And she would be perfect.

He approached, his breath quickening as each stitch came into clearer focus. He glanced at the tools in the corner but did not reach for any, though he was tempted by the billhook, a gleaming machete-like tool that boasted a curved blade along one side and an evil-looking hook at the top.

Later.

He traced his finger down her cheek, and the plastic of the mannequin caught ever so slightly. Dry. Not like skin, especially once it bore the blush of amour, the inevitable sheen of excited sweat. He ran a hand over the waist of the gown, and the gathered petticoat. He could almost feel the promise of her flesh.

But it wasn't time yet. She wasn't ready, didn't deserve to wear it. The girl still looked at him with blazing hatred in her eyes, a defiant rage that made his breath catch, his heart race. He deserved better. The men of their world deserved better. And if the women would not acquiesce, he'd bring them back to a time before they had a choice. When real men made the decisions.

I'm a real man.

He walked back to the iron cage and stopped just before the bars, where a large dog crate sat waiting. He bent and peered inside.

She was on all fours; her hair damp with sweat and oil—limp and disgusting. But it was red like Janice's—the color of power, of wealth—and glowing like the girl's eyes. She glared at him, and her cheeks flushed like she was ovulating, making his stomach drop and squeeze until he feared he might vomit. His jaw prickled with that old, familiar itch, and he resisted the urge to run for his needles and release the pressure by gouging the infernal boil. Too many, and he'd look like the savage he was. He wanted that to be a surprise.

Perhaps he'd grab the billhook after all. Nothing was too good for his number one girl.

But no...it was not time yet. Impatience was for weaker men, and though Michael had been weak, he had shown Adam how to bide his time. A gift here. A kind word there. Not that Michael hadn't made mistakes: he was so kind, so diminutive that the Acosta boy hadn't even remembered where he knew him from. But done right, you could draw a woman closer, closer, and they'd never suspect—they'd follow you wherever you went. He could be as patient as Janice, that fucking cunt. The reward would be that much greater.

He glanced at the stone wall. Patience. She'd give him what he was owed.

Near the stairs, it hung on a hook, the death mask, nose long and thin to protect him from her stench—pheromones could make a man insane, and he feared that heady stink as much as he feared the accusatory gleam in their eyes. Did they think they had the right to accuse him? If so, the mask would make them reconsider. The leather was thick and heavy and still smelled of the souls of the creatures it had been. One corner of the mask called to him, a tear he'd intended to fix. He wiped his hands on his pants and chose a shimmering needle from the kit, then ran his middle finger along each spool of thread. *Ahh,* the taupe was the one for the job: the hue would stand out nicely against the leather. His heart fluttered as he threaded. Perfection.

He shoved the needle into the corner of the fabric. It stuck. He pushed harder, feeling the stirring in his belly as he forced it, and when it gave, he sighed the needle through, watching the puncture deepen, the hole form. Like the boy. He'd felt the pierce of the spike, the initial resistance, then the give—and it might as well have been his own body entering the child. It had been the same with the woman. He'd taken the spike right off his boot for that one.

He plunged the needle into the mask again, and his dick got hard. He could almost feel the sword he'd tattooed there swelling, sharpening. He considered fucking the girl in the crate to teach her a lesson, but he didn't really feel like it. Sex was boring without blood. He glanced at the gown in the corner again, but went back to the needle, relishing the sharpness of it. Seamstress was synonymous with sissy, but the entire occupation was slashing and violence and stabbing. Was there anything more manly?

The tear was repaired in five stitches, and he carefully knotted the thread and replaced his tools. Then he lowered the mask over his face.

Much had changed since medieval times, but he could almost feel the ghosts still there, imprinted on the material of the mask, every soul sucked from a body via a too-thorough bloodletting, from plague, from childbirth, from injuries still ripe with complications and the promise of certain death should infection set in. He wished he'd been there to witness medieval life in all its glory. Sometimes he missed those days like he might miss a severed limb.

He bent to the cage again, seeking her face, and her eyes widened with fear and excitement and longing. The beaked doctor's mask was a symbol of status, and she surely knew it. Or perhaps she could feel how close she was to those who'd gone before, their souls almost touching her through the metal tip of the mask's nose, still stained with Shannon's blood. Maybe she was excited by the jester, superimposed over beak and hide, grinning at her with its fanged mouth. Hidden beneath the mask, he smiled.

Happy, happy, happy.

YOUR NEXT BOOK IS WAITING!

Get *HIDDEN*, the next book in the Ash Park series, at MEGHANOFLYNN.COM, then read on for a sneak peek!

"*HIDDEN* HAS IT ALL. SMART WRITING WITH A JAW-DROPPING TWIST. IT'S LIKE JO NESBO AND TANA FRENCH HAD A LOVE CHILD NAMED MEGHAN O'FLYNN."
~*AWARD-WINNING AUTHOR BETH TELIHO*

"Creepy and haunting...fully immersive
thrillers. The Ash Park series should be
everyone's next binge-read."
~New York Times Bestselling Author Andra Watkins

"Full of complex, engaging characters and evocative detail,
Wicked Sharp is a white-knuckle thrill ride. O'Flynn is a
master storyteller."
~Paul Austin Ardoin, USA Today Bestselling Author

"Nobody writes with such compelling and entrancing prose
as O'Flynn. The perfectly executed twists and expertly
crafted web woven into this serial killer series will captivate
you. Born Bad is chilling, twisted, heart-pounding suspense
that kept me guessing all the way up to the jaw-dropping
conclusion. This is my new favorite thriller series."
~Bestselling Author Emerald O'Brien

"Intense and suspenseful...captured me from the first chapter
and held me enthralled until the final page."
~Susan Sewell, Reader's Favorite

"Visceral, fearless, and addictive, this series
will keep you on the edge of your seat."
~Bestselling Author Mandi Castle

"Cunning, delightfully disturbing, and addictive, the Ash Park series is an expertly written labyrinth of twisted, unpredictable awesomeness!"
~Award-winning Author Beth Teliho

"Dark, gritty, and raw, O'Flynn's work will take your mind prisoner and keep you awake far
into the morning hours."
~Bestselling Author Kristen Mae

"From the feverishly surreal to the downright demented, O'Flynn takes you on a twisted journey through the deepest and darkest corners of the human mind."
~Bestselling Author Mary Widdicks

"With unbearable tension and gripping, thought-provoking storytelling, O'Flynn explores fear in all the best—and creepiest—ways. Masterful psychological thrillers replete with staggering, unpredictable twists."
~Bestselling Author Wendy Heard

LEARN MORE AT MEGHANOFLYNN.COM

HIDDEN

AN ASH PARK NOVEL

HE'S BACK.

Detective Edward Petrosky has always felt the pain of the world like a razor blade in his gut, even more so when he considers the killers who have escaped conviction. But he can't let that stop him, not after a grandmother is found murdered on her front lawn, the victim of some machete-wielding psycho.

The case is strange from the outset: no one heard a thing despite the public nature of the crime. An unknown child's footprints cover the property without a trace of the kid. And a grisly discovery in the basement has the entire police force stunned. Nothing makes sense. Whatever secrets their victim had, she'd taken them, quietly, to her grave.

But when another woman's corpse turns up with a familiar brand on her rib cage, Petrosky realizes the horrible truth: a killer he'd thought was long gone from Ash Park has remained, lurking in their midst. And who knows how many victims this butcher has collected? For those he's kidnapped, any day might be their last, imprisoned, unseen, with only their screams and a deranged lunatic for company.

Now Petrosky must risk everything he holds sacred to track the most sadistic killer Ash Park has ever seen, a man whose thirst for carnage extends far beyond mere bloodletting. But saving innocent lives will require an unbearable sacrifice.

One from which he may never recover.

GET HIDDEN ON MEGHANOFLYNN.COM

HIDDEN: An Ash Park Novel
CHAPTER 1

EDWARD PETROSKY FELT it before he opened his eyes that Thursday morning: the pressure. Some days, it was more a tugging in his chest like a motivated but sloppy panhandler snatching at his lapels. Today, an elephant was crushing his sternum. Tomorrow, it might squash him completely.

He hacked once, twice, then swallowed the slime and watched the predawn light spread slowly over the ceiling, trickling down the walls like dirty water dripping into a catch pan under a roof leak. *Drip, drip, drip.* Already the day was trying to make him insane.

The light reached the boy band poster on the wall above the bed, illuminating each gelled specimen with its frozen smile, and his heart seized, as always—but he'd never remove the picture. He welcomed that pain like an old, devoted friend. Other than the poster, Julie's room had been scrubbed of her, though her clothes were still boxed in his bedroom closet. He imagined her sifting through the slouchy socks and fuzzy headbands when she hit thirty, "Can you believe I used to wear that?" And she would have laughed. But now there would be no sighs of remembrance —all that was left were the clothes.

And that fucking poster.

A knock at the front door pulled him from thoughts of the clothes Julie would never outgrow, but Petrosky didn't move.

The knock came again. He rotated his ankles, trying to release the stiffness and the swelling. Maybe his chest would explode, the light would suddenly fade to black, and it would be done. But the light kept coming with the persistence of a leaky pipe—like that knock, begging to be acknowledged, when all he wanted to do was go back to bed and forget he was drowning under the crushing pressure of another day.

The knock came a third time, more insistent, each rap sending a stabbing pain through his skull. Petrosky grunted and pushed himself to sitting, the tattered comforter sliding from his leg to the carpet. The woman beside him stirred—maybe because of the sudden loss of the blanket, maybe because of the pounding from the kitchen—and shifted her weight toward the wall. She had taken her heels off but still wore her miniskirt under one of his T-shirts.

His stomach gave a liquid lurch. He swallowed hard to keep the sour awful from creeping up his gullet and shot an agitated glance at the empty bottle of Jack Daniels on the end table. And the needle beside it–empty now too. Empty for two years, the length of time it'd been since he'd allowed himself to partake. Four months since he'd set the Jack aside. He still kept both sitting on that end table, a constant reminder of the night he'd overdosed, and the morning after when his partner Morrison had found him unconscious on the living room floor in a puddle of vomit. The horrified look on Shannon's face, staring down at him when he'd awoken in the hospital. And the cost—he was still paying that off. Morrison had taken him to a private hospital to hide his sickness from the department. The kid didn't know when to give up.

He punched the Jack off the table and watched it teeter on one square side then tip onto the floor where it was saved by the comforter. Jack was one smug bastard. And rightly so—no matter how many times Petrosky tried to walk away, Jack stuck like an infection too deep to heal.

Petrosky staggered into the kitchen, not quite limping but favoring his left leg though he couldn't recall doing anything to injure it. He coughed again, phlegmy, gelatinous, and spat into the sink. The foam appeared angry, a mass of slime tinted pink by the night-light on the wall.

"Hang on!" he yelled at the door. If they wanted to come this early, they could wait.

Petrosky grabbed a slice of two-day-old pizza from the open box on the counter and chewed off a stale corner while he poured grounds into the world's most unreliable coffee pot—though maybe it'd actually work today. His wife had gotten the good coffee pot in the divorce, along with the good half of everything else. The coffee pot spluttered like she had when he refused to sign the divorce papers, and then it gave up—like he had.

He threw the front door open before the knocking could blast another round of pain through his temples.

"What the fuck is wrong with you?" Shannon's blue eyes flashed venom— his partner's wife, always the instigator. Stray snowflakes clung to one blond tendril that had come loose from her bun in the blustery wind, and her jacket billowed around her pin-striped suit despite her crossed arms. Her car was still running in the driveway. The kids were probably asleep inside, on their way to the sitter so that she could head to work at the prosecutor's office.

"Did you bring coffee?" he said.

"I'm not my fucking husband. And if you disappear like that again, I swear I'll slap the shit out of you."

"Well, good morning to you too."

"I'm not kidding, Petrosky. Morrison's worried sick. Says you dropped him at the precinct last night and took off. He's been calling you all morning."

"All morning? Where's he at?"

"At work. Like you should be."

A toilet flushed, and Shannon frowned as her gaze darted to the room behind him. "You have a working girl in here again?"

He raised one shoulder and took another bite of his pizza.

"Goddammit, Petrosky. You're going to lose your job."

But Shannon wasn't going to turn him in. Petrosky was the only one who knew about the man she'd killed. Not that he'd use it against her—Frank Griffen had deserved to die, would have in short order anyway because of the tumor in his brain. "So what if I do lose my job?" he said. "Without me handcuffing your husband to this city, you'd get a free pass to move wherever you want." *Away from that asshole ex-husband of yours.* Roger McFadden was the head prosecutor in Ash Park. How Shannon still worked with that twat was beyond him, as was the fact that his partner didn't seem the least bit concerned about Roger's obvious desire to make Shannon his again.

She clenched her jaw, and the needle scars around her mouth puckered—remnants from two years ago when a psychopath had sewn her lips shut. Still felt like yesterday, a sentiment his partner shared if Morrison's posse of guard dogs was any indication.

Shannon put her fingers to her temples as if the conversation was giving her a headache, too. "Listen, just…forget it, okay? You want to lose your job, that's on you. Just don't act like an asshole and make the kids…worry about you." She dropped her arms. "How about dinner tomorrow?"

"Soon."

She rolled her eyes and turned toward the car.

"Taylor, wait."

She reeled back to him. "I married Morrison years ago, you can stop calling me by my maiden name."

"Some feminist you are." Petrosky stepped back into the house and grabbed a box from the floor of the closet: a remote-controlled car that sang the ABCs when you drove it.

He thrust the package at her. "For Evie. And Henry, should he seem interested. Tell them Papa Ed will see them soon."

"You better make good on that, Petrosky." She stared at the gift like she thought it would be the last thing he'd ever give her. It just might be.

As soon as the door shut behind her, Petrosky grabbed another slice of pizza and watched three drops of sludge hit the bottom of the coffee pot. Then, he retreated to his bedroom, purposefully ignoring the pink princess night-light that cast a rosy glow on the countertop.

His blue button-down shirt seemed unnecessarily optimistic somehow like he was anticipating lunch with the fucking queen.

He hauled it on anyway, covering the tattoo of Julie's face that he'd had inked on his shoulder. The wound had stopped bleeding since he'd gotten it last year—but it would never heal. The buttons strained over his spare tire; hell, who was he kidding, this was no doughnut, but the real deal, earned honestly through fast food and booze. He could barely tuck his shirts in these days. He resisted the urge to kick the Jack bottle and heaved on jeans, gray sneakers, and his shoulder holster.

Petrosky turned abruptly when the phone rang and followed the peal of "Surfin' USA" to the kitchen, scowling at the irritating-as-shit ringtone his partner had put on his cell, knowing he had no idea how to turn it off. *Fucking surfers.* He snatched the cell from behind the coffee pot—last place he would have looked if it hadn't been ringing. "What's up, kid?"

"Hey, Boss. We've got a situation over on Pearlman, off Martin Luther King. Woman hacked up on her front lawn. Texting you the address."

"You know I hate tex—"

"Too bad, you old fart. I'm bringing you coffee too, so turn that ancient machine off."

Petrosky side-eyed the coffee maker, which was still belching steam into the air. There were three drops in the pot, same as when he'd left the room. *Son of a bitch.* He opened his mouth to give Morrison a snarky comeback, but the line clicked.

"Everything okay, baby?" The girl smiled shyly, like a little kid, but she wasn't a child. Old eyes stared at him from beneath mascara-clumped lashes, her frown lines caked with makeup. She'd removed his T-shirt to reveal a halter top and a skirt that wouldn't have been warm enough in May, let alone in the dead of winter.

"I have to run." He pulled his wallet from the pocket of his coat and peeled off four hundreds.

Her eyes widened. She took the money. "You don't want me to…do anything for it?"

"Buy a coat."

She stared at him, open-mouthed.

"Come on, I'll drop you back where I picked you up." He pocketed the phone, glowered at the empty coffee pot, and hauled on his jacket. Another day, another girl, another drive to leave her on the corner just as cold as he'd found her. Maybe today would be the day some perp finally put him out of his misery for good.

***

GET *HIDDEN* ON MEGHANOFLYNN.COM

"CREEPY AND HAUNTING... A FULLY-IMMERSIVE THRILLER."
~*NEW YORK TIMES BESTSELLING AUTHOR ANDRA WATKINS*

SHADOW'S KEEP

For William Shannahan, six-thirty on Tuesday, the third of August, was "the moment." Life was full of those moments, his mother had always told him, experiences that prevented you from going back to who you were before, tiny decisions that changed you forever.

And that morning, the moment came and went, though he didn't recognize it, nor would he ever have wished to recall that morning again for as long as he lived. But he would never, from that day on, be able to forget it.

He left his Mississippi farmhouse a little after six, dressed in running shorts and an old T-shirt that still had sunny yellow paint dashed across the front from decorating the child's room. *The child.* William had named him Brett, but he'd never told anyone that. To everyone else, the baby was just that-thing-you-could-never-mention, particularly since William had also lost his wife at Bartlett General.

His green Nikes beat against the gravel, a blunt metronome as he left the porch and started along the road parallel to the Oval, what the townsfolk called the near hundred square miles of woods that had turned marshy wasteland when freeway construction had dammed the creeks downstream. Before William was born, those fifty or so unlucky folks who owned property inside the Oval had gotten some settlement from the

327

developers when their houses flooded and were deemed unin-habitable. Now those homes were part of a ghost town, tucked well beyond the reach of prying eyes.

William's mother had called it a disgrace. William thought it might be the price of progress, though he'd never dared to tell her that. He'd also never told her that his fondest memory of the Oval was when his best friend Mike had beat the crap out of Kevin Pultzer for punching William in the eye. That was before Mike was the sheriff, back when they were all just "us" or "them" and William had always been a them, except when Mike was around. He might fit in somewhere else, some other place where the rest of the dorky goofballs lived, but here in Graybel he was just a little…odd. Oh well. People in this town gossiped far too much to trust them as friends anyway.

William sniffed at the marshy air, the closely-shorn grass sucking at his sneakers as he increased his pace. Somewhere near him a bird shrieked, sharp and high. He startled as it took flight above him with another aggravated scream.

Straight ahead, the car road leading into town was bathed in filtered dawn, the first rays of sun painting the gravel gold, though the road was slippery with moss and morning damp. To his right, deep shadows pulled at him from the trees; the tall pines crouched close together as if hiding a secret bundle in their underbrush. Dark but calm, quiet—comforting. Legs pumping, William headed off the road toward the pines.

A snap like that of a muted gunshot echoed through the morning air, somewhere deep inside the wooded stillness, and though it was surely just a fox, or maybe a raccoon, he paused, running in place, disquiet spreading through him like the worms of fog that were only now rolling out from under the trees to be burned off as the sun made its debut. Cops never got a moment off, although in this sleepy town the worst he'd see today would be an argument over cattle. He glanced up the road. Squinted. Should he continue up the brighter main street or escape into the shadows beneath the trees?

That was his moment.

William ran toward the woods.

As soon as he set foot inside the tree line, the dark descended on him like a blanket, the cool air brushing his face as another hawk shrieked overhead. William nodded to it, as if the animal had sought his approval, then swiped his arm over his forehead and dodged a limb, pick-jogging his way down the path. A branch caught his ear. He winced. Six foot three was great for some things, but not for running in the woods. Either that or God was pissed at him, which wouldn't be surprising, though he wasn't clear on what he had done wrong. Probably for smirking at his memories of Kevin Pultzer with a torn T-shirt and a bloodied nose.

He smiled again, just a little one this time.

When the path opened up, he raised his gaze above the canopy. He had an hour before he needed to be at the precinct, but the pewter sky beckoned him to run quicker before the heat crept up. It was a good day to turn forty-two, he decided. He might not be the best-looking guy around, but he had his health. And there was a woman whom he adored, even if she wasn't sure about him yet.

William didn't blame her. He probably didn't deserve her, but he'd surely try to convince her that he did, like he had with Marianna...though he didn't think weird card tricks would help this time. But weird was what he had. Without it, he was just background noise, part of the wallpaper of this small town, and at forty-one—*no, forty-two, now*—he was running out of time to start over.

He was pondering this when he rounded the bend and saw the feet. Pale soles barely bigger than his hand, poking from behind a rust-colored boulder that sat a few feet from the edge of the trail. He stopped, his heart throbbing an erratic rhythm in his ears.

Please let it be a doll. But he saw the flies buzzing around the top of the boulder. Buzzing. Buzzing.

William crept forward along the path, reaching for his hip where his gun usually sat, but he touched only cloth. The dried yellow paint scratched his thumb. He thrust his hand into his pocket for his lucky coin. No quarter. Only his phone.

William approached the rock, the edges of his vision dark and unfocused as if he were looking through a telescope, but in the dirt around the stone he could make out deep paw prints. Probably from a dog or a coyote, though these were *enormous*— nearly the size of a salad plate, too big for anything he'd expect to find in these woods. He frantically scanned the underbrush, trying to locate the animal, but saw only a cardinal appraising him from a nearby branch.

Someone's back there, someone needs my help.

He stepped closer to the boulder. *Please don't let it be what I think it is.* Two more steps and he'd be able to see beyond the rock, but he could not drag his gaze from the trees where he was certain canine eyes were watching. Still nothing there save the shaded bark of the surrounding woods. He took another step— cold oozed from the muddy earth into his shoe and around his left ankle, like a hand from the grave. William stumbled, pulling his gaze from the trees just in time to see the boulder rushing at his head and then he was on his side in the slimy filth to the right of the boulder, next to…

Oh god, oh god, oh god.

William had seen death in his twenty years as a deputy, but usually it was the result of a drunken accident, a car wreck, an old man found dead on his couch.

This was not that. The boy was no more than six, probably less. He lay on a carpet of rotting leaves, one arm draped over his chest, legs splayed haphazardly as if he, too, had tripped in the muck. But this wasn't an accident; the boy's throat was torn, jagged ribbons of flesh peeled back, drooping on either side of the muscle meat, the unwanted skin on a Thanksgiving turkey. Deep gouges permeated his chest and abdomen, black slashes against mottled green flesh, the wounds obscured behind his shredded clothing and bits of twigs and leaves.

William scrambled backward, clawing at the ground, his muddy shoe kicking the child's ruined calf, where the boy's shy white bones peeked from under congealing blackish tissue. The legs looked…*chewed on.*

His hand slipped in the muck. The child's face was turned to his, mouth open, black tongue lolling as if he were about to plead for help. *Not good, oh shit, not good.*

William finally clambered to standing, yanked his cell from

his pocket, and tapped a button, barely registering his friend's answering bark. A fly lit on the boy's eyebrow above a single white mushroom that crept upward over the landscape of his cheek, rooted in the empty socket that had once contained an eye.

"Mike, it's William. I need a...tell Dr. Klinger to bring the wagon."

He stepped backward, toward the path, shoe sinking again, the mud trying to root him there, and he yanked his foot free with a squelching sound. Another step backward and he was on the path, and another step off the path again, and another, another, feet moving until his back slammed against a gnarled oak on the opposite side of the trail. He jerked his head up, squinting through the greening awning half convinced the boy's assailant would be perched there, ready to leap from the trees and lurch him into oblivion on flensing jaws. But there was no wretched animal. Blue leaked through the filtered haze of dawn.

William lowered his gaze, Mike's voice a distant crackle irritating the edges of his brain but not breaking through—he could not understand what his friend was saying. He stopped trying to decipher it and said, "I'm on the trails behind my house, found a body. Tell them to come in through the path on the Winchester side." He tried to listen to the receiver, but heard only the buzzing of flies across the trail—had they been so loud a moment ago? Their noise grew, amplified to unnatural volumes, filling his head until every other sound fell away—was Mike still talking? He pushed *End,* pocketed the phone, and then leaned back and slid down the tree trunk.

And William Shannahan, not recognizing the event the rest of his life would hinge upon, sat at the base of a gnarled oak tree on Tuesday, the third of August, put his head into his hands, and wept.

GET *SHADOW'S KEEP* ON MEGHANOFLYNN.COM.

"MASTERFUL, STAGGERING, TWISTED... AND
COMPLETELY UNPREDICTABLE."
~*BESTSELLING AUTHOR WENDY HEARD*

Learn more about Meghan's novels on
https://meghanoflynn.com

ABOUT THE AUTHOR

With books deemed "visceral, haunting, and fully immersive" (*New York Times bestseller, Andra Watkins*), Meghan O'Flynn has made her mark on the thriller genre. Meghan is a clinical therapist who draws her character inspiration from her knowledge of the human psyche. She is the bestselling author of gritty crime novels and serial killer thrillers, all of which take readers on the dark, gripping, and unputdownable journey for which Meghan is notorious. Learn more at https://meghanoflynn.com! While you're there, join Meghan's reader group, and get a **FREE SHORT STORY** just for signing up.

Want to connect with Meghan?
https://meghanoflynn.com

Made in United States
Orlando, FL
18 September 2024

51686521R00202